D0710143

YOU, ME AND THE INSECTS

MYSORE, INDIA

BARBARA HENNING

SPUYTEN DUYVIL
NEW YORK CITY

Acknowledgements: This book is a work of fiction. Any resemblance to actual events or persons is entirely coincidental. All of Harihara's lectures, however, are based on teaching I received from Shankaranarayana of Mysore, India. My deepest gratitude to him for his lectures, advice and guidance. *Parama rishibu namaha.* Deepest gratitude also to his mahugu-rus, Sriranga and Srimata.

Special thanks to Lewis Warsh, Esther Hyneman, Dawn Merrill, Bob Henning, Harriette Hartigan, Jan Zimmerman, Tod Thilleman and Sylvia Rascon for reading this text and offering invaluable suggestions for revision. Also, thanks to *Mark(s)zine* for publishing an excerpt.

Library of Congress Cataloging-in-Publication Data

Henning, Barbara.

You, me and the insects : Mysore, India / Barbara Henning.

p. cm.

ISBN 0-9720662-6-8

1. Teacher-student relationships--Fiction. 2. Americans--India--Fiction. 3. Mysore (India)--Fiction. 4. Gurus--Fiction. 5. Yogis--Fiction. 6. Yoga--Fiction. I. Title.

PS3558.E4966Y68 2004

813'.54--dc22   2004013932

for Allen Saperstein

New York City. Thursday, May 18th. The edge of a photo sticks up from the stack. I pull it out. Lenny's grey sweatshirt with the hood up, face hidden inside, a dark misshapen circle with eyes, nose and mouth almost but not quite visible.

A child lies beside him with her head outside the frame of the photo, perhaps resting on someone else's lap. The child's legs are bare and comfortable in the sun.

Inside his hood, Lenny's hiding agony. Behind him, the grey blue horizon of sea and sky. This was in the summer before his illness made him completely immobile. Josh must have taken the photo right after he graduated from highschool. They were spending a day on a tourist boat off Montauk Point, watching for whales.

I study Lenny's face, draw the dark circle of the hood and the unknown girl's relaxed legs, then pick up my tea cup and look out the window on Tompkins Square and the steady stream of East Villagers hurrying down the street. I had hoped to finish these sketches before leaving for India, but now that's impossible. I'll take a few with me—this one for sure—but the rest will have to wait until I return in September.

1982, a whole year without a single image. That was the year Lenny and I separated and he and a friend opened an after hours club, the Dancing Dog, in downtown Detroit at Temple and Woodward. It was open only for six months, and he lost money. Still it became a popular hang-out for the Cass Corridor crowd, Detroit's counter-culture community of beat artists and political lefties. I think that's when Lenny really started slipping back into his drug habit. I jot down a note inside book #6 to look around for photos, walk over to the sewing machine, stitch the binding with purple thread, and then pack it away in a plastic box in the bedroom closet.

The afternoon light makes an elongated reflection of the venetian blinds on the living room wall. No matter how difficult the situation, some truth is revealed with the help of the sun. One afternoon when Lenny was lying in his hospital bed and I was sitting across from him, sinking into the old ruined red sofa in his living room, the sun streamed through the 6th Street window in his Brooklyn apartment, revealing a layer of dust over stacks of little papers and knickknacks randomly piled on his corner table. We were watching some show on television, an overweight young woman revealing a secret about her boyfriend while he sat huddled beside her.

Lenny turned over on his side and looked at me.

"You know, Gina, sometimes I really feel terrible about what happened between you and Dave, you know, just because of me being sick you two broke up after being together for five years. But then I think—hum, there's nothing to feel bad about. In fact, I probably did you a favor." He raised his eyebrows, and we both laughed.

Our relationship was like that. Even when we split up and were seeing other people, and Josh and Jessica were going back and forth between our apartments, even when we were arguing ferociously, we were still a couple for life. After fourteen years of separation, I sat by his bedside in the apartment when he was dying and we held hands.

Now, I sketch his hands in my notebook, as I remember them.

*

Friday, May 19th. It's 10:00 p.m. and the doors to Black Eyed Suzie's are locked. After teaching my last drawing class for the semester, I quickly finish a plate of tofu and vegetables. Ram, the busboy and my friend, walks by with a stack of dishes. He asks me if I need anything else.

"Ram, I have a question. Do people want to go barefoot in the mountains in Nepal in the snow? Or are they too poor to wear shoes?"

"Yes," he says, "their feet are like animal feet. They don't want shoes. They like the ground." Everything about Ram's demeanor is quiet and kind, his eyes, his hands. He came back from Nepal with a poet friend of mine last year and now he's working two jobs to send money home. He walks softly through the room in a pair of American sneakers.

"If you come to Katmandu," he says, "stop and visit my sons."

*

Monday, May 22, 2001. This morning I step out the door of my apartment building at 7 a.m. and walk through the park under the spreading oaks and elms. I'll miss these trees, I think, as I pass by the young man who practices Tai Chi everyday and then pass a few homeless unrecognizable men sleeping under tattered blankets on the park benches. When Lenny died, the day after a spring storm, these sidewalks were cluttered with pollen and young leaves. As I walked our dog, Peggy, every leaf and detail were vivid as if with his death, the screen of my mind had been wiped clean, and I could finally see objects as they really were in the world, luminous. Now the memory of that day creates a screen of its own.

At the 8th Street East exit, I pass the church I've entered only once before, last year, to attend a funeral service for a friend who died from an overdose of drugs. I can't walk past that church and its yellow bricks without thinking about Jack. He was a talented artist, a sweet human being, only thirty-six years old and dead. Two doors down I ring 1R and Manny buzzes me into the yoga shala. I am the first to arrive today to this empty room, adorned only with a photograph of Ramaji, Manny's guru. I lay my mat down in the corner where I always practice and then I stop for a minute to talk to him as he finishes sweeping the floor.

"You know, if Harihara accepts me as his student, Manny, there's a very good chance I may never return to this practice again. Should I do that? I am afraid to make this change."

He smiles and cocks his head a little like an Indian.

"Yes," he says. "Harihara is a yogi of the highest caliber. This is an opportunity for you to heal your back and take your yoga practice to another level."

Every morning in this studio I complete a rather rigorous yoga practice with five to ten other people. The only sounds in the room are the sounds of our breathing and occasionally Manny's quiet instructions to some individual student. In badakonasana, the soles of my feet are joined and then opened as my knees and thighs press against the floor. Manny leans his entire weight on my back. "Don't be afraid," he says. "Just breathe."

*

Wednesday, May 24th. Phone message from Dimitri in Russia. *I worry for you in India alone, Gina. We will see each other again. I will try to come to New York in September. Please do not forget me. Love for you Dimitri. Love for you. Take my phone number in case you need to reach me right away.*

I haven't seen him for four months. I put a few photos of him into a little book that I will also take with me. Perhaps I am falling in love again and this time with a young man who lives on the other side of the world.

Does age really make a difference? he asked when I left him at the airport. I guess the borders of time and space are just illusions. Perhaps, I use the word "perhaps" because I don't know exactly how I feel about him. From a distance, I watch myself eat dinner with him, make love, walk through the New York streets. Perhaps after these five years of studying yoga, I have learned how to move more carefully in the world with my emotions. Perhaps now it is impossible to *fall* in love.

*

Thursday, May 25th. I settle into my window seat on the airplane and begin writing in a new Nepali notebook. My dear friend Artie, a writer and publisher of some of my little art books, urged me to take my laptop and some writing books with me on this trip. "Instead of concentrating so much on your drawings, this trip why don't you write down everything you see and do. Everything," he said emphatically. After Lenny and I had moved to Brooklyn and the children were spending half the week with each of us, I met Artie at an opening at the Drawing Center. He had just split with his wife and he suggested we take his three children and my two to the park together the next day. After that we started a six month love affair and a twenty year friendship. He's a novelist, who has influenced many writers and artists with his ideas—he has certainly inspired me many times.

And so I am writing this record as I look out at the horizon of cement in the airport.

Jessie and Josh are probably still at the gate to the terminal. They drove me to the airport, happy to be with each other even though a day earlier they were involved in an intense argument. They are in their early twenties now, but when they are bickering, I feel like a frustrated parent of teenagers. Ever since Lenny died, they have been sharing his apartment with one other roommate. New York City apartments are scarce and so family members are often forced to stick together. Every three weeks or so they have a fight about who is cleaning what, and they call me so they can make the argument a matter of three instead of two. Last night was one of those nights.

"Please don't involve me," I begged. In a few months, after I return home, Josh will go to India where he will spend a year studying at an American school in Bangalore. After that, he'll graduate, return to New York and probably find his own apartment. Last night I was worried that when I was ready to board the plane, there would still be a lot of tension between them and as a result I'd be anxious, too, but today as always it is over and we are all happy.

I kiss them both goodbye, then look back and see a little bit of Lenny in my two lanky children. They will be fine without me.

"Bye Mom" Josh yells. "Be careful around those cows."

*

30 minutes outside of London, 260 miles from landing. One long nap with two meals. The first lap of this journey completed, the next one more difficult because it's much longer.

At the end of the last trip, I had just emerged from culture shock. As I sat in the back of the white Ambassador, waving to Dimitri and Isabella, my departure felt premature. Now, I want to go deeper into my yoga practice and learn what I can about yoga from the teachers in India.

Last night on the phone, my girlfriend Vivian talked about the possibility that as you live through your lives, you encounter the same souls but in entirely different roles. That's why suddenly you are drawn toward some particular person. Your soul remembers.

"Gina—you probably knew Dimitri in another life."

My brain feels as if it will burst through my forehead. I drink water.

What is a spiritual life? Accepting one's mortality and being in the present with a sense of balance—as a part of the whole and as a witness.

Time to destination 001.

Lenny—I take a breath and close my eyes—I've brought none of your body with me, but you are here in my heart and mind.

*

From London to Mumbai, the lady beside me is reading a book with a print of Krishna on the front and a large print inside in some Indian script. It's in Malayalam, the language of Kerala, she tells me later. I can see verses. "*The Bhagavad Gita?*" I ask. She is surprised that I recognize the images pasted into her book: Shiva, Hanuman, Sita and Krishna. She will not eat the rice dishes on the plane because they are not fresh, but she eats old cellophane wrapped bread and butter. Her husband is pleased to point out the names of the spots flashing on the movie screen—Taj Mahal, airport in Mumbai. Then they tell me the names of hotels in case I ever visit there again. Last year, I spent a night in Mumbai before going to Bangalore. I stayed in the YWCA Guest House, a nondescript, safe but unfriendly place. The city is big like New York and much more westernized than old world south India, like in Mysore. On the way to and from the airport, we passed through the slums. They are stunning in their simplicity and filth—endless miles of little huts and tents.

The young man who was sharing the cab with me explained, "Well they are not as poor as they look. Look at many of the huts and you will see antennas for televisions. Even on the tents. Yes and many have cable because they are the people who work for the cable companies so they know how to tap right into it."

"And this makes them not poor?" I asked. "They have a very poor water supply, no sewage systems, filthy, unstable walls and roofs that can be blown away."

"But they have jobs and money for food," he said. "And they accept this as where they are in this life, so they are relatively happy. It is the middle class who are unhappy in India because they want more and more."

Mysore, India. Friday May 26th. After the plane lands in Bangalore, I sit in the waiting room, jotting down notes. When I look up and see Vanessa, a young woman from New York, struggling with a big green case and two boxes.

"Hey you," I yell to her. "No one told me you were coming to Mysore this month."

She joins me in line and I offer to share my cab with her. This is Vanessa's first visit and she will be here for two months working with her guru Ramaji, who she has never met, but who I practiced with for one month last year. He has trained a lot of yoga teachers in the United States over the last twenty years, and many of his students' students, as well as new teachers, make at least one trip to Mysore to practice with him. Vanessa has just finished a year of yoga teacher training in New York.

The baggage return and money exchange are both slow and inefficient, as is most of India. (Try not to be impatient and just let the centuries unfold.) As I wait for my money in the exchange booth, I calculate what I should receive, and when the man gives me the rupees, he shorts me a few hundred.

"More," I say, and he shuffles his bills, pretending he is in the process of giving me the money when in fact he is trying to short change me.

I roll my baggage up to the official who asks about the contents of the box Vanessa is pulling behind her. "Books for my guru," she explains. That's all. That's customs in Bangalore. We roll our luggage out of the area, finding Jeevesh at the door waiting with a big smile and a sign with my name. I wave to him.

"Hello, Gina. Welcome home."

"Vanessa, this is Jeevesh."

He takes our baggage and then another man, Ravindra, goes one way around the car and Jeevesh the other way.

"Wait," Vanessa yells, thinking Ravindra is some stranger who is stealing her bags.

"It's ok, calm down," I say. "He's our driver."

Then from around the corner, two little boys appear with dirty hands and raggedy clothes, offering to help with our things. Jeevesh doesn't want to give them anything when they hold out their hands and I don't have small change yet. I ask him to please give them something. They did do some work. Their hands are black with filth. Usually, I don't give money to children who beg because of Thich Nhat Hahn's appeal to westerners not to train third world children to beg. But these children are not exactly begging—they are working.

"How is Subrata?" I ask Jeevesh as Ravindra begins to right-hand steer the white Ambassador out of the parking area and onto the street. Vanessa and I are in the back seat.

"Oh, she is fine." He turns to Vanessa and begins a sales pitch about the meals that Subrata cooks in their home and how all the yoga students come to her for breakfast, lunch and dinner. There is a whole industry in Mysore providing every possible service for the western yoga students, who will pay more than Indians for their services—rickshaw drivers, laundry men, tailors, landlords, coconut salesmen, cleaning women, etc.

He tells us his three children are doing very well in their studies of computers and business. As he looks straight at Vanessa who is wearing a big floppy white hat pulled down over her curly hair, he reminds me that they also provide internet service in the house.

On the way to Mysore, we pass through the tropical world of southern India with ramshackle buildings, tents, and women in col-orful saris walking barefoot with baskets on their heads.

"It looks a lot like Mexico," Vanessa says.

"Yes, Isabella talked about that last year."

"Isabella?"

"A woman from Mexico, who was here last year. She could speak very little English and I could speak just a little more Spanish. We became close friends and I spent my first two months in India speaking Spanish with her. She used to talk about the similarity in the food, houses and tapestries. Maybe it's because of the tropical climate."

"The worst place I've ever been," Vanessa says as we pass by a straw hut and a man wearing only a lungi, sitting on a stool in front, smoking, "is Albania. A very low quality of life. A beautiful land sprinkled with square cinder block shelters for people. So poor."

"Hey, watch out!" she hollers as Ravindra passes another cab and almost collides with a bus.

"Calm down," I say. "This is just the beginning of the ride. It's best not to look out the front window."

An hour later, we turn right, pass some grass huts, and head toward a roadside restaurant with a metal roof, twenty plastic tables and an outdoor kitchen with fried breads and vegetables simmering in big pots—dirty by our standards but not bad for India.

"Now I understand first hand why the Indian cab drivers in New York are so reckless. They got their training here," she says. "He drives like a maniac."

Jeevesh orders a lot of oily fried food, samosas and dosas.

Vanessa and I discuss our respective relationships and our relationship to sex and how this affects our practice. I tell her that my decision not to see the man I was dating last year had partly to do with the exhausting nature of our sex life. I knew if I were to see him, I would not be able to practice vinyasa yoga any longer. I don't tell her this, but I was also frightened about the way my day-to-day life would change if I were to live with a man with such a strong personality. As much as I liked him, I couldn't take a chance at sacrificing my freedom. I've often thought that my decision was also my loss.

Vanessa, who is about thirty years old, is involved in a relationship with a man she loves, and she finds monogamy difficult. We wonder if Jeevesh and Ravindra can hear us talking. We are afraid they might be shocked by our sexual freedom. But they are continually surrounded by Americans, many who view their trip to Mysore as a vacation. They probably already know a lot more about American sexual practices than we think. Many Indians seem to think that a lot of American women are prostitutes; this is due as much to marriage and dress customs (we don't cover our arms and legs) as it is to western television and music videos that capitalize on women's sexuality.

We decide finally that they don't understand English well enough to make sense of our discussion, so we continue talking. I talk a bit about Dimitri. How can I be in love with someone who is so much younger than I and who lives on the other side of the world? Perhaps that keeps me safe, in love, and far away. Actually, I tell her I like the idea of loving someone who only comes home to me only every three or four months for a week at a time. There is a joyful meeting, a lovely time alone and then the period of longing and expectation. It could be a perfect relationship at this point in my life.

This arrangement is quite different from the way my relationship started with Lenny. In 1972, I had just moved downtown to the Cass Corridor in Detroit to continue with college classes. It was between Christmas and New Years. I was sharing an apartment on Willis Street a few doors east of Woodward with Shirley Wilson, an English major. The neighborhood was kind of dangerous, with many street junkies and alcoholics hanging around on the corners. At night I'd wrap my blue pea coat around my body and walk quickly one and a half blocks to Cobbs Corner Bar to read and drink a beer. More than once as I walked that block, I was stopped by the police, who questioned me to see if I was a prostitute. An undercover operation was in effect at the time called STRESS, and there were a lot of complaints about the police illegally entering innocent people's homes and stopping them for no apparent reason. A number of shootouts had occurred. Anyhow, the second time I walked down to Cobbs, the police stopped me. I answered their questions, showing my ID and explaining that I was a student. When they finished interrogating me, I walked quickly down the street.

I sat down at the bar and ordered a "small" beer. The bartender was a tall lanky guy with a beard and a long red braid. "A small beer, eh?" He smiled at me.

I smiled back. He was cute.

"What's your name?"

"Gina. And yours?"

Lenny came home with me that night and he stayed for nine years. For many years we were inseparable.

"Watch out, Ravindra!" Vanessa yells again, leaning over the front seat as we swerve around a cab and back into the left lane just as a bus comes barreling by us.

As we pass through the countryside, I notice that what seemed exotic to me last year, now seems rather ordinary. Traveling to Mysore on the early morning train last year, I was in a daze. It was as if I had fallen into a dream.

"Why aren't you practicing with Ramaji?" Vanessa asks as she sits back, giving up with a sigh.

Well, I explain to her, I did that for a month last year and it wasn't for me. Too fashionable, a little bit too much like high school summer camp, and on top of that he's terribly expensive. Yes, there's a lot of energy in the room from so many advanced students practicing together, but I'm not patient enough for everything else. I am hoping Harihara—a yogi who worked with my friend Peter last year—will agree to work with me too. He worked very closely with Peter, helping him design a practice that wouldn't injure him anymore. Peter says that even though he had studied yoga for years, including teacher training, he never really experienced yoga until he met this teacher. His teacher isn't interested in working with a lot of western students, but occasionally he might accept a student who is serious and isn't jumping around from one teacher to another. I wrote him an email and he wrote back, saying he'd meet me to prepare my astrology chart and then we could talk.

When we arrive at the hotel, I unpack and immediately telephone Harihara. The woman who answers the phone explains that he is out of town for a week. I'm disappointed, but I decide that while I'm waiting for him to return, I'll practice with Mr. Jayaraj at his school, which is fairly close to the hotel.

*

I'm lying on the small bed in the room on the first floor next to the lobby, sound asleep.

There's a knock on the door.

It's Frank, a young man I know from New York. He looks different after traveling for several months. His face is thinner, his head shaved, and he seems calmer and more mature. I stretch out on the bed and listen to him. He is enjoying his time in India he tells me. How is it different here from Nepal? The yoga, he says, and ordinary life. Tourists and sightseeing are not that pleasurable.

We have lunch together at Upahar. I order rava idlies, but the waiter tells me they do not have them so I order what I assume is a thali, the standard Indian lunch, a combination of different dishes. Then I notice the waiter putting rava idlies on another table. I point to them and change my order. He doesn't understand my accent. Frank expects a particular lunch but is served several puffy breads with a lot of oil and some of the potato/cauliflower mix that I like, even though it is a little too spicy for me. He is a bit short tempered with the waiter.

"I told you," he says sternly, "I wanted this." He points to the menu.

I tell him I'm moving to a larger room and I want to buy kitchen things. He knows someone who is leaving, but she might have sold everything already. He volunteers to take me on his motorcycle over to Shreepurum to see if his friend wants to sell her kitchen belongings. The bike won't start at first and he has to coast down the street to get it running. I'm tense on the back because I'm not sure I trust Frank as a driver. The roads are bumpy and there are many big rocks scattered around and people driving recklessly, cutting very close to other vehicles, bikes and pedestrians.

The woman Frank is looking for isn't home, but in the apartment next door he starts a conversation with a young English man, about Mysore, the other students and Ramaji. Something about the tone—a kind of youthful bravado— makes me think that perhaps I'm too old for this group. They suggest tea and Frank says he will go out and buy some milk. He asks me if I want to stay or return to the hotel. I decide to go back to the hotel and rest.

On the back of Frank's bike, with a big bottle of water between us, I hold on to him. The last ride I had on a cycle in Mysore was last year with Dimitri, sailing around the Mysore Palace at night. I was exhilarated and frightened as I held my arms around his body. He drove very fast. It must have been a Sunday because the palace lights were on.

That's enough for today. I'm going to turn off the computer, move candles near the bed in case the lights go out, and prepare for sleep.

*

At 4 a.m., I wake up to the sound of a bird—a chickadee I think—and I do a little warm up practice to try to stretch out my spine and my back, hoping to relax the muscles and the nerve in my calf.

In the lobby, Raju, the morning attendant, is asleep on the sofa under a blanket. No tea yet. I return to my room and make a bottle of saline solution to clean my sinuses. The little plastic netti works better than the ceramic one because the nose is longer and thinner. I brush my teeth with myrrh powder, a simple antiseptic herb that tastes good. A simple approach to eating and care of the body is something I've begun to learn through my yoga practice and my trips to India. I guess it is congruent in some ways with my life as a child, growing up in a working class suburb outside of Detroit. My father was a factory worker at Ford Motor Company and my mother was a housewife. Our life was simple in part because of our lack of money. Five children, a very sick mother, and one small income created limits for us. Even though I was the oldest, all my clothes were hand-me-downs from my older cousins. My room was a little corner in a half finished attic. There were hardly ever any second helping with our meals. Nothing much was ever thrown out. Besides lack, there was the protestant ethic my mother brought to our life. Don't waste anything. Don't be extravagant. No ornate saints and relics in the church, just God, the minister, the congregation and your knees on the floor.

When she was dying—I was twelve years old—she fell out of her hospital bed trying to reach for a vision of Jesus. A simple life, but what made it different from the simplicity of yoga is that the intention was not directed toward health and happiness. Instead the emphasis was on austerity and obedience, saving your soul and your money rather than experiencing joy and bliss. Pleasure was minimal. Maybe that's why I can never save a dime now. By the time a new paycheck arrives, I'm broke.

Soon the sun will come up and the morning chant to Sri Venkatesa Suprabhatam will wake everyone. It's time to wake up, clean the house, wash off the front steps, draw a design in front of the stoop and begin the morning puja rituals.

*

Raju unlocks the front door for me. It has just turned daylight. All is quiet. A man in a white t-shirt leans over the balcony of his house and smiles. I say good morning as I float down the street. Women in their colorful saris scrub the walkways and draw chalk designs, rangolis, in front of their homes. A dog asleep on the corner lifts up his head. He is surrounded by a clutter of garbage. Does he remember me from last year or do I remember him in particular or only his brownish grey breed and family. The black, crow-like raven-like birds swoop from tree to tree. Do they remember me walking this way? I must buy a shawl today to cover my head so they don't land on me.

The woman with tomatoes in a basket on her head passes by. "Toe-ma-te," she hollers.

When I turn left around Jagamohan Palace, I am surprised—the Hayagriva Temple has changed. Now it is white. This circle is one of my favorite spots in Mysore. In the morning it is very quiet here. Two barefoot men in white dhotis conduct ritual puja at the street altar. Crows wander across the dusty intersection. A policeman sits in front of the station that occupies a corner of the temple building. Slowly the traffic will increase until in the afternoon, you can barely walk across it—crowded with trucks, workers, rickshaws, and tourists cutting through to see the palace.

This morning, a western woman with a long blonde pony tail leans against the temple door.

"Is Mr. Jayaraj here yet?" I ask.

"His scooter is here so he must be inside."

I climb the steps and enter the space of the shala. I love this place with its ancient, dusty, cathedral-like rooms. The photographs of yogis with the garlands of flowers draped around them. Let my practice here be easy on my spine, I think as I take off my sandals and set them next to a pair of men's shoes. I walk past Mr. Jayaraj's office, the padlock in place, and open the door to the women's room. There is my little corner from last year. The doors to the pranayama room are unlocked, but no one's there yet. Back into the main men's room, I lean against the wall and wait. An Indian man enters quietly and begins to take off his street clothes. And then Bill arrives—the man from Ireland who I met yesterday and who my yoga teacher, Manny, suggested I talk to if I have any computer problems. He's been living in India for some time. He is perhaps my age, stocky with a muscular body, one of his front teeth missing. He smiles. Yes, India for a long time.

I greet Mr. Jayaraj, and he's at first his distanced self. "Hello, yes, hello, follow me." He waddles into his office and sits down facing me. The office is cluttered with papers, dust and little brown bottles. I ask him how much he charges for a week (1500 rupees, an equivalent of about $35). I pay him and present him with a little book of drawings, number five of an edition of twenty that I made last year; there is one drawing of him standing in his clean white dhoti and shawla looking over the center margin of the book, and there are also many sketches of the other students from last year, a few of the Indian men who were studying with him, and numerous dogs and cows who congregate outside the shala.

He is happy to accept the book. He puts on his glasses and sits for a few minutes, examining it. Then he leads me into the little room to the left of his office and we start again. I'm so happy to be in the temple with the breeze from the smoky street and the sound of Mr. Jayaraj teaching a new student the opening chant.

*

Sitting on the stoop of the corner store, I talk with Nayanashi, a woman who is worldly as a result of years of interaction with western yoga students. She even speaks a little Spanish. She asks about Isabella. Nayanashi's thin, quiet father sits in the corner of the store, silent as always. If she speaks to him in Kannada to ask about some product, he answers in one or two words. He often seems sullen and unhappy sitting in the shadows. He reminds me of my father who sat in his chair in the living room, sleeping away every evening in the months following my mother's death. I've never met Nayanashi's mother. Perhaps there is a death behind his unhappiness, too. The family sells water, some groceries, ghee and oils from bulk containers. The little store is dark and dirty and not very well stocked. I believe the family survives on purchases by yoga students staying in the hotel.

*

In the years prior to studying yoga, I experienced a lack, a visceral longing for love, care, and someone to make me feel whole again. I was depressed. Even as I cared for my own children, I couldn't recover from my mother's death. She was the nurturer in our family, and when she was gone, I was alone, the oldest, the one my younger siblings looked to for care. Lenny reminded me of her. He also was kind and loving. She had red hair, he had red hair. They both had problems with mitral valves in their hearts. I guess I'm simplifying a bit with this analysis, but the point I'm trying to make is that after we split up, for a long time I didn't know how to be happy. Everywhere I looked I saw what would soon be lost. I was grieving.

Lenny and I used to take our yellow van down to Eastern Market on Saturdays and shop. I'd never eaten cashews, avocados, asparagus, mangos, blintzes and borscht. He loved to shop and talk to vendors. I'd never listened to jazz before. He took me to hear

Charlie Mingus in a little club on Woodward Avenue. Jazz was an integral part of our lives, with Lenny's many musician friends in and out of our apartments. With my white suburban working class background, I arrived downtown, starved for culture and Lenny introduced me to a whole new world.

*

The new email station down the street from the Kaveri Lodge takes forever to connect. But this place is clean, spacious and airy as opposed to the cramped, toxic place around the corner. So I wait. It takes time to learn how things function here.

Two roosters outside, one following the other. I make a quick sketch of a very elegant rooster who struts around in front of the astrology shop. Motorcycles pass by, slowly but surely. A woman, no maybe a young teenage girl in rags with two children covered in dirt appears at the window with her arm outstretched.

"Hello money," she says.

"No," I say, shaking my head. There are too many people begging and I don't know when and who I should give or not give to.

8 p.m.—walk along the road—with many bikes and rickshaws. Now and then a truck. I'm a bit melancholic tonight since there are hardly any yoga students staying in the hotel, and the students who are around this year are much younger than I am and their concerns are quite different from mine. One must share some base with another to be truly amiable. Otherwise it's just a gesture. Isabella and I met at Ramaji's on our first or second day in Mysore last year. Instantly, we were friends even though we couldn't speak fluently to each other. I think we recognized a shared artistic view of the world. Plus, as she said in a recent email, we are both unlucky with love.

*

Bill tells me that the person who usually practices beside me, Elijah, is learning to be a chiropractor and perhaps he can help me with some adjustments on my spine.

"Tomorrow, I show you more," says Mr. Jayaraj. He hands me new copies of the chant and the poses.

Out of the temple and so happy. People say hello to me as I pass. I think they recognize me from last year.

Right now there are the sounds of a family talking outside my room and a little Indian child running past my door, his feet slapping against the floor. I'm drowsy. Perhaps it's a good idea to rest before running errands. Perhaps it's a good idea to run errands before the afternoon sun heats up. The end of May is the hottest part of the year. I hear the sound of the brooms passing over the floor in the room next door. When I return Mahadeshwara tells me that my new room will be ready in just one-half hour.

Around the corner at Iyengar's restaurant, the young waiter I like so much floats over, tips his head without speaking, indicating that he wants my order.

"Keshraba and Cho Cho Bath."

"Yes, tea," he says, his head tipping back and forth in a sideways figure eight to indicate yes, yes, of course.

"I'm so happy to see you," I say. I'm not sure that he remembers me.

Iyengar's Mess is a Mysore Brahmin establishment. The rooms are like halls with long tables, benches, shiny and clean, high ceiling with purple walls. In the back, there are dark, dank rooms full of barefoot men wearing lungis and carrying tins of food as they pass from one room to the next. Perhaps they make food and take it elsewhere. I will return to the hotel, I think, move, bathe, rearrange my belongings, eat some bananas and papaya, sit down at the computer, and then rest before I run errands.

The day has slipped away. After napping for several hours in the afternoon, I curl into a ball. My joints are sore because the mattress I'm sleeping on is only a few inches thick. Since yesterday, the condition of my calf has not changed. I stretch out, then roll into a ball again.

Downstairs, I ask Rupesh if it's possible to switch mattresses with one of the other beds. He comes upstairs and surveys the bed, shakes his head in a sideways figure eight and points to some mattresses in the hallway. I ask him if we can put one on top of the other in my room and move one frame out. This will give me room for my kitchen. He does not look very happy about this, but he yells for Suresh, who does not come, and then together we push the frame into the hallway. The room looks very different, not as grand, and the mattresses, one on top of the other, do not make a bit of difference in terms of comfort.

I stop at the email station. The internet is moving very slowly. The blue line hangs there on the bottom of the screen for five minutes more. Finally, I pick up emails from Jessie and Josh and lose an email from my subletters. Then the whole thing freezes up. I'm frustrated. The woman in the email station isn't helpful. She doesn't speak English, she's always giving me dirty looks, and I hear her refer to me as "Auntie," which I think is the equivalent of "Old Lady." I give up without sending an email to Dimitri and quickly move over to the dingy email station next to the chemical fertilizer shop, where I try again.

After spending close to an hour and a half on the internet, sending only a few notes, I walk along the main road by the palace toward the vegetable market. Along typewriter row, I avoid bikes and cows and other vehicles. The sun is beginning to get hot. I stop at the pharmacy and buy some hand and body soap, and then search through the other shops along Sayaaji road for towels and blankets. Finally at Temple shop, where the old man sits at the sewing machine in the front, I look at blankets. They unfold one, spread it out, then another, then another.

I'm uncomfortable with the clerk opening thirty blankets all over the counter. When you enter an Indian store, the shopkeeper immediately starts opening up every blanket or sari until they are piled all over. I then find it very difficult to say, well, I'm not interested in these, maybe tomorrow. Someone explained to me once—it is because Indians are very hard workers. They want to make a sale. They will open up one hundred blankets if necessary.

Finally, I select a red and beige design that is a little busy and not traditional Indian—more like an American Indian print. The old man begins to cut the pillow cases off and sew them on an old black machine.

To the corner I go and then back again, looking for the store where they sell the silk scarves. A little boy whom I used to talk to last year is a little bigger, but he's still selling incense on the street. He wants to know my name. When I duck into a store, he sits on the curb waiting for me. When I've finished shopping, and I'm climbing into a rickshaw, he catches up with me. Against my better judgment, I give him a few rupees. I would give him more, but I have no more change.

The rickshaw man is unusual. He tells me before we leave, "This will cost 10 rupees." Last year, they said 15 even though the meter would read 10. When we arrive at the hotel, I give him 15. He is happy.

I feel awkward about money here. I'm not sure whether it is a good idea to give money to people who are asking for it, and it is difficult not to become irritated about being accosted all the time.

One of the difficult tasks for westerners in India is to learn how to avoid or accept difficult and inefficient situations without becoming irritated and emotional. We are so used to our individual space and time; the level of efficiency necessary to support these simply doesn't exist in India.

The market is grueling. The flowers, especially the jasmine and roses, are beautiful, but this morning all the vegetables are covered with flies. It is hard to imagine eating anything. I am searching for dishes, cups and silverware. People are knocking into me and yelling at me. My love for India is receding. A good lesson. Do not go shopping mid-afternoon.

As I climb out of the rickshaw, the tailor, Suhas, walks out of the hotel lobby. He waves and smiles and within minutes he's at my room, wanting to make clothes for me. I say hello, ask about his family and tell him that I'm not in a hurry to make anything this year. I tell him this even though I have only two things to wear. Who needs a wardrobe of skirts, blouses, pants and dresses? These then require closets and big apartments.

*

In the first few years Lenny and I lived together, we wore levis, t-shirts and army boots. Because we wore the same size, we shared everything, even our torn up, patched levis. And we kept everything mixed together in one dresser. When I became pregnant with Jessie, though, my body changed and then so did my aesthetic—big blouses and flowing granny dresses. That's also when Lenny decided to cut his hair. I came home from class one afternoon and he was sitting in a chair in the middle of the kitchen. A girlfriend of mine was standing there with her scissors, his red hair was all over the floor. I guess he was preparing to be a father.

When I first met him he was light and humorous, his spirit and his step. He loved me from the first time he met me even though I was skinny, a little hunched over and a little depressed. And it didn't matter to me that he had a drug habit. At the time, that was just the downside of a tender, politically-aware life.

*

It's Friday morning, 4 a.m. My light is the only light on the floor.

I eat an imported apple from Australia, order tea and then do some stretches for my spine, a little preface practice before I leave for my regular practice. I'm so stiff, the bed is so hard, and my sciatic nerve is burning from the long plane ride. I am turning over and over at night because of my joints. I'm going to find a better mattress somewhere.

Then the sound of a deep man's voice over a nearby loud speaker, saluting the greatness of God and Mohammed and summoning Muslims to morning prayer. I'm reading *A Source Book in Indian Philosophy*, and I note there is no section on Islam, and yet Muslims are everywhere.

A light feeling of moisture, perhaps a promise of rain, more than likely though just a subtle shower, promising monsoon season will soon begin, but not today. As I walk along Chelavambu Road, the women congregate with their red plastic water jugs to take water from the well and carry it back to their homes. We, the wealthy tourists, are staying in a hotel with running water.

I like the yogashala-temple building better in yellow. The white will soon become dirty. Perhaps this is just a primer and the yellow coat will reappear next year.

I am a little startled by a motorcycle turning in front of me. In the afternoon, traffic is crazy, so many vehicles, pedestrians, and people breaking the laws of street order. Soon I'm going to join them. I'll buy my burner for cooking and rent a scooter. Monique explains that the key is not to react to anything. Just keep going. That is the hardest thing to do, practicing yoga in a very chaotic situation.

At the temple, I climb the stairs, put my sandals next to several other pairs of sandals and men's shoes. There are three or four Indian men beginning their practices. They never seem too consistent with their vinyasas, breaking away often from their practices to talk to each other.

I decide not to lift up and jump back but instead to lean forward and jump back. It's slightly easier and perhaps better for my back today. I won't push myself today since my foot is very heavy and my calf is heavy too. And my neck is a bit crooked. I sound like an invalid, but actually I'm doing better every week since I injured my back in January, herniating a disk as I practiced asanas as calisthenics exercises rather than as yoga. The practice goes well even with all the interruptions from Mr. Jayaraj, who is not sure I'm really doing what I should. He keeps stopping and teaching me the sequence that he thinks I have forgotten.

*

Outside the temple, I sit on the stoop and wait for Elijah, a very thin man who is able to do the umpteenth series. His face is covered with freckles, his hair is long and pulled up on his head in a disheveled manner. I'm not sure if he is from California or Australia. When he was practicing next to me, I tried to imitate his very smooth, deep way of entering into the asanas.

He is just starting his chiropractic studies, he tells me after class, and he's not experienced enough yet to make adjustments, but there's a bone man two streets from the hotel, close to Double Road.

He thinks, though, that I can slowly correct the problem with my yoga practice. He shows me how I can lean over all the way with my hands flat on the floor, legs straight and let my neck hang freely and then swing the neck to the right, to the left and then back and forth deepening the swing. I can feel my neck cracking and when I stand up I feel so much better. "You can learn to make your own adjustments. It may take longer but it will probably stay longer."

As the afternoon progresses, my calf is less tight, but my lower back is very stiff. As I read, I extend my legs against the wall and then I switch to reading on my side rolled into a ball. Funny, as soon as I believe what Elijah has to say, my back begins to recover.

*

I'm the only person at Subrata's. I order chai, Indian breakfast and a bottle of water. Subrata is her ever ready business self. Yes, our motorcycle is used only by us. Talk to my son. Yes, of course you would like to wash your hands. Come inside for some soap.

Each day, I'm hoping more and more that Harihara will work with me. I'm anxious to work with someone who isn't in the business of making personal money by teaching westerners yoga, so there can be a clear spiritual relationship between student and teacher. Mr. Jayaraj is a lovely man, but I don't feel I'm learning anything new from him, and I need some serious help with my back and my practice.

Jeevesh tells me Matthew is in the back bedroom, working on the computer. I see the back of his head and his long gray braid.

"Hello, Gina, I was wondering when you would come around."

I tell him I'm not practicing with Ramaji this year. Instead, I'm hoping to begin working with Harihara.

The part of him that was there to greet me as a colleague recedes a bit.

I lie a little and tell him I cannot afford Ramaji's fees when in fact that is only a minor factor. Even if I were wealthy, I wouldn't practice there again.

He explains that Ramaji charges so much (seven hundred U.S.

dollars a month) because many teachers come here for a few weeks and then go out and teach his series and make a lot of money.

I practiced yoga with him the year before and I have some drawings of him in my book. Even though I am skeptical about the business he conducts, I did enjoy his humor, and I want to give him a copy of the book. I tell Matthew I have a gift for Ramaji and I will take it to him during conference, but I'm not sure what to say to him. I guess I could tell him the truth, that I am practicing elsewhere.

"No," he indicates, "No. You say you are going to do some traveling. Tell him that. Don't burn your bridges. Don't tell him you are practicing with anyone else."

"Hum, in the book I also include drawings of Mr. Jayaraj."

"Don't give it to him!" he says, emphatically. "As Ramaji would say, tell the truth unless it will hurt and then don't lie, don't say anything."

Well that sounds like a philosophy that could keep someone from speaking up about any problematic practices, I think to myself, as I walk back to the hotel.

*

I speak to Mahadeshwara, the manager of the hotel, a very sweet man with round lips and a round face, his forehead always marked from a recent puja. He is a challenge to communicate with though, since he can't speak English very well and my American Midwestern twang doesn't sound at all like English to him. I tell him I'm looking for Monique, a young woman from Philadelphia, whom I met last year.

"Monique," he says, "Monique is on the telephone." He points at a door.

I peek into room #1. She is huddled over the telephone. She looks up, waves and smiles. "I'm talking to Dennis."

"Come up to room 10 when you are done."

I remember that she talks on the telephone for a long time even on an international call, so I begin my bath with the pitcher and a large pail of water. Some people call it a shower. It's neither a shower nor a bath, simply pouring pitchers of water over your body, sudsing up and rinsing off with more pitchers.

Monique is beautiful as usual, wearing a tight black shirt, skirt, a shawl, and her long shiny black hair pulled into a thick tail. She wants to take my clothes, she tells me when she comes upstairs and make copies for herself. Funny Mysore yoga student activity. Can I use your pants? your shirt? The fabrics are beautiful and the tailor is so cheap, but it can become a time consuming activity, looking for fabric in the heat and talking with the tailor. Some activities like shopping for food, eating and this and that can consume the entire day.

Monique sits in my chair and I stretch out on the bed. "Gina, you seem like you have been here forever."

"In some ways, yea, but in other ways, I feel like a stranger."

Then she takes me on her scooter to pick up a burner so I can cook in my room. Why, I wonder, are all the men standing around, as if they are on vacation? Why are all the stores closed? Perhaps because it's not yet eleven o'clock. This is the store, but it's closed. I will come back later.

I hold on to Monique as we slow down, turn and move smoothly over the streets. I'm studying how she drives because today I am planning to pick up a scooter from Anoop.

Lenny and his older brother, Jacob, are standing on a cement ledge and the country behind them recedes down-hill into a gentle white fog. Perhaps they were visiting with his uncle in Wisconsin. Lenny told me about these trips. Jacob is standing on the left side, wearing a striped t-shirt and baggy pressed pants with dress shoes. He has a serious look on his face while his left hand is draped around his little brother's shoulder. Lenny is about six years old and he has his right arm around his big brother's waist. He's casually leaning into a curve as he poses in his bermuda shorts with a kookie scrunched up face. The clear focus on the boys as opposed to the fog in the background accentuates the temporary nature of that moment.

The drawing I've made catches Lenny's curvy quality and Jacob's straight arrow approach. And that's the way the rest of their lives went too, Lenny always avoiding the norm and Jacob follow-ing it. The light is on Lenny's skinny calves.

I put the drawing and the photo into the puja space in my room and then I go down to talk to Mahadeshwara. He tells me that all stores will be closed today until at least 2 or 3 o'clock because of a strike, a bundt. Okay. Well since I can't cook now, I decide to go to Iyengars Mess. The place is full of men. They seat me at a table in the main room, and the men at the table next to me sneak looks at me and then snicker.

I'm wearing a white, short sleeve shirt and my shiny, green syn-thetic ankle length skirt. My only pair of pants is drying on the roof. Why are they staring at me and laughing? I'm covered. Perhaps it's because I'm not wearing a shawl. I must cover myself with a shawl or some of these people are convinced I'm a prostitute. As I finish eating, I promise myself to avoid Iyengar's at lunch time. It seems to be a man's spot. Then as I walk outside, I notice a few women eat-ing in the back room. That's where I should eat, in the women's room.

Whew. And it's so hot outside.

In the hotel lobby a group of westerners are seated around the coffee table, chatting. I sit down. Emily is worried about a rash she has on her face and arms. She's from California—thin, long brown hair, late 20's, dressed in very tight clothes that must create perpetual problems for her on the street. Brandy from California is traveling around the East, in Thailand, Burma, India. He is a newly trained acupuncturist and a serious yoga practice is something new to him. After this journey, though, he's planning to return home to open a yoga center and an acupuncture room. He wants to go to Jayaraj's in the morning. I tell him I will take him the first day so he knows where to go. He is a tall, handsome young man with light brown hair combed to the side. When I look in his eyes, though, he does not look back. There is a very tall couple from Australia, both about six feet tall. She is somewhat cool and removed. I drink a cup of tea.

Now I take Amy, a young woman from California who is staying in the hotel, for a walk to show her around. We stop on the stoop of the store that sells the burners. It's closed up tight. There is an ominous mood on the street because of the water strike. A man from the B.J.P. party is on a hunger strike. Do not give away the water of Mysore or there will not be enough for the people. The party threatens to cut off the water to the homes of the officials if they don't stop giving it away. Groups are hanging around on street corners. I see feet through the store gate. "What do you want?" "I wanted to buy a burner. What time will you open?" They are interested in selling me the burner even though they are breaking the bundt. I ask them to carry it to the hotel since it's too heavy for me.

When I return to the hotel, I feel awkward. The boys in the hotel probably earn in three months about the same amount of money I have spent on this burner and they manage to feed their entire families.

"Do you have a burner like this?" I ask.

"Oh, no. We use kerosene."

I'd burn down the hotel with a kerosene stove.

A young man, who works as an accountant, engages me in a conversation in the lobby. What is your work and yours, etcetera, back and forth. He is off from school for the summer and working in an office.

"How much is your salary?"

I'm a little stunned. If I tell him my salary, he will think I'm rich but I'm not. "Well, I'll tell you my rent," I say. "$1,100 for an apartment about half the size of this lobby."

"What is yours?" I ask.

"About 500 rupees for the same size."

"So that means I pay 100 times as much for my rent as you do. Even though we make what seems like a large amount of money, we also have a high cost of living."

Later I think this is a bit of a lie. I'm also able to live much better than he. I can rent my apartment and come here, for example, and buy new clothes and a computer. If I spend $5 here, I'm being extravagant. That is about 200 rupees. I spent $30 on the stove.

The hotel accountant, in his dusty shoes and red shirt, explains: "Yes, many Indians go to the United States, work very hard, save money and then come back to India to live off of it for the rest of their lives. They prefer to live here." That's something I have thought about although I've never been able to save any money. I'm going to try to sleep for a little while before practice.

Suddenly my foot is tingling all over the place like something is waking up. Please wake up foot, wake up wake up wake up. Let me lie down and concentrate on my foot.

*

After my mother died, my aunt gave my father a bag of old clothes and shoes from my cousin. I was excited about the turquoise quilted skirt, but the pair of clunky saddle shoes did not appeal to me. They are your size, my father said. Please Dad, don't make me wear those shoes to school. We were wearing little flats and pantihose, not saddle shoes. I had a worn pair of black flats, with two holes in the soles. Whenever necessary, I stole nylons from the drugstore, telling my father they were from my mother's drawer. He wouldn't listen to me. He forced me to wear those shoes. I remember standing behind the house, looking at those big clunkers, and then walking around for the entire day, hiding part of the time in the woods a few blocks outside the neighborhood. Finally, my grandmother—my father's mother who was living with us at the time—came to my rescue. She argued with him and then she bought me a new pair of flats. When I was with Lenny in the early 70's, I wore army boots.

*

Well, this isn't the first time I've ridden a motorcycle. Why am I so nervous about it? The year before I met Lenny, I bought a used Honda 125 and my brother taught me how to ride it and tune it. I used to love riding on the freeway with my hair blowing in the wind. That was over 25 years ago. I remember shifting the bike with my foot and riding it on the freeway without a helmet. My brother and his friends let me tag along with them once in a while when they were riding around Belle Isle. I say tag along because most of my brother's friends were riding Harleys and I had a hard time keeping up with them. When Lenny and I moved into the house on Avery Street—before Jessie was born—he bought a Honda 350 and we used to ride them together. For the winter, we stored them in a garage on Third Avenue. One year when Lenny had to go to a family funeral in Wisconsin, someone called me up and said the garage was wide open and our bikes were sitting there, waiting to be stolen. I telephoned a friend, Joe, to help me walk the bikes over to our yard. The bikes weren't tuned up and the plates had expired so we couldn't legally ride them. We had to walk, cutting through a rather desolate neighborhood between the university and Avery Street.

The Detroit Police stopped us with their guns drawn. "We had a phone call about a robbery of two motorcycles."

I showed them the old registrations and titles, but they refused to examine the papers seriously. They handcuffed us and put us in the back of the car. A black guy and a white girl stealing motorcycles. They put Joe in the hole and sat me in the middle of the station in handcuffs, laughing and ridiculing me. A girl stealing a motorcycle! Finally, someone checked the registration, released Joe and drove us with the cycles back to Avery. In the spring after Jessie was born, we sold Lenny's 350 to a friend who later crashed it into a house and broke her jaw. We left my 125 in the basement of the flat when we moved.

*

Here I am on Monday, a full day later. I have eaten some fruit, washed dishes, killed a few mosquitoes and taken out my clothes for practice. I have also spent some time thinking about how to stay organized, healthy and self-sufficient in this room. Cooked dinner last night and some of it's left in a container on the shelf. Ghee, rice, green beans, carrots and cashews. I think it's all still good this morning without refrigeration.

Harihara doesn't return until June 4th. So I'm here for at least five days more unless I visit Swami Bramadeo in BR Hills. I think maybe it's important to stay put until the heat is washed out with rain. These men in the lobby really bother me though, staring at the sexy videos on the TV and making little grunts. Mahadeshwara notices me and turns the station to what seems to be a golf tournament. The men are swarming around the lobby. Please go away. Go eat dinner. I won't even look at them. I hear the word "American" and then they are back here sitting around me. Political men, says Mahadeshwara—Oh how I long for home today.

*

I fall asleep waiting for the morning chant. For some reason it doesn't begin until 5:45 today. I wake up with a start. I promised to take Brandy over to Mr. Jayaraj so he knows how to get there. I throw on my clothes, including the awkward scarf.

During the practice, Mr. Jayaraj comes over to me regularly and interrupts, "You did D? Like this?" He spreads out his hands, bends his knees.

"Yes, already did."

"You did like this?" He demonstrates surynamascar and loses his breath. Actually, despite his belly, he is much thinner this year than last.

He passes in and out of our room, and into the other little room with the two American women practicing and then into the very large room with the Indian men. Brandy is sitting on the stoop watching. At first, I'm the only person practicing, but then Bill and Elijah come. My mind keeps straying. I imagine paying some women to come here and clean the room, pound the rugs, sweep, and clean the huge cobwebs up in the rafters.

A bird flies in the window and lands up on one of the beams.

Chant, move, rest. Was it a good practice? Yes, I think so even though I was leaning forward more than up.

So many little critters in the hotel room this morning. Perhaps it will rain and there will be water for everyone. Ants, large ones, little red ones, mosquitoes. I will pick up some mosquito netting to cover the windows, I think, and some tape.

And so, I say goodbye for the day to Mr. Jayaraj, and he asks me about my "friend."

"I just met him."

"You take him with you now. That is sufficient. He has seen enough."

"Ok." I signal to Brandy, who is leaning against the wall, absorbed in watching Bill in yoganidrasana, lying on his back with both of his feet tucked behind his head. "He wants me to take you with me."

Back at the hotel, I shower and change clothes, and go downstairs to wait for Monique. Brandy is sitting in the lobby too, wondering where to find an ATM. This I would like to know, too, just in case of an emergency. Monique comes in beautifully dressed again—hello, hello. Last year when I first met her, she was on the roof with Anna and me, talking about how as a child her father, who practiced Buddhism, taught her every evening to review her day in a reflective, meditative way. It was evening, I remember, and we were leaning against the edge of the roof watching the black birds swirl around in the Mysore sky. Her father married her mother in Cambodia during the war and then they had a baby. When she was one year old, the family moved back to the states. Monique invites Brandy to have breakfast with us and we talk about the day and how she can help me learn to navigate traffic with the scooter I'm going to pick up later.

*

Last year Isabella and I would sit outside at this café and say "Paris" with a French accent and laugh. We could hardly understand each other but there was so much included in this—two artists imagining they were sitting at a café in Paris when in fact they were on this dusty, dirty street while cows and horses and oxen driven carts passed by. To us it was very funny. We would sit in the plastic chairs, brush the flies away and drink chai. Today, she is in Mexico and I haven't seen her since last August when I left Mysore.

*

Walking down a street in Shreepurum today, I run into Roberto, a man from Cost Rica, who arrived in Mysore last year and is still here. He greets me with a big smile.

"Hello," he says, "you were the first person I spoke to last year when I arrived. Gina, isn't that your name? How long are you here this year?" He's a short, wiry, animated fifty year old man with tattoos all over his chest and arms. He saunters along the road lined with big Indian houses, totally comfortable wearing only his blue boxer shorts.

"You must stop by my house," he says, "and have some tea."

He tells me he has rented a little cottage down the street for five years. He is practicing yoga with two of the teachers in Mysore, and he is doing very well. His wife is in Minnesota learning English.

Last year when I met him, he was frantic about finding a place to live in and a place to study yoga. I remember when he and his wife, a very tall African-English woman, appeared in the hotel lobby. Every time I saw him, he had a list of questions to ask about what he should do to become instantly adept at yoga. Just practice, Roberto, one day at a time. Go to Jayaraj and start tomorrow. I want to be able to teach yoga when I leave India in four years, he said. Don't start out wanting to be a yoga teacher before you've even become a yoga student, Roberto. And which book should I read? Who should I work with?

This year Roberto seems a little calmer. I tell him that I will stop by next week to visit.

*

In the afternoon, I hail a rickshaw to Shivanand's. Last year he gave me tabla lessons. There is a group of people waiting for lessons. Shivanand is so busy that he looks a little stressed. Last year, while I enjoyed an introduction to tablas, I realized quickly that it was not really my art form. I never was able to relax and play. I give him a copy of the book I made and he is happy.

I sit on he floor watching the lessons for a little while and then I catch another rickshaw to Nilgeris for groceries. It's a 40 rupee trip, circling here, circling there. The driver doesn't understand me, I don't know where I am, he doesn't know where we are, and I'm frustrated.

"Continue straight," I say. Perhaps I will see something that rings a bell. Nothing familiar. Just one Indian street after another. I'm in some neighborhood I don't know, perhaps on the far side of the palace.

"Stop," I say, giving him his money and a tip and flagging another driver to take me back to the Kaveri Lodge.

In the hotel, I call Anoop and ask if I can pick up the scooter tomorrow morning instead of today—when I'm rested. I'm a little afraid to manipulate it in this traffic. At the corner store, I buy ghee, salt, water, and honey, just enough to cook with the vegetables and rice from the market.

Upstairs, I try to figure out a way to clean vegetables, chop up things and cook without making a mess. Of course, a mess. This is new for me, cooking on the floor.

Fall asleep at 7 p.m.

*

The bliss of the street and the breeze on Monday morning. I walk under the sound of the morning salutation. Three women pour water and sweep the stones in front of their homes. Another sits with a little boy on her lap and a cup of milk. She smiles at him and he clings to her. A woman walks behind me, hollering *Mallige*, the Kannada word for flowers—a basket of jasmine on her head. All is quiet except for the sound of birds, her call, footsteps and the brooms scraping the cement.

I have started a new series of animal drawings and also doors with rangolis. I snap a photo of a beautiful pattern outside a turquoise house.

Practice was wonderful even though right now I'm tired and my back hurts a little. My chiropractor, Steve, would say that this is good because it's an honest pain at the root of the problem. Mr. Jayaraj was adjusting Bill and there was something interesting in the image. Two burly, older men, one adjusting the other, both in meditative states, both with little pony tails, one Irish and the other Indian. I receive some pranayama instruction from Mr. Jayaraj and then Bill asks me over for lunch.

Lots of bites on my arms. Must go look up which herb to put on them. Tea Tree Oil. All over my arm.

At lunch, Bill smokes cigarettes like a fiend even though he has been practicing a rigorous yoga for ten years or so. Maybe that's why he's coughing so much every morning. The deep breathing and exercise are probably cleaning out his lungs.

"No one has ever gotten sick from my salads," he says, as he saturates the tomatoes with lemon. "This is an effective antibacterial." The vegetables still have dirt on them, but he pressure cooks them so everything is steamed. I hesitantly eat his lunch, and then at home, I take a big dose of grapefruit seed extract. I did enjoy the salad, but the filthiness of his living conditions (the house was damp, covered with mildew and dirt) and the smoking was too much. Also, he has an obvious shelf of books on tantra and sex, and I thought I saw him looking at my body out of the corner of his eye while he cut up vegetables. Since I wasn't interested in him in that way, I was a bit relieved to finish, thank him for lunch and return to the hotel.

Rickshaw fiasco to pick up a map from Ashok Books and back. These bumpy rides. My back hurts from rickshaws with no springs. Where is Mohan, the rickshaw driver from last year? At Anoop's email station, another young man asks me—"How much is your rent at home, Madam?"

I could keep a record of only the sounds outside my room—a scraping sound from the yard underneath the roof outside my window, the sound of water running in another room, two children talking in the hallway in one of the Indian languages, and a quiet chant from the Hindu temple in back of the hotel.

Anoop's uncle comes by at 7:30 p.m. with the scooter. He is going to take me out and let me try it. In the dirt median of a double road on the outskirts of town, I turn it on, hit the pedal to bring up the gas, a man on an ox cart goes around my left, and then I drive very tentatively, unsure and unsteady.

After two or three wobbly tries, he shakes his head and says, "Madam, you will be dangerous on the road because of nervousness."

How could I have forgotten how to ride a motorbike? I'm thankful for his analysis. We arrive back at the hotel and I'm surprised when he asks, "So do you want the bike?" I thought he wouldn't allow me to take it, but I am the final judge.

"No. I'm going to accept your suggestion, Ravi. If I'm dangerous, I will not do this."

I must remember, in Mysore, do everything like NYC—always do only what is necessary to reduce your anxiety and heat. Do not go downtown in the middle of the day when the sun is beating down on your head. That is why there is a rest time in tropical climates. One must not come to India to learn yoga and instead destroy oneself.

Right now it's noon and I'm cooking rice and vegetables on my burner. It smells so good. The propane slowly increases in strength, causing a slight burning. Last year Anna of Germany gave me good advice about how to live here. Cook for yourself; dress for the weather and culture in light baggy cotton with kadi shawls and sleeveless sari blouses; swim in the afternoon; take rickshaws not scooters; between one and three rest; and be cautious about your relationship with other yoga students, who are mostly interested in stimulating the lower chakras. For the most part, she was very helpful, interesting, and friendly, but then just as I'd start to be comfortable with her, smack, she'd hit me in the face with an unexpected harsh criticism. When I complained about exhaustion due to a bout of dysentery while we were at an evening dance performance, she turned around and caustically chastised me—You're always complaining, Gina. Maybe she was correct—I don't bear illness well.

Once when I was practicing at Jayaraj's, Anna started yelling because some students who weren't serious about yoga were chatting. By the time she left the shala, she had told off four people, including me and Mr. Jayaraj. Later, she apologized. Another student, who was a doctor and who was staying in the little room on the balcony, told me that she was actually very ill and she wasn't acknowledging it. The doctor was quite sure that Anna was a hemophiliac suffering from hepatitis, which she had picked up in India. I feel Anna's tough, realistic, bitter and irritated presence here even though she is gone. I'm staying in the room beneath hers, the room where she was recovering last year.

Restless sleep last night after the nervous motorcycle ride. Took some valerian and then slept until 5:30 am. This morning one of the yoga students at Subrata's explains to me that the little red spots on my arms and legs are from ants. There are ants in the hotel and I should buy some ant chalk to put around my bed and at the edges of my room. I remember Isabella doing that.

Oops, check the rice. Odd, how I enjoy cooking for myself, especially here on the floor. This is odd after years of raising children and not enjoying cooking much at all. Lenny and I used to take turns. Of course, there wasn't the same easy availability of restaurants as in New York. And we didn't have enough money for restaurant dining anyway. Neither of us were chefs, but we had our specialties. Lenny made a spicy chili, some fried chicken liver dish, baked eggplants, and he was very social, often inviting groups of friends on Sunday afternoon for a brunch that would last all day. I would try to cook dishes the children liked, macaroni and cheese, rice with broccoli and cashews, plain vegetables. The only time I ever enjoyed cooking was the year before Jessie was born when we were sharing the house with my brother and another friend. We used to bake bread and make casseroles. It was a communal affair. After we moved to New York, Lenny and I had to work long hours, and so Jessie and Josh ended up being raised for the most part on carry-out food. They never liked much of anything I cooked anyway.

This morning, I stop to ask Raju if he can bring me tea every day at 5:15 a.m.

"Yes, 5:15 a.m," he says as he walks through the first floor hallway of the hotel, heading back to open the back gate for someone.

I wonder what his life is like. He has no front teeth and he's tall, bulky and slumped over. He nods to me in a very servile manner. Does he have children, a wife, a home? Where does he live when he has his one day off each week?

It's very hot outside and I'm worried about the red bumps. I decide to wear a sleeveless shirt and the light Krishna shawl that Vivian gave me when she returned to New York City last year from Northern India.

I'm so hot, I cannot practice yoga in this tight shirt, so I go into the little room and strip down to my sports bra.

"Is this all right, Mr. Jayaraj? I'm the only person here."

"Yes, it's fine. We are only interested in your asanas, nothing else. We are used to the way you people dress. That is why I have this room for the women and that room for the men. If you want adjustments, I adjust. If you are uncomfortable, I do not."

"I want adjustments."

The practice is strong and Mr. Jayaraj gives me advice about massaging the painful area in my back.

Why did I come here? To think differently. To remove myself from the place where I am at ease so I can see differently. Here in the newspaper there are book reviews and editorials referring to tantra and yoga. Yoga is an integral part of the culture.

Let me go now and take my laundry off the line. The sun is so hot at 2:00 p.m. that everything will be dry in half an hour. I'm going to run so I don't have to shut the window—hoping a monkey won't visit my room while I'm gone for five minutes.

I call Harihara's house again. He will not be back until June 4th.

*

Wednesday. It is so hot outside that if I walk a block, I must run back to the hotel and hide in the room. And I am mostly alone.

What can I learn from this solitude?

Sitting on the floor, cutting up vegetables with rice and cooking them in a little pot. Life can be so much simpler than we make it in the USA. Do we really need a big stove? I sit cross-legged and eat my lunch on the floor right beside the pot I cooked it. Then I clean everything in the plastic pail in the bathroom, dry the dishes and put them on the bottom shelf next to the burner.

I can stand up from a squatting position now without even touching anything. This is an improvement after the herniated disk. Just lean over on the flat of my feet and stand up.

Sitting cross-legged on the floor, I open the little bag with Lenny's photos and flip through them until one stands out. A side view of a gawky little boy with a brush cut, about ten years old. He's leaning forward after having thrown something into the space in front of him. His mother stands behind him watching with a concerned look on her face. I'm sure she was worried about him from the day he was born. His left hand is extended toward the left edge of the photo and his knees are knocked near the bottom. He's concentrating as the sun reflects off his mother's white blouse and then streams across his face. Other relatives stand around in a little group on the grass.

Was it a horseshoe he sent flying into the air?

Perhaps his mother is worried because he always used his left hand instead of his right. "Why won't he take a good job working for the telephone company?" she asked me when I was twenty-two years old and had just met Lenny. "He's not the type," I remember saying, "to work a straight, tedious job, for a utility company. Lenny was in the hospital then recovering from endocarditis, a bacterial infection in his blood caused from using contaminated needles. When he walked around the hospital in his hospital gown, with his long red braid and beard, holding on to an IV stand, I would call him Moses.

Now I make a sketch of Moses.

*

Lenny had heart surgery before I met him, along with a history of using heroin. During the nine years that we lived together, I was for the most part unaware that he had continued on and off with hard drugs. When I met him, I was experimenting with psychedelics and other non-addictive drugs, but because I was concerned about his well-being and didn't want to be a bad influence, I stopped taking drugs after a year or so except for the occasional use of marijuana. When Jessie was born, I stopped that, too. I knew Lenny was selling marijuana, drinking and maybe taking synthetic heroin once in a while, but I didn't realize the extent to which his drug use continued until many years later in New York when one of his friends told me the details. It was easy not to worry about him—he always worked, took care of the children, and when we were together in Detroit, he was like a father to me, protecting me and encouraging me to finish school and continue with my work as an artist.

I remember laying my ear on Lenny's chest the day after I met him and listening to his artificial valve click. That little piece of equipment was keeping him alive. We were so happy to have found each other. At the time, we were both alone and lonely, and we made a family for each other. I remember staying after hours in Cobbs Corner Bar with him and the other workers, drinking and dancing until five or six in the morning.

*

I ask the lady tailor down the block if she can make me a few sari blouses without sleeves, but a bit longer than the ones she is used to making. I'll buy the fabric. She looks at me as if I'm absolutely crazy, to want a sleeveless blouse. The Indian women look so hot wrapped in those saris. Her little blouses look a little like sexy bras with weird sleeves, and the fabric is really awful looking. In general saris are beautiful but the blouses leave a lot to be desired. In his travel book, William Dalrymple criticizes the Indians in Bangalore for being so resistant to the Miss World contest and women parading around in bikinis, the wicked influence of the west. After all, writes Dalrymple, less than a hundred years ago many Indian women went bare breasted. Perhaps it was the British, with their Victorian ways, who contributed the sari blouse and then helped institute some of the Indian sexual restrictions on women. Or perhaps only the poor women went bare-breasted.

*

I have breakfast at Upahar's and write a note to myself that I want to photograph the street from this table, looking out the door of the restaurant into the alley across the way with the cows and the women hanging their laundry. If it comes out right, there is a frame of the coca-cola cooler and the restaurant machinery.

Received an email from Dimitri today. He's back in New York teaching a workshop on kalari, an ancient martial art taught in Kerala, and preparing to fly back to Russia. He says he misses me a lot when he walks past my apartment. Then I send an email and it doesn't really go through. Or does it. I can't tell.

*

I take a different route to Jayaraj's, down the one way road and then up the truck road, a different experience, past the bars and the men sitting outside, drinking, after a long night. Hello, they say to me, smiling, as they lounge around on the stoops of the hotels. Then into the temple, up the stairs to the yogashala and that active dance of one and a half hours.

Right now my toes are numb and tingling.

Mahadeshwara calls a rickshaw for me and tells the driver where Dr. Anand's office is in Saraswati. I recognize the road as the road to the university. Only 15 rupees, he tells the driver, and then I give him 20. He is happy. The gates are pulled down on the doctor's office. I sit on the stoop beside two men until a little girl comes along and starts working at unlocking the doors. I help her push one metal gate up and then she invites me in. The office reminds me of the other ayurvedic office near the hotel, nothing pretentious, plastic chairs, candles lit because all the electricity in Mysore seems to have gone off with the brief and intense rains late this afternoon. There are only a few religious images in Dr. Anand's waiting room. It's kind of dark.

The thin girl tells me that her name is Akasha, she is twelve years old, and she has four other sisters and one brother. Her brother is a baby and three of her sisters are married. There is one child and one sister is pregnant. Akasha can expect to be married at about 17 years old. She is curious about my life and family and where I come from.

She asks me for a country coin.

I have one, a dime. I give it to her.

She tries to turn on a battery-run light that simply is not working.

"It's new," she says, tipping her head from side to side.

Dr. Anand is very capable with English and quite attractive. He tells me I look much younger than I am.

"The yoga," I say.

We talk a lot about my back. He says he is going to help me. We'll start with some medicines and salves. "Be careful," he tells me, "with forward bending and back bending."

"Careful? That is what I do every morning."

"Well, if anything hurts, stop."

If I can find three other students, he will run a class from 4:30 to 5:30 three times a week on the fundamentals of ayurveda.

I return home and Mahadeshwara is standing outside. He instructs me to tell him whenever I need a rickshaw and he will arrange it. Then the teenager, Kumar, passes by the hotel and after greeting each other—I haven't seen him since last year—he instantly asks me for money to help him buy his books. His grandmother told him that she had seen me. I was the woman who brought them the fruit basket and money last year. I do not like that he comes here and instantly asks for money. He's fifteen years old and he has learned to beg to the yoga students. The students are partially responsible for what has happened to this young man. He is slowly being ostracized from his own community. I've heard that often he doesn't go to school, he doesn't attend his yoga classes and he spends most of his time mooching off western yoga students. Last year, he was hanging around an American student with a drinking problem, who involved Kumar in a motorcycle accident in the middle of the night. He looks much younger than he really is, but soon he will be an older teenager and the students will not be interested in him. I wonder what will happen then.

An Indian man from Kovalum, who is staying in the hotel and practicing yoga, asks me where he can find decent food. I take him over to Iyengar's Mess. And then in the dark street, busy with rickshaws, motorcycles and pedestrians dashing here and there and swerving to avoid each other, I step gingerly around the potholes and right into a pile of cow manure.

The water isn't running in the hotel because of the perpetual electricity problem.

The Indians keep asking me why I am here. They are unable to understand how I could be traveling alone in this country. Where is your family? Yes, you have freedom, they say, but you are alone. I do not feel alone, I say, and I like my freedom.

The Tibetan settlement in Bylakuppe is a few hours away from Mysore. Vanessa and I leave the hotel about 11:00 a.m. and walk over to buy her a cotton shawl in a kadi shop on typewriter row, a little back street with many men working on manual typewriters. Then we take a rickshaw to the bus station. It is very hot and we are carrying a lot of bags. In the station, we try to get information regarding which bus we can take to reach Bylakuppe and where we can find it. Hardly anyone speaks English and it is chaotic with people milling everywhere.

Take this bus, says one person. Take another, take another. Get off here and take a rickshaw. Where? Kushalanagaratna. Or something like that. Finally we get on an old bus, stupidly choose a large seat, and within ten minutes an overweight grandmother and her four year old crying granddaughter squeeze in beside us. I'm squashed between the grandmother and Vanessa with my legs propped up on the back wheel cover.

The old woman leans on top of me. My shoulders are touching my ears as we begin a wild two hour drive through the country side outside Mysore.

"Good thing," I say to Vanessa, "we are not sitting in the front. This way we experience the swerves but with no anxiety over the dangerous driving."

Someone told me that buses in India are responsible for 70% of the accidents. They are reckless because they are paid for the number of trips they make a day rather than the amount of hours the drivers work.

The further we get into the country, the more visual and kinetic the relief. The air is clean and just looking at a horizon that isn't full of other human and animal bodies brings a sense of calmness.

Finally we arrive in Bylakuppe, a stop before Kushalanaratna (or whatever) and we ask a rickshaw driver how much he will charge to go to the monastery. 50 rupees. 50 rupees? Come on. He is the only rickshaw around though, so we agree to pay him. And then the longest, bumpiest, most impossible trip, down and around little paths, over rocky unpaved roads, around oxen, country people walking with baskets and pails on their heads, and monks in burgundy robes. Bump. Bump. No wonder it costs 50 rupees to go from Bylakuppe to Sera Monastery.

We are greeted at the Hospital Guest House by Sonam, a young man who cares for the rooms and guests. He sits at a plastic table on the veranda chatting with us. I remember him from last year when I came to Bylakuppe with two other yoga students in a taxi. He is a relative of one of the monks.

*

On the top steps of the Tibetan temple at Sera Monastery, we listen to the monks chanting.

Down below there are hundreds and hundreds of pairs of sandals on the steps along with a shiny black dog lying on his side. His feet dangle over the step as he snaps occasionally at the flies. Perhaps he is the French lover of the other black dog with the wiggle—named Frenchie—who lives in the hospital guest house.

We are sitting near the top of the steps and there is a powerful sound from hundreds and hundreds of seed mantras and a deep resonant echo. Below monks, nuns and others walk toward the back of the temple. A Tibetan couple climb the stairs and sit to listen, too.

The most astounding image is the horizon surrounding us, little odd shaped clouds passing from fields to mountains. The distance is immense. The sky is so open that you can see that, yes, you are standing on the earth in this particular spot and all around is a temple, and you are so small, listening to the sound of the monks rolling over the fields, om mani padma hum, om mani padma hum.

*

Now I'm in the room with a mosquito coil burning, a hard

mango, a scruffy wool blanket, half a bottle of water, and no book to read. I've been reading myself to sleep ever since I was a child and my mother took me to the library on Saturdays. She was the only child of nine to graduate from high school and she wanted me to be successful. When I was nine or ten years old, I was reading Dickens in bed, scrunched up next to the hall light. Now I fold my hands over my chest and remember the smell of paper.

*

At 5:30, dreaming about Sera Monastery, I turn over and realize, yes, I'm here again, covered with a wool blanket and some old worn sheets. I hear the morning sounds of cleaning, pails, clanking, water pouring, and rags hitting the cement. In the background more chanting. The air is wonderful, clean, a relief, no burning cow dung. Birds cawing. So nice to be in the country, especially this country.

I knock on Vanessa's door.

She says she slept horribly because she didn't take the sheet from the other bed to cover herself and she is sure there are fleas in her blankets. She borrows my shampoo for washing her body.

"Do you have any tissue?" she asks.

"I have it here in case of an emergency. Usually, I just use water."

She says she uses her hand.

"I guess," I say, "I'm loose enough so the water alone works."

Outside I decide to buy tea from the restaurant downstairs. No one is at the desk. There are piles of Tibetan bread and eggs on the counter. One monk is eating.

"No, no tea, no one until 7 a.m."

We take a trip to Camp #1, where we wander in and out of little shops. I am looking for some particular Tibetan skin cream for my girlfriend Vivian, but they don't have the same products here as in Dharmasala. I buy a shoulder bag and a set of meditation bells, and then we approach a little tea stall.

"Somewhere to sit?" Vanessa asks The Tibetan shopkeeper carries white plastic chairs up to the roof for us. Again the view is absolutely stunning, the horizon in all four directions with oh so many birds, clouds and trees. We sip sweet tea and tell each other little details about our lives. Her boyfriend is Jewish and she is Italian Catholic. There are some problems with her mother, who doesn't want her to marry him. I tell her about my family and Lenny.

My father was already used to my being a rebel. After running away from home at eighteen and living with an Italian Catholic pool hustler—My father didn't like people who were Catholic, Jewish or Black—and then living with another guy, I thought he might be used to the fact that I wasn't following along his path. I brought Lenny over to the house for a birthday party for my stepmother, and after I introduced him to everyone, my father turned his back on him and refused to speak to him for six months. Later, I learned that his anger was less about his being Jewish than the fact that we were living together and not planning to get married. Lenny didn't hold a grudge. Maybe he was hurt, but he never said so. When we left the house that night, my father was asleep in his recliner. I looked at Lenny and said, "I'm sorry." In the years that followed, things changed and they even played poker together occasionally, and Lenny's mother would come to my father's house on Christmas Eve. Eventually he gave up prodding us to get married. When my father was dying, six months before Lenny's death, Lenny called him and they talked on the telephone in a very loving way.

"I thought you were married?" Vanessa asks.

"Well a few years after we were split up, he needed my dental insurance so we got married then. Nothing changed."

"You're crazy, Gina."

We take a wild rickshaw ride back to our rooms. Boom, boom, boom goes the rickshaw over the holes—my back starts hurting. If this keeps up, I'll never be able to have sex again. I'm tired. My nose is running and I'm having diarrhea again. I try the grapefruit seed extract, one dose, and now it's time for the Chinese curing pills. I really think that this is caused by the oily food they prepare here. Last year I ate one meal here and I was instantly running to the bathroom. Lots of rice and curd might help, but I think I need to go back to Mysore to my room so I can cook for myself and see Dr. Anand. In the future, I'm going to carry all my food with me. I love the mood and life here, but I cannot eat their food.

The library is supposed to open at 8:30, but there are locks on every door. I peer into the room through a window at a big pile of books, torn up and thrown around the floor. The other library opens at 2:00. I will try that one. On my way back to the room, a little black dog walks confidently along the road. The dogs seem very intelligent and not as psychologically dependent upon people as dogs are in the United States. Something in their eyes announces their independence. They are not as destitute and skeletal as the dogs in Mysore. They must eat better.

So the day has gone and I'm sitting here on the bed in this little second story room on the ridge of a hill with Tibetan life on both sides, listening to the men in the courtyard and the children on the other side of the room chanting.

*

Not feeling great so sleeping a lot. Wake up and walk over to the secondary school library and take out a book entitled *Tibetan Buddhism, From the Ground Up.* Take notes in my journal. Sleeping, reading, eating a banana and some apple juice from Vanessa. Two more doses of Chinese curing pills. Then we take a rickshaw to the women's nunnery.

When we stroll into the center of campus, we are a spectacle. All the young women and children stand around looking at us and laughing. It does not look like a woman's nunnery at first because with their shaved heads and robes, the young girls look just like boys. And the women, too. I guess in fact there isn't that much actual difference between men and women. But the women's facility is much poorer than the men's—the land is scrubby and unattended, the buildings are not as ornate or well-kept, and their movement is confined or perhaps they are protected by the large fence surrounding the campus.

My stomach starts to rumble. I ask a young woman if there is a bathroom. She escorts me across the campus. "Bathroom, bathroom," she keeps saying over and over and all the young children around her start to laugh.

I look around and the whole nunnery is laughing at me. Everyone is aware that I must go to the bathroom. I follow my escort to a little house near the gate. A man answers the door, looks at me and gives her a key. I'm then escorted to a door that is marked, "Guest Bathroom." Inside I carefully tuck in my shawl and slide my clothing up around my hips. The whole nunnery waits outside.

*

A woman who speaks English, Tenzin Choden, tells Vanessa that not long ago she was allowed to escort a woman named Sandy from Los Angeles around the monasteries and the community. Tenzin has only been here about four months. Before that she was in another Tibetan settlement in northern India. Before that she was with her five children. Her husband divorced her and then she became a monk. Her mother who is seventy-five is raising her children. Her plans for the future, she says, are to stay here for a while and then go into the forest to a cave to meditate. I hope her mother lives long enough to raise her children. Tenzin seems young except for a few lines around her eyes. I'm sure though that she is at least ten years younger than me. We leave, promising to stop by in the morning and take a letter to the post office for her, a letter to Sandy.

As we leave the main entrance of the nunnery, we pass a little shop with a tea stall so we sit down and order tea, and then we wait a very long time for our service, sitting outside in plastic chairs and looking at the gate to the nunnery and the wide open fields. After drinking our tea we decide to walk along the road in the falling darkness.

How far are we from the guest house? I wonder. It didn't seem so far in the rickshaw but we are walking and walking.

I talk about how odd it is to be walking in the dark in an isolated place in the country where we know little about where we are or which wild animals or wild people are here. I'm only half serious and just talking from my imagination in a way I talk with my closest friends. I have absolutely no fear.

Suddenly, Vanessa laughs at me. "Oh, come on, Gina."

I'm hurt because of her tone. "You know, Vanessa, sometimes you talk to me with a condescending tone, as if you think I am a silly old person and you are my caretaker."

I'm old enough to be her mother, but not in need of care.

In the middle of the night, asleep on the cot next to the window, I jump when suddenly, boom, Sonam turns on the porch lights while simultaneously the monks begin chanting in their rooms. There is a lot of talking downstairs in the courtyard. Maybe this is what happens on Friday nights. I keep getting up and drinking water. Even now as I write this, I feel a bit dehydrated.

Sera Monastery Hospital Guest House is a beautiful place. Contemplative young and old monks on the street. A quiet hum of talk. I think it would be meaningful to come here alone, bring my own food or a way to prepare food, to meditate, to draw the monks, to spend my days reading books on Buddhism. All around the world, around the globe, and still my mind is very busy making plans for the future.

In the morning I knock on the wall between Vanessa and me. She shows up at the door a few minutes later. While I'm dressing, she sits at the table on the landing.

"I'll be out in a minute."

She writes a note for Tenzin, giving her our addresses. I yell out how to spell her name.

We are waiting for the rickshaw to leave the monastery. Someone promised to meet us here, but of course the driver never appears. We are sitting on a stone ledge drinking tea. Vanessa says that last night she thought she was expressing love because I seemed anxious. Forget it, it doesn't matter. It's just my ego. Perhaps this moment is an initiation into a stage of life where I begin to be the child and the children begin to be the parents. We hug each other, climb into the rickshaw and bump along in our rickshaw zig zagging across the rocky terrain.

At the nunnery, Vanessa asks, "Why won't you go in? Don't you want to see them chanting?"

"No," I tell her, "I don't want to be an observer today. My stomach is still rumbling."

So I wait outside with the rickshaw man, who has red and white checkered cushioned seats. He tells me that he is a Muslim and he asks if I'm Christian. We have some little dialogue about religion. I can't remember exactly what we talked about even though it's less than 12 hours later. Vanessa comes back and I write down the name of the women's monastery so I can send some books when I'm back at school.

We then take another long wild rickshaw ride to Kushalnagar (the correct name of the city near the monastery) where we are to pick up the bus. Sonan sends us to a three star Indian restaurant where we could have breakfast. When the driver takes us to the door of the hotel, we pay him 90 rupees for the ride, and then we go inside only to find out that it will not open until noon. Then we cut across the street and over a littered field to the lot with all the buses (all five of them), a little shelter, and a few shanties selling pre-packaged food.

"Is this bus going to Mysore?"

"Yes," says the official, "but there are no seats available."

"Will there be another one soon?"

"Yes, at 9. Stand right here."

We wait for a while and then decide to ask someone else.

"I think the bus over there goes to Mysore."

I run around the bus to the right to find Vanessa, who is kindly carrying my heavy backpack, just as I used to carry my children's bags when they were young. She is looking for me on the left. We go around and around and then we find each other in the middle and get on the bus. Always like this in India. One person tells you to wait here and another there and then finally you discover something in the middle. We take a seat for two so we won't be so squashed. We are comfortably chugging along with the bus full of people. The bus tips and curves and speeds along avoiding trucks.

The countryside of India is beautiful until one comes to the little camps and fields littered with garbage. Especially noticeable are the blue and pink plastic bags. If everyone reached over and picked up two pieces of garbage, it would be clean. An easy organization of garbage cans and bins for organic waste for animals. Why hasn't the government done anything about this? Nonetheless, large parts of India are beautiful and untainted. The cows in the countryside are generally fatter from the abundance of grass, and they seem to enjoy roaming freely.

*

Someone says to me, one day you see a little goat chained up to a door and the next day he is gone. He has been eaten. Today while on the bus, a big dirty hog came sauntering out of a yard.

*

From the book on Buddhism that I was reading at Bylakuppee: "The truth is, as soon as two individuals meet, parting is inevitable" . . . Santidesa tells us:

> Casting all aside, I must depart alone
> ....
> But my foes shall cease to exist
> Friends shall vanish
> I, too, will perish
> So will every thing pass from existence

*

After about an hour on the bus, we stop in a small town and a large group of people get on the bus. One older woman is holding a child. There are no seats. Vanessa signals that she will hold the little girl. She is about two years old, nervous at first, staring at her grandmother and then relaxing, the way a frightened animal might turn on its back becoming passive. Her eyes are open very wide. We give her a cracker. Finally she relaxes and falls asleep spreading out over Vanessa and me. She has dark, oiled hair with a little red flower woven into the tail on her head. Her father and grandmother stand in the aisle, laughing and pointing at us as they talk in their own language.

When we are almost to Mysore, Vanessa shakes the child, waking her a little and then she passes her to her grandmother. The child sits up, a bit groggy, and the grandmother whispers to her, telling her, I'm sure, that she was sleeping on the white auntie's lap. The child laughs uncomfortably as if she finds all this just too much to believe.

Just as the bus arrives at the outskirts of Mysore—with its smoky air and crowds—my stomach begins to feel better. Maybe I just like home and Mysore is my second home. The bus stops to let some people off close to the hotel, so we grab our bags and exit. Then we catch a rickshaw over to the hotel, drop my things in the room and head to Iyengars for breakfast.

An hour later I walk home, glad to finally be alone. No matter how much I enjoy spending time with people, I'm always happy to be alone when they leave. Perhaps this is the result of raising two children while living the life of an artist and a teacher. Every year I spend more and more time alone working on my projects and less time chasing after my desires. Where are you Dimitri—oh so far away on this planet and even in my mind. When I was younger— even ten years ago—I would be consumed with thinking about lovers. Now I find it satisfying to watch Rupesh clean my room, sweeping the floors with a little handmade broom, making the bed, and then washing the floors with a pail and rag. I sit out in the hallway waiting for the fan to dry the floors. He takes my sheets and towels to be washed. After the floor is dry, with ant chalk, I draw a circle around the bed, around the sink and around the doors.

At Gopala's email station, I take off my shawl, fold it into a square and check my mail. Jessie writes saying that she glanced into a window yesterday, saw her own reflection and thought it was me. I know that feeling. I used to see my mother in me and then after a while I stopped seeing her and I only saw me. This was after I had crossed the border, had become one year older than her death age of 36. I remember sitting in Greenfield's Café on Seventh Avenue in Brooklyn on my birthday, working on some project. It was raining. I looked out the window at the parked cars and it struck me—I did not have to live her life any longer. I was not an ill, abandoned, over-whelmed dying woman with five children. I was going to live a long life, my life. Well, it took a lot of years to realize this. I hope Jessie doesn't have to wait that long.

"Who's calling?" I say my name again and the woman tells me to call back after ten minutes. I call back in thirty minutes and he comes to the phone. I tell Harihara who I am, and he says, "Can you come over right now?"

I'm very tired, my hair is a mess, and my clothes are dirty from the trip. I know I'm expected to say, yes, so I say, "Yes." I straighten myself, brush my teeth, go downstairs and Mahadeshwara signals a rickshaw for me, gives the man directions, arranges the fee and sends me off.

It's quite a long way to J. Prakash. There are many turns. I'm not sure where I am. We pass the neighborhood of Ramaji's yoga shala, turn right, going further into an area of large houses with fields around them, and then an even more suburban area, almost rural. Still scrubby, dusty land though. The driver asks me questions about New York. He tells me the United States is beautiful. He has a very limited English vocabulary. He stops and asks other drivers for directions until we finally arrive at Harihara's street. The driver stops a woman in front of her house. She peers into the rickshaw staring at me, and finally she asks if we are looking for the yoga teacher. Yes. Around the corner.

There he is waiting in front of his house, tall, lanky and serene, dressed in a white dhoti and shawla. The driver asks if he should wait.

"Yes," and he gives the driver some instructions in Kannada.

I'm to follow Harihara to the side of the house and remove my shoes. He opens a door, and in the hallway he has two straw mats on the floor, one placed in a vertical position and the other horizontal. He sits down on the horizontal mat in half lotus, arranges his shawla and asks me, "Are you well enough to sit on the floor?"

"Yes, of course," I say. I sit opposite him and we quietly study each other. I remind myself not to overtalk, to jump in and fill in every gap with talk, to interrupt, one of my personality faults, thinking too fast and preempting others.

He is a thin and serious looking man in his fifties. Maybe a little older, maybe younger, kind of ageless. He is somewhat delicate.

He asks me, "Why do you study yoga?".

I tell him for peace and a vibrant sense of being in the present. I tell him when and how I came to study hatha yoga—when Lenny, my ex-husband, was dying, how we were friends even though we were separated, and how yoga became connected with dying to me.

He looks at me, ponders and asks, "What would you like from me?"

"Whatever you are willing and able to give," I say. "I know that you don't usually take students during this part of the year. Any studies of the Gita, Sutras, asanas."

He talks about how he wants the full attention of the student, not a divided study, how the heart relationship between student and teacher is very important. One should not always be switching from one teacher to the next. He asks me if I'm a teacher of yoga.

I tell him no but explain how my study of yoga has affected my teaching and work.

He pauses, ponders and looks at me. "At this time of the year I can only meet with you three times a week and then you must conduct the practice two and sometimes three times a day in your apartment. This will involve several hours."

"I am willing."

"We can begin on Monday at noon and after three meetings we can evaluate. I will be unhappy if you are disappointed, but the heart must be there between teacher and students."

I ask him what I should wear.

"What you have on now, but cotton clothes. Cotton, wool or silk only. That will be sufficient for now. Also, will you be willing to change your diet? It will be very simple."

He studies me and asks if I smoke cigarettes or drink alcohol.

I assure him—"No, not for years." Then I thank him.

The sweet and slow rickshaw driver is waiting for me outside.

He drives back to the hotel, stopping once to say a few things to some young women along the way, and then he takes me home to the hotel.

"How much," I ask?

"How much you think?"

This makes me nervous so I call Mahadeshwara and he tells me, 70 rupees all together.

I give him 75. And then he says he will come tomorrow.

"What is your name?"

"Shivapa."

*

In the *Star of Mysore,* on Wednesday. Title: Girl Excels. Title: Case of Sexual Jealousy. With the arrest of the culprit the police have solved the mystery behind the murder case which led to various rumors in public circles . . . a long nurtured grudge . . . some years ago they developed close contacts. C. introduced D. to his niece who was a student. . . the former developed a relationship with the girl whom C. loved and wished to marry . . . In the meantime the girl's parents came to know about the relationships and they sold property in Mysore City and settled in Napoklu Village in Kodagu district. The girl was later married off .. . . Deeply disturbed . . . C. nurtured his anger and decided to kill D. . . C. purchased an iron rod.

*

Today is Sunday and unfortunately last night I could only sleep a little. The men across the hall were making such a racket, laughing, talking and bumping around. They sounded like a bunch of drunkards. I felt a little afraid to leave my room when I heard this noise, but finally I went downstairs and talked to Mahadeshwara. He explained something to another boy there.

"What did you say?" I asked.

"I told him that foreigners are smooth. They need it quieter.

These men have some function, only for one night."

I think he went upstairs and told them to be quiet. Funny way of expressing it—foreigners are smooth. That means we can't sleep unless things go smoothly, I think, because maybe we think too much.

*

This morning, I wake at 6:00 and decide not to practice because I'm going to begin with Harihara tomorrow at noon. What was this morning like? I think I went back to sleep. I was a little cold. Oh, I remember. I woke up several times during the night sick. At one a.m., I went through all my envelopes and found the literature on traveler's diarrhea. The only thing to do is to fight it. Sometimes it takes a few months to get used to the change in climate and bacteria. I guess I'll be healthy right around the time I go home. Use the Chinese herbs, garlic, grapefruit seed extract, etcetera. And then wait it out. Drink hydrating drinks. Eat bananas, rice, grains. I remember my grandmother telling me that a little cheese helps, too. I sleep a little more. I want to go out, I think, and buy some oatmeal. I sleep in the pants and shirt I bought from the Tibetan woman, very light cotton blue pants with little mirrors—and the mirrors are falling off, one by one, a little glue and one stitch, about 20 mirrors almost all gone.

I ask Mahadeshwara if he knows where I can buy oats. He doesn't know what oats are—like rice and wheat, a grain, I tell him. Is Nilgeris open? Not until 10, he says. Try the other stores. No one knows what they are. I need to find the word in Kannada. I walk back and forth and then decide, ok, I'll go to Subrata's.

I catch a rickshaw on the corner. The driver begins to talk to me in English. "You are a yoga student." He is a husky older man. His rickshaw is familiar looking and very rickety. He turns and smiles at me. He has a red puja mark on his forehead.

I explain to him that I'm not studying with Ramaji. Who? Harihara. He doesn't known Harihara. When we pull over to Subrata's (He knows who she is and where she lives), he turns around and asks me if I know Jean S. Yes, I know Jean from New York City. An actress, African American, yes? He talks about his daughter's wedding and how he wants to contact Jean so he can set the date for the wedding. His name is Surya and his rickshaw number is 2266. I tell him I will send an email to someone who will pass it on to Jean if he'd like to give it to me handwritten. Yes, he says and then he promises to pick me up at 9:00, but he never shows up.

I say hello to Jeevesh. He tips his head and immediately recommends the Indian breakfast of flat rice with no spices. But it's loaded with spices. I ask him to take it back and give me porridge instead, ginger tea and bananas.

There is a little group in the dining room. We talk about this and that—yoga asanas, breathing, aches and pains, etcetera. Then they all leave and I'm waiting for the rickshaw driver. Subrata sits down and we have an extended conversation about religion and the meaning of the deities and their relationship to the oneness of god. Their deity is Venkateshwara, a manifestation of Vishnu. An image is framed above the dining room table. He has a blue face. She goes on. "There are many ways that lead to the same place, this includes all deities and religions and disciplines. One's whole life is written underneath the skin on your forehead," she says. I like the idea of a text being written underneath one's skin. I keep wanting to insert the possibility of will—even that can be written under the forehead. Perhaps there are multiple possibilities.

What do I remember from this conversation? The possibility that you suffer more if you resist the story that is written under your forehead. Always when you start something new, thank Ganesh and do a puja for him so he brings success to your endeavor. Like you— she says—perhaps, you think you will have breakfast with Subrata and give her your money, but perhaps something happens and you go somewhere else and someone else goes to Subrata. I can't remember all this and I didn't quite get it, but I do know that we are signs of her success. Perhaps we are already written under her forehead. Sometimes Indians don't understand the western mentality though, and goof up their relations by being too insistent about making a sale. What happens then? Perhaps the possibility of an erasure.

On the street, I run into Mary and Whitney, two yoga students from New York City who are staying with Vanessa. I stop in their apartment to use their bathroom. I see Vanessa's room, a little room completely dominated by cobwebs and a mosquito net. Their apartment is old and charming, but dusty and full of mosquitoes. Lots of yoga students have stayed here and their boxes are stored in the corners with their names penciled on the front of each one.

I walk along the side street and stop by the Pathabi Apartments to visit with Monique. She is in the living room playing tablas as she listens to a cd. Gary Kraftsow's book on viniyoga lies open in front of her. I'm comfortable here and wishing I could stay with Monique, but she already has a roommate and companion. A very thoughtful thirty year old. I like her.

"Can I take a shower here?"

"Sure." She gets me a towel.

I'm a drifter, drifting around neighborhoods in India, eating breakfast, using someone's bathroom, using someone else's shower.

"I wish I could live here," I tell Monique.

"Maybe you can take this apartment after Janice and I leave. It has a great shower. There is so much air."

"Yes, yes, I will," I say, but now, I think, home is here in this hotel room where I am typing this journal. I'm concerned that I might be too isolated in that neighborhood after Ramaji and all his students leave. After all most of the westerners in Mysore are here to study with him. And this hotel room is very comfortable here. Yes, I think I will remain here.

*

Cooking a very bland rice and vegetable dish. I turn the propane too high. Poof. I can see how this could be very dangerous. Door bell rings. It's Frank. I tell him I was looking for him today. He takes my picture, sitting on the bed. His camera is on a stand and it takes 15 seconds to take the photo with the light and whatever else he is doing. He's going to take a lot of photographs of cows, too, he says. Cows and yoga students. He is thinner and more attractive than he seemed in New York when he was coming and going for corporate America. He must go. He's here. He's gone. Frank diligently guards his feelings and thoughts so that I hardly ever experience any real communication with him, just his brief presence.

Reading Sri Aurobindo and drifting in and out of the text. Then shift to the computer—sitting here cross-legged on the bed typing these entries. I go downstairs for a tea and a lot of students come in: Emily, Dennis (a musician, not a yoga student), and Brandy (he's reading Ayn Rand and talking about how great capitalism is). We go up on the roof to see the lights. Vanessa and Whitney arrive with cookies. They say they wish they were living in the hotel.

In the sky, there are hundreds of birds, ravens I think, big black birds.

"No," someone says—I think it's Vanessa—"they are bats."

"Yes, of course, I remember those bats from last year. They perch on the tree over there sometimes."

We all look up into the sky—I'm lying flat on my back—as hundreds of bats swoop back and forth across the sky and the palace lights come on, these beautiful ornate steeples outlined in light. The bats spread out their ribbed wings. And then it's time for yoga students to go to bed. Practice starts at 5 a.m. Up and away they all go in their black rickshaws. I'm here in my black nightgown, spread out on the bed, thinking about dressing again and going downstairs to the lobby to read.

*

Today I ask Harihara if it is disrespectful for me to address him by his name. "Yes," he says.

"What should I call you?"

"Maybe sir. It would be better if you call me sir."

"Sir? It's so British and cold sounding."

"Well my Indian students call me Acharya so you can call me Acharya if you would like."

So, Acharya, it will be, esteemed teacher.

Acharya explains that we westerners suffer from diarrhea

because we are not used to the heavy oils the Indians use for cooking. The reason I have the sinus problem here he says is because I'm not used to such a mucous intensive diet as they eat with all the rice, fruit, and milk. Yes, that is true. I have very little milk at home. In fact, at home I now eat mostly raw vegetables, fruit and nuts.

*

A day later. Wash some clothes in the bucket in the bathroom and hang them at 6 a.m. Carefully step around the sleeping bodies on the roof to hang the clothes. Sit on the stoop and quietly draw the four men asleep in a line on four mattresses. I decide I can't bear that trip over to Subrata's. Iyengar's won't open until 7. Tea downstairs. Reading and cleaning. At 7 a.m., some keshraba and uptma. I don't think I can eat this again for a long time. It's too oily and spicy. For a while, morning will be the oatmeal I purchased. Acharya tells me to do my usual practice in the morning starting tomorrow in my room. So I will not be eating so early again. Then meet with him at 12 noon again and he will change my morning practice. That will be interesting since for the past three years I have been doing the same morning practice with only variations in the stopping point, adding asanas and then after the injury subtracting a bit.

I spend much of the morning sorting and straightening out my room and then walking over to the tailors. Acharya has told me that one should spend the hour prior to practice in a very peaceful activity, but this morning I find myself downtown looking for this and that, passing through the market and all the vendors calling "Madam, hello Madam." I walk through, with a little nod, but not attending to their calls. Last night as I listened to Brandy talk about how harried he is from the calls on the street, I realized I was harried last year, but now I practice a little yoga in the market. I purchase two mangos and a papaya from a fruit vendor. I ask the man at the bag booth if he has soap dishes and miraculously they appear. Now I know why one should not listen to people who tell you to take nothing to India. It isn't the money—it's the time and energy you spend setting up your living space. This time, I will store everything in a trunk at the hotel and next year I'll bring back my clothes with me.

My entire way of dressing is going to change because of Acharya's instructions about wearing natural fibers. The synthetics interfere with the vibrations in your body, especially during practice, but then also throughout the day.

All day I've been thinking about the teachings of Aurobindo. What stands out for me is this sense of the front of the body being a flurry of thoughts, intense activity and short circuiting ideas and emotions, and the back (from the sacrum up—right where I've been injured) is the seat of consciousness, the witness, where we can learn to retreat. Throughout my half hour meeting with Acharya, this was in my mind. The idea was powerfully present even as I walked down the street, stepping around people who were napping in between selling this and that household item or baskets of fruit.

I pick up all the items on my errand list. The bookstore is closed so I will have to come back another time. Let's see, I have headed toward this bookstore at least three times in the last few days and each time it's either closed or I'm stopped by the heat or some other mission.

Back at the hotel, my nose is running again and I need to brush my teeth. They have no bottled water. "Madam it will be here in ten minutes." Lying flat for ten minutes, I decide to get dressed, go down the street and get the water from Nayanashi's store. I come back, brush my teeth—I wish I knew how to wash things without worrying about getting a viral or bacterial infection. I simply use the tap water for washing the dishes, dry things well and hope for the best. If I had to boil that water, too, I would be here forever.

How can my nose run like this? Drink some more echinacea water. I think this little bottle of herbs and this packet of herbal pills will last until Wednesday when I see Dr. Anand again. Either the sinuses will simply adjust or he will give me some new remedy. I sit and wait for Shivapa to pick me up.

Shanmukha asks, "Why don't you use my rickshaw?"

"I have already made an arrangement, Shanmukha. If the driver doesn't show up, I will let you know." The last time I waited for

Shanmukha, he never showed up.

At eleven fifteen, Shivapa arrives. He has a glint in his eyes and a natural smile. Driving slowly and cautiously, he avoids every pothole with his new rickshaw. He is kind of a dreamy rickshaw driver. And he wants to take me to J. Prakash every time I go. It's a perfect half hour to spend before practice. You never know what could happen. A woman meets a beautiful dreamy rickshaw driver, and they secretly fall in love. How can she marry him, though? To marry is in some way to cut your children off from your little tiny retirement benefit. One must marry someone who doesn't need it. And the rickshaw driver certainly needs it. Or take out a larger insurance policy for the children.

I ask him on the way back to the hotel if he has any children.

"No," he says, "first I must have a wife. Do you have any children? Are you married?"

"No, my husband died. Yes, I have two children." I go on about them.

He asks questions possible with his limited twenty-five word English vocabulary. "One boy?"

We come back to the hotel and Mahadeshwara explains that he should come tomorrow at 11:30. I think perhaps he is a Christian. He doesn't seem Hindu. Although he did stop some Hindu school girls to talk to them yesterday. He's definitely much too culturally distant. But it would be an interesting story. He was so sweet to the little boy at Acharya's house, teaching him how to read the newspaper in his rickshaw.

I thought at first the little boy was Acharya's son, but in fact he is his nephew. Acharya has no children. He smiles then and says, "But I have so many children."

In the vestibule of his house, I sit cross-legged on the straw mat and he tells me all about yoga.

"Yoga," he says, "is making the mind peaceful." He talks quite a bit about the busy western life-style as opposed to a life of yoga.

"This yoga," he says, "is about being relaxed in all parts of your body while you are in the asana. The only effort is in keeping the spine straight. One thing he says that is quite interesting—"You can measure the success of your practice by the length of time you want to sit peacefully without thinking afterwards, by how easy it is to meditate. If you feel as if you have just had a cup of coffee, it was not a successful practice."

He instructs me in ten different poses with varying breathing patterns, one short pranayama and then a two minute rest.

Then that dreamy ride home with Shivapa and his green eyes.

I'm more peaceful as I go about my new set of errands, eating lunch at Upahar, two rava idlies laced with vegetables and lentils and served with coconut chutney. After eating, I take a rickshaw to look for women's underwear without elastic so no synthetic material will be touching my body. No such animal exists. I end up at KR circle and walk over to Ashok Books, where I buy an ayurvedic cookbook and order a few more books recommended by Acharya.

I stop at Lakshmi Silk. While I'm there, two yoga students, Virginia and Anna are looking at silk. Anna glides over toward me, "Hi what are you buying?" she asks. "What are you doing? What will you make with that? What books do you have in your bag?"

I don't know her and I want to be as protective as possible about my new practice with Acharya so I don't tell her I'm trying to find out how to make underwear without any synthetic ingredients. Besides it would require lots of explanation, and it sounds kind of crazy. I begin to look very closely at a red sari to let her know that I'm absorbed in what I'm doing.

"I can make anything for you Madam," the tailor says. "Just make a drawing. Silk, cotton, anything."

I defer. Another day. I wave to the students, duck down the back stairs and out the door.

*

Yesterday Vanessa asked me why I ever left Lenny. I've asked myself that same question many times. He helped me finish my bachelor's degree and he encouraged me to go to graduate school for an MFA. As I went deeper into my studies and into my work, I met other students who had similar interests in art and theory. At the same time, Lenny wasn't coming home regularly. He was running concessions in art fairs and selling ice cream and popcorn off a truck on the southwest side of town. A group of his friends worked with him. I could always find him at night if I wanted him—in the Del Rio Bar or one of the other bars on Cass Avenue. We started sleeping on opposite sides of the bed. Ok, this analysis makes it sound inevitable. He was going in one direction and I was going in the other. That's what I told Vanessa, but still at the border line between this and that, we had two children together. And we loved each other. When I told him a few times that we needed to talk and he shied away and avoided really talking, why didn't I insist? Why didn't I insist that he go to a drug treatment center? I could have looked at him and screamed, "Do you love me? Do you love your children? Come on—please—this is all going to fall apart." That is the woman I am now, but was not then.

Instead, I tried a few times and then when he refused to talk, I turned around quickly after nine years together and found him another apartment. I wanted a sex life. I wanted some excitement. I wanted someone I could talk to about intellectual and philosophical ideas. I wanted something different than being a mother with an absent partner. Like most people in my culture and time, I thought one should move on if a relationship wasn't working. I remember one day when I opened the door to the van, sat down beside Lenny, putting the groceries from Central Market at my feet and arranged my skirt around my pregnant body. I smiled at him. I didn't realize I was in the middle of the most important relationship in my life. And instead of fighting to keep it, I found him an apartment, sold the house, and moved with Josh and Jessie into university housing.

In the last year of his life, when he was in the hospital bed and we were finally talking openly to each other, I asked him why he wouldn't talk. He said, "Well, Gina, you always used to lock yourself up in your studio." It's odd how perception and memory work. He thought I was the closed one.

I asked him why he continued to use heroin. He said, "It's the only way I ever felt normal."

*

I run into Roberto in Nilgiris and he invites me over for tea, mu tea. He's a little frustrated today, complaining about the dirt in India—they live like pigs—and the tricking nature of many Indians. So I ask him why he stays here. He tells me he wants to learn yoga, to recover from many years as an alcoholic and a cokehead. He has traveled all over the world working as a travel guide. He was so screwed up, finally, that he took people to the wrong place and so he was fired. His life was falling apart. His third wife (who I met last year and who is now in Minnesota) went back to the states and he came to India. He feels he can't leave India for a number of years if he wants to stay straight.

"What about your wife?"

"She'll wait for me. We have a lot of history." He offers me a piece of brown bread. "Here dear, eat this, it will make you very strong."

He looks down at my feet and notices that I am barefoot. "Don't take off your shoes. The floor is too cold." He quickly dashes into the living room and returns with my sandals.

His little apartment is quite charming, spotlessly clean, with a little yoga room, a very well supplied kitchen with equipment to make tofu and cartons of seaweed labeled and stacked in the rafters. I tell Roberto that my friend Peter stayed here a few years ago.

"The place was filthy after all the yoga students dropped in and out for short stays."

I lean forward with my chin in the cup of my hand and listen to him talk about his macrobiotic diet and how difficult it is to obtain the food he needs to follow it. "I saved my liver and my life, dear, with macrobiotics and with Krishnamurti's advice. When I first read a book on macrobiotics, it seemed so scientific and logical. Since then I've stuck with it."

He invites me to stay for lunch, a bowl of soup with tofu, buckwheat flour, soy sauce, sea salt and a few other vegetables. It isn't very tasty but it is definitely hearty.

Then he gives me a ride back to the hotel on his motorcycle. His bike reminds me of a monstrous house fly, a fly from outer space. Roberto's knee is bothering him. I ask him why he doesn't get a smaller bike, one that isn't so heavy. He tells me that he has this bike so he can ride out into the country every morning. I hold on to his torso, and he is so slim it feels almost like holding on to nothing. He weighs himself everyday and adjusts his diet so that he doesn't gain a single gram.

*

Today, June 5th, at 5:25 in the afternoon, I'm sitting on my bed writing even though I'm sure the bed is a tamasic place and the vibrations coming from it might interfere with the writing, which is probably intermittently rajasic and sattvic. I'm sick, though, and I need rest, so maybe the two will be all right. This morning I woke up with a heavy head, especially above the eyebrows. Nonetheless, I wash clothes, clean my body a little, order tea (I can't have anymore tea, Acharya says, because it's the exact opposite of the state we want in yoga), straighten the room, and lay out the carpets for my morning yoga practice. One day he is going to watch me do my asana practice. I'd better keep strong in the practice . . . I feel I'm attending to it weakly during this week of different illnesses. Before I start the practice, I have to drag the carpet around here and there because of a space problem in the room and because I like facing east.

The monsoon has arrived and it has been overcast and raining all day long.

My mind is wavering, thinking of my yoga teacher, Manny, imagining doing a different practice in his studio, thinking of Acharya, thinking of Dimitri, thinking of my children, thinking of this and that. I do watch the thoughts, and at the end of the practice, I'm tired and I quit early. My head is so heavy. I bathe again and wash my hair. Oh such beautiful hot water when one is choking from so much mucous.

Surya rings the bell with my last tea.

I make oatmeal with cashews and cut up a mango and a few tiny bananas. A good breakfast to eat in one's room.

*

So solitary. It's raining and I'm walking down the street in a rain poncho. I look like a spectacle, a tall blue tent. In an email, Manny tells me he now has fifteen students at night and that my chiropractor, Steven, asks about me. There is a beautiful note from Isabella telling me how happy she is in Mexico City working as a yoga teacher and she's not quite sure where she will be going next. I love reading her emails in Spanish. She tells me to visit Pondicherry. An email from Dimitri—Namaste! Dear, Gina! Thank you for your short, but a very hot last letter to me. We will meet each other soon. The trip to New York was good. I'm still planning to come in the fall. And I'll be happy to see you then. How is your spine? I'll do massage for your back soon. I love you also. Namaste. Dimitri.

*

I notice a huge burn mark in the altar area of the hotel room— a little sunken shelf in the wall—where I burned a candle last night. I could have burned down the hotel. Lack of attention. When I was twelve, I was gabbing away with my sister while I was ironing my skirt and I leaned on the iron. Forty years later I still have a light brown spot on my arm. Attention. I didn't realize Lenny needed and deserved my full attention even though he couldn't give his attention to me. Once I met with a psychoanalyst to discuss another relationship that was failing. He looked at me and said, "Gina, to enjoy love is to enjoy giving without expecting love in return." He was someone I really respected, an older, intelligent, compassionate man. Wow. I'd always been functioning with this lack, this huge desire, wanting to be taken care of, to be loved, to regain something I had lost when my mother died. In the meantime, the problem was me— I didn't know how to love.

*

Acharya listens to me chant the "Asota ma" chant. "I will teach you chanting later," he says, I think, noticing how weakly and perhaps incorrectly I pronounce it. He talks a lot about how incorrectly and incompletely yoga is taught in the west. As I learn more, I can see this clearly. I tell him about my thoughts during my morning practice, worrying about not practicing with a group or a teacher, and he talks about the importance of one-to-one teaching and occasionally meeting with your teacher so he can observe you and add more poses or change techniques. I think this visit to India is going to change my life. Quieter. Alone.

Outside it's cool and the winds are blowing the coconut leaves back and forth. A crow caws.

*

Shivapa arrives a little bit late and it is raining very hard, pouring and pouring as if a dam has broken apart in the sky. I sit in the back of the rickshaw under my poncho. Yes, now I'm a big blue tent with a white face at the top, propped up in a rickshaw. He goes so carefully and it's cold out. Last year I didn't wear a jacket once. But then everyone was saying that the monsoon was not as it should be. Today in the paper there is a long article about how they need better scientific warning about the exact timing of the monsoon because of its effect on their economy.

I've just counted out some rupees for Acharya as a donation for the many hours he will spend calculating my horoscope. I tell him about my past with Nagma, when Lenny and I traveled as young people, how I assisted her in preparing and selling astrology charts in the carnivals. Her father, a Muslim from India who lived in Detroit, had taught her the art of astrology and palmistry. Lenny was working as a carnie at the time and I assisted Nagma by talking to people and looking up the location of the planets in her box of books. I think vedic astrology is more of a science, but I'm not sure.

Harihara smiles. With him, the science surely comes from a yogic way of knowing.

*

Another cup of tea with cumin, pepper, coriander seeds, turmeric and ginger. I need to make a fresh batch of herbs. In the background, the faint sound of the horns of rickshaws and the sing song rhythm of the water filter in the kitchen.

In bed, I stare at a photo of Lenny—he is about eighteen years old and he looks exactly like Josh. If Lenny had never shown me this photo, no one could have convinced me that it wasn't Josh. He's sitting at some event with one of his uncles, maybe his mother's brother, who lived in Chicago above a little party store. Lenny always looked up to him, and here he is absolutely at ease and happy, looking directly into the camera, his hands folded and resting between his legs. The really poignant part of the photo is his uncle's face—tough, working class, a perfect face for a bookie in a movie.

*

This afternoon when I return from Acharya's, I walk down to the email station again to check my mail, to respond to Dimitri and Isabella, and to write a note to Jessie. There is loud American music playing next door. western life style is more prevalent than is apparent at first when one looks at the people. For the old, poor and beaten Indians who are driving their skinny, damaged oxen with their heavily loaded carts, a western life style is very distant, a sound from a window. The middle class have much more contact with technology, and they are more cosmopolitan and therefore more western even though they don't look it when you see them.

Soon I must change my clothes and do my yoga practice.

Once a week, Acharya says I must give myself an ayurvedic bath with sesame oil. In the morning, rub the oil all over my body and massage it in for 10 minutes to half an hour and then wash it out with hot water and something called shikake pode. I purchased something that sounds sort of similar but the package says it's herbs for dandruff. I'll have to ask him again. I've done this before but it was oily, slippery and difficult to clean. But now that I've been told to do this again, yes, in a day or so I will.

I clean up a little and decide to go out once more and have the photograph taken for Acharya. A rickshaw there and then one back. Both of the drivers are aggressive. One swerves and tries to knock into a woman he seems to know. She is carrying a basket of oranges on her head. After having the photo taken, I acknowledge, yes, this is how I look. I can't even try now to be a young swank sexy looking woman, if I ever could. Now I'm rather austere and serious looking, perhaps because of the ten pounds I lost this month. I imagine Acharya putting the serious little photo on the sheet of paper with my birth information and then putting it in a stack with photos of a lot of other smiling students. Happy photographs. I have a sinus headache in mine.

Then I walk around the corner and into the fruit market.

Uh oh, the boy with the incense starts dogging me again. "Please I can't talk now. I'm not feeling well."

"Do you want to buy some incense, sister?"

I'm stern. I'm mean. I do not want to be harassed. Go away.

Today, a lot of people are calling out to me. Perhaps it's because I'm not well and therefore I do not look as focused. I'm bothered a little bit by the way I spoke to the boy. I'm not sure how to behave. I give him a few rupees, but I know he wants more, ten rupees and lots of conversation. And I'm not sure if I am helping or hurting when I give him money.

I'm going to wear my yoga clothes in the rickshaw even though I'm unsure about the affect the rickshaw might have on the vibration. I'll unfold my yoga mat—never use it for anything else, otherwise it will carry those vibrations. I did use it as a carpet for a few days, but I washed it with hot water. And Isabella carried it around India. Let me see now if I can recognize the thoughts that enter into my practice like thieves that are caught in the act and then sneak out the back door and run away. They do steal your peace, Acharya.

Return after practice and wash clothes. The practice was very sweet. Remember something important that Acharya told me—"On the inhale, experience strength. On the exhale, experience lightness."

*

Open the door to my room today and surprise—there's an angry teenage monkey standing in the middle of the room, growling at me. He looks so fierce. In his hand is my papaya, half eaten. I scream and run down the hallway. The hotel boys clamor up the stairs and chase the monkey out of the room with their brooms. From now on, I'll remember to lock the windows.

*

Shortly after Lenny and I met, we found an apartment on Willis Street, a first floor, two room apartment with big French windows in a building that was in terrible disrepair. A good percentage of the people in the building were either students on limited budgets or welfare recipients, which was probably the case for most of the people living around the university. We were living off food stamps and working as the supers for the building, collecting rent and cleaning the halls—we had little or no repair skills. Lenny also worked as a bartender and I worked part-time in the university as a student assistant and also as a nude model for the art department. Sometimes we sold marijuana to make a little extra money. When we weren't working, we were often with our friends at the bar listening to music and talking politics. I finished a few classes every semester at the university.

When I try to remember Lenny on Willis Street, I remember him helping me cut up zucchini to make a big pot of mixed vegetables, including three different types of squash. So easy to cook and the colors were beautiful. When I'd come home from classes, I'd walk around the corner and he'd be sitting in the window waiting for me, often chatting with someone sitting on the stoop. One time when he was working as a bartender at Our Place on Third and Willis after the bar closed at 3:00 a.m., and after several vodkas and orange juice, he chose to lie down on the sidewalk and pretend he was dead. I was very frightened. I tried pulling him, but he wouldn't move. What was there to be afraid of? At 3 a.m. in this downtown Detroit neighborhood, there were the police and the criminals. Finally when I was near tears, he opened one eye and laughed at me. "Come on, Gina," he said, poking me. Lenny was always teasing me, but I've always been a rather serious person, who doesn't enjoy being teased. That was probably part of the reason we were together.

After a while, we decided to rent a large flat on Avery Street. At first my brother and another friend lived with us. It was like a farm house, with three bedrooms, two living rooms, a kitchen and a basement. Another group of young people lived upstairs. It was when we were living on Avery Street that Lenny developed a serious interest in working at carnivals, circuses and street vending. He bought a popcorn cart and set up in front of the university when school was in session. I made thousands of caramel and candy apples for him to sell. Our house was littered with sacks of peanuts, boxes of cups and crates of apples.

I remember coming home to the Avery house after having taken a hit of acid and watching the Watergate trials on television with my brother and another friend. Turning on the TV was like opening a window to a room where politicians and newscasters existed in a different universe, an underworld, where they had no power over us, but only thought what they were talking about was real. We rolled around the room laughing at them. When Lenny came home, I was keyed up and anxious because I wanted to stay straight for him, but here I was in another universe. He was staying away from drugs then, he never liked psychedelics, and he especially didn't want me to do drugs. "You can't handle it, Gina," he said when I was huddled up in the living room, "So don't take them anymore."

We'd been together for three years when we learned I was pregnant. It seemed like a natural and acceptable consequence of our love. At the time I couldn't imagine being with anyone but him. We decided to have the baby at home. Jessie was born in the back bedroom after three days of labor with two midwives coming and going. I remember looking at Lenny's face as he helped me breathe. Inhale. Exhale. He was worried and tired. Now, I look at a photograph of him holding her right after the birth, his little girl. He was in love with her from that moment. No matter how bizarre his habits, he always managed to be there for his children. When Jessie was away at college, he called her sometimes three times a day. She told me once that whenever her phone rang, before she'd pick up the receiver, she'd tell the other girls in the dorm—"That's my Dad calling."

Then we bought a house around the corner on Commonwealth Street, on a land contract, one thousand dollars down and a hundred and fifty dollars a month. I was just finishing my bachelor's degree when I became pregnant with Josh. Josh was born in an upstairs bedroom after three hours of labor. Jessie was there. She claims his first sound was, "Ma."

Once we drove down to Key west with the children and one of Lenny's friends to sell lemonade at an art festival. We were pulling a little camping trailer. Jessie threw tantrums all the way there and back. Josh took his first steps on the beach in Miami. And I realized on this trip that I didn't enjoy following carnivals and art fairs. I'd had enough of that life. It was Lenny's passion, not mine. I liked staying home and drawing.

Then we were robbed. A friend of Lenny's, who was painting our house, hired a teenager who lived down the street to assist him. The kid must have seen our friend hide the key. He came back and stole a lot of money—maybe a thousand dollars—which I had stupidly put in a dresser drawer. The thief was known in the neighborhood for B and E's and burning garages. We went to court. I remember walking Josh in his stroller and the kid stopping me on the street and glaring at me in a threatening way. Lenny and some very hulky friends cornered him, threatening to kill him if he didn't return the money. The money was never returned. The girl who claimed she had seen him break into the house was asked to take her glasses off in court. The jury was convinced she couldn't see well enough to identify him. He was let off. Then Lenny started drinking more, and perhaps he was using heroin again. Shortly thereafter, I found him an apartment around the corner from us. Two years later, I read in the newspaper that the teenager had died in a garage fire that he probably had set.

*

I walk over to Upahar for lunch, again forgetting Tuesday is a Brahmin holiday. They are closed. I buy a small bottle of water from the store next to the restaurant, prop my rain poncho over my head and drape it over my bag. Light rain. I circle around to Iyengar's Mess and into the main room. All men. I look in the back room. Women and some men.

"Madam." I hear Mahadeshwara's voice. In the back, he is sitting beside the young man with the false arm who works as an accountant and does the hotel proprietor's books.

"Can I join you?"

They give me detailed instructions on eating thalis. First, there are no chilies in the two items on the plate so they are edible. Pepper, Acharya tells me, is usually fine to eat. So dump the rice in the middle. Take away all the little bowls and use the chapatti to eat the food.

The accountant asks for a spoon, so I ask for one too, and when the chapatti is gone, I eat with the spoon. Mahadeshwara is very tidy, eating with his right hand. He instructs me to drink the soup. "It's very good for"—and he points at the area at the top of his nose.

I take his advice and drink it.

Then they add the very strong chili mixture. I skip that. Then yogurt or buttermilk is mixed with the rice. And so it's a meal.

One waiter stands beside our table, smiling, raising his eyebrows and motioning to me by tipping his head.

Mahadeshwara informs me that Indians never leave tips in restaurants unless it's a very upscale hotel. But I'm not an Indian, so expectations are different for me in this restaurant that is frequented by yoga students.

*

Wednesday, June 6th. I just prepared dinner, peeled carrots and beets soaking in lemon juice, dahl and rice soaking in water, green beans and cilantro in cooking water. It takes so much time to cook in this hotel room. I'm learning everything new and how to do it on a little burner. I want to learn how to cook chapattis, too. Acharya tells me it's better for me to cook for myself, but Iyengars is ok. It's better than the other restaurants. Perhaps because it is a Brahmin restaurant, they don't cook with as much garlic and onions as other restaurants do.

Let me back track. One eerie moment last night. I decide after my practice (which was much too late so that I find myself eating dinner at 7:45) to go over to Iyengars and have chapattis. It is dark and the street is a bit ominous. The men stare at me when I'm eating. There are people at three other tables. I look up from my plate and they are all staring at me.

On the way around the corner, it is very dark. I step carefully to avoid big piles of cow manure. There are many motorbikes and rickshaws and people walking here and there in the darkness. Half way down the block, the electricity goes out. There is an element of loneliness that excites a little bit of fear in me. Others are busy going where they go. I'm wandering home from a late dinner alone. Last year, I was always with Isabella or Dimitri. I wish Dimitri would come to Mysore but because of his martial arts studio, he doesn't have time.

(Oops as I type this, the lights go out. On and off they go.)

Sleeping is difficult—at 10 p.m. the men across the hall come back and they are so loud that I yell out—"Please be quiet, I'm trying to sleep." I yell from my bed knowing that the sound will go right out the grates around the top of the room. Some laughter. I'm not sure they even hear me or even understand what I am saying.

I remember one thing about my dreams. There is a horse. I am riding her and I am petting her. I love you, I am saying. Perhaps this has something to do with missing my dog Peggy or perhaps it's the result of seeing many animals on the street with so much despair and hard work.

*

One bookstore doesn't have the books I am looking for and the other is closed from 1-4 every afternoon. I cut down the street by

Jayaraj's yogashala and around the courtyard into the back street, passing a very old wiry man wearing only shorts and sitting smoking on his cart—a small covered wagon with very large wooden wheels. He is dark and thin with a little cloth tied around his head. He looks tired and frustrated. If I had my camera, I could take his photo. It would show something very profound about India. His ox is skinny with a heavy yoke upon her neck and sores on her body. A young man zips around him on a motorbike. There are some other young, healthy looking men pulling heavy carts, too. I imagine their futures as similar to this old man's. I walk a few more steps and there is a large healthy looking black cow walking with a sense of direction and speed (for a cow). Her tits are swollen with milk. She must be heading home to give. Then a large truck with an empty shell comes throttling down the street, honking at us to move over. As it speeds by, the driver leaves behind a cloud of smoke. I pull my white shawl up around my face. Then I turn the corner to the street of the hotel and a big truck is blocking the way. I step around mud puddles, move over for motorbikes, jump out of the way of honking vehicles and step into the hotel.

"Good day, madam."

take off my clothes, still unclear about how to handle this requirement about clothing. These are the clothes I wore for morning practice and in the rickshaw. I suppose I can go on wearing them for everything except for yoga practice in the room at 5 p.m. (It's almost 5 p.m. now). I begin reading *A Search in Secret India*. Acharya prefers that I not read anything this summer unless he suggests it. Put away the other books about yoga. I think he doesn't want contradictory teachings about yoga to interfere with my experience, which depends upon my confidence in his instructions.

He watches my practice and says that I'm not receiving the true flower of the yoga. In my rest period, my mind is working too hard. I must give myself the oil bath tomorrow morning, follow his instructions about eating mango always with curd, a little ghee with each meal, and no tea. In fifteen days I will be experiencing the rose, the flower, the goal of yoga, a quiet mind.

I'm a little defensive. This reason. That reason. I feel uncomfortable being watched. But the truth is that I have not developed that part of my practice. And that is what I'm here for.

He tells me he often has reading groups for the Gita and other texts, but for now it will be just me.

I ask if he wants me to organize a group and he says, no. If they come, yes, but no encouragement.

He is a lovely man. I give him a donation and two photographs of me, one when I was about five years old and one from yesterday.

"No hardship?"

"No hardship," I say, worrying if I have perhaps not given enough. Worry is a thief, too. It steals your clarity of mind.

*

Let's review the night and day before I lose everything in the cumulative mind heap.

The days are taking over. Reading more. Drawing less. The night before last (Wednesday), I took a rickshaw to Dr. Anand's office. On the way, I asked Shivapa to stop at Geetha books to look for the books Acharya had asked that I read. They looked around and had none of them.

It's raining lightly. I step around the puddles and crowds to find the rickshaw and then we head over to Saraswati Purum. Somehow Shivapa knows how to get there even though he doesn't know the exact place. He comes from the opposite direction. I see the big empty field and the hospital across the street. "Right there. Are you sure you want to stay and wait?"

"Yes, Madam."

I wait for the doctor and talk to the little girl, Akasha. She is very fastidious, cleaning and arranging everything on the shelves and desk. She is wearing the same slightly worn skirt and blouse she wore last week—a calf length turquoise skirt and a western blouse with long sleeves.

"Do you have a country coin?" she asks.

"No, not today sorry, maybe next time."

"I like your nail polish," she says, "bright blue."

She shows me a string of old fake pearls that someone gave her. She holds them up and looks at them with great admiration, asking me if I want to look at them.

"Yes." I look at them and try to see pearls, but I see only plastic. To her they are beautiful.

"I like your nail polish," she says again.

"I will bring it for you next week." I'm not going to wear nail polish anymore. Why put any unnatural substance on my body. I look down at my toes. I want to ask Acharya about my shoes. He was looking at them rather intently the other day. They are a sturdy pair of rubber sandals. "I should not wear them?" I asked.

"Not for yoga," he said. He is wearing leather sandals. I know that leather is more organic, but what about the cows? I must ask him about the cows.

The doctor notes that I'm in stress due to the cold and he gives me some new medicines to take. He instructs me to drink only hot water. No cold bottled water. I have found this impossible, though, because I'm not at home and I need to drink something. Also, I'm a lazy cook. Boiling water to drink over and over. I just don't have the habit. That's all it is, establishing the habit.

Next week he will adjust my spine and perhaps I will take lessons in ayurveda from him. We again discuss the hormones I'm taking—I tell him they are synthesized from soy and yam products to mimic the hormones in a woman's body. He is not happy, but says I can keep taking them for the time being. Later he will give me herbs. I mention I'm taking vitamins. He says—you only mentioned the hormones. To me vitamins are like food. To him they are synthesized and so enter your body in an unnatural way.

*

Later that night I go downstairs and order a ginger tea. There is a group of six men hanging around the lobby watching television and leaving no room for me to sit so I bring the tea back to my room.

I pass Brandy in the hallway. He too is on his way for tea. I tell him about the mob in the lobby and we decide to have tea together in my room.

I sit on the bed and he sits in the chair.

This morning at Subrata's he was defensive about admitting he is a beginner in yoga even though he was sitting with a group of very advanced teachers and students. Now he talks about how much he loves Ayn Rand and *Atlas Shrugged* and how he's an advocate of free enterprise and all the plans he has to start a big yoga acupuncture and yoga center in southern California.

"Who will teach the classes?"

"Oh that won't be a problem. I'll hire a crew. There are a lot of unemployed yoga teachers, especially in California."

I ask him if he is one of those persons who weaves huge projects in the future. Yes, he says, but unlike my father, I actually do them. He continues with a list of his accomplishments.

*

Sleep. Coughing. Waking. Dreaming. Taking Dr. Anand's herbs. Well that was a few nights ago. Last night I slept very nicely, falling asleep with the peppery cough pill under my tongue, waking in a trance to go to the bathroom and then back into bed. Then the morning chants. Today and yesterday are mixed up in my mind.

Artie asks me in a letter what I see when I look out my window at 2 a.m. Rooftops and the top of a coconut tree. I have no idea who the family is or what they do beneath that rooftop. I tell him about the streets and the fact that I have never been out at 2 a.m. The only people on the street are probably drunken men. Most Indians go to sleep early and rise early. And so do yoga students. Acharya told me once that many Indians will not take a rickshaw after ten o'clock because they are afraid of the drivers. Perhaps they will be robbed or murdered. I guess Mysore is different after dark. One day I will wake up at 2 a.m., go downstairs and walk around the corner for my report to Artie.

I woke up yesterday and prepared for the oil bath. First I wash my nightgown and hang it in the bathroom. Every morning so you don't begin the next night with the vibrations from the past, rinse out your evening clothes. I'm starting to become used to washing clothes at night and in the morning. They don't dry well enough now though because of the monsoon. So in the morning I take them on the roof. There is a woman staying on the third floor who wears a blue sari. She stands outside her door often and stares at me hanging clothes. I wonder what she thinks. And why is she always standing in the hallway like that?

Back in my room, I open the bottle of sesame oil and spread it over my head and body. It feels wonderful. I look in the mirror in the main room. I don't look so good under the florescent light, kind of green, but in the bathroom, I look fine. I enjoy spreading it over my breasts. I enjoy my body covered in oil. Then after 20 minutes, I open the herbs with my knife and cut myself. (Even as I try to be calm, I'm continually dropping things, cutting myself, and losing things!) A thought steals my pleasure—Will I absorb some amoeba in the area of the wound? I put a piece of alcohol cloth under a bandage on my finger, and continue sprinkling the herbs and massaging them into my skin and then bathing with shampoo and soap.

Then I walk down the street to Anoop's, check my email and write to Artie, Mark, Miranda and others. The email station is closed, but the man in the STD phone booth opens it for me. The first message is from Josh, telling me that my dog Peggy has been ill and vomiting, that Mike took her to the vet and he said she had eaten something bad. She wasn't moving because she was so old. Josh said that when he and Jessie visited her, she became happy. I felt suddenly so unhappy that tears formed in my eyes. When I left I was worried about leaving her because she is so old. She might die while I'm gone. I cannot stop crying. I call Josh in Brooklyn. He tells me she is ok, he has just talked to Mike and she is perfectly fine now. I'm overwhelmed with emotion. But it feels like a cleansing. The day is just beginning. I go back to my room to rest and regain my composure. I hear Acharya saying, "It is your duty to be joyful."

In *Search for Secret India*, Brunton writes about the amazing peace and knowledge that yogis find in their practice. I take out a photo of Peggy running happily through Tompkins Square Park, make a new sketch and add it to the little collection of animals.

*

When Mei-Luen walks through the hotel lobby, Mahadeshwara calls me, "Madam, Madam."

I introduce myself to her. I am a bit raggedy, my room is a mess and I feel a little bit of stress. Mahadeshwara refers to me as the Mother of the Kaveri Hotel, I guess because I have returned and because I took care of some students last year, telling them where to go and what to do.

*

"You will be a mother someday," my mother told me as I sat on our green couch holding my newborn sister, Terri, in my lap. I was six years old. When my mother was feverish and ill, stretched out on the couch, I put a cold washcloth on her forehead and combed her hair away from her face. Look after your brother and sisters, she told me when she went into the hospital. I was eleven and I was carrying motherhood as a burden, at least it seemed like a burden to me then and on and off for many years. That's why I cringe a little when Mahadeshwara calls me "Mother of the Kaveri" or in the 70s when people called me an earth mother. That's why I burst into tears one time at a meeting when someone said to me, "Stop mothering me." Is there some fault in my personality, some weird twist, some karma from a past life that insists I always be the mother?

On the day Jessie was born, I was wearing an old terrycloth bathrobe (the same style that my mother wore). I picked up the baby and walked through the hallway. My hair was matted against the side of my face. I stopped midway and felt the presence of my mother very strongly. It was as if I were my mother and the baby were me, and we were starting over again. Now you are a mother, I heard her say. When the children were small, I was a loving, untroubled mother. A week after Jessie was born, Lenny said to me one night when I was nursing the baby, "Gina, I never told you this, but I was worried. I wasn't sure you'd be able to handle this. But you are fine."

Later when I was alone with two young children, six and three years old, I would sometimes despair over the situation. It seemed too similar to my experience as an inept twelve year old mother to my brothers and sisters, who were five, six, eight, and ten. But after a while, Lenny became better at sharing the parenting, responsibilities. Jessie, Josh and I survived their adolescence and our bohemian ways, I think, because of the cracks and fissures in our family. When one parent was on the edge, they were able to escape by running to the apartment of the other. Lenny and I were always on the telephone with each other, trying to do the best we could for them. I worked hard when they were young to keep my freedom as an independent female artist, as a sexual woman, and as a non-traditional but attentive mother. Once Jessie wrote a paper comparing the mother in Charlotte's Web to me. She wrote, "Her mother is a cooker, my mother is a draw-er."

*

Acharya asks me to do my practice in front of him on a straw mat. I like the straw mat. But I'm a little distracted, moving slowly, thinking strength, lightness. He says, do only two sun salutations A & B. My body is moving quickly, fluidly, but I'm a little out of breath. At the end of the practice, he tells me it is wrong for me and that I will have perpetual back problems if I continue with it. Tomorrow, he will make changes. At one point his little nephew tries to get into the room. He puts him out and holds the door closed with his foot. The child is screaming. He wants his uncle to come with him. Acharya is smiling. Children sounds do not bother me much either. During graduate school, I learned how to read theoretical texts in the middle of child chaos. He interrupts me to talk before savasana, the final rest pose. By then I can hear Shivapa and the child and now I'm a bit distracted and worn out. He is correct. I do not know how to quiet my body. Yoga has not done that for me yet. Is this a hardship for you to come here every day? No, I say, that is why I came to India, to practice with you.

Ride back with Shivapa in that dreamy coasting way. No honking, no jarring stops. I'm starting to recognize markers. A skinny man with two oxen and a heavy load is curled up, sleeping on the side of the road.

And so the day progresses until my five o'clock practice in my room. I eat my dinner in stages so I can have some vegetables without a lot of cooking. Cook the ear of corn I bought from the man pushing the cart down the side street here. Then I eat a raw carrot.

I ask Mahadeshwara to tell Mei-Luen that I'm at Iyengar's Mess. I eat dinner and walk back to the hotel. Rupesh informs me that she has already gone to Iyengar's. I realize she must be at the other Iyengar's Lunchroom on Double Road, so I head down the street and find her mid route. We talk about Anjali's mother, who can't speak English, who is so loving. She was an important part of my trip last year, an old woman from Delhi who was spending time in

Mysore with her two daughters who now live in Singapore and in Germany. She opened her big arms and became the grandmother of everyone on the third floor. It was natural for her.

*

Shivapa and I drop Mei-Luen off at Subrata's so she can meet the other yoga students. Then he takes the back roads to get to where we are going. He cuts through little neighborhoods, gliding around holes rather than plowing forward like the other drivers. He is a truly eccentric rickshaw driver. Most drivers plow forward, bouncing their passengers up and down. Not Shivapa. He's a roller and a weaver. I really like his style. Even so, I believe I'm soon going to rent my own scooter so I'm not always so dependent on someone else.

When I arrive at Acharya's, his wife Jayashree greets me and asks me to sit on a chair in front of the house. He is not here yet. I ask her about the fabric used in clothes and she explains that elastic is ok as long as it's covered with cotton so that only cotton touches the body. Also we talk about shoes. Your feet should only touch animal skin, she says. I ask about the cows and she says in India leather shoes are made from cows who die naturally. That's interesting, but from the responses I've had from shoe salesmen, I think it's only partially true.

Some women stop by the house, leaving their sandals on the stoop and a rickshaw parked outside, then leaving minutes later. The house is very austere with photographs of great yogis on the walls. Young male students in dhotis and shawlas are walking up and down the stairs at the front of the house. Jayashree returns and tells me that I will have to do my old practice by myself. "Today go to the side. Perhaps my husband will return before you finish."

I hang up my things, unfold the straw mat and even though it feels strange, I begin. Each strangeness has its own built in thinking pattern—so many thieves busy trying to make the present into an event—and I want to recognize them, so they leave and I can be as vibrantly here in this room as possible.

I complete the whole practice, and right at padmasana when I'm about to begin the meditation, I hear Acharya's voice. Minutes later he appears sitting on the ledge.

"I'm so sorry. I must warn you that this will happen on occasion since I'm so busy."

Then we talk. I tell him that it was nice practicing here alone too (with the mosquitoes, the narrow walls, his seat covered with a cloth, a lawn chair packed into the area). It's an odd little space that he has made for his private yoga sessions. I talk about the secrets in secret India. "Have they all been revealed?"

"No there will always be secrets. No matter how popular yoga is, the true secret of it will only be known by a few. Those who are meant to know do not have to seek it."

I talk about how the last time I meditated in front of him, the minute I closed my eyes, there was a burning yellow circle in front of my face, almost too intense for me to continue. I tell him how when I would do my little bit of meditation after morning yoga in the states, I was starting to see an eye and the iris was full of light.

He advises me that I should note these things but not become fascinated by them. Just note them. Do not concentrate on them.

We are both happy. I'm happy that he showed up before I left because I like him so much. I talk about the motor scooter idea and how I'm going to work on that. Then he has a very long phone call and he's unable to return to the little practice room. As I'm preparing to leave, Jayashree brings me a bag with some very tasty cooked jack fruit in it. I eat it on my way back to Agrahara.

*

Walking over to the fruit market, I notice that when poor people beg—most of them are old—many Indians give them a single rupee. I think I gave the same man one rupee in each lane of the market. They don't have an organized social security program in India, only begging and the help of social programs offered by ashrams, so I think it is important to give old people something.

I walk through the market, totally calm no matter who is calling

to me, no matter what I encounter. I step out with my bags and signal a rickshaw. Usually I ask before I ride, How much? I forget to
do this today, and when the driver takes me home, I hand him ten
rupees.

He says, "No, fifteen," and I say, "No I go there every day. It's
ten rupees."

He follows me into the hotel. It's a matter of principle.
Mahadeshwara engages him in an argument. "Madame please give
me five more rupees," he says.

"Only if Mahadeshwara tells me to."

"Ok, Madam, now he is begging, so you give him the five
rupees."

Later Mahadeshwara explains that the man went from demanding to begging for the five rupees. He is wrong, but when begging,
give. I ask what I should do about the children in the market area
selling incense.

"Buy the incense,' says Mahadeshwara.

The fruit store owner says, "No, say no, I'm not interested. They
are not good boys."

If I buy the incense every time I appear in the market, I will be
surrounded by a crowd of boys. I will have no peace of mind.
Maybe Mahadeshwara doesn't understand what it is like to be a foreigner on these streets.

On the corner near the hotel, I'm looking in a little store for a
jar of peanut oil when a group of children start talking to me. One
points at a cookie. "Will you buy me one of these?" I count the children—seven—and I buy each one a cookie. They are happy, skipping, jumping, following me down the street. Very young. Perhaps
four years old. I cannot escape the fact that I'm from the west and
loaded with money as far as they know. And they are simply children at the corner store, wishing for something sweet from the
adults who are around them. We would beg from our mothers. They
are begging from me, a white auntie. Perhaps by doing this, however, I'm teaching them to beg whenever they see a westerner.

*

The telephone house is a sprawling suburban Indian house next door to the telephone office. The larger part of the house is divided into rooms that are rented mostly to western yoga students. Many of the houses in this neighborhood serve as rooming houses for foreigners visiting India. Three flautists are playing in the middle of the common area. Twenty five mostly young white westerners, many dressed in saris or lungis, sit in lotus poses smiling and perhaps meditating to the flutes. They look identical to the group that was here last year. Even our smiles look the same.

*

Surya delivers my laundry to the room and then he hobbles back to his room on his crutches. I have never seen anything like this. His bones were severely broken, so they put a metal rod into his leg and gigantic screws into his flesh and bones that now have to be removed. It looks very unprofessional and painful. I give him a mango.

This is my third Saturday here. Bells are ringing. I have bathed and had an oil bath, washed my sleeping gown, practiced pranayama during nadi shodana with some difficulty, since my left nostril refuses to be completely free. I have discovered that if I breathe very slowly, I can still practice. In meditation, a large black circular form slowly takes the outer shape of an eye, then the iris, then the pupil. I watch it without fascination, without attachment. Thieves are the sounds of the world including that dripping faucet in the bathroom.

A few doors down, I climb the steps of the turquoise house. A little girl meets me halfway in her school girl clothes, dressed similar to a catholic school girl in the U.S., plaid skirt, white shirt, her hair in braids. She hollers something to her mother, who appears at the top of the steps. Curd? Yes. No, a small. Small? Yes. Three-and-a-quarter rupees. These quarter rupees are like pennies in the states. It has taken me two visits to India to realize that I can buy milk products from a woman two doors away.

"Hello, good morning Mahadeshwara."

"Good morning Madam. How are you?"

"Fine and you."

"Oh, Fine."

"Mahadeshwara, can you tell me—how do you know when you buy shoes that they have been made from cows who have died naturally?

"Yes, yes."

"Is there a law?"

"Yes, a law."

"How can you know for sure?"

"Some tablas are made from cows who were killed."

"How can you tell for sure?"

He shakes his head left and right and I never can tell what is yes and what is no. I don't think he understands me. He steps outside to buy strings of white flowers from the man passing by the hotel to make a puja to Lakshmi for success, lighting incense and sprinkling camphor water. To Ganesh. To Vishnu. These are the deities in the lobby.

Something brought me to this computer—It was the dream I had last night. Something about a little baby coming into my life from somewhere and I keep taking him to different places to sleep where he is not happy. A mat on the floor. A crib with some major problems that I can't remember right now. We are also at some performance. I reassure him. All will be well. I, too, am the baby, looking. I'm performing. I'm collecting tickets. I'm watching a parade. Where is the baby? There is also another child, Jessie I think, who is very comfortable with her bed.

Cooking breakfast. First a mango cut up in a cup, then a package of curd. Then the blender. Voom. Everything is mixed. Then I cook oatmeal, ghee and cashews. Bland but healthy.

A walk down the street. A little email from Josh saying that Peggy is fine. I send him three emails. One with news of the day and such, one asking if it's ok if I send him an email, teaching him something about Tibet and India, and then one telling him to call to check on his financial aid. I also send a quick message to my brother. I wonder if he and his wife are staying together or going in different directions. Jerome, a friend from graduate school, sends me a formal message mentioning he will be in New York. I let him know I'm in

India. We used to be close, but now we are becoming more like acquaintances.

I come upstairs and begin reading when someone knocks at the door. I'm expecting Monique but it's Vanessa and Whitney. Vanessa was going to give me a lesson on the scooter, but she can't do it until Tuesday. I tell her that Monique will help me. Then Monique comes upstairs and we sit and talk about her plans to move to Hawaii. Whitney and I both know an artist whose cat died during the quarantine in Hawaii. Monique has two cats. Then we talk about mother-child relationships. I talk a lot about my relationship with my daughter and Monique talks about her mother. Whitney and Vanessa do not say a word about their mothers. I wonder why.

Now I'm going to tell Shivapa that I'm not going to need a rickshaw because I'm getting a motor bike. I feel bad telling him this because I do like him.

8:45, the sound of light rain and many people on the first floor of the hotel, talking.

Acharya was very busy today and he kept running into the practice room and telling me asanas to write down in my sequence which I'm now supposed to do for fifteen days. There were mosquitoes and ants all over the floor where I was practicing. I must remember to put pennyroyal on my arms before I go there. His little nephew kept pushing open the door and demanding Acharya's attention and he'd start screaming when Acharya would shut the door. Such a funny busy yogi life. And Acharya is sick. He says that it's because they are cleaning today and dust is everywhere. But I think he is sick and needs to see his own ayurvedic doctor. But who am I to say what the ayurvedic doctor needs? I keep thinking I should go home and let him be. I tell him that whenever we have appointments and he feels unable to meet with me, he should call the hotel. Tuesday should be better because his nephew will be in school.

I'm unsure if the next meeting will be alone or with another student. He gives me a new sequence, which is quite different from what I have been doing, and he also tells me that I should be waking up at 4:30 a.m. and allowing an hour before practice and an hour after the practice before eating. What else did he say? "Your asana practice should take no more than one half of your strength and no less than one half if it's to truly be effective. If you take more, the result is exhaustion and ultimately illness." I must have appeared exhausted to him when I demonstrated because I was also ill. I usually don't feel exhausted, but I must admit I use more than 50% of my strength—maybe 60%.

I tell Shivapa about the bike and he seems very disappointed. He tells me he wants to go to America and he asks me if I have an American dollar. I guess his imagination was working, too. Unfortunately, I don't have a dollar, so I give him two quarters and tell him to call at 11:00 to see if I will need him on Tuesday. I'm hopeful I will be proficient enough on the scooter to transport myself after tomorrow.

*

I am reading Rama Krishna when Mei-Luen knocks on my door.

I walk her over to Jayaraj's yoga shala. Then we go into the KR circle madness. I order a silk nightgown, buy some cotton underwear, a little pad of paper and a book on Mysore yoga which is a little bit informative, a little bit bitter and defensive, but mostly beautiful in its reproduction of old illustrations from the palace.

I become more and more short-tempered as people approach me, stare at me, the heat, the crowd. At one point, I am in a narrow crowded street and I am wedged between two trucks, an ox driven cart, and a dark man with a beautiful body carrying an unbelievably heavy stack of sacks on his head. When I watch them, I wonder why India hasn't taken to using such things as hand carts. Wouldn't that save the bodies of these men?

I feel so sad every time I think of a particular pose that Acharya has taken away from me. The balancing poses, for example. No forget those. I have been doing this practice for almost three years, every single day, and now I wonder about the future and how my body will change.

I come home and rest a little bit before I do the afternoon practice. The meditation is becoming easier. Then I cook some little green lima bean-looking peas, I don't know what they are called, with rice, salt, garlic, cilantro, ghee and turmeric. I call downstairs to ask for an order of chapattis. Rupesh is happy to bring me chapattis. If I only want the chapattis, he gets the rest. I'm happy to make him happy. Then I eat a big bowl of food and that tastes very good. I wonder about the garbage from carrot peels and the extra food. I ask if there is a place to put it for the animals. Yes, out in back of the hotel. I dump the remains of my dinner on the street for the cows and dogs. Mahadeshwara and I look down at rice and peas and carrot skins. I wonder if it should have been given to a person first.

*

Meditation this afternoon—the black circle outlined in gold starts getting smaller and a pinprick appears inside and is filled with gold and then for just a brief minute there is a woman's face in the lower left side. I think it is my mother's face. Acharya says that the energy between child and parent is very strong whether they are on opposite sides of the planet or one is dead and the other alive.

*

In Monique and Jackie's apartment, I tie the little scarf around my head to hold my hair back and then I go out and practice riding the scooter again. They are both laughing at me. I think I look like an old hippie. Well? I keep trying to be a lady but it doesn't work.

*

You're in New York City in the East Village reading on a bench in Tompkins Square. Take a taxi to LaGuardia Airport. Take an airplane to London. Transfer to Mumbai. Transfer to Bangalore. Take a rickshaw to a train. Take the train to Mysore. Take a rickshaw to the Kaveri Lodge on Chelevambu Road, right across from Dolly Men's Fashions, next to the unmarked little dingy store. Walk through the lobby, up the stairs to the second floor. Push open the door to room ten. A woman is curled up on the bed, reading a book with the title, *A Search in Secret India*.

Rupesh knocks on the door. "Madam, home?"

"Yes, just a second." I put on my blouse.

"Home? You're going home? When do you come back?"

"7 a.m."

"Return, when do you return?"

"7 a.m."

I can't figure out what he wants. He stands there with his glasses on and his jacket over his arm. "Wait a minute. Do you want to use the scooter?"

"Yes."

"How far?"

"7 kilometers."

"Go ahead." He has a wife and two children whom he hardly ever sees. And he makes hardly any money. But, probably with western tips, he does better than most people at menial jobs in India.

*

Practicing riding the scooter in Shreepurum on the dirt roads. Turning around. Turning left. Turning right. A little shaky. When I was nineteen and first learning how to ride a motorcycle, I flew over the top of the bike and hit the fence. I had a slight concussion. I continued riding. I used to take it on the freeways in Detroit with no helmet, 55 miles an hour with my hair whipping in the wind. So why so difficult now? A little riding and I'm in the swing. It's actually easier than walking, scooting around cows, people, bicycles and rickshaws. Roberto says to me, if you can ride a cycle in India, you can ride one anywhere in the world. At the circle, I go smoothly right around the policeman.

Eating chapattis and curried peas at Upahar with my fingers in a much sloppier way than the Indians. I sneak a little help with my left hand. I put on my glasses so to be a little removed from the others, especially the men who sit across from me and who feel so uncomfortable about my presence. I guess I am a strange bird. If any other tables become available, they have no shyness about getting up and sitting elsewhere. Proprietors come right over and reseat Indian people if they end up sitting across from me.

Monday morning. Wake at 4:30 to the alarm. Push the snooze button. Sleep. Push it again. Sleep. Push it again. Then knock it on the floor. Oh well, the alarm is broken. I wake up and it's sitting right on its base, push in the battery and it's working fine. This alarm is indestructible.

In the bathroom I run the water. It's hot! Fill up the pail, wash out my nightgown and hang it up to dry. Pour hot water in the little blue pitcher over my head. Hot water is beautiful. Yesterday it was so cold. Shampoo. Suds. Scrub. Rinse. Wash out handkerchief and blouse from yesterday. Scrub with a little plastic brush. These little domestic acts are so satisfying. Just caring for yourself in the most simple ways possible.

The morning yoga practice was better. I remembered thinking that I was not getting hot from it because it wasn't demanding enough and then I thought to myself—put your heart into this practice as it is. I started understanding it. I almost did it as Acharya wanted except that I inserted a few jump backs. I want to ask him to keep the vinyasas because they make it feel more flowing, at least until the navasana poses. They provide a segue between unsimilar positions. But the whole thing doesn't take long enough. Only 35 minutes and the pranayama is 20 minutes or maybe 22. Then I finish, lie down and go back to sleep. I'm sure that is not a good thing to do. But I can't eat for an hour and I have not adjusted to waking at 4:30 a.m. I have a difficult time going to sleep early enough. I think I should stay awake. I have been dreaming a lot more here and my sleep is much sounder.

The door bell rings and I'm involved in something, some dream. It's Rupesh with the keys to the scooter. "I'm sorry madam. I didn't want to disturb you earlier."

"Did it run ok?"

"Yes, very nice. Thank you."

The scooter is very heavy. I try to push it out to start it and I almost drop it on the other side. Rupesh grabs it for me. I bravely turn the gas up and coast down the street, turning right and heading for the main road where there are so many animals, people and vehicles.

*

Madam, the man from Naveen Travel is on the telephone. He wants to know if you are interested in a tour.

"No, Mahadeshwara, tell him I'm not. Last year, they stood me up at the airport."

The day I arrived in Bangalore last year, I was alone and I was exhausted. The man at this same agency had promised to send a man to meet me. He was supposed to be in the airport with a sign with my name. But he was not there. I kept walking in and out of the main door of the airport. Whenever I walked out the door, groups of drivers surrounded me, asking me to come with them for this amount of rupees or that amount of rupees.

No, no, I said, having heard about these men. Still I was confused and unprepared. Where is my driver? Should I go to a hotel? Which hotel? Should I rent a taxi and go to Mysore? Which taxi? There was a stand inside the lobby for taxis but I didn't understand then that these were government regulated taxis. The guard at the gate kept telling me to just sit inside and wait, Madam. But I was so tired and there was nowhere to lean my head, and everyone seemed a bit sinister.

"Where is a pay telephone?" I asked the guard.

He pointed to a building outside and around the corner. I dragged all my luggage over to this building and I still didn't see a pay phone.

"Pay phone?" A man pointed to a phone on a table.

I gave him the telephone number and he connected me with someone at the travel agency. It was 4:00 in the morning, the man must have been sleeping. He was surprised that no one was in the airport.

"He will be there very shortly," he said. "Just wait, Madam."

I waited and waited and finally I asked at the desk when the next train would leave for Mysore. 5:30 a.m.

A very young man, maybe fifteen years old had been pursuing me to take me to the train station. He seemed honest and innocent, so I decided to take the train. The young man helped me carry my bags to the back of a parking lot where he had a very old white car. He had given me a price for the trip. I can't remember how much right now. He got in the passenger side of the front seat and another man climbed into the driver's seat.

I was a little bit worried about the second man.

"My brother," he said. "He is the driver." They had trouble starting the car. They had to get out of the car and wire something under the hood. Finally we pulled out of the airport and started chugging along on some deserted dirt roads.

Someone inside my tired and confused head said to me, "Gina, are you crazy? It's the middle of the night, and it is very dark outside, you're on the other side of the planet and you have just gotten in a car with two strangers and you are driving away on a deserted road." Because I was so tired and my ears were plugged up from the airplane trip, I was too disoriented to be afraid.

Then my young friend handed me a little card with the rates for the trip. They were twice as high as he had quoted me in the airport. I was angry even though the price was still low compared to home. It was the lying, the trickery involved.

It took quite some time to get to the train station, but when we arrived, I refused to let them carry my bags because I was irritated about the deception. So there I was, tall, white, blonde, tired, carrying a lot of baggage.

I pushed open the door to the train station. Yes, it was a train station, but quite different from anything I had ever encountered in my limited travels: an ancient building, crowded with people wrapped up in saris and lungis, lying on their sides, sleeping on the ground. One thin old man was sitting in a lotus pose with a turban on his head. He stared at me as if I were a visitor from outer space.

I stepped around and through the people, saying, "Tickets? Tickets?"

Someone pointed to a window with bars. I waited in line. "Train to Mysore," I said.

I couldn't understand the clerk, and she couldn't understand me. I gave her money. She gave me a ticket. I didn't know where I was going or when. I looked around. I was so tired that I thought I was going to faint, but then I noticed a woman in the line wearing glasses. Glasses. Perhaps she speaks English.

I asked her if she was going to Mysore.

"Yes," she nodded her head, and adjusted her glasses.

"Will you take me with you?"

"Yes, of course." She bought her ticket and her husband joined us, leading me through some very dark corridors into a black tunnel where we boarded an old train with open cars. This was not second or even third class.

She was going to Mysore for a job interview and she wasn't very happy about it. Her company was transferring their business. Now I know why she was unhappy. I love Mysore, but I think you might have more freedom as a woman in a bigger city like Bangalore.

On the train last year, I was tired and stunned by the world I was seeing for the first time. Very thin, dirty people begging and crawling through the cars. People selling food out of dirty buckets. We were gliding past rice paddies and fields of coconut trees, neem trees, and women carrying burdens on their heads. Barefoot.

I arrived safely three or four hours later. The woman helped me find a rickshaw, and she instructed me to pay the driver no more than fifteen rupees for taking me to the hotel. But as is India, when we arrived, he asked for thirty rupees. I didn't know how to stand my ground yet, so I gave it to him. After all, and this is the problem—it's only seventy-five American cents.

That was a year ago. Now I'm a regular, the mother of the Kaveri as Mahadeshwara calls me.

"No, Mahadeshwara, I don't want a tour organized by Naveen Travel." I didn't know then that Indians often say "Yes" even if the truth is "No"—either to cheat you or to please you. "Yes, Madam, we'll be there in fifteen minutes" might mean, "No not until tomorrow."

*

Two oxen reclining next to the stone fence around Jagamohan

temple. Facing opposite directions, they are chewing and their faces are pressed together.

A cow trying to climb up a little hill of red dirt near a construction site. I must take my camera with me from now on.

I can't get the bike over the curb to start my journey. Rupesh comes outside and soon so do all the other men and boys who work in the hotel. I'm about to get on the bike. "Wait a minute madam." Someone whips out a cloth to wipe the rain drops off the seat.

Tuesday, June 13th. I'm sitting cross legged on the bed listening to the sound of sweeping in the hallway and down in the house next door. Here I feel so close to my life, the actual simple needs of my body—washing clothes in a bucket, pouring water over my head, cutting vegetables and cooking in a little tiny space on the floor. I feel protected in this room.

Now I'm sitting on the floor as Rupesh sweeps and makes up the bed. He takes a rag and water and wets down the floor. Then he turns on the fan. I study his movements because this is the way I am going to clean when I return home, using Rupesh's cleaning asanas. Sometimes we understand each other, sometimes we don't.

Mei-Leun comes by to ask me more questions about where things are and how to get there. I call and arrange Shivapa to pick her up at 4:00 today.

Then I ride the scooter to the gas station and purchase oil. The man helps me and then he spills gas all over the bike. I'm so hesitant, but still I pull out of the station slowly, crawling along the edge of the road as the traffic passes by, honking. Even though I'm early, I head directly for Acharya's house. When the bike is moving I feel absolutely steady. What is difficult though is going around corners and circles and dealing with someone who passes closely when I'm within inches of hitting a pedestrian.

I arrive half an hour early and walk to the edge of Acharya's neighborhood near a big house with some little shanties behind it, rows of coconut trees, and people moving here and there between the shanties. I snap a photograph and sit on a stone on the corner of two streets, noting the countryside so close to the city. I take out my sketch pad and draw the horizon. People stare at me or force themselves to walk by without turning their heads as if to erase me from their street.

A little boy stops on his bike and asks me my name, "What

country? Country coin?" I ask him to stand still for a few minutes so I can catch a quick impression of his profile and the horizon behind. I give him my pen. Happily, he rides away.

Sitting on Acharya's porch, I smooth pennyroyal and hazelnut oil on my skin and wait for his arrival. Jayashree sits across from me and we talk about what she does with her day. They never eat in restaurants. Cooking, this is her job, she says. She feeds her husband, family and the Indian yoga students. She can make many kinds of food and she enjoys her work. She has a Masters in Sanskrit Studies, and for nine years she taught ladies yoga, but now she has too much to do in the house. They traveled to the U.S. once and Acharya spoke at several very large yoga centers. He and Jayashree didn't like the way yoga was being taught in the U.S.. She occasionally mentions something about life in NYC. "I like it here," she says.

"Is Acharya a professor?" I ask. "Yes of Sanskrit and literary criticism at the university. He teaches yoga, Sanskrit and literary studies."

Acharya arrives in his white dhoti and shawla. Students move around inside the house. We go into the little yoga area and talk. I tell him the story of my leg, how I hurt it and healed it by doing yoga, and how I enjoy this habit of practicing in the morning, meeting my friend, walking over to the shala together, sweating together, etcetera. All those things about yoga I love, and yet I know the old practice is not quite right for me now.

He says I need not discuss this with others because they will not want to hear me, but this practice is correct only for a few people—those who want to lose weight or those who want only to gain strength. Some though are so accustomed to the practice that it is difficult for them to stop.

We talk about how you can know if you have reached the 50% mark. If you are sweating on your upper lip and under your arms, you are above the 50% mark.

"You have to take into consideration all the things—weather, location, job, everything. They all affect your relationship with your yoga. And the practice must be adjusted taking into consideration the whole context, including what you eat. You must take into consideration your particular constitution. There are seven constitutions, vata, pitta, kappa and their combinations. A person with a lot of phlegm is very flexible. He does the poses like rubber. You must not compare yourself with this person. A person who is a vata person . . . "

"Am I?"

"Yes—vata is stiff and you must take your body into consideration. Yes, of course you can do extra poses if you want, but they are not necessary. And like medications—if one is not necessary and it will do you no harm, do you take it? Perhaps you will need it later and it will not be as effective then because you have used it so much now. So it is with the asanas. Later when you are aging, you may need one of these asanas. Only do what is necessary now. This is how we look at it. Do this practice for one week and then I will watch again.

And he tells me that I must breathe slowly. I'm completing too quickly.

We talk about my diet again. "Are you eating cashews?"

"Yes."

"A lot?"

"Yes, everyday."

"That is why your mind is so busy. You must stop eating them immediately. You can eat almonds if you take off the skin and eat only five a day. Indians eat very few cashews because they know this."

I tell him that I do not like the flavor of ghee.

"Ghee?" he asks, with a look of surprise as if he is amazed that anyone would not like ghee. "Where do you purchase it? Perhaps it's not of good quality. Cut it in half. Half a teaspoon every meal."

Then after more talk about individual poses, he tells me to do my pranayama practice again. He interrupts me. You are breathing too quickly.

He leaves the room and then returns with some papers in his hands. "Can you help me with something? Do you have time?"

"Yes, of course, I'll help you with anything."

He has written an article in English and it needs a little editing.

Then he asks if I know of Phyllis, a woman who is staying at Sudarma House. I know the house. He returns her calls and they won't take a message.

I volunteer to stop by the house on my way home and leave the message. Take your rest, he says.

After five minutes, I pack up and begin my journey. One day with this scooter, and I'm already a messenger. I take another route and find myself somewhere I have been before. Perhaps in a dream. Maybe I was walking in this area with Isabella last year. We were looking for a beauty shop here, I think, to have our legs waxed. I emerge on the double road. Which double road? I turn left, slowly, holding up traffic as usual and then I'm near Subrata's house. I zip by a house of yoga students and ask for directions. Inside the yard I find a student who will take the message.

Then I'm back here in the hotel. I can't get the bike over the curb. Mahadeshwara does it in his bare feet while the accountant gives him advice. The men in this hotel are sweet, but I miss the old manager, Krishnaswami. Last year, when I first came to the hotel, my ears were plugged up and I couldn't hear anything.

"Sit down and wait, Madam, your room is not ready," Krishnaswami yelled at me so I could hear him.

"How much money now?"

Part of the problem was that I was not attuned to his English-Indian accent and he didn't understand my mumbling American words. As I sat on the chair across from the counter, an Indian family with a little baby entered the lobby. They stood there staring at me and smiling. Finally, the woman signaled to me, nodding her head and pointing to the baby.

"Would I hold her baby?" She was a fat baby girl dressed in white.

"Sure, yes, of course."

And then the cameras. An American woman holding their baby. Then this other relative next to me. Then that relative.

Then I was taken to my room by one of the boys in the hotel. I checked the bed as I had been instructed by a friend. The sheets looked old. I asked if they would change them. Quickly, they changed them, but now I know—they were completely clean. The old man who comes in the morning beats, soaks, scrubs and hangs them in the sun. But they are very worn.

When I settled into my room, I met some other westerners from across the hallway, a woman I knew in New York. She quickly took me on the back of her scooter, introduced me to Subrata, and then she took me shopping for food.

There was another man in the hallway—I can't remember his name now, I think it was Jack. He was from New Jersey and leaving Mysore in a few days. He was very unhappy with his yoga experience. He talked about how he had received little or no attention from his teacher during his entire month in Mysore. He complained that Ramaji was making mostly adjustments on women students and neglecting the men. I tried to ignore his criticism (I think I was a little short with him) because I didn't want to start my practice with a negative attitude, especially after traveling half way around the world. I found out a few days later though that Ramaji did adjust women almost exclusively, but it didn't seem overtly perverse to me, just a little pat here and there. He seemed rather humorous and somewhat paternal. I remember sitting on the floor in the afternoon meetings embarrassed however by the quality of many of the students' questions—often naïve and disrespectful of Indian culture. Ramaji laughed, read his newspaper and called people upstairs to pay for their yoga lessons. After a week or so I started feeling uncomfortable, as if I were a fake sitting there—paying so much money just to be allowed to do my practice in a space that did not feel particularly sacred to me and where I received very few adjustments, maybe because I was an older woman. My experience practicing in New York shalas was far more sacred.

I often wish I could experience the devotion that some of my friends in New York express for Ramaji. Last year as the month progressed, I came to feel as if I was participating in a structure that felt like a bad encounter with a rickshaw driver who was trying to take as much money as possible from a foreigner. And this seemed contradictory to me—the transmission of an ancient spiritual practice in exchange for a lot of money from people who don't quite understand the exchange rate. I expressed this in an email to a friend who wrote back, "Well, Gina, for me, the money isn't an issue, I love him and it's worth it to me."

Where does that leave me? Here, lying flat on my back, my foot vibrating from the nerve damage, lower back a little sore—I think perhaps all of these new vibrations are coming from riding the motorcycle with tension in my arms and neck and hitting those bumps. Slower tomorrow.

I read through Acharya's manuscript once, editing it. It's about metaphors of the ocean, moon, ripples in Kalidasa's work and in physics. I have never read the work, but I've seen the metaphors used in the sutras and the Gita.

*

Tomorrow is today and I think today is Wednesday, June 14th. Acharya will not be here on the 16, 17, and 18th. I must use this time to work on my projects or to go somewhere. I could go to the jungle. A little turbulence is in the ocean right now as I sit across from Maureen, a woman from southern California who arrived a few days ago and is staying for three weeks. She asks me my age— 49. She is 49, overweight and made-up. We talk about our injuries. I don't want old age to mean I'll be a feeble person, sitting around chatting about illnesses. I have not been a feeble person so far and I don't plan to be one in the future.

This morning I wake up at dawn instead of 4:30. The alarm does not work (I was so happy when Acharya told me that an hour before dawn is the best time, but I should not make myself wake up. I should wake up naturally.) And so at 5:30, I arise, take an oil bath, a regular shower, pour laundry detergent on my chest by mistake, and then do my practice. My leg stops hurting after the practice.

At 11:20, I ask Rupesh if he can bring my bike around to the front. I'm ready to leave.

He takes off and I'm standing in the front of the hotel, waiting and waiting.

"Where is Rupesh?" I ask Mahadeshwara.

"He took Surya to the bus station."

"What? He didn't ask my permission." I sit there and wait. Why didn't he ask me first? I hate being late, especially when Acharya is expecting me.

I'm almost ready to catch a rickshaw when Rupesh pulls up and I let him know that I'm angry. I wish I hadn't been so emotional with him, though, because he is a sweet person, he was doing Surya a favor and anger is usually not expressed so overtly in India. Also, we Americans have such a different sense of time.

Then I jump on the scooter and go to Acharya's with my shoulders tight. But the bike riding is kind of soothing. You have a problem, you must scoot in and around the world of pedestrian India and not hurt anyone or yourself. Somehow you go over the bumps and arrive in front of your teacher's house. And you tell Jayashree that you are perfectly able to sit and wait.

Acharya is busy with his astrology consultations. I'm told to do my practice in a different room inside the house. I'm glad to be brought into the house. There are photos on the wall of a youthful Acharya doing yoga in amazing poses and other stunning child photos that I think are the same as those in Jayaraj's shala.

"Who is he?" I ask him later.

He tells me he is another student of Krishnamacharya. This must have been his teacher.

I ask his name again.

He mumbles a name quickly, making me think that he doesn't want me to know.

"Sri-who?"

I still couldn't understand him. "Was he your teacher?"

"Since boyhood, I studied astrology and ayurveda with my father. For five years without interruption, two times a day in the late sixties and early seventies, I studied asanas and pranayamas at the Sanskrita College in a yoga class with Mr. Pattabhi Jois who was working there as a yoga tutor. Because I was also a student of Sanskrit, I went through in detail many basic yoga texts and their commentaries. Later, for many reasons, I searched throughout India for a mahaguru, studying with many teachers. My search brought me back to Mysore. What I teach, the theory of yoga and every practical like asana and pranayama is influenced highly by the thought, words and activity of my teacher and his wife. My heart feels deepest gratitude to this divine couple, Sriranga and Srimata."

He nods to me and points at a photo in the hallway of a seated yogi. This is his teacher, not the boy in the photos.

I hand him his manuscript with my editing. He thanks me and then asks me if I'm bored.

"No, not bored, sleepy a lot though."

He mentions that we have slowed my system down. Less movement.

Then I understand something quite profound. Your ability to realize your soul can be enhanced by adjusting your food and your activities.

When I was doing my pranayama practice at Acharya's, the eye was quite pronounced. There were eyelashes and it would form and dissolve, form and dissolve.

*

I'm on the bike, cutting down one road and then another, quite confident now. Then I'm on a beautiful country road. I love this—people look at this strange woman with a scarf tied around her head, zooming through their villages. Green, green everywhere. I must have gone too far, I think. Finally, I turn around and decide to go back to where I made this turn. I stop along the road and my decision is confirmed. I'm going the wrong way.

Getting directions from someone who doesn't speak English is curious. Sometimes a crowd forms around me.

"Palace," I say. "Shreepurum," and then they point.

I finally recognize some houses. I turn right and come to a stop in front of the bakery. In a plastic chair, I sit outside and eat spicy, baked vegetable pastry and mango with milk. I am exhausted, hungry and I need a break from the bike or I wouldn't eat this food. Acharya tells me that because of my particular constitution, I should always have mangos with curd and I should avoid spicy food. Then

I ride on further, try to make a left at Upahar, but I end up in the little neighborhood of the hotel. I park the bike, sit in the lobby for a rest and then walk back to Upahar. I order one idli, receive two. I ask for the check, and the waiter brings me a tea. Then he brings me the bill for two idli and a tea. I eat the one idli and decide to pay the bill because he might get charged for it and it's so insignificant in terms of my money (10 cents perhaps).

A man stops me on the street to ask me where I come from and what my name is. He points to a button he is wearing—Talk to Me if You Want to Lose Weight. Funny. All one needs to do in India to lose weight is eat in restaurants and suffer from traveler's diarrhea for a few weeks. I tell him I don't need to lose weight and then I'm on my way home.

When I see Rupesh, I tell him I'm sorry I was angry. Please just ask me first though so I know what is going on. He tells me that he had been very worried.

I nap and read *Autobiography of a Yogi,* an account of Yogananda's amazing experiences. And then I do my evening breathing practice, kind of quickly. Probably that mango drink. Whenever I move quickly, I'm usually busy thinking.

Then I scoot over to Dr. Anand's office. He gives me another herb to help repair the nerves in my leg and he checks my leg movement. He too is very busy and in a hurry. The class he discussed last week has not been organized. All in all this has been an Indian day.

Night is here again.

*

Last night I was tossing and turning. Perhaps the estrogen maintains my youth. Perhaps without it I will fall into old age. Or probably I will not sleep well for two weeks. I take the pills. I'm not ready to stop yet. After all, Elizabeth, the secretary of the Art Department, was stooped over in pain. They told her she had osteoporosis and gave her estrogen and calcium. Now she is much better. But then again, I'm not eighty years old, living with osteoporosis.

This morning I wake up a little bit after dawn and take a hot water bath, straighten the room, and begin my practice with the vinyasa segues between the poses. I'm hot, but I'm not sweating too much. It's a good practice. In savasana, I look into the eye and I say, one day you will suck me out of this body. Then tears flow. I do my pranayama. It is beautiful, but I'm sad and confused. What will I lose? All but this burning something that is pulsating through my body. Perhaps I will lose this new boyfriend. He is lost already, on the other side of the world, lost even when he is here. Our energies meet and then disperse. I'm almost half a century old. Perhaps I will live a long life like my great grandfather. Perhaps I'm here with Acharya to step over into the second half.

I roll the scooter out of the yard and ride over to J. Prakash, stopping at Subrata's on the way to tell her I will be back for lunch. Then it starts sprinkling so I ride quickly toward my teacher. I park the bike and take a seat on the porch.

Jayashree is there. "Hello, how are you?" She seems a little irritated.

"Fine and you."

"Yes," she says.

I ask her how Indians usually answer that question—

"Very well, thank you."

Like the British, I think.

Acharya meets me in the little yoga room. He sits on the side as if he must run away any minute. "How are you? How is the cold? Is it gone?"

"Yes, and yours."

"Well it's better. But I'm allergic to some flowers right next to this spot."

"I thought so," I say. "I was hoping you weren't allergic to me."

Anyhow, he suffers and teaches. So many lessons today. He asks about my morning practice and I tell him about my sorrow. He talks about attachment and how there are some attachments that are positive for you and some that are not, and the task is to move the attachment to something that will enable you to have a quiet mind and experience great joy through meditation. Great joy. We will work on this.

I must tell him all about these moods I'm experiencing, he says. I express a kind of grief over losing my astanga yoga practice and I think perhaps this maybe a signal about the beginning of old age.

"You *are* still practicing the eight limbs," he says, "with just some small changes. You have not lost your practice." He tells me many things about yoga and the goal of it.

We talk about the U.S. yoga shalas and I tell him about my friend Vivian who was just hurt across her midsection doing Mariasana D. "Oh, no," he says, talking about the difference between exercises and asanas. "Asanas are supposed to bring you peace, not to disturb you. Yes, they are exercises in the sense that you must have a strong body for meditating, but only in that sense."

He uses the lake metaphor to illustrate his point. "If the goal is to project an image on a lake, and there are ripples, there will be no image. You do not want to create ripples in your mind by doing a wild asana practice. You want to have a strong practice. Your pranayama practice will require strength, too."

He then asks me to do my pranayama practice.

He stops the pranayama asanas before the meditation, adding a new pose, a very complicated pose with my fingers closing my eyes, mouth, ears and nostrils. I breathe in through both nostrils, block them and hold my breath for as long as possible. Very complicated. Then another eight breathes in padmasana.

"That's enough for now," he says. "I will not be here for three days and maybe one more." He is taking his senior students and traveling nine hours on a bus to a two-day yoga camp for Indians. He does this with no pay. It's a mission of sorts.

"I do these often," he says.

I look at him and say, "You have a good life."

"Yes, yes, I have a good life."

We smile and he tells me to sit and rest. He leaves through the little side door, pushing it shut. I don't hear his footsteps as he moves through the yard and into the house. After I rest, I coast along the Indian roads back to Shreepurum for lunch.

That was 24 hours ago. Today at Subrata's, Emily asks me if I would show her some of my drawings. "Of course, come over, knock on my door," I say. "I'll give you a little book."

And then when we are talking about stages of life and which ones are good and which aren't, I say how much I like the age I am at now. Vanessa and Emily look forward to their thirties.

"Yes, they were good. That's before I was into yoga, though. I was into sex back then."

They start laughing. And Emily mentions that her mother is just a little bit older than me, but so different—thirty years of an unhappy marriage. I tell them a little bit about my life from eighteen to twenty-eight, running away from home and living with a pool hustler, on and on about those years with Richard, then with Lenny, and then school and children. Much different from their mothers' lives, they say.

*

I stop by Whitney's house. We plan to meet at the American Pizza Shop at 6:30 and then chat with the men at Raman Travel to see what the trip into the jungle might be like. I arrive a little early and check out the cost—so expensive for 24 hours. Then I notice the photograph on the wall next to the tour, a group of overweight sedentary westerners sitting in a circle at the ok corral after their trip into the jungle to look at animals. This is not the way I want to go to the jungle. Maybe we should just leave the jungle be, so the environment isn't ruined by two more visitors.

At the restaurant, we eat western fast food with western prices. One piece of pizza, or maybe it's really two pieces for $2.50. Cheap in the west. By Indian standards, quite expensive. And it comes with very exclusive waiter treatment. Funny contrast. The fast food look and taste and then this funny service. Because people are paid so little in India, they can afford to have many people working here.

Whitney is a sculptor and we know some of the same people in NYC. We talk about them. It's dark when we leave. I tell her that I don't feel competent enough to give her a ride on the back of the scooter, so she catches a rickshaw home.

I'm not sure how to get back to the hotel. I cut in the direction that seems right, through the busiest craziest streets in the shopping district and then KR Circle is a nightmare. The circle is full of cars and rickshaws and motorbikes going around like a mad merry-go-round, six bikes thick with smoke filling the air and all five streets flowing into the circle with traffic, moving very fast. I need to get close to the circle so I can continue going straight. I try but I'm pushed over to the left. I don't want to turn left. I'll never get back home, I think, so I pull over with the pedestrians and they crowd around me on all four sides waiting to get across. I crawl across with them when the policeman signals for us to go. And then I'm again in the middle of the pack of vehicles heading up Sayyaji Road. One more circle to maneuver and then left into my neighborhood. I find myself going the wrong way on a one way street. It's dark, and when I go slowly the lights on the bike dim, but I continue around some trucks, just missing a big hole, following my instinct, until finally I come to the hotel. Instead of asking someone to park the bike, I go around the back and literally slam into the gate.

Raju opens the gate and signals me into the last spot.

I come up stairs, shut the door, whew! All that for a piece of pizza. I survived. And I wonder the next morning why I had difficulty sleeping.

*

In the morning, I find myself stiffer than usual and unable to do the poses as well as I can when I'm warm and practicing more asanas. I continue, however, and finally I become very hot when I practice the pranayama, especially the last one. I must ask Acharya for the names of these poses.

I miss Lenny terribly. When I think about the pupil in the eye during my meditation, I think, well perhaps this eye is simply a reflection of my closed eyes. Then I realize that Lenny went out that pinprick. He clung and clung until his body was covered with bedsores, more forming every minute and his lungs were almost completely full of fluids. He clung there in family shared agony. And then like a baby emerging from its mother, with a sudden push he emerged. We helped him leave with a little speed, whispering, goodbye dear Lenny, goodbye. I miss you and all your fumbling, disorganized, loving ways.

*

Saturday. Yesterday, an article in the paper reported that dowry deaths are fifteen times more numerous now than they were several years ago when dowries were outlawed. There are many loop holes and many wealthy-educated men and their families participate in this bribery of their wives' families. When the money isn't forthcoming, some of them douse the woman in gasoline, light her with a match, and she is disfigured for life, if she lives. Maybe he looks for a new wife then. Mahadeshwara tells me that if I were to walk through the halls of the hospitals, I would see many women who have been burned like this. I'm sure some are the result of kitchen accidents. In an email, Artie tells me about a Puerto Rican freedom parade, how a group of twenty men ran through Central Park randomly attacking women. Whew.

This morning my practice is better, a little more flexible, but kurmasana is almost ludicrous—my crooked arms and legs all tangled up with each other. I'm so stiff without the preparatory poses. The pranayama though is powerful and heating.

In the afternoon, I'm full of thoughts and plans. Call Terri, Call Terri.

I call Shivanand. Come over Gina at 1:30.

At 4:30 I call my sister, Terri, and wake her up—yes everything is ok. We haven't talked for so long. Email me Sis, I tell her, because a few minutes here is $5.00.

What else can I say. I was leaving Shivanand's house and suddenly he shows up beside me on his motor scooter.

"I'm your escort."

I laugh and he pulls over to the side and disappears behind me.

I worry about him on the scooter since he has such a hard time seeing anything. He holds a book right up in front of his eyes to see what is written there. He needs a cataract operation and some students collected money to help him, but he has still not gone to the hospital.

When we are sitting in his living room eating, I notice he has a lot of bruises and sores on his legs. What are they from? I ask Monique. From sitting for many hours playing tablas. I watch them play tablas together. Shivanand, could you teach me singing? Out comes a harmonium, which I have never touched, and suddenly I'm receiving lessons from Shivanand on the Indian scale. I love singing with Krishna Das in New York and now Shivanand tells me he will help me stretch my voice.

A new young woman is in the house this year, Appa's wife Nanda, a daughter-in-law for Shivanand and Aishwani. She serves us tea. And she is fairly fluent in English.

"Is it a love marriage or arranged?"

"Love."

"Good," I say, not at all understanding if this really is good, or bad.

"Is it good?"

Manjushri, the younger daughter, explains, "Parents always want arranged marriages. The dowry is usually money or sometimes a vehicle."

I guess Shivanand will have to find a dowry for the two girls without the help of a dowry from his son.

"Later we will have a celebration for them, a big celebration," he says.

Monique tells him that when his daughters finish school, she will help them if they come to the U.S. That is a big promise. She is definitely becoming a member of their family.

"Who else do I have?" asks Shivanand, "but all of you?" He is a lovely spirited man—His smile, his joy, his wild tabla hands and a house that seems to be on the verge of collapsing. The ceiling in the kitchen is leaking. The animals are a bit thin and flea ridden. His daughters are always busy and happy preparing themselves for school and studying. Today the older daughter, Arpana, is copying over Om Namoshivaya 5000 times.

"Why?" I ask.

"Just as an exercise."

"Will you continue with your schooling?" I ask Nanda.

Government university costs only about 1,000 rupees a year, but the books are expensive. I think the task is to gain admittance and that means passing the tests.

She isn't sure, yet. Maybe she will take sewing lessons instead.

*

The Muslim chanting is so eerie and beautiful right now, like the church bells at home ringing around Tompkins Square Park. Sometimes your own way of addressing the sacred becomes mundane, just routine, and you have to go all the way around the world to hear it again.

*

Sunday. I have almost been here for a month. I left home on May 23rd. Today I experience a large wave of homesickness. The Indian life on the street seems a bit mean and dirty this morning. Which it is. I wake up, do my practice and feel stiff as if I'm not pushing my body enough and as if I am losing something. Thoughts. Where is Dimitri? Why hasn't he been writing me? Lots of thoughts. I forget two poses. Instead of the morning meditation being the strongest, the evening is, even though I rush through, thinking of breakfast, lunch and dinner.

Take the bike out, jerking around the corner and heading over to Subrata's for breakfast. I see some people sitting at the table and

I walk right into the house without taking off my shoes.

"Gina, please remove your shoes."

"Oh, yes, sorry." Emily, Vanessa, an older man I've seen around before, and a new arrival, Carl, are sitting at the table. The young women are laughing, quoting Ramaji, "No money, no prana." Emily is openly critical of the way his fees keep climbing, but like many others, she wants to study there so that she will have months of experience with his program and be more diverse with her teaching when she returns home. Well, I'm happy I'm not a yoga teacher and am free to make a detour.

Then the older man, whose name I can't remember, asks Carl, "Are you still practicing with Harihara?"

"Did you just arrive?" I jump in, questioning Carl, excitedly. "Harihara told me about you. I'm practicing with him, too. I want to talk with you."

Carl is wearing a traditional Indian cloth, a dhoti, around his hips and an American tee-shirt. He's trying to eat his fruit and yogurt on a plate with his fingers, and he is coated with yogurt up to his right wrist.

"You're really enjoying eating that with your hand aren't you?" I say. Well, it was quickly apparent that Carl was not one of the fashion-oriented western yoga students here to remake his body fashionably with yoga asanas. He's a little bulky and somewhat ordinary looking, in a pleasant Midwestern way. I'm sure I'll get to know him as the month progresses. He's living in a house in J. Prakash. He says that Acharya discourages most students from living there because he thinks it's safer to stay in close touch with other westerners. Carl tells me that Acharya saved his life. When I ask him how, he just smiles and tips his head back and forth like an Indian.

*

Emily comes to my room and I give her a copy of my book. She is very excited and then I take her as my first passenger on the scooter over to Shivanand's house. Every time I turn, it's hard to get my balance with her weight added to the bike. When I stop, it's much heavier. We crawl around the circles and turn onto the roads until finally we make it to his house.

Up the stairs with all my things. He puts a tray in front of me. I put everything on it (bananas, coconut, money, camphor, candy, etcetera) and then he says—

"Gina, where are the flowers?"

"Oh, I forgot the flowers."

"How could you? Flowers are essential for a puja."

He sends his daughter, Manjushri, out with me to the street. We find a flower man, but all he has left are a few tattered roses for five rupees each. We take five of them and then we need to buy some puffed rice. She calls it something else. They use it for cooking and it's part of the puja.

Back at Shivanand's house, I put all the items on the tray and he prepares a rather ornate celebration to begin my study of singing. He puts some powder on the head of a statue of Saraswati, then he prays and walks in a circle, burns the candle wick, throws water here and there and offers food to each of us. He gives me a tray and I take it around to the others and while all this is going on, I'm moved to tears. There is something about this man and his family that I love.

His old mother is sitting on the couch. Granddaughter-in-law gives her food. She eats rice and then she dozes off with her glasses slipping to the side. Shivanand leans back with his glasses a little crooked. He looks exactly like her, just a little bit younger. She also looks a little like my father's mother when she was old and living in our house.

A little while later, Shivanand plays the harmonium and I sing: Sa ri ga ma pa da ni sa ... Sa ni da pa ma ga ri sa ... sa ri ga ma sa ri ga ma sa ri ga ma pa da ni sa ... Sa ni da pa sa ni da pa sa ni da pa ma ga ri sa. It's a beautiful feeling to sing this simple scale. Then he makes me play the keys on the harmonium. This year I'm not as nervous so I will take my voice, this warped instrument I was born with, and discover what sounds can be made with it.

I drop Emily off at her bike and then pass through the Agrahara streets. Even though it's only 4:00 p.m., I decide to park the bike for the night. I ring the bell and Surya opens the gate. Zoom, zip, parked. This is becoming a habit, too.

I finish some of my animal drawings and then begin an assignment for Artie. He wants me to write a history of a project that I finished a few years ago, *Cass City*, a collection of rather dark drawings of old friends from Detroit as they hunch over the Song Shop Bar. I am working on my notes when suddenly something goes wrong. This has happened to me before. The file begins to duplicate itself and it becomes longer and longer and longer. Just as I'm trying to discover the logic of it so I don't lose the file and these emails forever, there is a knock at the door.

It's Maureen, the woman from California. She comes in with her shopping list. She is here for three weeks, to buy as many things as she can and she loves dressing up in saris. I try hard to be kind but all I can think of is the file that is perhaps being eaten up by the computer. Finally, she leaves to have a tea. She is looking for a partner, but I will not be it and yet perhaps I'm the closest she can come to what she wants. . . simply based on my age. Finally I bring the file up, figure out what the first section of it is, copy that, paste it into a new file and delete the old. Then I copy that and the other file onto a disk to take to the email station.

The door is locked.

"Tomorrow, " says the man sitting in the phone booth next to the email station.

"Tomorrow? Last week she was there on Sunday."

"No difference. Not today. Tomorrow."

So then, I think, dinner. Where? I should cook, but the little store on the corner has no vegetables left. I go to Iyengar's. Another chapatti. There is no one in the restaurant except for the workers and they are busy carrying huge containers of food in and out of a truck in front. Something about the huge containers discourages me from eating there. I have been eating too many chili peppers lately. My colon is raw.

I return to the hotel, climb the stairs. I realize that I have forgotten to do my evening pranayama practice. I call Subrata and tell her I'll be there for dinner at 6:15. I practice, thinking about this and that. When I'm in child's pose, it seems as if I can go forever in that pose without breathing, and then I think food, I think walk, I think motorcycle, I think walk...

At my age, a traditional yogi retires from his life as a householder and retreats to the forest.

I dress and walk down the road.

There is something sinister about everything at dusk today. So much garbage on the street. Monday a.m. is cleaning day so things are at their worst now. The cows look a little abused, dirty, tied up in their own dung, eating garbage. Some man who is at a tea stand comes over and says things to me in a language I can't understand—he has a look on his face as if he is provoking me. I'm glad I cannot understand him. I just walk along.

Emily is at the dining room table reading Jeanette Winterston's *Written on the Body*. We eat and talk. She tells me about her terrible year with all kinds of bacterias and parasites from not caring for herself and then she tells me how she finally weaned herself off the western medicine, but she is now eating a lot of sugar. "Stop it," I say, "if you don't want candida to flair up." I tell her how I'm trying to stop taking the hormones I have been taking for five years but I'm a little frightened about it as if the fast and hard yoga and the pills can keep me young. Anyhow I head home. The food is very good at Subrata's. I think it's where I should eat if I'm not eating at home.

And so it is night. Before sleeping, I need to stretch.

*

Today is Monday and tomorrow Acharya will return and perhaps I will be able to figure out why I'm here again. This morning I woke up and remembered a very intense dream about a friend from New York, Rosemary. She had been accused of stealing and she was in a court, which was also a lot like a church or a large auditorium. I decided to stand up, unannounced, and defend her. Later I went to my father and told him, yes, I did the same with your son, my brother, Bruce—my father had been accusing him and I had defended him, too. Yes, my father said, and you were right, Gina. This was a vivid dream.

*

I wake up at 6:30 a.m. My waking hour is getting later and later. Yesterday, Emily asked me how I could possibly sleep with the windows closed and the fan turned off. I can't figure out how to sleep with the wind blowing on my cheek, I told her. But then there were mosquitoes buzzing in my ear and it was so hot. She told me the fan will keep the mosquitoes away and then you can leave your window open. So last night I took a blanket, turned on the fan and slept. I remember getting up once in a dreamy way and peeing on my foot. I poured a bucket of water over my feet and stumbled back to bed, back to the dream world under the fan.

I turn on the hot water, fill up the bucket, and then I squat over the toilet. I miss my rigorous, singing yoga practice where my body sings and bends, so I will practice my New York yoga today—as an experiment, I tell myself. I cover the bed, straighten up a little bit, brush my teeth with myrrh powder (so much better than toothpaste). And then I pray to the sun, suryanamascar and begin my rigorous practice, swinging back and forth and up and down. I imagine lying to Acharya and saying I did the shorter practice, but I know that is stupid. He's my teacher. Of course I will tell him. With that thought, I skip some asanas and add what he has added. Then I rest.

My body feels alive, vibrant, perhaps not so calm and quiet as before, but I like vibrant. I practice the pranayama, too. Not so vivid of an eye, but still that pupil flickering and in the background the cosmos.

Here I am. Here I am.

Then I stand up, dress and step outside with my umbrella. After buying some curd from the lady down the street, I peel some mangos and place them with the curd in the plastic cup. I take out the portable blender which I brought with me from New York. Voom, a cup of mango lassi, which I slowly eat with the little teaspoon.

Then I cook some oatmeal with raisins and a little bit of cloves, which get stuck in my teeth since I didn't grind them enough.

The room is a bit of a mess, with dirty dishes in the bucket and dirty clothes on the floor in the bathroom. I step outside again with the umbrella and stroll down to the email station. The old woman is leaning over and wiping down the floor. I step inside and leave a big footprint.

"I'm sorry," I say. She smiles a toothless smile and I turn around and place my sandals on the ledge. She cleans and I smile at her and greet her with my hands in prayer position. She makes all kinds of signs toward me. Hands on her forehead in prayer, at her heart, opening up. We both smile. When the old lady leaves, the woman who manages the shop returns.

"Should I give her money?" I ask. "Is she poor? How old is she?"

"No we pay her." she says. "Perhaps 70 years old."

So thin. "Does her family take care of her?"

"No, they pushed her out of the house. Her daughter-in-laws don't want her."

Two emails, one from Josh commenting on my notes on Indian dowry deaths and asking a million questions about his preparation for India. One from Vivian telling me about her recent date, the state of her injury and other things. I love both of them. There is also a note from Kirtana at the school in Bangalore. We'll see each other when I pass through Bangalore at the end of July. I print many pages of the notes and pay the woman. Now I don't have to worry about everything being lost.

Then I walk around the corner and over to the Palace square, where I buy a little pair of scissors and a tiny stapler. Oh, the wonders of organization. Home I clip apart each email and sort them into envelopes. Words, words, words. I reread the emails from Dimitri and find maybe a little evidence of longing. Maybe I was wrong about him all along. Maybe this affair has really been just that, a short affair, and any other thoughts have just been part of my active imagination. As the days pass, I notice I think less and less about him.

Rainy today and cool. I ride the scooter over to Shivanand's for Monique's birthday party with his family and about five other yoga students. I give her one of the beautiful silver bracelets that I bought the week before. She is pleased and happy.

Someone tells the story about the swami in the hill who is completely swamped with tourists who visit him during his morning puja rituals. Perhaps it was a very quiet place when he took up that cave. Some young Indian men were talking today while he was doing puja and he told them to be quiet or leave, something like that. They turned back and yelled at him—you just like the westerners and not we Indians. Then they cursed him. He went back to his puja.

"Don't you see," I say, "we are privileged wherever we go. If we are in a store, we are waited on first. Others are asked to leave. And at ceremonies in India, Indians talk. That is common." But maybe I am wrong. Maybe these boys were simply teenagers behaving badly. Or maybe both of us are correct. Nanda and Manjushri serve us a little meal and some sweet tea. Afterwards each of us practices with Shivanand. He gives me a new lesson, making me play it on the harmonium. Start on the key of D—sa ri ga   sa ri ga   sa ri sa ri ga ma pa dani sa sa ni da sa ni da sa ni sa ni da pa ma ga ri sa. I like singing.

Just as I notice I'm getting smoother and more comfortable on the scooter, surprise, it begins to rain. This is new, avoiding puddles and all. On top of that, when riding the scooter over to Shivanand's, I put myself into a cloud of smoke—so much pollution, especially from the rickshaws and trucks, black diesel smoke pumping out of broken mufflers. I wonder how many deaths could be avoided with a simple law requiring mufflers and emission control. Yes, money. Still I don't believe it would be impossible.

I pull over and put on my jacket and continue on my way to the railroad station and then over to hospital circle. I turn onto the narrow red dirt road, cluttered with people and cows. As I park by the house, I notice some men across the street scowling at me. These damn westerners. I'm ignorant about the hate I see occasionally in the eyes glaring at me. I'm told that up north, more people hate westerners than here.

I zip up my black jacket. Spent some time today studying a snapshot of Lenny when he was about sixteen or seventeen years old, wearing a black leather jacket. A little bit of the tough guy—he was probably already going downtown Detroit with his friends and experimenting with drugs. He looks happy. His hair is slicked back and his eyes are light grey in this black and white photo, but light light blue in life. He's smiling as he stares directly into the camera in the booth, probably in the dime store. In direct contrast to the slicked back hair and black leather jacket is his face, human, vulnerable and happy.

*

I remember the first day Lenny took me to his friend Pete's apartment on Myrtle and 3rd Avenue. The hallways were dismal— old chipped paint and dirt in the corners. We took the elevator up to the 5th floor and walked past some teenagers sitting near the window. When Pete unlocked the door, I could hear four locks crank open. The apartment wasn't much different from the hallway. Some old sofas and chairs with the stuffing loose. Pete, an older black man, was happy to meet me and show me the several scars from gunshot wounds on his body. "So you're the girl I've been hearing about. Lenny's my man. Be nice to him," he said with a deep guttural voice. A desperate looking woman, dressed in a tight red vinyl skirt came in and went in the bedroom with Pete for a few minutes. When she left, Lenny said, "Gina, you stay here for a few minutes." He kissed me on the cheek. Maybe he was buying drugs from Pete or selling him something. At that time, I didn't think much about it. This was the hidden world, the back room of Detroit where jazz musicians gathered and life went on. I didn't want to be excluded, but I now know how lucky I was that Lenny loved me enough to keep me at least one room away.

A week later, Lenny went into the hospital. That's when I met his mother and his brother. His brother Howie warned me not to go out with him. Lenny had been in a lot of trouble and he wasn't changing his ways. I looked at his brother's shiny new car and his big suburban house, and I didn't give his warning much credence. After all, Lenny was more than his drug problem. He was Moses, too.

*

Today is Tuesday, June something or other. I will see Acharya for less than a week and then he leaves for five or six days! I'm definitely going away in this period, perhaps to Auroville, perhaps just to visit Swami Bramadeo, perhaps to Bombay. The damn fan is going around to keep the mosquitoes out of here and I don't like it. I came here with one injury and now I'm discovering that my body is full of aches and pains. The clicking in my knee, for example.

Acharya says, "You are going to have to do the things I teach you every day for the rest of your life or all kinds of symptoms will occur.

Dr. Anand says, "Well that type of clicking is a pre-sign to osteoarthritis, which most people get after age 50."

I'm going to stick with Acharya's diagnosis. Yoga fo ever. I had a crash course into the second half of my century in January when I decided to bend this back a little too far. It was lovely moving so energetically like that for those few years and I still want to be able to do it. I will.

This morning, after finishing my asana and pranayama practice, I take the bike out the gate, over the bumpy curb and around the corner to Subrata's. I'm planning to hook a camera around my neck and just flash photos here and there for the record of life on a scooter in India and then perhaps another series of drawings. It's much easier to move on the scooter than on foot, as if this is the correct speed and all the pedestrians and animals are slugging along, bothered continually by those who are zipping by.

I'm a fly! I cut around the rickshaw and park outside her gate in the red dirt. Off with my shoes. Inside. Who's there? Carl, yes. Did we talk about Acharya? A little, and then he said in a day or so he wants to have me over for lunch—yes, so we can talk.

Back to the hotel. I wait too long to remember this day from that day. So fast the details of life noticed and then forgotten. Right this minute missing home, a clean bath, and a walk with Peggy in the park. I have so many little insect bites on my body, little red bumps, not nasty itchy lumps.

I straighten up and leave early so I can put gas in the scooter. Then I'm floating over the pavement in and around animal driven vehicles and large smoky trucks and buses. The Indian countryside. Turn left into Acharya's neighborhood, slow down. People are out for a little stroll. I park right behind his bike. My hair is windblown. I'm not at my calmest.

Twelve noon exactly. He directs me into the little cave- like room where we talk, but then he is interrupted. Someone has arrived for an astrology chart. In and out. Back and forth. I'm not impatient. I knew this was going to happen.

"I have finished your chart but we will not talk about it for another week."

Yes, all the students from the other teacher are crowding in to have their charts completed before they leave.

"By the way, I won't be here between the 27th and 2nd," he says.

Six days, I think. "I want to go, too," I say, but he shakes his head.

"No, not possible. Lots of problems."

Because I'm western, I think, a spectacle, a woman, all kinds of problems.

One very stark memory is sitting cross-legged across from Acharya. He looks so serene with his eyes looking right into mine, like half moons. I want to tell him everything, but it isn't necessary to talk.

Fat or skinny, says Acharya. Don't even think about it again. You will never get fat if you do this practice. You will never be skinny if you follow this sequence.

Today I'm in the computer room in his house on the straw mat and I'm secretly watching Jayashree sitting on a mat quietly reading.

"I don't like change," she said a little earlier, sitting on the porch in a beautiful green cotton sari. "I wear the same bracelets always. I use the same thing on my skin. Everything to have a quiet mind. I never put any products on my skin except cucumber, milk and sandalwood." She describes how she mixes turmeric with a little lemon and puts it on her forehead with some ghee.

She is sitting so quietly now.

"I don't like change and I never change. As I was when I was twenty, I'm now."

She is very likeable.

I'm too much of a westerner to ever become a yogi like this. Life in New York is all about creating new projects and meeting friends for dinner in restaurants. I'd have to move to an ashram or be reborn as an Indian yogi.

"Your chart is ascending. Don't think about another life," Acharya says, smiling. "You should keep your focus on liberation."

*

I wish I could capture the experience on the motor bike, buzzing along at a speed where no one can stop and bother me.

Once in a while, I hear some child yell, "Hello, what is your name?"

I'm there and gone, zipping over these streets with this wide variety of vehicles, someone whipping an ox, pulling a cart that must have been built a hundred years ago. The driver is nearly 70 years old, or at least he looks that old.

Tomorrow I'm going to travel with the camera around my neck and take random snaps. Usually I don't like the spectacle I create, taking photographs of people, but on the scooter it will be just fast snaps.

Before I travel to Acharya's, I follow Mahadeshwara's directions to find the hospital. I ride around the palace and into the craziest part of town and no hospital. Go that way. Go this way. I don't understand, says the blank expression. Finally I arrive in a totally different neighborhood from where I was sent and there is the hospital. Dr. Anand is outside talking to some other doctors.

"Sit down inside," he says.

A huge cockroach walks around me. I keep my eye on him. The hospitals and clinics are dirty compared to those in the U.S. and they seem to be technologically deficient or perhaps we are just too complicated. The walls haven't been painted in a long time and there is mildew over everything.

He finally reappears and hands me a bag of what seems to be flour. "Take this. Go into the main hospital, take the lift to the ayurvedic wing on the 3rd floor. I will meet you there."

Up I go with the elevator man.

"What country are you from?"

"U.S.A., New York City."

"Ok." That's all, just an idea needed, to figure out who I am and what I stand for.

Then I turn left into the ayurvedic wing—lots of beds with tattered plastic covers, a few covered with blankets. Dr. Anand appears and introduces me to an aid, Nimisha, who goes into a room to prepare some therapy for me.

An old woman in a turquoise skirt, a man's short sleeve old shirt and a brown sweater totters over to me—definitely in pain. She stands in front of me and stares at me with a little smile. She has a white line on her forehead, I think indicating that she follows Shiva, and her teeth on one side are missing. On the other they are growing out of the left side of her gum and flopping over her lip. Dark circles surround her eyes.

I look down. What can I say? What can I do?

A young woman lies flat on the bed. Fear is in her position. Her family surrounds her. A few other women take their plates into the bath to wash them. I'm sitting on Bed #27.

A very tall, dark and sinewy woman in a sari moves around the ward doing tasks, cleaning and collecting plates. She is either a relative of the young woman or someone working in the ward. She gives me a disapproving glare as she glides past me.

Then I'm called into a room down the hall. Nimisha holds a big mound of dough in her hands. Dr. Anand tells me to loosen my pants and lay on my belly on the table with my head on a pillow that is as hard as the table.

"Relax," he tells me, "it's important to remain relaxed." Dr. Anand massages the area, hesitantly.

Then Nimisha makes a long tube like form with the dough and molds it into a circle or a corral on my lower back, surrounding the area where the disk was herniated. She pours three brown bottles of oil into a pan sitting on a little crusty gas burner on a table beside the bed. She absorbs the oil into a cotton rag and then drips it into the circle on my back.

"Hot? Too hot? Bearable?"

She makes a little pot of oil on my back and then she absorbs it again with cotton, squeezes it back into the pan, reheats it and drops it on my back again. This goes on for half an hour.

She goes longer than I had expected. And then she massages it into my skin and down my leg into the foot. Oh, I wish she could just do the whole body, but that foot needs work, and right this minute it is feeling lighter than before. Then she has me stand up and take off my pants. She hooks up a hose to the top of a pressure cooker on the burner and begins spraying my leg and back with hot steam.

Finally, I tell her I must go. We will meet for this therapy for seven days. This is wonderful, but in the future I want to finish earlier so I can be at Acharya's on time, without anxiety.

When I come downstairs, I ask a policeman, "Where is

Madyruachara Road?"

"Go that way," he points toward the statue of Hanuman.

I realize I'm already on the double road near Shreepurum. I zip on over to J. Prakashpurum

It's another one of these days when Acharya is busy with an astrology consultation. Jayashree tells me to go into his study and practice on the straw mat. The practice is fast, so fast and then I can hear him standing in front of me and then footsteps retreating. I hear a muffled conversation taking place. I find it hard to concentrate under those circumstances. I stop and he is standing there again.

"How is your practice? How is your back and leg?"

I ask him questions about how many pomegranates to eat each day.

"One for fifteen days and your mind will definitely be quiet by then. You must do your pranayama slowly, holding your breath for longer and longer. If you must count to start out, ok, count, but the goal is not to count."

I want to talk to him, but he is standing up and Jayashree is reading in the other room, so my questions will have to wait until tomorrow.

I forget to do my evening practice because I decide to take the motor scooter into the market area to see if I can ride into a busy section. Later in the lobby I talk with Maureen a little bit about her friend who owns a big wine distributing company in India. He is picking her up tomorrow and taking her out to dinner.

Frank stops by and we walk over to a shop on the double road so I can buy a mosquito net. When I return home, I'll leave it in Bangalore for Josh or wrap it up here for my next visit. I guess there will be a next visit. Here I am on the floor in my nightgown with a white shawl draped around my shoulders. There are thousands of little bites all over my arms and upper back. They must bite me when I'm sleeping. My upper back and thighs are covered with some kind of pimples. I have tried tea tree oil. I've tried aloe vera. Now it's grapefruit seed extract. Next the doctor.

It's near bedtime. I'm going to do my practice even though it's very late in the day.

*

I lean forward with my elbow on the table and my chin in the cup of my hand.

Roberto is roasting buckwheat in a pan on the stove and telling me a story.

"Man, I couldn't believe it. I was supposed to transport this car, a white and red pin-striped Cadillac, and the man handed me the keys and a petrol card to top it off. I drove off and picked up my friend and this lady and we had a ball. All over the country. The U.S. has beautiful roads and everything is organized. A beautiful rich country. Forty five days later we showed up in Santa Barbara and some guy in a gas station called the police. They deport me, send me back to San Jose on an airplane. For free." He smiles at me and pours the newly roasted buckwheat into a large plastic container and sets it on the shelf next to all the other neatly arranged boxes and jars, each one labeled and dust free.

"You've really had a life, Roberto."

"Yes and next week, I'll make you bread."

*

Today is Thursday. I pay my hotel bill of 1,565 rupees. Madam! It has been a strange day. I had difficulty sleeping last night. There were mosquitoes inside my net and they were in a conversation with me all night. I woke up at 4 a.m. and started puttering around the room. I couldn't take a bath because the water was cold and so after cleaning a little and straightening my things, I began to read *The Gospels of Rama Krishna*. Interesting Indian-yogi life, but if this is yoga, and it most certainly is yoga, reading it teaches me that I must adapt yoga to the life I live in New York City, a life devoid of Hindu rituals and social structures but full of our own.

Finally hot water. I rub oil on my knee and then do my practice. During pranayama, I fall asleep in a seated position. So I quit, climb into bed and sleep deeply for an hour.

I make my breakfast and take the scooter over to the hospital for my second treatment. The same woman is there, but I see clearly that what at first looked like teeth hanging over her lip is in fact one very large tooth. I wonder why no one ever removed that tooth.

More people here today. It's quite pleasant having Nimisha put the hot oil on my back and I have to admit that my back feels less stiff after the treatments. I feel a bit harried, though, and right this minute I wonder if perhaps I've picked up another bacterial infection or an amoeba or another parasite. Of course, it could just be a headache from not sleeping well last night.

Riding down the narrow street toward the pink hospital buildings, I pull over to the side to let a procession pass. It is either a funeral or a wedding. I don't see a body so I'm not sure. The people have their faces painted and the men leading the parade are playing flutes. I skirt around them. Later at Subrata's, Matthew and I hear the instruments again.

"A funeral," Subrata explains.

"But where is the body?"

"Right there in that chair."

"Sitting up?"

"Yes Brahmins are always carried upright. Others are lying down flat."

*

When Lenny and I talked at his bedside, he told me that he was in shock when he first came to New York in 1983. He liked the excitement of the city and he loved to shop and vend. To get a high all he had to do was put a token in the subway, walk down to Avenue B and he could buy anything he wanted.

For me life in New York was economically demanding—I had to work lots of office jobs while teaching at night—but the presence of so many artists was exciting. New York seemed very alive while Detroit was deteriorating and dismal. There's a reason why the blues are so strong in Detroit. For Jessie and Josh, living in New York meant they could negotiate the neighborhood and city much more freely and often without an adult escort. The opportunities to live and learn were much better for us. For Lenny, though, I'm not so sure that New York was a good thing.

A year or so after we moved, he turned bright yellow from alcoholic hepatitis or a recurrence of the drug-related hepatitis he had in Mexico in the sixties. When your liver isn't working, toxins are released into your body, and you become irritated physically and mentally. The doctors told him he couldn't drink anymore. I thought he was going to die then. His life was too dark for the children. So Josh and Jessie started to live with me permanently and saw him every night or every other night for dinner.

Eventually the yellow color started to fade. He was going to AA meetings and taking the children with him. He began a methadone program, and his life became more steady. Methadone helped him even though it became a substitute addiction. I suppose it's no worse than the legal antidepressants so many people are taking now.

Ten years later, his skin started turning yellow again. Cirrhosis. The liver never really heals. He was working in his music store in Brooklyn. His partner called me up and said, "Gina, you better get over here. Lenny's not doing well. I think he's dying."

*

I wonder how safe it is for me to go into an Indian hospital with all the sick people there. I like the experience but it makes me feel a little crazy, doing so many things in one day and negotiating traffic on the bike.

The trip to Shivanand's is the worst. The streets are a nightmare. Then sometimes he works with me for only five minutes. Today, I was there longer because he wasn't home and I had to wait for him. All the women were sleeping in the living room, and they invited me to lay down on the sofa which I did. Three people sleeping in the living room and two in the music room. How many people sleep in this apartment at night? Twelve to thirteen. This is a small one bedroom apartment. Everyone clears out of the bedroom for the music lessons. At night, one person must be curled up on the floor next to another. I suppose my encounters with Shivanand have been the most gritty and real of all my encounters in India. His flat is a funky Indian version of a poor jazz musician's apartment in the East Village in the 1960s. And here the whole extended family lives.

There must be thousands of accidents on the road to his house. Big holes and cracks and everyone trying to squeeze in. I ride past KR circle and it is quite uncomplicated today, but then the road to the hotel is blocked by construction. Just enough room (one inch to spare) to squeeze the motorcycle through and then immediately I have to pass over a pile of muddy sand. Too much to even try to explain. Only a video could adequately portray the chaos.

Dr. Anand wants me to come by to pick up some cream for my left leg, but right this minute a trip to his office sounds like too much work.

*

I decide to leave the hotel and catch a rickshaw to Raman Travel to reserve a seat for an August 1st return to New York from Bangalore. I dash into the travel agency, trying to elude the troops of begging children, some of them controlled by mafia organizations and some who are really poor. It's hard to tell. But they are trained and they follow and harass you here. Some of them look much younger than they really are. A fourteen year old often looks like a western eight year old. The rickshaw is an easy ride this time. I sit in the office while they sell a jungle trip to a family and call a yoga student to tell him that they have given him $500 too much on a money exchange. Lucky for them, he's a very honest student. Then I eat pizza at the pizza shop. This is soothing because it reminds me of home.

Later, I take a rickshaw to Saraswati to pick up some solution from the doctor and a rickshaw back to the hotel. The whole thing is quite easy. I have a very nice conversation with Dr. Anand. He says that sometimes the hot oil massage treatment can turn the herniation right around. I notice that I do not feel as stiff in my lower back. He would like to go to New York, but it's difficult to leave his patients and he figures this trip will come naturally when it is the right time.

I enter the hotel lobby. Maureen is sitting on the sofa. She wants to rent a scooter and go into the country with me. I tell her I'm really overbooked this week and have some drawings I want to finish.

Here I sit late at night, studying a black and white photo Josh took of Lenny in his kitchen. Josh always likes taking black an white photos. Side view—in the middle of the frame, Lenny reaching into his cupboard for something. He's wearing a baseball hat over a tiny pony tail and his belly is swollen a little, so the photo must have been taken the year before he became ill.

On the left are shelves of cans and spices and all the dishes in the sink.

Every so often, when the children were young, I'd go over to the apartment and clean and arrange things, throwing out old cans and garbage in the refrigerator, which he had hidden from the roaches. A pot on the stove with a little steam. The refrigerator's on the right with some blurry square, probably a photo of the kids or one of their drawings. And in the middle is Lenny's head looking upward and the light from the window streaming in so that there are no details on his face, just this amazing light and the outline of his head with his arms reaching up to take something out of the cupboard.

I like remembering him like this. The window is a burning square of light.

*

Today is Friday. In one half hour I go to see Acharya. Perhaps he'll be there for me or he'll be with someone else. Surely, though some words will pass between us. Last night I slept well, waking only twice to crawl under the mosquito netting and feel my way into the bathroom. Tuck it in, that's the key to building this tent, so no mosquitoes torment me all night. I woke up twice looking up at the netting. I kind of like it, like a little womb. At 5 a.m., I straightened the bed and put the mosquito net in the corner. Then I crawled into bed for another hour, waking up to take an oil bath and complete my yoga practice. I'm just moving with this practice according to what feels right.

The pranayama takes longer, maybe 31 minutes. Counting helps me slow down, but Acharya says that too is a way of thinking.

The man in the house where I buy the curd smiles at me in between yelling at one of his children to get dressed. Houses are dank and mildewy. It is surprising that the bodies walking out of these houses look so clean.

Two little girls smile at me and say, "Hi, what is your name?" as they climb into the rickshaw waiting downstairs and their father hooks their lunch tins on the side. Five little children sit in the open car and rickshaws full of children turn corners on every block.

I finally figure out a way to put the camera around my neck and disguise it with my shawl. Then I take off, ready to photograph Mysore. I'm zooming down the road to the pink hospital when around the corner comes an oxen driven cart, taking up all the room. Another photo of the backs of many women, walking toward the school and hospital in their colorful saris and shawls. And then I put the camera in my bag. There were only two shots left on the roll.

Getting used to Nimisha and the oil treatment. Today was day three, and she was singing.

I sing a little tune, too, and she laughs.

We try to talk to each other with very little shared vocabulary. Breakfast? Yes. You? No. No? When? 1:00. That's lunch.

She rubs my leg up and down in a hearty way and then sprays it with hot steam. I keep wishing she would do both legs, but perhaps this uneven massage is needed to even out the uneven injury. So tedious the details of this injury. It is this injury, though, that has brought me to study with Acharya. If I had not hurt my back, I would never have met him.

I ride back home, find my roll of film, load the camera and repack my things. The corners and U-turns on the scooter are becoming easier. So are the circles. What looks like chaos is actually a very orderly affair. Everyone is coming into the circle thinking they might have to stop or slow down, and the key is to merge. If it is bigger or faster than you, give in.

I have to admit that on the way there, I was a little dangerous because I was focused on what I thought was unusual—two men, for example, carrying a baby cow between them on a motor scooter. Snap. Did I get it? I'll find out tomorrow. A funeral. Many different carts and people carrying all kinds of baskets and boxes on their heads. The most dangerous thing I do on the cycle: when I am in a fix, I simultaneously brake with the left hand and turn up the speed with the right. It is a panic reaction. Good thing the brake is the one that works the best.

Lenny would be terribly critical of me if he could see me now, riding the brake, riding the clutch. Don't ride the clutch, he'd say. Oh well, Len, there is probably something to say about my caution. While he wasn't very cautious about how he lived his life, he always tried to provide a safety net. In his last months of his life, he asked me, please, don't let me suffer. He had a stockpile of methadone and morphine in his drawers, which he told us to use to speed up his death if he were to go into the hepatic coma the doctors predicted. He begged me to please not let him stay alive in a coma.

I want to talk to Acharya about this.

I coast around the corner smoothly with my brake constantly engaged.

*

When I arrive, Acharya is meeting with Emily for an astrology consultation. I hear her voice. Jayashree sends me into the study to do my practice. I move so slowly, counting and breathing very methodically. Near the end of the practice, he appears. I hear him blowing his nose. He sits down across from me and studies me. I try to keep no thoughts in my head even though I know he is staring at my eyelids.

Today it is Acharya who wants to talk. Food advice. "For sleeping, you must have yogurt with every meal and ghee." He wants me to make it myself.

"In the hotel?"

"All right," he concedes, "you can purchase it from the milk stand." He says mango and curd are for me, no one else. "For others mango and milk is better. Some few asanas are good for everyone, but most other things vary."

I tell him that one woman I talked to about his astrology reading was impressed by what he knew about her. She was very happy, and she wants to come back and study with him. I hope he doesn't become too popular.

That will never happen, he says, because he doesn't want it to happen. Please don't talk about me with too much praise, he pleads.

I explain that most of the students in Mysore are very attached to a group experience, so I don't think many would be willing to give up their present practices for a solitary one.

I've been thinking all day about the word "God," this great force and state that encompasses destruction, preservation and continuance of NESS—that which is behind all the emotion and thought. Turn off the noise and there is a hum. Stop humming. Crash. Keep humming. If one can keep focused on (hum) (time) with the necessary destruction and creation—one will not lead a false life, suffering will be minimized, joy will be greater.

"Can I do my pranayama practice on the floor in my office?" I ask.

"Yes," he says, "but be certain you are not wearing anything except a natural fiber."

We talk about my concern that I become a bit frenetic when I have too many activities planned and the world around me is crazy.

"Ok," he says, "add ten minutes of savasana to the beginning of your pranayama practice. That will take care of that."

"My foot is numb."

"There are four little exercises I will show you."

"I can't sleep."

"Add three servings of curd."

"I have a lot of mucous."

"Put a little ginger and turmeric in the curd."

Whew. Everything is so simple.

Indian students are starting to arrive and I can hear Jayashree cooking in the background. The door is closed and I keep asking one question after another to hold him. But eventually, the western lady is sent home.

I don't realize that I am riding right by Ravi's house (the sweeper in the hotel), across from the silk factory—wherever that might be. He tells me in the hotel that he has seen me riding past his house several times and he has called out for me. Tomorrow I will look for him.

My stomach is growling and I am on my way to Subrata's for lunch. I give Mei-Luen a ride on the bike and immediately I become tense. The bike doesn't work like it should with someone on the back. But I am better at it now. She sits very close to me. Part of her way of being is to ridicule in a kind of loving way. I've kept my distance from her because of that, but I like her spunk. I am often skeptical of people at first and then surprised that I was so wrong.

We go shopping together after that—for fruit and then to other places around the fruit market. She laughs at me as I almost drop the bike with her on it. She is a bit rude to old people who are begging. That bothers me. But then it might have something to do with whatever life is like in Singapore. Finally, we make it back to the hotel.

And later at night I give another woman a ride home in the dark. Ok, now I can take passengers.

After that pranayama and rest.

*

There are three other men in the restaurant, and they are all staring at me as I begin to eat my idlies. I am a little fed up with it and I mention to the tall skinny waiter how difficult it is sometimes, with everyone staring at me. He says, "I treat everyone the same. And you," he advises, "you just concentrate on your food." Good advice.

Then off to Shivanand's concert at Lakshmi house. I do have a mind that never stops. If it does, some sorrow comes in. The concert is beautiful. A woman singer, smart and it's great to see a woman in charge in India. The harmonium player is a man I've seen at Shivanand's many times. Sweet face, white hair, white hat, white clothes, beautiful music. I'm so happy that I casually rub Shivanand's back, and I think later that perhaps that was not an acceptable public act for Indians. Perhaps I embarrassed him.

*

My feet, arms and face are brown from the sun. One more month and I'll be black. I must buy a hat. My thinking is filled with I must buy this—I must buy that. All the things necessary to make myself comfortable. Then I bike over to the ayurvedic wing of the hospital.

As soon as I sit down on a bed in the ward, a man approaches me. He is very tall and lanky with a large curved nose and dark sunken dreamy eyes. Then he starts to talk.

"Yes, madam, what country are you from? Ah, America, I love America. I love Jesus Christ, too. Yes, a beautiful country. I have seen it in the Hollywood films. Not like here where there are so many fanatics and corrupt politicians. So filthy. America is clean. I know. I know. My father was a professor and he was in New York at Columbia University. I have studied history and political science. Have you traveled up north to Varanasi and Vrindavan? That is where all the Americans go. How many days in Mysore?"

He is a bit overwhelming, talking so fast and leaning over me. "So you are here in India for another month and you are a teacher and an artist? What do you teach? Those of us here don't think much of American art and literature. It is the British or Naipaul. So how many more days will you have your treatment?"

Nimisha comes toward me. Instantly he pivots and returns to his mother's side—I think she is his mother—an old woman, calm, lying in the bed with her sheer shawl around her head and her shoulders. Beautiful.

He talks very slowly to her. "Yes," I hear him saying, "the rest of the world is starting to learn about ayurveda."

Nimisha points at her head to indicate that he is not right. He seems intelligent, but that doesn't mean he's sane.

I slide off the bed and stand up. Into the massage room.

"Are you ready, Nimisha?"

"Yes," she says.

An stooped old man hobbles out of the room in his bright blue lungi, carrying a cane. I realize that we all lie on the bed on the same cloth. Oh well, this is India, land of not many resources to be enjoyed by ordinary people.

Nimisha and I don't speak the same language, but we find a way to communicate with each other. Today, when I lift up my head to turn my face from one side to the other, she arranges my hair around my ears like a mother does for a child. She is singing and tapping and I start to tap along with her. She laughs and drips the hot oil on my back while I keep trying to rearrange my arms—the joints in my shoulders and neck are stiff and creaky. I hope this is a temporary state of affairs. I stand up in my underwear and shirt and she sprays hot steam all over my back and legs.

So many people stop by and peak in the door while I have this treatment—a western woman having an ayurvedic hot oil treatment. Or just a western woman half dressed. I limp out to the motor scooter and zoom back to the hotel.

Ten Men are on the roof, sitting around the open door to a tiny room. They all stare at my bare shoulders with big grins. Why did I wear a sleeveless tee-shirt to come up here and hang my clothes?

"What's the matter—you've never seen a woman before?" I snap.

Everyone is glued to the sexually enticing music videos of swaying erotic women on tv, but on the street, you must cover up everything. Men can wear Indian or western clothes, but women only punjabis or saris. Maybe I shouldn't say "only" since they do have the freedom and beauty of color.

Here I am, drinking a chalky green drink, the powder I bought in a health food store in New York. Maybe this will help my creaky joints. I wonder what vitamin or mineral I am lacking here that is causing the funny noise in my knees.

I ride my bike over to Acharya's. I can't remember the ride except yes there was more traffic, especially rickshaws loaded with children. It is Saturday—some children have no school. Some have a shorter day. Also the shopping districts are busy with pedestrian traffic. One mishap today. In the afternoon, when I am riding up and down the streets in Shreepurum thinking about moving into a house, I head straight for a piece of brick and turn the gas up instead of down. I weave around, almost fall, swerve, and catch my balance.

"Oh, Madam," someone hollers. I was in a bit of a state.

I arrive at Acharya's, take off my shoes and sit on the porch.

A young Indian man comes out, "Oh!" he says when he sees me, then he turns and goes back into the house to tell Jayashree that I'm here.

She comes out to talk for a minute. I tell her that Carl is coming. "Oh, good."

Then Acharya pulls up on his scooter and calls to me, come.

I'm to follow him. He's already way up ahead and around the corner before I get the bike started and he is not sitting straight! He must be tired.

I take off with the kickstand down.

"Gina," Jayashree calls to me, "be careful."

Up the stand goes and around the corner I go, following him about a mile or so over to the house Carl is renting. Inside, a very large and empty house. One room with a mosquito net. Another room with his computer on the floor and the room we are meeting in—two mats on the floor. Acharya sits down and we sit across from him. Carl is wearing a lungi. When Acharya starts talking, I notice that Carl is signaling yes by using the exact head motions that Indians use.

Acharya asks if we have any particular subjects we would like to address.

"Theory, I ask, or practice?"

"Theory." And then some little joke about the practice-theory relationship.

Acharya begins to talk about *The Bhagavad Gita*. "Gita is song. This is the song of god. Krishna advises Arjuna. It is divided into three parts, Karma yoga, Bhakti yoga and Jhana Yoga. In this book, the advice Krishna gives Arjuna is also advice for anyone to live by."

I begin by asking questions and making comments and we swerve away from the text to discuss issues of ahimsa and destruction to animals and people and how god is expressed more in humans. I am asking many questions to provoke a discussion about how violence might be excused in the Gita.

Suddenly Acharya looks at his watch, stands up and leaves.

The discussion lasts only one half hour. I am a little shocked.

"Is that all?" I ask Carl.

"Yes. We are to come back tomorrow at 12:30."

Acharya asks me not to tell anyone else about this class unless I check with him first.

I don't say anything, but I wonder if perhaps he is leaving because I was engaging in this conversation about ahimsa.

I hang around and talk to Carl. "Why are you staying here for a year?" I ask him as he is washing dishes. He is living very far away from other westerners. "I want to learn how to quiet my mind," he says, "and the Indians know best how to do that." He was running a successful architectural firm and now he's going to stay here and write some books on architecture in the U.S.

We go on his roof and look out over beautiful Chamundi hill, beautiful except for the litter of blue and pink plastic bags in the meadow between his house and the mountain.

He thinks I should try to rent the apartment in Shreepurum. Right now, though, as I sit here writing, this hotel room feels like my little cave. I'm fine right here.

*

The next day, as I ride around Shreepurum with Carl's beautiful space in my mind, I consider renting Monique's apartment. I decide, yes, I'll do it. When I call Anoop from a phone booth, though, I discover that he has already rented it to someone else.

I stop and say goodbye to Monique. She mentions another apartment. I'm suddenly a little crazed with the idea of finding an apartment. I can tell I'm not moving with a quiet mind.

I begin to run errands in the city. And this is work, riding a motor scooter in the terrible air and avoiding all those bumps and the traffic and pedestrians. I do it though—pick up the bag which needed to be repaired in the fruit market. "Hello, madam." "No thank you."

Pretty smooth. I emerge on the other side of the market and walk over to pick up the photos. For the most part they are mundane and repetitive. I drop off another roll of film, which is probably even worse. Then I see Amy and I ask her if she knows of any apartments. Yes, come over to her guru's at 6:00 and you'll see the man who is leaving his apartment.

A little boy approaches me.

"Hi, I remember you from last year."

He's selling incense.

"I don't want any incense," I tell him. "Yes, last year. You are taller."

"Yes, I'm older. I'm thirteen now."

I try to give him some money. He won't take it if I don't take the incense.

"Ok." I say, "but this incense is lousy."

I give it to Amy.

The boy holds my hand. There is something utterly sweet about him even though I'm sure the act is meant to persuade me to give him money. It must have been his brother to whom I was so sharp with a few weeks earlier.

When I finally make it home, my whole body is sore, hot, sweaty and smelly. I strip and lay in bed for an hour. I want to be at home.

Except in the morning, I did not have a quiet mind all day today. During both pranayama experiences, people knocked on my door— first Vanessa to cancel our plans for today and then at 5:30, Maureen asking me to go to dinner at the Park Lane Hotel which I did on the motor scooter. I got to know her a little, but the ride was fraught with anxiety. On the way back, I couldn't see the street and the scooter was hard to manipulate with someone else on the back and I needed to avoid giant potholes. It was especially intense when we turned the corner behind the Raman Travel block and we were crawling along with fifty or so smokey buses. We made it though. And now I am here on the floor typing and the mosquitoes are biting me like mad. I am going to crawl into the net soon and read Ramakrishna.

*

Today is Sunday—a rather long, hot day.

Nimisha calls me into the room. She is treating the woman with the one tooth hanging over her lip. She has made a little circle of dough around the woman's eye and is pouring hot herb medicated oil into the circle. I sit on the opposite bed and try not to stare.

I suggest that they treat me on the bed rather than waiting for the rock hard table. So I am on a bed beside the older, very ill Indian woman.

When she jerks, her son smacks her legs to help her be still. I'm sure they don't want any hot oil to seep into her eye.

I am very quiet even though my mind has been noisy lately. These treatments added to my day are making me a bit frenetic. A potentially calming process, but too much time spent on the motor bike.

I take the road from Subrata's house all the way to J. Prakash—straight there. I see two accidents—a motor scooter hits a bicyclist and then a motor scooter hits a young cow. The calf staggers over to the side of the road, a little stunned with a few gashes in her leg and side. No one attends to her. Just go your way with the rest of the wounded Indians.

Acharya tells us more about Arjuna and *The Bhagavad Gita*. "First some words about education. You need not open the worst side of our lives—placing it into new hearts and minds." He talks a lot about Krishna waiting for Arjuna to reach the moment in his life where he asks the important question. The point is that nothing should be taught without the quest for knowledge. The teacher can provoke the student. However, there should be no providing of information without the question. Here Arjuna is from the warrior caste, the same class that kings were usually from.

"According to yoga, the ripe heart in a student is revealed by the question. The problems will all be solved if we address the mind, body and universe. Use mind and body as instruments to understand who we are."

"Krishna is a direct incarnation of the gods. We are all incarnations but not so direct and so our capacities are less—because our forms have been twisted and such through many rebirths."

At some point Acharya tells me that I think and talk too much and I should just listen.

Ok. I hear that. I've been told that over and over ever since I was a little girl.

Right now I'm lying in bed typing and my body is out of sync. The right side is beginning to suffer a little. I hope it is a muscle and not related to the disks in my lower back. I am running around too much on the scooter in the heat.

Most of Ramaji's students are leaving this week, so soon Mysore will be quieter.

Two gates, two water towers, two coconut trees. In the early morning I look at Ed's apartment and take his landlord's phone number. I try to make the phone call at Subrata's but she is overly curious about my phone conversation because, she would have liked to have made the connection and collected a finder's fee. The western industry—you can't avoid it if you are in Mysore and you're a foreigner, especially a yoga student. So I go to a phone stand to make the call.

*

Today is Monday. I think it is the 27th of June. When I wake up my back is not hurting as much as it hurt the previous night. The ibuprofen and all the ointments and the cold packs and the rest. I think this is related to not walking enough. Tonight I will go for another walk. When I move to Shreepurum I will walk over to the avenue to pick up my vegetables and fruits instead of biking into the large, amazing and toxic fruit market in the center of town. I am moving to the suburbs. Quiet. Perhaps.

Breakfast at Subrata's. Jeevesh tries to get me to discuss the apartment I found, implying that he should have been consulted. Perhaps what seems greedy to us is acceptable here. As an experiment I start talking to him about my children and his look drifts away. No real interest. Just business. Every time he talks I skirt the issue of the apartment. He is not the manager of these apartments. He did not find it for me. He found it for Ed. He doesn't deserve two finder's fees. Sometimes I feel awkward around them because they are often overly eager to make a sale. But I continue to come here to eat because the food is clean, healthy and it tastes good. And that's unusual in restaurants in India. Today a few yoga students are sitting at the dining room table talking about their teacher, Ramaji.

"This morning he grabbed me and whew, shakti right up my spine. I screamed and he said—You ok? Hurt? Hurt? And then I just pointed and he laughed." Laughter. I'm eating my porridge. "Today he said to me as he was leaning on me in baddhakonasana—last week? Rupees? I paid him $700 yesterday." "I should help him with his bookkeeping. It's such a mess." "What can I say. It's his system and it works for me." "It's changed my life." "I'm learning so many things." "My back hurts today. I thought he was going to break it." "We're going to rent a car and follow him from Colorado to California." "I've got to figure out a way to make some money." I eat my fruit. "Did you see how deep I got into kurmasana today?"

*

When I decided to move to New York in 1983, I told Lenny that I'd help him figure out a way to make money there. It's a big city after all, with lots of possibilities. I wanted to move because Detroit was becoming a dead end for me. I had just finished my MFA at Wayne State University and a painful dramatic relationship with a boyfriend. The community was incestuous and I was participating, sleeping with too many friends. I needed to leave. The children were doing well with school, but they could do that in New York, too. A friend had moved to the city with her child and dogs, and when I visited her, she was happy, involved artistically, building stage scenery to make a living, and her daughter was doing fine in a nursery school in the Village. A whole different mood in New York. I wanted to go. Lenny and I had visited several times when we were younger. He loved the city. He wouldn't promise to move, but I knew he would because he would follow Jessie and Josh wherever they went.

I left the children with him in Detroit for five months. Jessie was seven and Josh was four. My absence was hardest on Jessie. Even though she loved her dad and he stayed out of the bars during that time to be home with them, she really missed me. We visited back and forth several times, wrote letters and talked on the telephone almost every day. I knew what it was like to be separated from my mother, but I couldn't figure any other way to make the move without leaving them in Detroit for a few months.

I filled my station wagon with books, art supplies and clothes and stayed with my friend in the East Village for a few weeks. It wasn't long before I found an apartment in Brooklyn, a job typing for the Legal Aid Society, as well as some part-time teaching in art departments at a couple of colleges. When I looked around the neighborhood in Brooklyn, I thought Lenny could open a music store there. There seemed to be a lot of artists and musicians moving into the neighborhood, and he had a truck-load of old jazz records and tapes. So I rented a little store front for him and helped him get started.

The music store became a gathering place in the South Slope. Musicians and people who loved jazz would stop by on their way to and from the subway. Before long he was selling all kinds of things besides records and tapes, anything he could find that was a good deal. At one point he bought a crate of vitamins. They were set up on the shelves right beside the Miles Davis records. He bought an old copy machine and stocked office supplies. The place was very disorganized, but he managed to make a living and keep the store running for 14 years. The kids often hung out in the back room after school. Every six months or so I would clean, organize things, and update his accounting. I did it because of Jess and Josh—I wanted Lenny to be stable for them. He seemed to enjoy running the store even though he often complained about having to go there everyday. Maybe New York wasn't so bad for him. Even though drugs were easily available, he became more rooted here in terms of his work.

Lenny had a funny habit. He'd hide money and then forget where it was. He was always worried about the future and he didn't like banks. I first discovered this years earlier when I was cleaning our basement on Avery Street in Detroit. I found an envelope in the rafters with five hundred dollars in it. When I asked him about it, he was relieved because he couldn't remember where he had hidden it. He also liked to save rolls of change. The year before he died, I had to go through his store very carefully looking for money he might have hidden years earlier. He needed the money because he wasn't earning anything anymore. That money lasted six months.

*

I scoot over to Acharya's. Jayashree comments on how much she likes the shopping bag I'm carrying. It will last you fifteen years, she says. I think, maybe I'll buy her one like it but then I wonder—she probably has had the one she is carrying for so many years that she wouldn't want a change. Then she sends me into the little yoga room. Acharya sits down with his handkerchief. The flowers are bothering him today.

"What are you putting on your skin?" he asks me.

"Hazelnut oil, pennyroyal and citronella for the mosquitoes."

"Yes, I use it, too. Do not put too much on your skin. Just a little. Just as it scares the mosquitoes away, it also steals your calmness."

Maybe I'll dilute it with more oil.

We talk about my practice. I ask questions about certain pranayama poses and breathing.

He asks if Carl and I talked and I said Carl told me to keep my legs in lotus during our class discussions so energy doesn't escape from my body. Acharya smiles.

I describe how important my community relationship with other yoga students in the U.S. is and how I fear I will lose something by only practicing alone in my apartment.

"Oh, yes. Well, ok, you can practice with the group, but only if you do this practice. No other practice."

He tells me that we won't meet until Sunday.

I tell him I am moving into a new space, that I have decided not to concentrate on the injury anymore, and that I have been having some treatments to my back at the Ayurvedic Hospital.

He says it will take a long time for this to heal. After the first four positions in my pranayama practice, he instructs me in another breathing asana, taking a position similar to Janiurasana A.

I like changing my body with these breathing exercises. Today my mind is quieter than usual.

We talk for twenty minutes and then he goes back into the

house. I can hear talking and smell food. I feel a little euphoric as I coast along the smooth highways of J. Prakash.

At Subrata's, Emily tells me she wants to go to the market. So do I. So I invite her on the bike. She is looking for a precious stone. We follow advice from Jeevesh and end up in a place above KR Circle with all kinds of interesting stones and necklaces. I also follow her into a silk store. Emily is kind of irritated with the people in the store and on the street. She has reached her limit with India, I think. She is downstairs with a tailor who I know is not very good. He seems afraid to get close enough to a woman to measure her accurately. Emily is yelling at him.

"He is an idiot!" she tells me.

"Don't give me any excuses," she tells him. "You didn't know what you were doing. I'm not paying for this. You better bring it over to the hotel at 6:30. And it better be correct."

"He's an idiot."

I've had glimpses of this behavior before with her, and I remember many times when I became extremely irritable and impatient with shopkeepers last year. I feel sorry for the man, though, who has promised something he can't possibly deliver.

Now I'm much smoother on the motor scooter with someone on the back. I drop her off in Shreepurum and come back to the hotel, pick up some money and go back to the fruit market to buy some fruit for a few days. I hope the decision to move is correct.

Back here, eating fruit, reading, napping, pranayama (kind of a quiet mind), waiting downstairs in the lobby with the tailor who is waiting for Emily. She is young and beautiful with thick long brown hair. When she walks through the door, she has an angry expression on her face. She is geared up to fight with the tailor. He follows her upstairs to my room and returns, hanging his head, still holding the dress over his arm. Whew.

We go around the corner to Iyengar's to eat, meet Vanessa, and then she's back here with the tailor again. She gives him no money for his work, but she accepts the dress for the fabric. Unhappily, he leaves the hotel.

What is this about? Perhaps he's playing a trick on foreigners, promising what he can't deliver. That's possible. What I notice, though, is that many well-behaved westerners reach a level of frustration here and go into crisis as they demand the efficiency they expect on a daily basis at home. It does not exist here.

The young man in the email station has learned how to turn on the switches and put in the password. He moves as if he is illiterate and has just been given responsibility for the switches in an atomic energy station. On tip toe. I send an email to Dimitri, asking where he is and what's been going on. I tell him the date I'm returning to New York and ask if he has any idea when he will be there. I wonder why he hasn't written in so long.

*

Nimisha gives me the last massage.

Creaky joints on that table for sure.

A smooth oil treatment with a lot of people coming in and staring at me. A whole group of doctors and nurses and everyone else.

Last day, I think, picking up my head and staring at the frosted windows with many holes in the glass and a big piece of board nailed on one side.

Lift up and slowly move my right arm—rotator cuff a little stiff in this position. Neck stiff too.

Then we are done. My leg feels much better.

I slip her 250 rupees. I hope that is enough of a tip and not too much. How is one to know? We take each other's hands. She is a kind woman.

I go for a walk to pick up some things in the market. Stop and send an email to Manny asking him what he thinks about my future relationship to my New York yoga practice after all this.

As I walk down the street, Maureen approaches and asks me where I'm going. I tell her. She is going to KR Circle.

"Can I join you?" she asks.

The highlight of our trip is an argument in Pares Café about whether bindes, the symbols women wear over their third eyes, are cultural, religious or just fashion items. Of course, they can be any of these, but she sees them only as fashion items. We are on the brink of another argument about whether asanas are purely physical or spiritual when I decide that it is stupid to talk to her about these things.

She tells me she is going to buy a lot of Indian items, store them in a warehouse and eventually open a store somewhere in California called MYSORE. My head is sore. She thinks we are highly compatible when I know that our mentalities are on opposite sides of the planet. Still we have dinner together and accomplish various chores and amicably come home. She leaves tomorrow.

It is so hot, I peel off my blouse, wash my face and do my pranayama practice before Vanessa and Emily arrive. It is a beautiful little practice. Even though I am involved in so much activity, I am feeling calmer.

Just as I am about to put the lock on the door, Emily arrives and plops down on the bed, placing her tablas on the floor. She is also leaving tomorrow.

We go downstairs and when Vanessa comes in, we take off on our scooters for the Ramakrishna Ashram bookstore. They are following me. I am speeding along. I think I know where I'm going, but after a while I know we are not in the right place.

One policeman directs us in one direction and another in another direction.

When we finally arrive at the ashram, Vanessa and Emily tell me I was almost killed twice. They go on about what a close call I had and to tell you the truth I am completely unaware of the vehicle that almost took my life. I tell Vanessa—I'll bet if you follow anyone in India, from the rear, it will look as if they are constantly skirting death. I apologize for not knowing where I was going.

The young man in the bookstore with the beautiful smile and a little pony tail is helping some other people find a copy of a book about Vivikananda. Suddenly I remember that he was in the bookstore last year, too.

I tell him and he says, "Yes, I remembered you the other day, too. That's why I said, How are you madam?"

I've always liked this ashram, the herb gardens to provide medicine, their schools for the poor, carrying on Vivikenanda message and all the work he did for India. Now I'm reading and enjoying Ramakrishna. Perhaps I'll visit the ashram in New York when I return to the states. I buy two books for my brother and the young man encourages me to buy a book about "The Mother" to read after I'm finished with the Ramakrishna books.

Then we scoot over to Samrat Restaurant. The next time I want to go to the ashram I must remember to head out the road that Samrat is on until I come to the statue of the little elephant and then go to my right.

Vanessa, Emily and I talk about boyfriends and taking chances. And then we talk about spirituality, and Vanessa leaves us to go to the Parklane to meet some others for a party.

Emily and I wind our way down a dark, potholed road full of speeding motorcycles and pedestrians. We move so slowly that several times the bike almost falls over. Finally, we emerge into the courtyard of Jayaraj's shala and then cut down a few streets to the hotel.

She retrieves her tablas from my room and I taxi her over to Shreepurum on the insane streets in the dark with the cows and everyone speeding and stumbling around.

I make it home for my last few encounters of the day. One, with Mahadeshwara, I show him a headline where the LEADER ENCOURAGES MAHADESHWARA TO RESIGN—he laughs. Some important political figure, yes, but a slap-happy joke.

"Be sure, Madam, to come back everyday for tea."

I am drinking ginger tea and reading the paper when Mei-Luen arrives. We talk about her day and then I ask if I can look at the clothes she has made.

We go to her room. The clothes are simple and beautiful. While I'm here maybe I should take advantage of Mysore (Is that what I want to do?) but I need to learn how to design clothes that I will actually wear when I return to New York. She has made many things from a few patterns. Beautiful baggy clothes that are suited to her little Asian frame. Will they look the same on me? I'm not sure. I may look like a tall tent.

She is one of these women who can make a room look good. Strings of flowers all around. The bed made tightly with a beautiful shawl over the pillow cases. My room looks like the aftermath of a hippie's weekend spent reading. We exchange addresses and say goodbye.

I buy a pair of Indian women's leather sandals and after I wear them and walk in them for a mile or so, my foot becomes muddy, flat, and part of the environment. Another day. There are about 31 more days before I leave.

I hear from Dimitri, a very brief email explaining how busy he is with his center, telling me that he isn't sure if he'll be able to come in the fall. I decide to be forthright, asking if he is having second thoughts about our relationship since he hasn't been as communicative as usual. I tell him I am afraid that what we have had between us might not mean so much to him. Otherwise he'd be anxious to see me and write more often. At night I am a little melancholic. Perhaps I'm projecting some old sadness about past relationships. Perhaps I'm talking to myself too much. Leave this alone.

*

Wednesday. Just like that the days roll around. Today all the westerners in the hotel have left. Mei-Luen knocks on my door to say goodbye. I do not see Maureen. She left early in the morning for a plane to California.

I wake up very late, at 7 a.m. My sleeping habits are doing what they naturally like to do—go to bed later and later. I wonder what they would creep up to with total freedom. I finished almost the entire primary series until suptakurmasana, easily, then the pranayama.

At Subrata's this morning, Emily was there alone with Subrata, sitting at the table singing chants to her—Subrata must have forgiven her for saying that she was too expensive.

As I pull out of the driveway, Jeevesh asks if I'm coming for lunch. No, I say. Well, most of these folks are leaving soon. It is cool and raining on and off today and I feel so calm in my room typing.

I'm happy about moving tomorrow. I've packed mostly everything into my suitcase one day early. I feel like drifting off into sleep right now, but if I do, I won't fall asleep early enough tonight, so I'm not going to.

I love packing up early so that I can prepare myself fully for the transition to a new experience, I say to myself as I take down the map of India, fold it up and put it in a plastic bag.

The boys in the hotel are sad that I'm leaving.

Mahadeshwara says I'm a very good, kind hearted woman, the mother of the Kaveri Hotel. When I leave India, he wants me to keep my trunk here until I return.

I put some water on my face. I must be in the kapha stage of digestion. Acharya explains that this is the best time to go to sleep, a little past one hour after eating. But in the morning it is time to keep active.

I take out the stack of photos of Lenny, remove the rubber band and one slips out, a beautiful young man, about thirty-five years old, holding fat chubby Josh with one arm and Jessie with the other. Jessie is making an ugly face, her three year old tongue pointed at the camera and her fingers in her ears. Her little Buster Brown hair-cut. She's happy in a rebellious way. Josh's arms are spread out wide, one little baby hand holding on to Lenny's tee-shirt and a very big smile on his rollypolly face. Lenny looks straight at me. The expression on his face says he may be angry at me for taking this photo. No smile, just those intent blue eyes. One of his curly locks hangs down the middle of his forehead. Maybe he had to be somewhere, some business with one of his friends. His beard is well-shaped and then that straight nose.

Ok, I'm doing what you want, now can we get it over with?

There is a strength in his body and his face that disappeared later in life as he started to lose his health. I think we were a bit overwhelmed with all our responsibilities around this time. It was maybe a year later when we split up. I start to sketch his eyes when the telephone rings. It is Shivanand asking me to come early.

Riding over to Shivanand's along the main road and circle, I feel as if I have really learned how to merge as everyone merges for everyone else. I am the only student today. We practice singing and he tells me he has been teaching tablas at the college for over twenty years. He has many students there. He wants to take me to meet the guru of the center. It is wonderful being with him. They call me into the kitchen to eat breakfast with them. It would be rude to say no, so I take a little, telling him that I just ate. It is a delicious little bread and some potatoes with spices, lovely. Then Aishwani, his wife, brings me a little cup of tea, which I accept but do not drink. I am not allowed to drink tea, I tell him. This is something he doesn't understand. A tiny spot of tea with five teaspoons of sugar in it. I leave it sitting in the corner. Then he leads me in singing. It is lovely even though I can not go above the lowest range—my voice is so low. That's ok he says. I wonder why my speaking voice isn't low.

Shivanand's kitchen is dank and dark like many of the traditional cement houses in India. His wife is sitting on the floor rolling little breads on a chapatti board. Another daughter is stooped in the corner, stirring some of the vegetables. The daughter-in-law is washing dishes in a pan on the floor in another corner. The other daughter is fixing her hair in a mirror in the living room. His son is resting on the sofa. In this house there is furniture in the living room instead of straw mats, probably to entertain all his western students. His old mother is sitting downstairs on the stoop, lost in a reverie.

I leave Swami Shivanand's house happy that I can sing in one register on the harmonium. That means I have promise.

Swerving around the circles into the main drag, six motorcycles thick and no problem, back to the email station. No computers available. Mary and Whitney are busy sending emails and they look long and literate, so I decide to go back to the hotel, pack up my books, and go over to Mr. Anoop's to work on his machine even though his place is such a mess. The smell of pesticides, flies everywhere, dirty tables. Surprisingly, the keyboard works today—well kind of works without capitals and other necessary codes.

Thursday, June 30th. This journal is a record of the changes in my state of mind. Right now my head is pounding. I have changed my living location. This place is large, spacious and potentially calm except for the sound of ongoing traffic on the street, engines revving and the constant honking of horns. I am trying to think of the coming and going of the engines as the coming and going of the tide. I hope it quiets down out there before it gets too late. Despite the noise and my anxiety, this feels like an ideal place for writing and drawing. The floors are empty of furniture, only straw mats and a little mattress in the bedroom. There is a front porch and a back outdoor area on top of a roof. It is a solid place to stay.

Practice ok this morning. Eating oranges, pears, pomegranate juice and curd for breakfast. Email station. Many little notes and then I write a long letter to my friend, Artie. It is lost when I hit one wrong key. I give up and decide to rewrite it later somewhere else.

Shivanand's house. I'm singing with him and then sitting in the kitchen at a metal table eating breakfast with his family—rice, refined oil, ground nuts, tamarind, and so many different spices. So good. Today, they do not insist on giving me tea. I hear Rick practicing in the other room—sari ga ma pa da ni sa.

*

The noise of the overhead fan masks the street noise, just like home in NYC where the air conditioner masks the 7th Street noise, the perpetual line of young people passing by my window as they party between two bars, one on each corner.

Packing and packing. Just as I finish my practice, I realize I have piddled around, it is late, 1:20, and I told Subrata I'd be there at

1:00. So I rush to a conclusion and in an irritated way go over to her house—Marilyn has left me a note—I want you to take me to your yoga teacher. I can't take her to my yoga teacher. He doesn't want me to bring people to him. I thought she wanted to go to Shivanand's house.

So I finish eating rather quickly and go over to Sudharma house where I find her reading in her bed, *Autobiography of a Yogi*. She wants an astrology chart. I give her Acharya's number and tell her how to get there via the map. She will need an appointment. We chat a bit and I say goodbye. I come back home and do another practice very early because I know I'm going to meet my new landlord and Mohan, a rickshaw driver I used last year, at around 5:00. Everything is packed. I hang out around the hotel talking to the boys (as they are called even though they are men) and Mahadeshwara.

He often yells at Prakash, the youngest of the group. Perhaps he is about twenty.

Prakash gives him a sassy teenage look, narrowing his eyes.

I don't understand their words, but Mahadeshwara looks over at me and says, "He is the only one here and. . . ." He puts two fingers to his mouth to indicate he went to eat and he looks at his watch and shakes his head.

Prakash rolls his eyes. Like a father and sassy son.

I give each of the boys 300 rupees as a tip for all their help while I stayed in the hotel. Mohan helps me take the bags and we talk a little bit about his misunderstanding with my friend Isabella. Mohan's wife was teaching her English. I say, "She thinks you still owe her 700 rupees."

"Not so," he says, mentioning that she had an Indian man staying in her room and that it was not right for Elizabeth to go there. "Elizabeth went there twice and Isabella wasn't there, but this man was there." And so on and so forth. He is very nervous talking about the situation with me.

I tell him that in America if you are not married it is perfectly acceptable to stay with someone of the opposite sex if you choose to do that.

"Really?"

"Yes," I say, "probably most of the western couples you meet here are not really married."

"No, Madam?" As if he doesn't really understand, but I think he does.

I understand though—there is a big problem with an Indian dating a westerner here. Last year Isabella was very angry about the racism. That's what she called it when a friend from Kerala was visiting her in the hotel. The hotel manager, Krishnaswami, wouldn't even look at him. If she had been seeing another westerner, there would have been no problem. I'm presuming the problem with Mohan was partly Isabella's lack of skill with English, as well as Mohan's lack in English, partly Mohan's pushing the situation so he could make more money, and then his moralistic stance about her daring to have an Indian lover, and, to make it even worse, to have his wife see this.

Last year, I used to purposely give his wife fictional works about the situation of women in India, hoping she would read them. I think that she was in no danger since he quickly turned around and resold the books before she could look at them.

I've moved into the apartment. Mr. Nutan promised to be here at 9:30 but he is late.

*

After shopping at Nilgiris for detergent and then walking over to the fruit store for vegetables and fruit, I walk home in the rain, carry up my groceries and then take all the clothes out on the roof with my detergents and wash, wash, stooping over from the hips as I see the women do here all the time—very good training for yoga or vice versa. Laundry strung across the roof. So much more pleasant without an army of hotel men watching me.

Someone downstairs is playing a beautiful solo on an alto saxophone.

Shivanand takes me up the scale one note at a time. Tomorrow he's going to mark the harmonium and have Mohan bring it here so I can practice.

When I arrive, the women are busy moving around the apartment conducting puja, ritual worship, attending to photos and images of the deities and their ancestors, as well as other sacred spots in the house, with incense, camphor water, flowers, vermillion powder and sandalwood paste.

Shivanand is talking to two men while I wait . . . it sounds like business.

Then they leave and he goes into the kitchen, pulls off his pants, puts on a lungi. I can see him. It doesn't matter. I have seen him walking around in his underwear in the house many times. How could it be otherwise in a house with so many people. Everyone can see everyone. (I just noticed that they have a refrigerator in the living room. That was not here last year.)

"Where, Shivanand, can I purchase a pair of leather sandals and be sure that the cow died a natural death and wasn't murdered for the sandals?"

"In a store very close by—run by the government—they assure you that the leather comes from cows who died naturally. And they have beautifully made shoes."

So I buy another pair of sandals. This one with good vibrations.

*

My new landlord, Mr. Nutan, has a big smile and he is carefully manicured and sweet. He wants to know things about me. What type of work do I do? Where is my husband? My children? Whom do I practice yoga with?

He meets me at the house with his mother and the cleaning women. They are busy shuffling dirt around, sort of sweeping.

Oh well, it is somewhat clean. I notice she takes the rag out of the dirty water from washing the floors and then she wipes off the kitchen counter with it. I'll rewash that later.

I feel comfortable in India, especially here in this house. I am sitting on the bedroom floor now and there is a huge coconut tree outside the window, loaded down with thick yellow coconuts. I think they are overripe. I'm very happy in India and very calm.

I'm resting on the mattress in the living room, listening to a flute downstairs and suddenly a wave of sadness. I'm on the other side of the world, content, and then I am flooded by a memory of lying on the mattress in the Willis Street apartment. Big windows that opened onto the street. I'd sit on the window ledge and people would stop by to see us, especially the jazz musicians from Our Place. I was making a flier and doing a little work for the band—what was the name of that band? Pete William's brother Dexter was the trumpet player. I used to sit at the bar, listen to jazz and poetry performances, and watch Lenny smoothly handle all kinds of altercations between prostitutes, pimps, street people and college students. I remember him turning the lights off and on demanding that everyone leave when some guy hit another guy over the head with a pool stick and guns were drawn. I ran behind the bar, down on the floor. Without a gun, Lenny was able to get everyone out of the bar and lock the door. He was always smooth and the street people respected him. We never knew, though, what happened once they got outside.

*

Last night I slept, happy to wake and cough and not hear everyone else in the hotel coughing, happy not to smell cow dung burning thickly in the air, happy not to encounter so many curious people in the hallway. I was awakened by the sound of traffic, honking, engines revving and squealing sounds, instead of the beautiful chanting from the Hindu temple loudspeaker behind the hotel.

The sheets the tailor made for me are of lovely, thick handwoven cotton. And I like sleeping on the floor on a narrow mattress. It reminds me of Gandhi's bed in his house in Bombay, where I visited last year. All I need is a spinning wheel. When I wake up, I take a bath and then finish my practice in the living room with plenty of room to spread out my arms. I am not sweating at all. I must tell Acharya that I think I should have more asanas. In a moment I'm going to turn off this machine and go for a walk, come back, cook and read Ramakrishna.

I walk into Shreepurum. There is a padlock on Vanessa's place. They have all gone somewhere. Everywhere I walk, groups of men—gathered around tea stalls and motorcycle shacks—stare at me and laugh. But when I walk into the neighborhood on the main roads, it feels like a country estate compared to the neighborhood around the Kaveri Lodge. Part way, I stop to buy a green coconut. The man hacks it open with a big curved knife, leaving a black edge from the knife. He hands me a straw with his dirty hands, and I think, oh well, this juice is supposed to be really good for you.

I walk around, accumulating sores on my feet from the new shoes and from struggling to climb uphill as I slip out of the sandals. As I walk along the median, I pass a cow whose horns are stuck in a drooping wire. She keeps shaking her head to try to get untangled. I look at the wire. The cow isn't electrocuted so I guess I won't be either. I reach up, almost petting her face, we look each other straight in the eyes and I untangle the wire. I guess my capacities *are* greater than hers today, I say in my internal conversation with Acharya as I try to argue about the possibility that animals might be experiencing samadhi. She says thank you and I walk along, carrying a plastic chair I purchased for the front porch. Home, I set the chair on the porch, take out Ramakrishna and read.

Such a beautiful book, this gentle, sometimes mad soul speaking and singing wisdom to the gathering of disciples around him. He experiences ecstasy and samadhi from the sound of a bird or a thought of God. He needles whoever comes before him, breaking the web of their egos. I wish he would needle me because, reading this book, I love him and I want to love him, but I am troubled by the way "women and gold" are described as the biggest problem for a man who is trying to live a yogic life. If I substitute men for women or lust for women, still I come up uncomfortable for two reasons: one, I do not believe or I do not want to believe that the sexual act necessarily involves a depletion of one's prana, thereby increasing the strength of one's worldly illusions and taking one away from an awareness of our ever present spirit. I also do not believe that men and women should stay apart from each other. Maybe for monks it is appropriate and was necessary in Ramakrishna's time, but for the rest of us, I think sexual relations can heighten the awareness of the spirit between and around us if we approach them with care. This emphasis in M's book seems to be mostly written for male readers. He rarely gives to women—it is directed toward the men who gather around him—so I have to constantly translate it.

In the afternoon, while I am reading, the doorbell rings. Who is that?

I run down the stairs and ask through the door, "Who's there?"

"It's me, dear. Roberto."

I open the door and Roberto's standing there with a rose and a loaf of brown bread. A housewarming gift. Now we are neighbors. We go out on the porch. I give him the chair because his knee is still bothering him. I sit on the floor.

"Be careful of catching a draft," he says. "Sit on something. Put shoes on your feet. During this time of year, people here easily get sick."

I sit on a little carpet and then we begin talking about the students in Mysore and how it is important not to talk too much about Ramaji with them.

"They're crazy," he says. "I can't figure it out. Look at that Brandy paying Raviswami $1,000 for a little extra training in yoga. Now he'll want to charge the same thing to everyone else. So he taught him a few calisthenics exercises."

Our conversation strays into our history with drugs. He talks about his tough life, drinking, drugs, the beaches in South America. Once he took a lot of coke and he wanted to go to sleep and still wake up on time to open a shop where he worked selling gems. So he took a few valium and put the alarm clock inside a bowl so it would be sure to wake him. When he woke he noticed—shit it was 2:00 p.m. He was supposed to open the shop at 10:00 a.m. He went downstairs and found four tickets on his car. Shit how come four? It turns out he had gone into a coma and had been upstairs for four days. Where have you been, man? someone asked him. Later he went to the doctor. This is when he was living in Vancouver, I think, and to demonstrate how the medical system works there—he explains that he went to three doctors for a scan of his brain because he felt he had lost his short term memory. He was forgetting everything. Every week he had to call the locksmith to come and unlock his car to retrieve his keys. He had three scans and they all said, yes he was crazy.

I'm sure that Roberto is 100% vata. He's studying different facets of exercise and yoga all day long. First he practices yoga vinyasas, then swimming, then walking, then baking bread, then passive poses in his yoga room, then another yoga class . . . Whew, I'd be worn out.

He leaves, inviting me over any day between 2:00 and 3:00 or between 7:00 and 8:00 when his schedule is open.

*

I finish my practice, coughing a lot from the carbon monoxide and diesel smoke from the road outside. I think the task is to continue through interruptions without losing mental focus, act without thinking about it too much.

Then I begin to prepare for cooking. Wash the rice and dhal. Turn on the burner. It won't go on. Try again. The lights go out. Why? Because of the computer? No. I look outside. Not many lights on anywhere. One next door. Probably a generator.

I change the batteries in the flashlight and light two candles. Here I am with no electricity and no gas. Well, with little ado, I take the bike over to the Kaveri to bring my burner back to the apartment.

On the road, I think to myself—be extra careful. It is more difficult to see at dusk, but here in India it is terribly dangerous. Many close calls. It's so strange the way people come so close to you with no warning, especially nerve-racking when gigantic trucks come within an inch of you and in your state of shock you must not move over that inch. Good practice at keeping a quiet mind.

In the hotel, Mahadeshwara is conducting an elaborate puja, with puffed rice, bananas and coconut. He is burning a flame in a plate and approaching the grand photo of Lakshmi in many different lotus poses. And then over to Saraswati. Please bring wealth and well being to this hotel.

He is not as helpful as usual.

I take the burner out of the closet.

"Do you want a tea, madame a small tea, please, yes." Something about his pleading tone. "Yes, ok, a small tea."

A woman and a young man are sitting on the couch.

"The proprietors," Mahadeshwara tells me.

"Oh, I see." I hang around saying kind things about everyone who works there (the truth).

Then I decide to take a rickshaw, drop off the burner and return later in the rickshaw to drive the scooter back home.

When I return home, the lights are on. I make dinner with rice, vegetables, ghee, olive oil, spices and yogurt. I eat this unexciting meal on the floor in the living room and I am happy.

*

It is 8:00 at night on Saturday. This morning, I wake up later than usual, wash lots of clothes inside the house so no one can watch me work in my sleeveless blouse, hang them on the line in back, take an oil bath and then wash off all the oil with the dusty herbs, using lots of water.

After all that, I take the bike out to buy some yogurt and a block away I run into Frank on his bike. He invites me to a goodbye breakfast for Michelle and her boyfriend. At the party everyone talks about their different experiences with asana and pranayama. Michelle it turns out had studied some pranayama with Acharya a year earlier. "He made us do these *little* breathing exercises while we were propped up on our elbows, " she says with a snotty tone.

I cringe. I love Acharya and these little breathing exercises are the deepest things I have ever experienced. When I listen to Michelle belittle him, I have to stop myself from telling her off. A little internal attention to breathing helps.

Other than that moment, it is a pleasant gathering. We eat fruit and chapattis.

Then Rick and I take Mohan's rickshaw to Shivanand's, singing our sarigamas so loudly in the back of his rickshaw that everyone stares at us, especially when Mohan stops to put gas into the rickshaw. These two crazy westerners singing Indian scales.

When we arrive Shivanand says, "You are a bad lady, Gina, you are late."

I give him a big candy bar and he smiles, breaks it open and insists that I take two pieces. Tomorrow it will be oranges and bananas.

He sends his harmonium home with me to practice.

I take the main palace road and then turn right by the hospital. There is a parade coming down the street so I pull over for a moment, but then I watch the motorcycles go to the right and the pedestrians move over to let us through. In the middle of the parade, a gaunt corpse sits in a chair held high up above people's shoulders, flowers adorning his face.

Later, while I am walking across the street to dump my garbage in and around the bin on the corner, I realize that, yes, I am alone here, and I am already planning my next trip—for at least six months next time—and why, if I am so alone. Because I want to learn how to live and die with some kind of understanding, to reduce the suffering, to enjoy my life without drama, and coming to India is a way of stopping the mindless tasks of everyday life and concentrating on this—yes, this life, everything about it, constantly changing, lost, found, transformed—and nothing you have now, you love now, nothing will be here in the future exactly as it is now, this loved one, this shirt, this dress, this ring, all gone in the heap of change, like the amazing disgusting garbage which the cow eats as she ages and gives milk, walking down the street, swaying back and forth. So much drama. On Monday the men and women sort out what's left of the garbage and carry it away in their little wagons. The corpse that goes into the fire sitting up or lying down emerges as dust to be taken to the Ganges, dust and water rushing through India.

*

After Lenny stopped breathing, I turned off Louie Armstrong. We had played his tape "What a Wonderful World" over and over. His body was in the living room for about twelve hours before the men from the funeral parlor came. I was in a trance and not a yogic trance. I was frozen in absolute grief. Two very unprofessional men came into the apartment and clumsily transferred his body to a stretcher. They almost dropped him as they tried to get him down five flights of stairs. Jessie was sobbing in her room, with her boyfriend lying beside her. Josh was in the kitchen with his girl-friend. I followed behind the men. And then the door opened and it was a bright April day with lots of people outside. I was moaning and a teenager turned around and said, "Hey, what's wrong, lady? Did somebody die?" The stretcher went with his body into a blue van, and then around the corner the van disappeared.

I climbed the stairs, lit a candle and felt his presence still in the room.

*

I buy a rolling pin today for chapattis and the ingredients (sim-ply flour, water, salt and ghee) and I make a complete mess out of the kitchen. They come out fat and tasteless. Much more complicat-ed than I had anticipated. After I finish cleaning up the mess, I put most of them in a pile by the garbage heap for the cows, dogs and roosters. Then I sit down and read the cookbook. It is all so com-plicated and beautiful that it sends me right out the door to a restau-rant for palak paneer.

I talk to my downstairs neighbors. They are very pleasant young musicians who are now off on a music event at a festival somewhere in India. They want to meet Josh when he comes and jam with him. Josh plays the sax. But they have left and now I am in this gigantic house all by myself.

When they come back I promise to perhaps cook something. Me? I can't cook worth a damn. And in India where every woman can cook so well, my lacks will appear as craters in someone's taste buds. Maybe just a simple rice dish with peas and cashews. Yes, and then I'll try to cook one little chapatti every day until I learn how.

*

Today is Sunday, July 2, 2000. I am thinking that today is the 3rd and that I will see Acharya today. This has been a very long week without a yoga advisor. Acharya tells me I can't do so many things and then he disappears. I guess that's what it is all about.

I am walking down a road not far from here when I hear Carl call to me—"Hi Gina."

I walk over to the car where he is sitting in the passenger seat. The driver is a man dressed in a white dhoti and shawla.

I tell Carl I think we are meeting at his house today at 12:00.

Later at an STD phone stand, I call Acharya and a man at his house says they will not be home until the evening. So I have given Carl incorrect information. Later Subrata tells me that Carl has been trying to reach me by telephone. She gives me a number and I call him. We are going to meet at his house tomorrow at 12:00 whether Acharya is there or not.

I want to talk to Carl about women and gold, about renouncing one's love of sex and material objects, and how this is not my idea of yoga—if it is, then I am going to be living a lot of lives in the future.

Life as life itself, my friend Mark would say.

The divinity of the present, of maya and spirit woven together in one fabric, of one human in the arms of another, the divinity and that freedom.

This is ok, Ramakrishna would say, except it is too difficult for most people in the Kaliyuga era. We need the god of forms and to especially avoid women and gold, which represent lust and greed. I guess the "we" isn't "me" or "we westerners." It is addressed to his disciples, young monks and merchants in Calcutta in the 19th century.

I will consider this more later. My computer is running too hot now. I think I need to turn it off completely and let it rest. The stabilizer I ran out and bought today isn't really doing much for the computer.

Here I am at about 4:00 and I'm bored. I'm seldom bored, but today I'm bored. I'm going to do my practice, clean everything in my messy apartment, practice singing, look over my drawings from the first week, make a little salad of cucumbers and carrots, go to Iyengar's for chapattis, and finally visit Mahadeshswara and the boys in the hotel. That will be quite a bit to do. Then it will be time to come home and sleep.

Last night, I wrote a history of the *Cass City* Project for Artie—he's co-publishing an art book with a Detroit small press:

> I finished the Cass City collection of drawings in 1976. The Song Shop on Forest and Cass in Detroit had closed, and there was nostalgia on my part for a community that used to gather there. Eleanor, the elderly woman who owned the place, once mentioned that in the years past there used to be a lot of singing going on in her bar, but the years I knew were kind of dark and bluesy for the Cass Corridor and that's why soft charcoal seemed the best medium. Year after year, the same group with minor changes would gather in the afternoon, drink, and talk about art and social problems—students, professors, drunks, artists, writers, etc. There was, of course, mostly jazz and blues on the juke box. Here is Indian Joe completely smashed, with his head resting on the bar and the bag of books for his studies at Wayne County Community College sitting on the floor under the bar stool. Lenny and David tip their heads together, talking—maybe they are trying to figure out where they can buy drugs, or perhaps they're analyzing the political structure and inherent corruption of the city. Once a thriving automobile factory town with a strong union mentality, Detroit in the seventies seemed to be a deteriorating shell of abandoned buildings, littered lots and lost human beings. Here in the wreckage, Eleanor wipes down the bar. This couple dancing near the

jukebox—they are alive with the blue light of romance and alcohol. And that's me as a young girl sitting in the corner with two long braids, a coke, a cigarette and a stack of books on the bar. I'm reading a sociology book entitled *Marital Abuse*. It was a time of love, despair and beauty.

Even though this project and life seems so different from my new quest with yoga, there was still a search for some spiritual relation in the world. We were looking then with the help of drugs and alcohol.

*

I learn today that 2:30 on Sunday afternoon is the most terrible time to travel on Shivanand's road, the bumpiest most crowded road in Mysore. I learn that on a warm Sunday afternoon, people are in wicked moods.

Certain days, men glare at me, like today in the gas station when the man was going to pour oil into my gas tank—as if I am so stupid, a white woman, why not? I see the red glint in his eye. I see it in so many eyes today.

I arrive at Shivanand's. Arpana is studying. Shivanand is eating dinner. I lay down on the sofa and rest until I can hear the harmonium, and in a minute he calls me into the room.

"Gina, you come."

I certainly can't hit the "ri" key so he gives me some other easy lower scale and we practice the "sa-ri" several times.

Vanessa wants me to leave early to go to Pondicherry with her. I'm not sure. I want to wait to see what happens with my lessons this week. I don't think I'm going to leave early because I want to spend as much time with Acharya as possible. I'm going to check with him tomorrow about his schedule for the month.

I've just returned from a short trip to Agrahara to cash some traveler's checks. The hotel lobby was filled with a group of aged men. One of them had a blue cloth wrapped around his head and neck. They were all curious to examine my traveler's checks.

I am very unsteady on the bike. Actually, I was planning to go to the Parklane and eat palek paneer, but I was so unsteady on the bike and so many people were riding erratically that I decide to walk over to Iyengar's and have idlies.

A couple with two young children sit down next to me. I can tell that the three year old boy in the knitted hat is frightened of me.

Who is the white woman with the funny clothes?

He sits on his father's lap. So beautiful. Then they get up and move to a table across the aisle.

Right now the electricity in the house is weird just as it is weird in my foot. My foot is vibrating and the computer is vibrating. Lonely tonight. If I have to spend many days like this without any yoga instruction and just on my own, I think I'll move on. If I tell Acharya about this, he will probably adjust my diet.

wake up from many strange dreams—one, I am under the influence of an evil man. I can't remember the details. It must have come as a result of working on the *Cass City* book again. The second dream is about Josh. He is a young child and I have sent him off on a boat into the rough ocean, directing that he be put into the water to swim back to the shore. As soon as he leaves, I know it is a mistake. He will never make it. I am talking to someone about going after him and saving him when I realize that he isn't three years old, he is seven. Still, he is not strong enough for this journey. I am frantic. Then the boat returns. Lenny's friend, Mike is driving it. He would never really drop Josh off in the ocean, I think in the dream. He just took him for a ride and there Josh is, healthy, but fully grown, at least a foot taller than he is now, a giant and he is naked. He is climbing the stairs and talking.

I wake up at 6:00 and my bones are sore. Perhaps these weird cramps appear because I am sleeping only on one side or because the other side has the damaged nerve. Slowly I take various positions so that my spine becomes flexible. First on my left side, then my right, curled into a ball and then crouched up into child's pose. Finally I stand up.

I do the whole primary practice and my body feels good after this. The only poses I eliminate are some of the sun salutations and the final poses which I replace with the three that Acharya has added. Then I complete my pranayama. It is a long practice, and it feels right to me. My clothes are a little damp but I do not have sweat running from my body. I think I am learning how to vary the practice based on my condition.

I use Subrata's computer to send an email to Josh. There is an email from Dimitri saying he cares deeply for me, but he would understand if I decide not to sleep with him anymore because I want to protect myself from any future pain. He mentions that his mother and his brother are both pushing him to get married before he is too old, and they want him to have children. Children? But he doesn't know really what he wants to do. Some astrologer has told him that he should not have children because they will destroy his creative energy.

I telephone him on his cell phone; he is driving down a boulevard in Moscow and I am in a little booth in India; he pulls over to the side of the road and we talk. Oh the wonders of our age. We are happy to talk to each other. He is reassuring, expressing love, and so I decide to keep this relationship open as a possibility, following the heart rather than the head that says over and over, be careful, Gina, not only is he in a different part of the world, but he's also in a different stage of life.

*

I'm off to lunch with Carl at his house in J. Prakash. Maybe Acharya will be there.

I completely forget my pranayama. This is the first time I have skipped the 12:00 practice. I realize that if I go to Shivanand's and then go directly to a lecture at Carl's house, I will end up skipping it again.

Carl talks a lot about Acharya and Brahmin practices.

"Acharya is like having a senator as your teacher," he explains. "He could have thousands and thousands of Indian students. In fact he did have a large following, but he sent them away. He couldn't do his own practice which takes up most of his day. Acharya goes into a trance easily. He now has a group of young Brahmin men and a few women studying with him. After studying asanas here in Mysore for many years and at a very advanced level, his body began sustaining injury after injury. He stopped practicing and traveled around India, studying with other teachers. Then when he came back to Mysore, he found his true teacher. His whole practice became centered on the second yoga sutra—make the mind quiet. At some point Acharya decided to start teaching westerners. He wanted to know more about them since western culture was having a negative affect on Indian culture. So from January through March every year, he takes a few western students.

We talk about books—*The Autobiography of a Yogi*. I tell him how Yogananda's concentration on his miracles seemed kind of excessive to me. But that I really liked Paul Brunton's book. He talks about other books to read by Yogananda that are transcripts of his talks, *The Divine Romance, Man's Eternal Quest, Whispers from Eternity*.

About women and gold in Ramakrishna, Acharya said that this is the only point where his colleagues have problems with the book. Many of them believe that perhaps "M" embellished this message because it had more to do with M's issues than with Ramakrishna. According to Carl's understanding, one can earn money as long as it is done honorably and you are not seeking more than you need. Also, sex is appropriate with your wife.

"What about a single person, like me?" I ask. "That means I don't have a sexual life."

"You'll have to ask Acharya," he says.

"But I won't," I say, "because I come from a different culture and the rules of this culture won't work with mine, especially this rule. I just make sure that my actions don't make my mind too busy with thought or anxiety. That's my goal."

Carl is planning to visit Arunachala, the red mountain, south of Madras. It is a power spot in the world, the place of Ramana Maharshi, guru to Paul Brunton.

Then he cooks. He asks me if Acharya has told me about "precious" food—we have a discussion about sattvic, rajasic, and tamasic foods—not eating spoiled foods or meat; avoiding upsetting food like onions and garlic, and staying with foods that are sattvic, like rice, milk, mangos, etc. Sattvic foods are mild and precious, promoting balance and lucidity. Rajasic foods are passionate, excite the body and thinking. Tamasic foods promote enertia. They are heavy and take a long time to digest. He says that he has noticed a concrete difference in his meditation by paying attention to the way these three energies interact in his diet. If he doesn't eat onions and garlic, slowly but surely the smell of his sweat changes and he has a quieter mind. He teaches me how to make chapattis and a delicious sambar with gord and coconut, as well as rice and idlies. He makes a butter milk with cilantro and other spices.

If you follow Brahmin customs, he says, you can pick up things with your left hand, but you can only eat with your right hand. Once you pick a cup up with your right hand, it must go into your plate. Then the plates and cups you eat from are washed outside. The others are washed in the kitchen. It has something to do with separating the plates that saliva has touched because saliva is some-how intensely connected with one's mind. Then you must clean the spot where you eat by sprinkling a little water on the floor and swishing it around your hand to pick up any particles. Then take a rag and wash the spot where you were eating. Each person washes his own spot.

Carl sold his architectural firm because it was taking too much away from his peace of mind. His wife came here for five months, studied with Acharya, returned for a month and now he has come for a year. That sounds very strange to me. They are never together. Maybe a ritual trip to India is a part of a dissolving marriage.

Later, I ride around the edge of Mysore. It is such a relief, the open skyline, empty of people, coconut trees waving in the open fields. I do miss seeing Acharya, though. It is kind of lonely not see-ing him everyday.

*

July 4. It's about 3:00 p.m., and Acharya has just left my house. He came by to see if this will be a good place for our Gita meetings. I think he likes the apartment. I want to find someone to clean it. If the woman doesn't come here by this evening, I am going to start washing it myself in my own way. Rag, pail, soap. Maybe I'll do that anyhow. It will help me feel as if I am at home here.

The day. This morning's practice—a fly bothers me and I never really meditate sufficiently. Then I am in too many places. I do not have a midday practice, except for a meeting with Acharya; he adds a pose to my pranayama practice, in full lotus with arms criss-crossed behind my back and fingers holding toes. Four times.

Later I ride over to Shivanand's—the roads are again a dirty dusty smoky nightmare. Somehow I make it into the little alley that leads to his house, prop up the bike and climb the stairs. Women and men in and out of the doors on the first floor—dark, dirty rooms. Up the stairs and he is sitting in a chair drinking tea. There are troubled looks on all the family faces. Arpana is scowling. I wonder why. The younger one, Manjushri, is usually more lighthearted. Just as I am ready to go into the music room, which is a room for sleeping at night, Aishwani gives me a bowl of rice and a cup of milk instead of tea. Thank you, Aishwani. Then I go into the sweet little music room full of instruments. I sing and Shivanand fumbles on the harmonium. It is not his instrument, but he has moved my voice up a register. He asks me questions about how much money I make and I tell him exactly, along with my rent so he can see that this amount of money, while great here, is not so great there. Perhaps they are having money problems.

I leave and start out toward Carl's house. I realize that I have forgotten his little containers (from the food he gave me a few days earlier) so I return to my house before heading to J. Prakash. I love this ride by now even though today there is so much traffic. I think it is a holiday for some people and so the roads are very busy. When I arrive at Carl's after many near misses with buses and trucks, he is in his computer room with two Indian men working on a project. I wonder why he would think that Acharya would be happy discussing the Gita next to a room where men are working on a computer.

Acharya arrives late and apologizes. He stands in the middle of the room lost in thought, his head tipped down, his hand holding his chin.

"Perhaps we will meet tomorrow," he says.

I stand up. I don't know what he means.

Then he stands again very quietly with his head tilted.

I am secretly disappointed. I haven't talked to him in so long.

"How are you doing?" he asks.

I tell him that I'm fine and that I have purchased the leather shoes.

He looks at my feet, at the band aids under the straps from the sandals.

"The karma is biting you." Carl and he laugh.

I explain—"a cow who died naturally."

"Still the karma is biting you." He tells me to rub castor oil on the shoes.

I tell him I gave his number to two people for astrology charts, and I am a little bit lonely without many students around.

He stands thinking quietly.

Carl looks very concerned.

"Carl," he says, "I think we will meet here tomorrow. Today I want to meet with her alone to talk about practical matters and her practice."

"You follow me to my house. Yes."

Zoom, Acharya is around the corner and probably already home. I am chugging along at a pace I used to think was quick, passing the little shops, around the corner, the fields on the right and left, more little shops, the rickshaw stand with three rickshaws. I turn right into Acharya's neighborhood, park in front and he opens the door to the little side room.

"You wait there. I will be there in a minute."

I sit on the straw mat. His mat is gone. I think about some of my questions before he arrives. About the left heel in the perineum—always with padmasana?

"No," he says, "when you go into half padmasana, the left heel is relaxed and the right is placed up high. You can reverse this but not in pranayama. Otherwise it is ok to reverse it."

I ask about when I automatically go into a meditative state before I finish all the pranayama exercises. Should I hold myself back, finish the exercises or go with the meditation? I have to repeat this question a few times before he understands.

"Meditate, that is the purpose of the exercises, to reach that state."

Patchimotanasana—I tell him that it feels right to begin with that. After the warrior poses, my body wants this asana.

He then goes into a long talk about my body—a vata body—and the injury I have sustained. "This injury is going to stay with you always and it will return if you are not careful. The memory of that injury is in your body. You must keep your body warm and flexible. Some days you will be stiff and you must be careful and not push your body any further than it goes naturally. This injury can reoccur from forward bending or back bending. Other days you will be more flexible. Only you will know, so no one should ever touch your body and push you into a pose."

I talk about the cold weather in New York and how this injury happened on one of the coldest days of the year.

"Yes, on cold days you must do more asanas. You need to bend back and forward, but nothing extreme. No pain."

Then we talk a little bit and he asks me how many days I will be here—about 25 more—and he asks if the place I have rented is spacious. Later, he stops by and looks at the apartment.

"This will be a good place for our meetings," he says. "Will that be all right?"

"Yes, of course."

He sits on one mat. I sit on the other and we talk. He asks me please not to encourage other students to come to him. "If they come and ask, I cannot turn them away, and there have been problems in the past." He asks me not to say negative things about other yoga teachers. "Also, don't talk unnecessarily about me. Some may think, oh he is just working with westerners for the money. All money donated by students, I put into charities. Even half of my salary from the university is put into a yoga project, teaching yoga to Indians. Please we are only having discussions. I have my reasons for wanting to spread what I know. I ask him if he is training the young people in his house so they will go on and teach. Yes, so they will teach Indians. There are thirty young people."

I explain to him that there are only about ten western students in all of Mysore right now and they seem to have their projects already outlined so we will probably be working alone.

It was a sweet meeting.

*

I wish I wasn't such a terrible cook.

I cancel my appointment with Shivanand today. I tell him I'm going to come in the afternoon with Rick starting tomorrow.

Then I ride over to Nilgiris looking for castor oil for oiling my shoes. No, we don't have that. They look a bit irritated that I'd even ask. A man there tells me that he will come outside and point my way to an oil shop. Over there, straight after the circle. See the blue building and the yellow building and the awning. Yes. That is the oil shop. I bike over. It is a shop with two dirty men, one old and the other probably his son sitting in a hovel with twenty or so big filthy cans of oil. You bring your own container or they will put your oil into a bag for you. For one rupee I buy a little tiny bit of castor oil. I can't imagine buying oil from here and then eating it, although once I did buy some peanut oil from a similar stand—slightly cleaner—in the fruit market.

*

Acharya watches me do my pranayama. I thought I was doing very well except that a little cough was sitting in my chest. I saw blue. I saw yellow. I stop and he says, there are certain things you must do to improve. SLOW DOWN. I hear the words loudly like this, but I think he actually said—Stop the speed at which you are doing it. He took my notebook and wrote down Jeericadi Rasayana in either Sanskrit or Kannada. This is an herbal mixture that I should take half an hour before eating, and then some hot water or milk—2 x a day. For ten days. Wait two days he says and he may change the oil I am using for my bath to take my pitta down so I stop thinking so much. I have a feeling that if he knew the way I am drawing and writing everything down, he might tell me to stop that, too. But this is one of the purposes of the trip.

A beautiful young Brahmin boy stands by the door looking at me and listening to Acharya talk.

"Is there any touch in your day?"

"What?"

"Are you having touch from anyone?"

"Not really. I'm pretty solitary."

"Hands?"

"The little boys on Sayyaji Road. An occasional yoga student."

He explains that Indians don't touch each other unless you are children, parents, husband or wife because someone could have negative energy and send it to you through the contact. "This may not work," he says, "in your country where everyone kisses and hugs and such. You may have to forget this when you get home. If there is a heart-to-heart connection to the maximum, with nothing mechanical, then there will be no disturbance. If touch comes with love as a flood, then no disturbance."

I think back to the proforma hug and kiss I gave Frank the night before. We talked about these children on Sayyaji Road—"Avoid them he says. They just want money." Then I remembered that this morning Subrata put her hand on my shoulder. Clothing in between. Cotton is a conductor. Suhas, measuring me for clothes, inadvertently touches my arms.

I mention that I have boyfriends at home. I don't tell him I am looking for a husband, but I am. Nonetheless the boyfriends are always the impossible husbands. "One lives in Russia." He shows no shock. He says nothing.

He talks about contemplation and how for some it is easier than for others. "For Brahmins the capacity is inherited. We don't want excitement or adventure. For those in the west and other places, because of materialism, vata is extremely high. It takes a lot more work when everyone is so industriously seeking and controlling."

*

I am tired. Yes, tired. It is raining.

I roll the motor scooter into the yard after going out to buy some curd for my afternoon dose of quiet food. When I leave the gate open for 5 seconds to park the bike, a herd of four cows approaches the yard, and one very large black cow with horns goes into the yard and starts eating all the little greenery. Hey you, I say, but her front end is working its way into the yard, not toward the gate. And

I'm a little bit leery of those horns. Last year Anna told me several stories about cows who butted people. That's why owners often remove the cow's horns. So I leave the cow to her dinner. Upstairs I make a mango lassi, eat it with a spoon on the porch and watch the big girl have dinner, too. Finally her head is near the gate and I say, "Hey you, get out of here." She walks right out.

*

This photo of Dimitri was at the beginning of a roll of film I finished in Mysore. He's sitting in a chair in my apartment at my computer, typing, and looking into the computer screen. His image in profile, forehead leaning over, strong arms, black tee-shirt with the sleeves torn off. His image in this photo looks very similar to a photo I have of my old boyfriend David, and to my memory of my father, too. I'm often drawn toward masculine, single-minded men who eventually go their own way, leaving my heart, or perhaps its my ego, twisting and turning. Except for Lenny—he was more like my mother. Since Lenny and I separated, though, it's almost as if there is a book that is being written over and over again with the same theme and I open the cover and jump inside. It begins with ecstasy and ends with agony. I think I want a husband, but I don't want anymore of that drama. I close my eyes and sit in the middle of the room. Who am I? I say over and over and a little light starts burning between my eyebrows. I am who. And so is he and he.

Adventure is possible even if I never leave the house. These drawings, this notebook, these photographs. Here's Lenny and Josh with their arms around each other, standing on the edge of a landing that overlooks the mountains, almost a replay of the early photo of Lenny and his brother. These two guys are both a little curved though. Lenny has his leg crossed and he's holding tightly on to little Josh's arm. They are happy together. Jessie probably took this photograph. Lenny used to take them out for vacations in the mountains, to places children enjoy, like the Rocking Horse Ranch, places I would never enjoy. I was more involved in their education. He was deeply attached to them and that's why when the doctor said he had a few weeks left, he stayed alive for two months waiting for Josh to return from his semester in Argentina. So much love in the curving lines of their bodies. If you were out to dinner with him, and he had just ordered a plate of his favorite food, and you said, "That looks great, Len," without a second thought he'd give you his plate. Sometimes I wish he could have been a little more selfish and a little less self-destructive.

*

I read a little more from the gospel of Sri Ramakrishna. Before I go, I'm going to copy one passage:

> Maya is woman and gold. He who puts maya aside to see God can see him . . . I have seen with my own eyes that God dwells even in the sexual organ. I saw Him once in the sexual intercourse of a dog and a bitch. . . . Sometimes I find that the universe is saturated with the Consciousness of God, as the earth is soaked with water in the rainy season.

Yes, I like seeing that saturation in the world, even in lust and money. I guess the point is to avoid being mesmerized, enslaved or tricked by lust and money. And for most it is easier to just avoid the temptation, especially for those who see themselves as monks.

I just made dinner and it tasted surprisingly good. The chapatti pan is broken in and is now working better. Odd thing about my mind—the present seems like the present always has been and always will be even when I have watched that present change hour to hour. A few days ago, I said, I am not a good cook. And then today: Yes, I like to cook for myself.

*

I wake up at 6:00 a.m., sleeping longer than usual. Even though I woke up a few times because my bones were hurting and I needed to pee, it seems as if I have really been sleeping so much. But it feels good. I remember someone saying something about the less activity, the more sleep needed. I wake up, wash all my clothes, take a bath—I enjoy these standing baths. Yesterday, Jeevesh was dragging a bunch of coconut shells into the back of the house. I had seen him doing that before. I always wondered what they did with them, so I asked.

"We use it to burn a fire under our bath," Subrata said.

"You get in the bath?" I asked, confused.

"No, no, do you want to see?" She took me into their bathing room. A big tiled pot is built into the room with a space underneath for a fire. They have electricity in the house but prefer this. "It is so nice," she said. "Three times a day we fill a pot for each of us and pour the hot water over our bodies. It is a much better feeling with water made with a fire from coconut shells."

I tried to describe the modernized world of the USA. I think it sounded corrupt to her.

In this little apartment there is a hot-water tank that I switch on to heat the water that fills my pail. That's how I take my bath.

*

I arrive at Carl's house, and while standing on the porch, I see Acharya pull up on his scooter. He is so serene that all harried feelings leave me.

We sit down on the mats and he begins to talk about the Gita.

"It would take two years of constant talk and study to really come to any understanding of the Gita," he says. Then he chants an invocation in Sanskrit and explains that the whole Mahabharata represents the life of the human being. "The five Pandavas are representatives of the five senses. Krishna represents eternal truth and wise energy. The 100 Kurovans are partners to the Pandavas. There are 101 parts in the body. 100 cause problems. They are vicious by nature, including lust, desire, anger. They are all brothers. If you use these parts, you can become trapped. Only one part helps for realization, eternal truth, Krishna. The Pandhavas seek the shelter of Krishna.

"In the body, bad overcomes good, but sometimes it is defeated. The soul sees all. In the end of the story, vicious energy—one hundred kings—is overcome by eternal truths. A yogi does the same. He takes shelter in eternal truths, gets happy, wise, strong and wins against the one hundred. In the same way, if we relax more and more, automatically we take control of the senses. The more and more we dwell on eternal truth, the more we overcome weakness. Here the poet tells the whole gist of yoga as a story. Even common persons know that wise and vicious energy battle within us. They are indirectly influenced by reading these stories."

"This," Acharya says, "is one of the most wonderful poems in the world. The poet selects an exact example to explain the whole of life. It is coincidental that Krishna was reincarnated at that time. Hundreds of thousands of yogic secrets are hidden in this story. This is what I have learned," he says, "from the eternal teacher, Srirangar".

"We are going to concentrate on Chapter Six because Gina is here only for another month and it is about what we practice and how to keep the mind calm." He reads one shloka in Sanskrit and then talks about it. First he refers to the earlier chapters where Krishna taught Arjuna about Karma yoga, the yoga of action. "You must find a way to keep your energies in balance. And this can be done for the common man, simply through karma yoga. Usually when a man is 80 years old, he gives up everything in his worldly life, studies the holy books, pranayama, asanas and lives his life as a monk lives. Krishna talks about how an ordinary man might live his life following the guidelines of karma yoga—doing his duty without desire, without attachment to desire and his life will be equal to the sannyasi's life. The Brahmin households used to (some small number still do) keep a fire going always (called the fire sacrifice), day and night, year after year, and when they died they were cremated with this fire. Only a tenth of a percent of the Brahmins still do this. Living your life following the guidelines of karma yoga is the equivalent to keeping the fire always going. Before we can enjoy yoga, we must know what our duty is and how it should be performed."

Then there is a discussion about the importance of knowing what natural desires or decisions are, like eating, and then unnatural desires and decisions (those that are unnecessary). "If a man has a very poor appetite and he wants to eat oily foods, this is an unnatural desire. If an eight year old girl wants a child of her own, this is an untimely desire. If you are a dwarf and you want to marry a very tall man, this is unsuitable and will cause problems. It is difficult to determine sometimes. But the unnatural desires must be avoided as much as possible and there are many of them. One should aim to live a simple life."

He talks about how for the common man karmic duty is enough to bring energy in balance and to receive detachment. Everyone has the capacity for samadhi (detachment, liberation, peace), just as we all have the capacity for sleep. But unwanted desires and unsuitable actions hold human beings away from this samadhi. Perform karma yoga to again achieve balance.

It is a beautiful talk. I say hardly anything, but I feel peaceful. He says he will meet with me tomorrow to read my astrology chart. And he will be unavailable to talk about the Gita on Saturday and Sunday.

He stands tall and willowy in Carl's door, as he says goodbye.

I hear the sound of his motor scooter going down the street and around the corner.

I sit still for a few minutes and Carl invites me to stay for lunch. We cook rava dosa, mixing wheat and rice flour and yogurt into a thin dough, then adding salt, chili and cilantro. Carl puts a little ghee on the griddle, popping some mustard seeds and then pouring a circle of dough on the griddle with a little circle in the middle and a little more ghee.

We are about to begin cooking a dish with sprouted mung beans when his friend Mohanswami knocks on the door. He's a very sweet and cheerful man who is teaching Carl how to cook. Mohanswami wipes off the counter, puts a little sesame oil in a pan with some mustard seeds. Popping mustard seeds seems to be the beginning of most Indian dishes. He adds black gram dhal, a chili, the mung beans, a little water and then he lets the water boil out. A little scraped coconut, salt and lemon and it is a gourmet meal.

He whips up a desert. Standing at the burner in his bluish white dhoti, he stirs four strands of saffron into some keserebat. Keep stirring and stirring, he says, heat up some ghee in a separate pan and put some raisins and cashews in it and another tablespoon of ghee, heat and fry for a minute until the raisins are round. It is delicious but too sweet for my taste.

While eating, Carl tells me that he and two of his friends traveled with Acharya and Jayashree in an RV around the United States for two months. We talk about the gift it is to study with him and how hardly anyone else knows about him.

Carl's scooter is being repaired at Subrata's—so after we eat, he rides me over to Subrata's on my scooter. I don't feel comfortable riding the scooter with someone so much larger than me in the back, so I ask him to drive. I hold on to his torso as we take the back roads through the fields in the outer edge of Mysore. I think he would have felt more comfortable if I had ridden sidesaddle because lately he's very influenced by the philosophy of touch. Unfortunately, I would be terrified to ride sidesaddle with no one to hold on to.

Four nights have passed between the last entry and this one. After the first night, I wake up feeling excited about meeting with Acharya. I finish my practice, go over to the STD stand across the two roads and telephone his house. Jayashree tells me he will not be seeing me today because he had to leave Mysore and he will be out of Mysore until Sunday. So perhaps he will see me on Sunday. He will contact me. I can't be contacted, I tell her, since I don't have a telephone. So then you call here at 9:00 a.m. on Sunday. I can't imagine staying in this apartment until then with nothing to do but draw and record what I am doing. To do. That, I realize, is what my mind is overly absorbed with. Doing. What I have done, but especially what I must or will do in the near future. Duties. What is wrong is that I have no duties here and now.

So I decide to go to Bombay by train. A vata adventure. While I am waiting for Subrata to bring me my breakfast (toast, ghee, fruit, ginger tea, milk, yogurt), and she is so slow, I start talking to Jeevesh about Bombay and where to stay and how to get there. I have one and a half hours to prepare. So what do I do? I eat quickly, ask Subrata to make me some food to carry, pay her some money on my account, ride my scooter home, sort through everything, and pack my backpack with some clothes, toiletries, my computer, a few books. Then I go to the bank and spend 45 minutes cashing some traveler's checks. Where are you living? Who are you studying yoga with? You haven't come here before. Yes, last year.

After cashing my checks, I decide I definitely can't handle carrying this computer. Even though it only weighs seven pounds, it is dead weight and carrying it causes my lower back to become stiff. Back to the house, I put the computer into the closet and take out a sheet of paper with some notes about Bombay from last year. I switch my sandals. I wish I had never done that. For twenty-four hours my feet are sliding out of my shoes. I'm definitely not taking these sandals home with me. This has become one text that is dominating my interior mind when I'm meditating. . . I'm definitely not taking these sandals home with me. I'm putting this into a trunk for Josh with a note that says . . . I want to ask Acharya this and that. . . I want to buy a pair of these before I leave. . . . I want to finish five or six more drawings. Some thoughts about my future classes. My stream of thoughts is relentlessly doing-this-and-doing-that thoughts. And I do not need to think these thoughts. Perhaps if I make lists of the things I have to do, then I might not think the same thing over and over. It is as if they are done when they go on the list. This thinking problem is hereditary. It is your fate, Acharya says.

Just as I go around the corner, I see Roberto. I stop and tell him I am going to Bombay.

"Let me call, dear and make a reservation for you at the hotel I stayed in, The Bentley in Colaba. It's clean and safe. But be careful, Gina, with what you eat there. Don't drink any juice from the juice bars. They use bad water. A friend I know picked up a terrible case of typhoid in Bombay."

When I drop the bike off at Subrata's and pick up the food, Jeevesh helps me catch a rickshaw. They are very nice when it is on a one-to-one basis even though it is only a business arrangement. That's how it is in the hotel, too. Of course, economics are behind all actions—some kind of gift giving, receiving and expecting—but what's different here from New York is that people here often act as if they are really your friends and at the same time they are eager to take your money. Acharya explains that as commerce has become more and more important in India, "cheating" has also increased. I notice that the reaction to cheating on the consumer's side here in India is constant suspicion and resistance, at least with westerners.

I climb into the old rickshaw, the kind with the motor in the front and the boy (he is very young) tries to charge 20 rupees, but Jeevesh says only 15, so when we stop, after bouncing all the way there, he expects 15 rupees, and I gave him 20. If the meter had been on, it would have been about 9 rupees. I think I have been overtipping in India. (A heavy tipper in India is like a foreign mark in a *Law*

& Order show on tv in the U.S. We clearly understand why this heavy tipper has been marked for execution by a group of con men and prostitutes. After all he was an ignorant man, a *heavy tipper*.) No one wants to use the rickshaw meters because very devious drivers often take you far out of your way to get home just to run the meter up. Once someone was driving all the way around Mysore in the evening with me inside—and he wouldn't listen to a word I said. It was frightening.

In the train station, I buy my ticket (41 rupees) and someone points at the train. I climb in. They have horrible steps that are almost impossible to climb, especially for old people, very steep and with no angle. I reach out my hand to help an elderly Indian man, and he reaches out to me. He must not be a Brahmin, I think, since he immediately put his hand into mine.

On the train, I sit next to an older Hindu woman. She has her bag between us. My back pack is on the floor. A boy about twelve years old sits across from us and another smaller boy with his mother. What I remember about them is the beautiful way the young mother sits in half lotus in her blue sari, slumped over to one side sleeping. Her skinny son, in his very tight black levis and belt and angelic face, leans on her shoulder sound asleep with his mouth open. Many times during the trip, he reaches into the tight pocket in his pants pulling out a little zipper bag with some rupees inside to buy things to eat from the venders. They are selling samosas (he doesn't want those). He buys some fried cake that looks like a cookie but I think is some spicy grainy thing, mango drink, mineral water, tea, coffee, sweet cakes. I eat what I have in my bag, some chapattis.

She dozes and I read a little of the Gita, write a bit in my journal and then I doze, too, dropping everything on the floor, picking it up and looking out the window. The country side in South India—plots of land attended by men in lungis driving oxen. Women walking with water jugs on their heads. Tall wild grasses and coconut trees. Little grass hovels, cement block houses, a burning plot of land. A man stands looking at the fields with his hands behind his back, a white turban on his head. On and off rain. Beautiful river with ancient stones and women and children wading and washing clothes on the rocks.

The women washing clothes in the river beat their clothes against the rocks and then lay them out to dry on the rocks. Radha's mother came to clean my house yesterday. She was sitting on the stoop when I walked around the corner, a thin, rather pretty woman about my age or maybe even younger. Her son is in college. She cleans houses to help him get through, and some yoga students are helping, too. She can speak only a few words of English. She washes my clothes on the bathroom floor the same way the women wash in the river. She stretches out a piece of clothing and scrubs it with the brush against the ground, beats it and then rings it out. When she takes the clothes outside, she sees a spigot and shows me a rough block of cement, which is there for scrubbing clothes. I swear it seems a much quicker job to wash your clothes by hand and hang them on the line to dry than in the washer-dryer world of New York City. Of course, most of us don't have outdoor lines and spigots.

When we arrive in Bangalore, I step off the train and I'm surprised. This station looks very different from a year ago when I arrived in the middle of the night. It was full of poor people and travelers sleeping all over the hallways and along the tracks. No westerners then. The trains are old and the stations are dirty, but I am used to this by now. Everyday India is becoming more ordinary for me. Mid-day, the station is a bustling place full of traditionally dressed Indians as well as very modern (in the western sense) foreigners and Indians. Everyone is on their way somewhere. People come up to me to beg and when I say no and emphatically move my right hand at an angle from left to right, they accept no and leave me alone.

*

Now I'm in berth 33 on the Laknamyatilah express, an hour and a half past Bangalore, heading to Bombay, for arrival tomorrow afternoon. An old man across from me is sleeping with a little snore and a young man above him is napping quietly. The older Hindu man doesn't say anything to me. I don't think he speaks English. The young man is reading a biography of Indira Gandhi. He works for a company that manufactures trucks, he was born in Calcutta and he is now on his way to Pune.

I'm reading a book that was left in the closet of the apartment, *Papillion* by Henri Charriere—a riveting, mysterious true story that is probably not conducive to meditation, but which will help me pass twenty-four hours on the train. I'm in prison with him right now.

The man across from me is snoring loudly, continually, and he looks very peaceful. I hope I can sleep to his sounds tonight.

I love riding trains. India is vast and open. Most of it is empty even though it is overpopulated. If I were a poor mother with a babe or two, I'd much rather struggle here than in the filth of the city— but I'm sure I don't know what I'm proposing. She doesn't have that freedom. An unknown woman with babies appears in a village. I'm going to ask someone.

Despite the conflict in Pakistan and the rest of the violence in the world right now, the landscape outside this window is so peaceful, rolling hills with a few trees—mostly velvety green with some spots of red huts. Telephone wires follow the railroad about fifty yards away. Horses and water buffalo graze. Ridges of coconut trees and other bushes divide the land. A dirt road going off toward the hills with no vehicles. We are slowing down.

Some field workers, barefoot with saris tied up around their knees, heads covered with the scarf side of the sari. Big plants like cactuses. Slow. Some crop, small brown clumps. An orchard of low full trees like apple or pear. A man with four horses, his head wrapped, barefoot wearing only a lungi. Now no one as far as the horizon. The young man looks up from his book and says, "The British built the train system with our labor." I look into his dark eyes and back to the landscape.

The wheels make a soft clackity as we glide forward. Three lone cows. Dusty paths. The remains of a stone building with no roof. A patch of water. A little farm with a tiny hut. The little ridge is closer to the train now. A lone tree on the top. A man squatting with a staff and six brown and white pigs. Rocks, ridges of worn smooth rocks. Cows. A herd of sheep with a shepherd. A lone woman wading through a field at sunset looking down at her feet and the land.

I am looking west and the train heads north. Greener again. So close to this little mountain. Clouds and a burning sun. Fields in little ridges. Empty. No people, no animals. Along the track, one man driving two oxen with a cart behind him. Some larger mountains. Lots of taller trees obscure the view. Rubble along the edge of the mountain. Now again the velvety land in between. A scarecrow in a white shirt. No more mountains. Dust. Roads and some little houses. An old station. A fence made out of slabs of rock. Village here. Village gone. Far off a low ridge of mountains. Water buffalos and cows grazing inside some velvety green square. Five little black birds. Suddenly several big ridges with red boulders and no more green. They look as if they could come down in an avalanche. They spread out over the green land as we pass by. A flat cart with no driver and no animal. A white scarecrow with no arms. And it goes on like this.

It is seven in the morning now. The young man is still sleeping on the top berth. He reaches up, flashes the light to look at his watch. Still an hour and a half before Pune. The older man slept on top of his blanket all night. It was so cold in here with the AC pumping out of the ceiling and he didn't move very much. He just went to the bathroom to wash up. He smells like garlic.

I am sitting here in my baggy Indian clothes, blanket around my legs, writing and watching the morning landscape—pools of standing water—open fields and streams. A very low ridge of hills toward the horizon. It is still monsoon-like here. Cows. Some large thatched farm houses every so often. Trees planted along the edge of the plots. Slowing down. The train horn sounds. A group of squalid huts with cows—Muslim man milking a cow. He is wearing his flat white hat.

I am thinking about my life in New York City, thinking about leaving Manhattan and moving to the country.

So wet here. Three Indian men in long white dhotis, heads wrapped, tall, walking in the plowed field with their hands behind their backs, contemplating. Bare feet in the mud.

White birds in the mud.

A sudden crowded squalid village. Here and gone. Cement square walls on a hill. Some tents. Poor farmers living near the railway. One man walking away down the road with his dhoti pinned up at his waist, hands held behind his back. That calm way of walking.

Some factory or mill. A few trucks.

Into town. Lots of little rusted, mildewed tin buildings. Turquoise huts in a row. Poor living conditions. Such beautiful land and then a little slum. In station. Maybe I can buy bananas.

Pune–mile after mile of Indian slums. What are these? Tents made of scraps of mildewed material. One next to another. Buildings of rusted tin sheets sharing walls. Often no doors, just one open side with a tarp. Occasionally a television antenna. Mostly dark holes inside. A man asleep on a piece of cloth in the yard. Now the more affluent poor—three story yellow apartment buildings with mildew, rust and collapsing widows.

All of this of course is the backside of Pune—as seen from the railroad track.

We are leaving Pune. Thick growth now.

If I were Indian and poor, I'd crave a country hut and just enough to grow and eat.

The suburbs—middle class houses—some large, grander houses with a Muslim slum on the outskirts. Goats wandering here and there. Houses made out of canvas sacks, now all hidden by a ridge of grass. The lucky poor have rows of little houses behind a polluted stream. Now the countryside. A park with young men in black trousers and white shirts. Taller middle class housing with potted plants on the ledges. Laundry string. Big water tanks. Some wealth here. Air clean. The skeletal remains of an ancient temple. The real edge of town. A little tent town right next to a cluster of large well constructed houses. Gone. Green. Here and there a white square house. Fields. Farms. This is farmland. A man in white sitting looking at the sky. Drier here than the miles before Pune. Some puddles.

They make red bricks here. The land is red and the bricks seem to grow out of it.

Sitting in some station, the air blowing, blanket over my knees. The old man in the berth across from me has moved to an empty seat on the other side. He's uncomfortable being near me, I think. He can't speak English, I have no Hindi. He looks at me with discomfort in his eyes. I've offered him everything—a banana, crackers, cheese, etc. No, no. Ok. Perhaps he is a Brahmin.

Now much hillier. Little shacks spread far apart on light green hills in the sun.

We are in darkness, a tunnel. We must be moving through a mountain, emerging into light green, then fog, then gray sky, back underground again. It is breathtaking emerging into green.

Inside the train, despite the florescent lights, there is no gray desperation as I often see in the subways of New York. This is second class air. Poverty in some of the trains though where people sleep in every available spot, even the luggage racks. Patiently waiting. Indians are patient.

A hut down in the valley with a four-sided shale roof—reddish beside a straw roof. And a bright red sari strung up on the line.

Bombay. I am comfortable waiting for the last stop when someone suddenly tells me this train does not stop at Victoria terminal. Get off here and catch another one. I rush to unlock my bag and someone helps me get onto the platform.

How will I get a ticket and carry my backpack up and down several flights of stairs, running, without further injuring my back.

A kind man on the platform offers to buy me a local ticket several terminals away while I sit with my bag and his briefcase. He then directs me to the front car of the local, the woman's car. I never realized there were special cars for women.

As I start to follow the line of women into the car, the woman behind me pushes me so hard that I almost drop my bag and fall inside.

I yell at her—to hold on—I'm sitting here now on my backpack on the floor. Two young women with laundry bags sit on the floor beside me.

The train is almost full. It stops again, the doors open, and the women push their way inside as if they are preparing for war—just to get a spot. One old, thin woman with a long gray braid elbows her way in, and her face is fierce and determined. Whew, she gets on and she gets a seat. I've never seen Indian women so aggressive except for the women selling mats outside the market in Mysore.

Outside it is green and lush. I can smell the slightly toxic smell of Bombay thirty minutes away.

A beautiful young Muslim girl stares at me from under her black shawl. I smile at her. She does not smile back.

*

There are no rickshaws in the central part of Bombay. The city is a cross between New York, London and an Indian city. A cab takes me to the Bentley Hotel in Colaba, a British style hotel. The clerk is a short sweet man with one eyeball missing, a red cave in his face. "Madame, I saved you the room that your friend asked for. Yes, the cab driver charged you five times what is necessary."

I run out the door and yell at the man, "I gave you 100 rupees too much and you should know that I know that you cheated me."

The room is very spacious with a big mission bed, a table to work on, a standing fan and a chest of drawers. The breeze floats in the window with the sounds of sea birds and pigeons. They gather in the trees outside the windows, talk and argue all day long. I lay on the mattress in my slip, happy. I survived the train trip, and I feel at home here even though I don't know a single soul.

I buy another pair of sandals, but they need some work. I squat down next to the shoe repair man while he softens my sandals and sews the sides. He does all the work with a little tool and some waxed thread. Perfect, simple without any machinery or even a building. He is barefoot.

"How much?"

"100 rupees."

"100 rupees? That's very high."

"No madam."

"Well you did a good job and you need the money so even though it is higher than usual, I *give* it to you."

In the morning after sleeping very well, I finish my practice, very smooth and fluid with the asanas and sort of brief with the meditation.

Then I walk up and down the main streets in Colaba, shopping a little in the khadi shops. I buy an Indian dress, eat in a fancy Indian restaurant, and then back in the room to wash up and practice again.

At Mahalakshmi temple, I donate a plate of flowers and a coconut to the deity.

A few blocks from the hotel, a man tells me how to get to Elephanta Island. "Go that way to the Gateway of India, just a few blocks. It's where the British first landed. There are small ferries that take you there every hour or so."

An island of caves. When I arrive, I discover that Indians pay only five rupees while I must pay 400. Why?

"Because you are a foreigner. This is a new government policy," the man says.

"Well it's a corrupt policy."

Now I wish I had gone in to see the caves, but then I felt I should protest a scam organized by the government, so I turned around, and down I went, back on the boat and across the bay, past the giant ships and toward the sprawling city with the cloud of pollution over it. Terrible smells. Sprayed with brown water.

*

After spending a day wandering around the streets, shopping and eating in fancy hotels, I take the train back to Mysore. In my berth, there is a very tall CPA, with a stomach that almost intrudes into my side of the car, and his round wife. They eat and eat the entire time they are awake, buying every snack the venders are selling. She is chubby with a very odd-shaped head, oblong, like an egg, and very large eyes. He has so much difficulty getting up on the top berth. I think—this man could not possibly expect a long life with this way of living. I am a little repulsed by their continual eating.

When they talk to me directly in English I like them better. From what I can gather, she runs a little factory making objects out of plastic shopping bags. They both wear fancy gems with lots of gold on their fingers. Most of the trip, I try to read and sleep.

When I move around at night or wake up in the morning, she is lying across from me with her eyes wide open, staring at me, reminding me of the etiquette of privacy that I am used to at home and that is not a part of Indian life. Right now her husband is asleep above me and she is sitting like a Buddha in her red sari, staring out the window. Some poetic book of scripture is open on her lap. We pass by a station, a village of cinderblock houses where people are waking up, emerging with their plastic water jugs on their way to the pump.

*

From Bangalore to Mysore, I take the Shathabi Express, a fast first class train. There are very few people in my car. A tall man with a turban and western pants and shirt approaches me and asks if he can sit down beside me. I look at him and I know I won't enjoy this contact. "No," I say, "I'd rather not." He is in the process of moving his body into the seat when he hears me and stands up, surprised. There are many empty seats. I'm sure he was preparing to sell me something and I'm glad I told him, no. I see him pass through the car two or three times during my journey back to Mysore.

*

Three weeks left in Mysore. This morning I am feeling that time is too short. While I am in a hurry as usual, unable to sit still without thoughts and plans rushing through my mind, I am aware that I need to be here for a much longer time to go through this. I turn my laptop on this morning to try to make a list of all the do-this, don't-forget-that thoughts in the hope that putting them on paper will make me stop running through them constantly during my yoga practice. Acharya assures me that this type of thinking is quite common in the western culture. It is heightened for me now because I am aware of it. That is the first stage.

I am on the bed. The breeze is flapping the leaves on the window. As the morning sun rises, so does the amount of traffic and the noise outside the window.

I get up and ride all over Mystore (that was an appropriate typo: *Mystore*) and look for various things. Mostly I find every shop closed. There aren't many trucks on the road on Sunday so I am riding and the wind is whipping my hair. I am so much in the mentality of going home. Today it is hard for me to figure out why I am here. Without regular contact with a teacher, I feel I should be elsewhere. That's why I'm leaving everything for Josh. I'm not sure if I will come back.

*

I've been sitting on the bed looking in the mirror at the fading tattoos on my shoulders, a discus and a conch shell. They are a trace of the final day of my trip last year. When I asked Mr. Jayaraj if he could give me a mantra, he arranged an initiation ceremony in the temple downstairs from the yoga shala on my last day in India.

I arrived early in the morning and was instructed to wait in the temple and stare into the face of god. (I did look into the horse-faced God's face, Hayagreva, an early form of Vishnu, and later in the year, when I was meditating, his face seemed fused with my body, his eyes in front of mine, burning yellow circles, his nose pressing against the front of my breastbone.)

After sitting for an hour and a half in the temple and wondering what was going on—the sage was conducting a puja, performing rites in various spots—Mr. Jayaraj arrived with a group of men and women. They seated me on the floor in front of the sage, who was sitting in an ornate chair and then they gathered around us. I was instructed to make an offering in the basket, flowers, fruit and a little bit of money, and then to repeat the chants after him. Even though I was confused, I mumbled after him. During the ceremony a man brought over some hot coals and a metal branding tool. I wasn't expecting this, but both my shoulders were branded, one with the conch shell and the other with the discus. When I screamed and flinched after the first brand, the sage told me to close my eyes, a woman pulled up my other sleeve, and I heard some other women laughing. As I repeated his chants, I was in a bit of a trance.

Feed her, the sage said, and an old woman led me into the back hallway of the temple where she gave me some rice on a banana leaf. I wandered away into the street. Later Mr. Jayaraj wrote the mantra on a paper for me. He explained that I should not say OM. That is for men. I should say AUM since I am a woman. Now, you are my colleague, Mr. Jayaraj said. Less than ten hours later, I flew back to New York City with two very inflamed shoulders and a determination to return to India.

*

Ramakrishna writes, "But if the process has already become too rapid and violent, our experience suggests it maybe advisable to take steps such as a heavier diet, suspension of meditations, and vigorous physical activity, to moderate its course. . . . Meditation itself is no chance response to a chance stimulus. It is a systematic and willed modulation of consciousness that puts the body into harmony with itself and with the macrocosm" (94-96).

*

The doorbell rings and I run down and open the door to lanky thoughtful Acharya. He asks me how I am and I tell him about the trip to Bombay and now the diarrhea. He says to take only a little bit of the Jeericadi Rasayana instead of the spoonful. I want to ask him more, but the doorbell rings again and it is Carl. We all wonder if Jayashree will be able to find the house. Acharya thinks she will recognize his scooter. But still he goes downstairs to look for her.

Then he asks us if we have any questions.

I talk a bit about the Protestant ethic and all my thinking during my meditation about *doing*.

Acharya talks about how I should keep practicing and it will become easier to understand what I am thinking and to be able to be detached from that thinking. Then he discusses the 3rd and 4th shlokas in the 6th Chapter. "There are two types of detachment for yoga practice, one that is initial, called *apara*, where you detach yourself during your practice. The other is *para*, a final form. At this point you enjoy the presence of God after practice and all through your day."

God, I think, is present when you stop thinking and are totally in the present moment without the constant thread of thoughts.

"In *para*, one is a realized soul, in balance with sattvic energy. You can do anything and remain in balance."

I talk a bit about food. "You mean you can eat anything then and it won't throw your balance off?"

"Yes," he says, "but most sannyasis will continue to follow the guidelines because they know they are teachers and setting examples for others. Even Krishna, who is an incarnation of God and has no need for meditation, continues to practice for the same reason."

In the middle of this discussion, Jayashree rings the bell and I let her in. Acharya begins again. And Jayashree sings passages from the Gita.

"In the Gita," he explains, "there is a description of the original yoga—the yogis have different approaches. Some can remember the details of their dreams exactly as if they have just dreamed. A few can enjoy meditation with an inner turn whenever wherever. Others need to enjoy it only at particular times. Some have the ability to explain everything, all the variations. A yogarudha has an established mastery of the experience. This yogi acts on intuition, an internal source."

"The 5th Shloka is the most important. There are 700 shlokas in The *Bhagavad Gita*, but 100 are considered the most important. This one if I can explain it correctly is very important. You alone must uplift yourself. Try not to create problems for yourself because you are your own closest relative as well as your own enemy. If a bad thought is allowed to manifest into an act, it will hurt others and yourself." He talks a lot about conditioned minds—"they are preoccupied with thoughts that are not natural. They can't see correctly. One must remember that each mind has two causes for this: one, previous minds have given incorrect knowledge; and, two, in this life, false methods for understanding have developed. While guidance is often required, self capacity is available. The common man needs help, but still he can struggle. He is making a distinction between natural instincts versus conditioned behavior. For example you might wake up at a certain time when you are ready to rise. That is natural. If you are required to rise for your job or appointments, that is conditioned. In a quiet space, you need to understand which are your natural instincts (the body's call) and which are unsuitable and doubtful thoughts. Balance will eventually arrive. Even as you are searching for a teacher, it is best if your inner knowing points the direction. You need to tame your enemies, the mind through thought, the body through food."

This was the end of the session. Carl has a new haircut and he looks a little overclipped, not the way a New Yorker wants to look, but perhaps the way an Indian wants to look. He admits in our meeting that he too is driven by a Protestant ethic.

At one point Jayashree changes her leg positions by turning one leg from half lotus into half virasana, and then after some time the reverse. Thank you, Jayashree, I think. I cannot sit for an hour without my knees crying.

I mention that in the west we often say that women are more intuitive and men are more rational in their ways of knowing and acting.

"A woman may know what type of food to offer a child, but a man might know that a baby should carry a certain stone." He wraps his shawla around his shoulders and stands up.

As they leave, I touch Carl on his shoulder. Well, he is not really a Brahmin, just an admirer of Brahmin culture, so I guess it is ok to touch him lightly.

*

I scoot over to Pradeep's shop. He is a short man with gray hair and a round, kindly face. He wears a pair of crooked glasses. He is probably only about sixty years old, but he appears older to me because for some reason I think I am a teenager. He works at a sewing machine on typewriter row. In the Khadi shop where he works there are lots of beautiful hand-woven fabrics, and it seems to be one of the really old shops. I think they don't care much for westerners and the clerks here are not eager to take my money— although Pradeep is eager to sew for me. His sewing machine is in the shop next door, almost outside, right under a doorway. Behind his sewing machine is a room full of old manual typewriters and men typing. It is raining, but the rain misses Pradeep, his sewing machine, and the man beside him who sells laminated holy pictures. They are under a little ledge. When I pass by on my scooter, he is sewing the shirt he has made for me and he waves and yells to me, "Three o'clock."

"Ok." I am getting used to the scooter and the traffic so I wave to him, "Return at three o'clock."

Then I zip around the block, around trucks and young men carrying loads of potatoes and onions on their backs. I head over to Anoop's with a package for Swami Bramadeo, the knives and a note Manny gave me to mail to him. This is a big relief, something I don't have to think about for a while, something crossed off my inner list of do this, do that. Anoop is the first person to bring email service to Mysore, he tells me, but now there are many providers, and the students have forgotten him. His little shop is dirty, the keyboards don't work well, and there is a strong smell of pesticides from the chemical shop next door. These are the reasons why many of the westerners are unfaithful.

Anoop is a very likeable man. Last year when I first arrived in Mysore and I was ill and confined to my room in the hotel, he checked my email and brought copies to my room. He refused to accept money. Madam, it is my duty to help you when you are ill. Anoop reminds me of Lenny, with his friendliness, care and his disorganized way of conducting business.

*

I put away my art supplies and the photos and go out on the porch with the computer, hoping no one notices the blue square of light projected into the night. I fold it between my belly and my knees and close my eyes. I remember so clearly. We are in a kitchen at a friend's house in Highland Park. It's a New Year's Eve party. Jessie's about three months old, propped up on my hip while I'm leaning against the sink. My hair is short. It was starting to get into my face all the time and the baby was grabbing it, so I cut it off. Lenny's standing to the side talking to a woman I've never seen before. She swishes her long black hair behind her right ear. She doesn't know we are together and she's very interested in meeting him. I have never been jealous of him before. I watch them talk. He smiles, showing his front teeth and the slight overlap, his curly red hair, one lock falling over his forehead. His body is a little heavier since the baby was born. Lately we are so involved with the baby that we aren't as loving with each other. I don't remember if he came over to my side after that. Later, of course, we drove home together. Did I ask him who she was? If he were here and I asked him, he would say, "Come on, you were always jealous and insecure, Gina. Don't you remember?" We lived together for nine years and in that nine years I used to talk about our faithfulness as if it were an anomaly, as if we were different from everyone around us.

A few weeks after I told Lenny that our relationship wasn't working and I wanted him to move out, I stayed out all night with a man I had known for years, came home in the morning and found him, Jessie and Josh all in our bed together. He looked at me. "You have to do what you have to do, Gina." He was unhappy but he would never insist that I remain faithful or that we stay together. That would be outside the code of hip life. He believed strongly in personal freedom. Maybe that had something to do with why I never insisted he go through drug rehab. Later after we separated, he had a relationship—for six months or so—with a very young woman who had a child. When I met her, even though I had a boyfriend standing right next to me, I felt wounded. That's when a different kind of friendship began to form between Lenny and me. I went out of my way to be friendly with his girlfriend. My father was dumfounded when I invited her to a birthday party for Josh at his house. I think we always felt related and so we reinvented the family to fit our changing needs and desires.

*

I ask a question of Acharya—"Why is Ramakrishna so negative about the hatha yogis? Isn't hatha yoga part of the tantric tradition?"

"Originally Hatha yoga was meant for liberation. It was pure but gradually it has become twisted and become a tool for achieving different powers. In Ramakrishna's days many hatha yogis were demonstrating that they could burn themselves with fire and still feel happy or walk on air. Ramakrishna hated these things. Why do this? he asked. One day he was going to take a boat across the river and the hatha yogi laughed. I'll walk over water, he said. This is unimportant, Ramakrishna replied. Why so many years of penance for this achievement when a boat is already available? Wasted years of life. The yogi flew to one side. Better than all this penance for this siddhi, instead get a crow birth and fly over. Hatha yoga used for demonstration, for ego, is a twisted yoga. Pure hatha yoga, however, is for the whole and is good."

*

The door bell rings at 11 a.m. I go downstairs. It is Roberto.

"Hello my dear, I was wondering if you could do me a little favor." He is holding a paper in his hand.

"Yes, of course, Roberto. Come in."

"Could you print this exactly here for a man to copy? I'm sorry I cannot write so well in English."

I copy two passages by Krishnamurti. The first one says: "The land where humanity has attained its highest towards gentleness, toward purity, towards calmness, above all the land of introspection and of spirituality. It is India."

I copy it line by line. "Roberto, the other day ago you were complaining about India. You were saying, They are like animals. Everything is getting worse. I can't trust anyone here. I'm just counting the days until I go back to Costa Rica."

"I need to put this sign up so when I am negative, I can remember. And the other sign I'm going to put over my desk—There is really nothing you must be and there is really nothing you must do. There is nothing you must have and there is nothing you must know. There is really nothing you must become. However, it helps to understand that fire burns. And when it rains, the earth becomes wet."

I laugh at him and sip my tea. "Roberto, I have a question for you. What does salt have to do with calcium absorption? I'm worried because I had a bone density test and it showed that my hips are a little thin. Harihara told me that this is normal. As you get older your bones thin and they get brittle. And he told me only to use a little bit of salt."

"Well, I made a big mistake once when I was not following my diet correctly. I was in prison and I was eating way too much salt and I got ra – qui –tis- mo. Do you have that word in English."

"Rickets?" I ask.

"Yes, I was stooped over and a doctor told me that I would break all my bones if I fell down. I was eating too much salt and my blood was sucking the calcium out of my bones. When I got home, I instantly went back on my macrobiotic diet and I completely recovered. Don't eat anymore than half a teaspoon of salt a day. Thank you my dear for this lovely printing job."

He leaves and I think to myself, Roberto is one of the most eccentric persons I have ever met. On the fringes of the well-to-do foreign Mysore health club, there are some unusual people here who are coming to recover from their hard and fast lives.

*

First thing in the morning, I stop at the email place first to write a quick note to Vivian. A very irritating email station. The man always seats me at this computer where someone is looking over my shoulder reading my words and where I have to be scooted in and out in order for other people to get through. Today, my pitta is high and I am letting people know I am irritated. As I park the bike, a little girl (or more accurately a small woman with a demon face) comes up to me in the middle of the street with her hand stuck out, pushing into me in order to force me to give her something.

I say, "Not today, excuse me."

She starts grabbing my leg and grabbing my hand.

"You let go of me and go away," I say, as I yank myself out of her grip and dash across the street. Many of these children or small people have been trained by their parents or some mafia to behave like this. I am giving money only to the deformed and old people. No one else.

Then I ride slowly over to Acharya's for my astrology chart. On the way there, I am a little frightened about listening to a forecast of my future, especially from someone I respect. When I arrive, he isn't there. Jayashree and I sit on the porch and chat about yoga.

"I was like that fifteen years ago," she says, "sitting only for five minutes but now, one hour, two hours and sometimes more. Everyone knows. Do not interrupt me in the morning between six and eight or in the evening between five and seven. I am not available. This is the time to be quiet. You will see how beautiful your life will be."

We talk about hatha yoga being the asanas. Again she talks about the big yoga centers in the U.S., and how disappointed they were in the way yoga was being taught in the U.S. as an exercise program and as a business, with too much attention to the physical asana. Acharya says later that this problem is now in India as a result of contact with the west. He says that many of these yoga practices are body oriented and egoistic. "The object of yoga is to forget your body. They are receiving the medical aspect of yoga only, making their bodies healthier, but yoga is to make the system quiet and calm and to experience an inner light. Westerners may get a feeling of lightness through breathing and enthusiasm if asana and vinyasas are properly adopted. And this may be a good commencement, with a gradual shift to real yogic style. For that we have to appreciate."

When Acharya comes home, he says, "Give me ten minutes."

I love him. An hour, a day, a week, but please not a year.

He calls me into the little cave-like room and we sit down. An army of ants is marching up the wall in a straight line and then streaming around the light fixture.

He smiles and I say, "It's just you, me and the insects."

"Save that for the title of one of your little books," he says. Then he asks me to stretch out my hand and he studies my palm, flat and sideways. He doesn't touch my hand, though. He leans over and inspects it and then tells me to move back where I normally sit. He studies his papers, beginning first by discussing my character.

"There is a humor at the root. Sometimes it shows and some-times it doesn't. From the age of six to thirteen there was a wound and out of this wound, combined with this humor, came some sharp talking. This sharp talking could be harsh at times. But since 1993 that harshness has rescinded. You also have a noble heart. But you must work at making your talking smoother and nicer. Teaching will be an important aspect of your life. You will be honored for your teaching. In your whole life, education will be the most important. In a few years, however, it will take a new direction. And all of this is by the grace of your father."

"My father?" I ask with surprise.

He looks back at the chart and says, "No, by the grace of your mother, you will have a calm ending. From 2003-2010 there will be a golden period for you. From 2010 to 2028 you will be bothered by health issues, but they will not be chronic. With human effort they can be solved. It is possible to learn how to have calm and quiet even when the body is in stress. From 2028 you will be calm, quiet, and philosophical. You will live to be very old."

"Regarding your health, colds will be an irritating part of your life due to eating many mucous foods. Even pomegranates are mucous forming. Eat them with a little ginger powder. And due to digestive weakness, spicy foods stay too long in some section of your stomach . . . do not eat them too often. There is some problem with the anus, and later, I will teach you a mudra to help. Your feet will have pain because of vata. And you will have teeth decay so take care of your teeth. You will not be troubled by this backache, sciatica again, as long as there is no forceful twisting and turning. While you are not strong, you'll have moderately good health and no chronic illnesses. Regarding money, some money is coming from your mother."

I am confused by this. "There is no possibility of money coming from my mother. There is no money and no direct family lines left in that direction."

"Somehow in a few years," he says, "your income will raise."

"Relatives . . . there is a gap between brothers and sisters as there is in most families and it will last your whole life because of different tendencies. Children ... there is a good love connection for life with your children. Both of them will be ok in the future. He mentions Jessie's losing confidence as being a temporary thing that plagues my family from way back. And Josh is involved in proving himself with his peers but that, too, will be resolved.

"In a few years, all the fickleness you have will be much less.

"With your job," he warns me , "there is a little spirit plaguing you from somewhere and every three years or so someone at your work place will say painful things about you, bad things that are not founded on truth. You must not suffer too much. In each case, your character will survive and your reputation will be very good. Perhaps in a previous birth you did things without understanding their outcome."

Regarding my activities, he thinks I should use my creative energies with serious moral intention. This work will blossom in just a few years. He encourages me to work on larger works instead of the little sketches. But these are fine, too. Also he thinks I should use music regularly. Singing would be good for me.

I tell him that I sing kirtan regularly with someone in New York and I just quit with Shivanand because the trip there is too crazy. He says, "Perhaps Jayashree will teach you to sing." In five years, I will be living in a house that I own, tiny, in a small city in a quiet area. And I will enjoy it. I will have many noble friends.

My chart is ascending in that direction.

Regarding my past lives. There is some desert-like place with a dry wind where I was involved in music and education. There were some small mischiefs. As a child I was very naughty to my mother and disturbed her very much and that is why in this life I have not enjoyed "mother." Also a husband was disturbing to others' welfare and even though I could have stopped him, I did not. So therefore I have had problems in the family and in the husband area. I was rich, involved in music and dance and well known to the public. It is some place straight downward from Detroit. Dry winds and a garden. "Maybe Mexico," he says.

I ask him if I will have another husband, and he says, "No. And within a few years you will come to accept that and you will be calm, quiet and happy with many friends. Don't be crazy with men," he tells me.

I have to smile now. I gave him the words once when I told him I used to be crazy about men, and he gives the words right back to me.

He tells me to stay with my job. "It is a good job, stay there for life and you will excel in it and be known as a very good teacher." He tells me I will come to India many times. Then in terms of the concrete, he warns me to avoid wearing black, it brings too melancholic a mood. The colors I should wear are green, then blue, then white (or very light colors). I should wear a pearl in order to keep my mind calm. It will naturally calm me. And I should sleep with my head pointing east. And above all. Be simple. Don't think about a next birth. You have the possibility of being realized. Your chart is ascending. At some point he asks me not to discuss this reading with others. If I do mention it, though, I am not to be stressed about it, but it really should not be discussed.

That was a beautiful experience even though we were interrupted twice because two other students came to talk to him. I left his house, and now the group will meet here in my apartment in an hour to talk about the Gita. If this is indeed my future, it's not so bad. I can't help thinking about how drawn I am to people from Mexico, my friend Isabella last year, a dancer and sculptress, Jose whom I lived with for a year in Detroit when I was young, and many other friends. I traveled through Mexico in 1970. Even though my grandmother spoke French and I was encouraged to learn French, I studied Spanish in school. I wonder if there is any connection between my past life and my attraction to Latino culture.

When I ride off to pick up items in the city, first I go to the gem place to see if they have any pearls. Upstairs, an old man shows me a string of fake pearls. Then he shows me a pearl ring. I ask him if it is a real pearl.

"They say it is—from Japan and China, but who knows."

"Well, I can't buy anything under those circumstances. I'll have to wait until I get home."

I stop at the store on the circle to pick up a pair of pants I had ordered and they look awful, like black snow pants. I throw them into my bag and walk around the corner to another store, fuming a bit over these pants. They cost so much money.

The clerk in the other store asks me if I am angry. "Not at you," I snap.

I ask how much the fabric is and it is one half the cost of the fabric used for these *black* pants. I am showing my negative emotions in India. People laugh at you for showing your anger here. We are unused to bargaining and being tricked for every item we purchase. And we are considered ridiculous when we lose control of our emotions. Yoga. Repeat Namashivaya one thousand times.

I stop in the market to pick up a chapatti pan because Carl has insisted I will need it when I'm home, and then as I'm biking home, it starts raining. I pull over and stand under an awning until the rain stops. I stand there staring at the water and the trees across the street. A man is there, too. He doesn't make eye contact. I decide to go to Pradeep—he said to come today—even though I know he takes a whole day to finish things. He is sewing the skirt and I think it looks lovely.

"You were here yesterday when it was raining. And now you are here again and it is raining," he says.

"Yes, yesterday you took an extra day and now today too," I say. "I will see you tomorrow. Good bye."

Off in the rain with this new scooter that is lighter but more difficult to start. I stop at a fruit stand and buy a pomegranate, three oranges and a little papaya. Breakfast.

Home I am home.

*

It is the dark of night. I have just made three chapattis and vegetables. It was very good.

As for our discussion of the Gita—first Jayashree arrives and then Carl and then Acharya. Acharya and Jayashree sing the verses to be discussed. The 6th shloka of the 6th chapter: "The mind must be under control. It is like a horse and chariot that go where you want them to go. Or the mind will go on its own and that will be only a tragedy for you. The purpose of yoga is to use certain techniques to help control the mind. If the mind is out of control, it means the techniques are not working. There is something wrong with these particular techniques.

"The 7th shloka. The senses are dragging the mind down so you must conquer the five senses. To a yogi, the mind is also a sense. When one experiences joy from inside naturally, the unnatural desire will fade away. Why? Because unnatural desires are only potent because they end in pleasure. If one experiences such great joy from the inside, these others will be naturally eliminated. One is calm and quiet, but still burning with joy." He uses a metaphor of a stove, with the flames representing desire, and the burning coals the other joy.

He then talks about realizing God and I ask him, very hesitantly, "What do you mean, Acharya, when you say, *God*?"

Acharya looks at me and says, "For the yogis God is a bright light. We can't usually see it, but it is everywhere around us. It especially becomes visible and one with us when we are meditating. This white light is the god of the yogis."

I can accept that definition.

"Those who conquer the five senses are not disturbed by honor or dishonor or by cold or heat. The common man is very disturbed by these. The man who has control will not suffer any psychological affects. . . some objective effects, but they will be minimal. If he also has control over the correct chakra center, he cannot even be burned."

Then there is a long conversation about some miraculous things yogis can do as a result of this kind of control. And yet yogis don't want to display these powers and bring public attention to themselves. He talks about Sankaracharya's non dual philosophy. "His mother's body needed to be burned but there was no one available, so he brought fire from his nostrils. Man has many natural capacities to control senses and mind, but our fickleness keeps us away from this higher capacity." He also gives an example of a yogi who feels anger and minutes later calms down. "He is being used as a tool for an action."

During this discussion, the vedic astrology reading was in my mind. I am so tired right now and I want to read a little of the Gita before I go to sleep. Especially in my mind is this suggestion that I create art with a high moral purpose. I'm not sure what he means by high moral purpose. I am wondering if these notes and drawings can become material for a new series. I am very interested in the Mexican story. Could I draw from memories of a previous birth? I'm going to visit Isabella in Mexico in December. Perhaps something new will start there. Thinking about telling a story from a past life, some cold dry wind runs through my mind.

I'm lying here reading the Gita. I put it down and lift my legs in the air. What a journey I am on, I think, and Lenny you are the one who dragged me right out of my suffering life on to this path. With your illness and death, I set my other life aside to care for you and I began to practice yoga. Thank you, dear.

A turning point occurred when I was sitting on the D train on my way to Brooklyn, overwhelmed and missing my life with David—hanging out in cafes with him, going out to jazz clubs and intellectual lectures, dancing and fighting with him. Instead for six months I had been running back and forth between my classes at school, my house, Lenny's music store where I was working as much as I could to bring in money for him, and then to his apartment where I was taking care of him, trying to get him social security and health care. In that moment, I felt sorry for myself. "When will I get my life back again?" And then I heard an inner voice, "This *is* your life, Gina." I never again regretted what I had given up. Instead, I felt a rush of gratitude.

very time I have an article of clothing made, it seems to take about five trips, including buying the fabric and going back and forth, visiting the tailor, enduring the Indian crowds and streets. In fact, I'm not sure that there actually is any saving involved after all the hassle. Down to typewriter row, not open, over to KR Circle. Sit and wait for the tailor who never shows up.

I was going to eat at home, but after Subrata pleaded with me to lend her 1000 rupees because she needed it for her daughter's schooling, I have decided to eat breakfast there. I'll surely use up 1,000 rupees eating there before I leave.

I try to come home at 11:00 to do my practice before the discussion, but it is a little too late and it seems better to drink some batam milk and read Ramakrishna. Carl rings the bell. We sit for ten minutes and then Jayashree and Acharya are pounding on the door. I ring the bell. It works. I didn't know then that the electricity had been going on and off all day due to the heavy rains, which according to the newspaper, are due to the monsoon over the Bay of Bengal.

Jayashree sings but only a little. Acharya kind of mutters along with her. Jayashree is very quiet for some reason. I wonder if they ever have arguments.

"Here in the 8th stanza, Krishna talks about two types of yogis, one who is struggling to achieve, the practitioner, and the one who has achieved his gold, yukta. For him gold and mud are equal. He loses extra interest in the tools that helped him achieve his goal." Acharya talks about a yogi who uses a deer skin to practice on and that deer skin becomes very much a part of his practice. After he has become realized, though, it means nothing to him. The realized being also sees eternal truth everywhere—so his or her mentality to materials changes." (The "his or her" is mine. Acharya follows British English. For him, the pronoun "he" is indefinite.)

"The 9th shloka. A realized man sees everyone as equal, even relatives and close others."

I say, "Yes, I understand but it's hard to imagine."

Jayashree smiles.

"Each is responsible for their own uplift," he explains. "You do the duty with a different mentality when you realize that not only did this child come into this body through you, but they have their own karma, their own rebirths."

I ask a question about love.

"You love all beings," he says, "but some you love from a distance, like cobras."

We laugh. "There are differences in love. That is appropriate. This helps to keep a balance in society. Even with realized beings, this is true. We must maintain a balance in the universe. These are all inevitable sides of love."

I talk about Ramakrishna's great love for his disciples.

"He is different, though, because he is a spiritual tool, a realized person. It is the difference between a regular piece of iron and a magnetized piece of iron." He discusses the differences between attachments, natural and unnatural. "Unnatural attachments cause disturbances. A realized person eliminates all of these."

"10th Stanza. Practitioners should stay isolated. Maintain your loneliness. Human beings have an influence on your practice so that you can't focus well on it. So be alone. Live in your home, make only as many contacts as needed, don't use energy to develop more friendships. It's very healthful to be less influenced by others. You want to be able to remember calm and quiet. With the influence of others, this is difficult. Minimize contacts. Practice always in an isolated place rather than in busy quarters. Others should not look at you. Their looks influence and disturb. Thoughts are also caused by what you see, and even what someone else thinks creates disturbances. Practice in a studio is inevitable for a short period, but not always. The team spirit, yes, perhaps it is good for physical exercise. It is mechanical though and not for serious yoga practice."

Another suggestion he makes is to loosen your desires. "Obey this and have less possessions. Don't receive any material from anyone else that is not required. Why collect things? Give away what is not needed or you acquire lots of work . . . Possess as little as possible. Even if a relative offers you unnecessary money, do not accept it. Material objects have an influence on you."

I talk about my books.

"Not in use, give away," he says.

I tell him about Thoreau and he doesn't know about him.

"Yes, the Gita has been read by many world wide, but not always correctly."

Well, the be-simple idea has been with me ever since childhood. Protestant teachings are about simplicity and my mother's teachings were about simplicity and avoiding the traps of greed and accumulation. When I read *Walden* in high school, I was greatly influenced by Thoreau. I remember giving away all my old clothes and childhood toys. A year or so after I graduated from high school, I encountered hippie culture, wearing old clothes and resisting consumerism. Perhaps it was Thoreauvian yoga speaking through my mouth during my years with Lenny when I would try to persuade him to organize his life and give things away. He never wanted to part with anything. Our basement was full of old bottles, clothes, boxes. He was an old, loving beatnik, attached to material objects, friends and good bargains in the flea markets. This was part of our conflict. I wanted a clean, empty room. He wanted clutter.

Maybe this is why I was so drawn to yoga. Today however as a contradiction, I find myself running around acquiring the things of India. For the most part, I think, they are practical things. I am not accumulating fancy ornaments. Instead I am trying to purchase things so that I can take advantage of the savings, and if I want to wear mostly natural fibers from now on, it will cost me a lot of money in the states. Is this yoga simplicity or Protestant guilt speaking? Over and over, I must apologize for spending a dime. Like that. When I get home, though, I want to give away whatever I don't need to someone who can use them. An empty house so there are few disturbances.

I just had a very interesting lunch with Matthew, talking about yoga, sex, teacher training, materialism and the destruction of beauty through money. He even suggests that his teacher may have been tainted by the same thing, love of money. I am surprised because Matthew won't usually say anything critical about Ramaji.

After everyone leaves the house, I go back to pick up my clothes from the tailors. I refuse to try them on and just take them. I had ordered a skirt with side slits from Pradeep and instead he made big bulky unwearable pants with side slits. The pants the other man made for me cost a small fortune and they have a big bulge in the front as if I have a big penis. I am washing them over and over to see what happens and then I may leave them both here.

When I am walking around in the shopping area, a little boy selling incense starts following me, and eventually I give him a few rupees for helping me find something. Suddenly two other boys appear. They surround me, push me and talk in their language in a tone that is a little frightening. When they see middle class Indians shopping, they don't stop them, but if they see a foreigner, they follow with a persistence that is often hard to resist. Even as I get on the motorcycle they are asking me for this and that, surrounding me and yelling at me.

I leave quickly and decide I'll have more peace of mind if I finish all tasks connected to my departure as soon as possible. I zoom around the corner and park in a new spot and head up toward Gandhi Square. A girl with a monkey starts following me, refusing to listen when I say no. I duck into a luggage store and the man tells her to leave. I buy a cheap bag for Josh's stuff. Then I duck into the market (trying to avoid that group of boys again) and buy some vegetables for dinner.

Behind some horrible traffic and smoke (I am coughing), I finally make it back to my house. I park the bike in the driveway, go upstairs and spend the rest of the evening at home, breathing, meditating, cooking, eating dinner, reading Rama Krishna and sleeping. Oh mama. I move the bed so my head will face East, and then I have so many terrible dreams. Is it because I ate ground nuts at Subrata's? Is it because I am facing the wrong direction? The dreams are about my ex-boyfriend, David, whom I am trying to forget. In the dream, I keep telling him to get away from me. Leave me alone. He is with another woman, who is monstrous looking, and he is lying to her and hurting her. It is a disturbing dream. But I am telling him to leave in the dream. I am not unhappy about it. I just want to be away from him. So leave my dreams alone, David. Now I am finished with you.

That was yesterday. Today it is windy and rainy on and off and I keep taking the laundry in and out of the house until it is dry. Right now, I'm going to put the mat outside again.

In my meditation, I am back to five minutes and thought after thought after thought. I keep wondering if perhaps I was doing a better job in the hotel because I could hear myself breathing there and here the sounds of my breathing are lost in the roar of traffic. Maybe I should move into the bedroom. I am going to experiment with that tonight. After I wake up, bathe and practice, I go over to Subrata's, send a few emails, one to Peter, telling him to email Acharya, another to Josh. Then I eat some flat rice with ginger tea. At home, I sit on the floor and draw a sketch of the empty living room with the leaves of the coconut tree in the frame of the window. Then I start recording yesterday's details.

When Carl arrives, he tells me that the cracking in my knee is called meniscus cartilage—a little piece of gravel has probably broken off in the knee. They use orthoscopic surgery to remove it and then it will be fine. Before Jayashree arrives, I ask Acharya what my natal constitution is.

"Vata and Pitta—in almost equal amounts."

That sounds correct. All the time as he has been referring to my Vata constitution, however, I have been hearing him say my "WATER" constitution since they pronounce the "v" almost as we pronounce "w". And water is a kapha predominant element.

Let me finish Acharya's lecture before I forget anything. "You should find a precious sacred place for meditation. There are devices to best decide. But if they are unavailable, use feeling and the heart. It is bad to ever be near a burial ground. For some that is appropriate, for example for witchcraft, but for a goal of realization, move far way. Never meditate in a ruined house or in a house that has been kept vacant for a long time. Spirits and ghosts, old wandering human beings inhabit them and will trouble you. Even a few months with no inhabitant is bad. Houses are meant for people or cows. In the big cities, this problem may not be as relevant because the spirits won't go there—too much sound, light and energy. They'll leave immediately. There are certain trees that are bad and attract ghosts and bad spirits. Don't use a spot where wicked persons lived before. Use your mind to determine this—ask others—use common sense. In the earth there are certain unsuitable areas. You will need guidance for this. In ancient times they would keep the area sacred by brushing it and washing it with cow dung—the floor would be of mud. In very ancient times yogis used the cow's shelter for meditation. Brahmins and even other people drank cow urine and dung with ghee and sugar.

"What is sacred is different here than in the U.S. You must get help to be calm and quiet. There are certain materials that are important and can help your meditation. In Nepal, there is a sacred stone. Beautiful jasmine flowers create a sacred smell—picked from creepers and put in the place. Holy basil also helps. Use the leaves. Then there is a drawing made by white stones which gives an experience of the yogi inside the site of meditation. Never give your yoga seat to someone else, ever. Use only a stable platform or the ground. Nothing should be more than a few inches off the ground. Now asanas are more or less exercises. It was not always like that. Now they can be done almost anywhere. The Indians have a type of grass which grows to be about two feet; it has two sharp edges and it grows bush like—called Kusha or Darbha. Normally the yoga mat is made out of this grass. Then there is a white cloth and a deer skin. This is especially good if it is a brown deer with natural black spots. On this they sit and meditate. It is very sacred.

"To start, minimize all activities or they will disturb your mind. Stop all activity and unnatural desires. Stop eating delicious foods, merry making and unnecessary intellectual work. Sit in one posture and you will get a pure mind. This will happen gradually. It is possible for those who have duties to do this too, but they must learn to balance their duties with yoga. More rules and regulations are required. There is a particular time meant for this every day. You must have discipline at all times. The purpose is to purify the mind. All thoughts therefore must be eliminated at this hour so you can enjoy the experience with no obstacles.

"You must have a stable platform. Choose a comfortable position with no pain. By intention, stop all actions, no movement, even a little. The whole back bone must be kept very straight, vertical. There is a little curve at the base of the spine. Match this curve with the head, a very slight curve. Concentrate on the tip of the nose or the ego center between your eyes. It is recommended to focus on the tip of the nose at first. With the eyes closed, it is simpler. Even with the eyes open, the white light comes."

Carl asks about his spine curving down when he is tired from some pain in the back. "If your back starts hurting, lie down in savasana for 10 to 15 minutes, then come back to padmasana."

"Be calm and quiet prior to starting. Keep the mind calm and quiet with no anxiety, no fear complex. Be in a protected area. Don't be worried about how long you might forget your body and problems this might cause. Have a support person come to get you. Unwanted desires are obstacles. Have no interest in sex at that time. Have no one around you of the opposite sex. In ancient time when young boys were being initiated at 9-10-11-12, there was to be no contact with females. No sex urge arrives for at least ten to 15 years. If desire then, householder life is possible, get married, and then have sex only at suitable times. Be sure you practice in separate rooms so there is no distraction."

The doorbell rings. I run downstairs. It is a man trying to sell me mineral water. I have to tell him no two times. Then I come back and Acharya says, "The last one for today is the 16th Stanza. Contemplate on the divine. Do you have any questions?" He looks at me quizzically.

"No, no questions, just disrupted by the mineral water man."

*

It's about 8:30 in the evening. I believe it is July 12th, Thursday night. I am sitting in half lotus on the floor in the living room in the dark with no electricity. Neither of the candles is any good, but I do have a flashlight if I can find it. I crawl around the living room. Here it is under my jacket on the mat in the corner. I am about to sneeze. There is water boiling in the kitchen. Sneeze over.

I am going to get up, take down my map and find out the exact name of the double road this house is on. And the other cross road that takes one everywhere in Mysore. Vanivlas is the street with this house. Jhansi Lakshmi Bai Road is the road I take to go out to J. Prakash. If I'm going to scoot around, I need to become a local.

Check the water pump in the kitchen. Five more minutes. Lots of bugs today. Need to pick up some paper tomorrow since I am running out of notebook space. I am bothered by the astrology reading and the fact that Acharya says I am not going to have another husband. Should I accept this and just go forward? I am troubled a bit because I like physical affection from a man, more than the sex, physical affection. But sex is nice, too. Well I'm going to put this aside and read Ramakrishna, a great love-mad yogi who continually emphasizes the need for celibacy.

Today is Friday. I had a very difficult time sleeping last night and it had everything to do with what I was eating. I tried to draw in the middle of the night, but I couldn't sit still. I must go back to having more curd, no milk, no onions or chilies, and no banana chips or sudden impulse foods that inflame my system. I will take the gooey herbal mix that Acharya gave me. Vata energy is pounding a bit. I can feel my pulse in my fingers.

Five minutes to pour my mind into this machine before I do my practice. Getting ready to go home—in the last few days lots of thoughts have been appearing about my teaching and relations at school, and Acharya's prediction that every three years I will be falsely accused of something and then vindicated. Whew! I have had a series of incidents at the university that fit this description. I hope it is not this year. If I apply for a promotion, I'm worried something will occur. But when it does, I'm going to blink and do my practice. I also keep thinking about this house where I'm going to be living

three years from now. That seems impossible. I like living in my little apartment. And again the thought about companionship. Not to
have. It makes me sad and I want to resist the prediction.

And then the mundane thoughts about what things I should take
home with me from India—the kitchen things, a few skirts, and
some more nightshirts. That's all. Although maybe others will
appear because I am allowing myself to be so complicated and
worldly by shopping so much. When I arrive home, I want to change
my daily way of living, the living room empty of furniture with only
the futon and one cabinet with everything else in it and the desk on
the floor. I think this is impossible though because of Peggy's hair
and the dirt she tracks in. Why not? The computer can go into the
cabinet. Everything in the cabinet. And I'll give away many books.

At breakfast, Subrata's servant follows me around smiling as if
she is an off balance person. Or maybe she thinks if she smiles at me,
I will open up like a slot machine and pour wealth on her.

*

All afternoon I've been thinking about past lives, about this
other body I inhabited, this Mexican woman, a rich and successful
singer and dancer with a husband who did awful things to somebody and she just closed her eyes to it. And she was cruel to her
mother. Such a strange thing—this sense of having lived other lives
and the consequences from one to the next. I'm not sure if I believe
it, but just entertaining the belief gives me a shiver, and it changes
the way the moment registers.

I'm also thinking of a movement from the melancholy to the
quiet and calm, real light on life. Could I remember this life and
draw from these memories? Work on a moral issue, says Acharya.
The woman would be someone very much like me, differences, yes,
but then to be truthful and meaningful, sticking with what I know.
A young girl and her mother in a bedroom. The sun streaming
through the windows. Humor. Life is beginning again. By the grace
of her mother, gifts. The gift of the father, confusion. The birth of
harshness. This situation without a mother's love, the family in a

state of ruination. Not a good place for yoga. The normal prediction of the future. Sexuality. Music. Great Balls of Fire. The speed of fix that and fix that. Karma—doomed with men . . .

Maybe as an old woman in my past life, I talked to Krishna and he explained that, yes, I would be reborn in a cold climate in a working class family with many troubles. Curious thoughts. I must undo the furniture world of my apartment when I get home and buy straw rugs like these. Make everything simple. Type. Type. Type. Take the Hindu god, Krishna, perhaps he was a night shift orderly in the hospital where I died. No, in Mexico he would be the Christ figure, the same one who appeared before my mother in this life when she fell out of her hospital bed. Perhaps I died in a bed in a house in the Mexican desert. My children took turns staying with me. Can I remember their faces if I concentrate? The grand children, too. Perhaps I was walking in the garden when I had a heart attack. Perhaps, I was holding a rosary, chanting, Hail Mary, mother of god. He comes and I am one with the flowers. He leaves and I am alone. Maybe in the future, I will improve the strength of my meditation so that I can visualize people in my past lives and draw their images.

*

Tomorrow I must be sure to ask Bhavini if she found a ring the other day when she was sweeping since the ring I bought last year has disappeared and I think I remember a clinking sound as she swept the floor. On the train to Bombay, I was wearing my silver rings, one on each little finger and three others. The men across from me were looking at my hands and talking in their language. One of them asked me if there is any significance to the rings other than decorative. I explained that each one is meaningful. One was a gift and another was purchased in India. He looked at the man next to him and said, "In the west, jewelry is decorative." Apparently, most Indians wear jewelry for astrological or religious reasons or to signify their marital status.

*

Carl arrives first and then Jayashree. Acharya is late.

When he arrives, he begins immediately. "Any questions?"

"Yes," I say, "you finished with fourteen, contemplate on the divine, but . . .

"But what?" he asks, smiling and cocking his head.

"But, how? If you can't contemplate, what difference does the divine make?"

"You want to stop your thoughts through contemplating on the divine and if you stop your thoughts, the divine will be there. So just stopping your thoughts as you are doing in your meditation is a technique. A realized person is completely there. Someone might use pictures of the deities. They are soothing. Originally they were visualizations by sages of their meditative states. They provided the images as aids to others. Someone could meditate on a good dream or memorize the calm and quiet after a good sleep and meditate on that."

I ask about mantras.

"The problem with mantras is that they have to be repeated exactly, with the proper tone and pitch, and that is very unusual. It is a rare technique and not given often to students. A few Brahmins might meditate with mantras. Pitch variations must be exact. Just as a friend who is used to being called might come with a certain pitch and tone, he might not recognize variations. It can bring harm."

What harm? I wonder now.

"Yoga practitioners must give up all undesirable activities and concentrate on Self. Joy is there and it will increase.

"An incarnation is someone who has no disturbance in the body and so he can express eternal truths continually. The first discipline is to be sure to consume appropriate food and not more than is required or gradually you will become weak. Normally most people consume food for relaxation. Children normally will eat just what they need, but their parents push more food on the child. The second discipline is that you must enjoy loneliness and isolation. Constant movement for many is a disturbance, so minimize contacts, only those that are essential. Don't spend time developing contacts. With isolation, there is concentration. Contacts are all right for those who are less materialistic, since they have less engagement in activities. They are calm and quiet. Even if they do not practice yoga, these are people who naturally contemplate.

"The third Discipline: do not sleep more than is needed or you will achieve nothing. Six to eight hours depending on season. Overeating and overstraining affect sleep. Less sleep is required in summer. More in winter. Automatically. Also it is very bad to sleep less than is needed. For the common man, night is meant for sleep. Daytime hours are meant for work."

He then explains how a tamasic quality of mind leads to fat and how that person needs to exercise more and the body will heal the mind. I asked if depression is tamasic.

"No ragasic, and depression is more likely in vata minds because of activity, rather then no activity. If you eat too much, though, your mind gets dull."

At that moment, my downstairs neighbor starts pumping out a tune on his saxophone.

"Beautiful," I say.

"Yes," says Acharya, "beautiful, but melancholic and not good to listen to very much for a yogic life." He is referring to the instrument itself.

I try to talk about blues and jazz being music of longing that are in fact uplifting in their changes and overall affect. He isn't impressed with my argument.

＊

It is evening and I have just eaten chapattis, cucumbers and a mango lassi with oranges and bananas. It feels sufficient, but I keep longing for all the raw foods I normally eat. I must admit though that I am sleeping much better here and coughing less than I do at home. I'm going to study Gabriel Cousens book on raw and ayurveda when I'm home. When I tell Acharya that I want to eat only raw foods and no milk, he tells me to be sure the food is sattvic. This is most important.

Spent a lot of time today reading Ramakrishna and really taking a step back . . . his continual emphasis on the dangers of contact with women is somewhat disturbing. If she is your mother, do anything for her, even take an office job, but for your wife and children—absolutely not. Wife, children and family demands are the world stealing you away from god. Woman is the embodiment of these demands, of maya, he says, while men are part of spirit. . . "I may not be deluded by thy world bewitching maya." Anyhow here his emphasis is beyond my understanding of lust as a synonym for woman. I want to talk about this with Acharya.

Beautiful thank you letter today from Swami Bramadeo. It makes me think that I should visit there but not this time, next time. Time has passed and there are only a few weeks left. I am not going to continually count the days.

Acharya was unavailable today.

I park the motor bike on the gravel and garbage space in front of the house. I notice the three young American men from downstairs playing kickball in the yard. The evening sun is so bright in the west, illuminating a herd of sheep with a shepherd driving them across the street. The light is shimmering in between their legs. How strange and completely ordinary, a shepherd leading his sheep from this patch of grass to that patch of grass in a city with mostly tar and red dirt.

*

The little boy, or I should say young man with the round eyes and the big sell—who then turns into a monster hanging on me and begging me to buy incense—approached me today and I quickly sent him away. I looked at him and said very firmly, "No," as I pushed my right hand down and across my body. He turned and walked away. There is something final about the particular movement of my hand from left to right. Perhaps it is an imitation of a slap.

Shivanand says my voice has opened up a little. By the time you leave, you will still be low, but you will be open. Aishwani brings me hot milk instead of tea. Shivanand asks me for 100 rupees because he is going to Bangalore.

I am very sleepy, but I don't want to go to sleep until at least 10:30 p.m. because I am sleeping too much. I want to set the alarm clock, wake up at 5:30 and practice at 6:30. So I'm going to sit up and read for a while.

*

As I look over his notes on my constitution after meeting with Dr. Anand, I'm a little perturbed. I think I misrepresented myself to him in terms of my early physical activity. He thinks I'm a kapha-vata. I'm going to call tomorrow and ask if I can stop by in the evening and ask him a few questions about this report. He believes that the way I can bring my vata down is to bring my pitta up and that way I will be balanced. Ghee he claims is antivata, nourishing, and will not cause much phlegm at all. Curd will cause more phlegm. If I improve my heat, using the spices of ginger, cumin, moderate pepper, coriander and turmeric that will help.

He suggests that when I get home I buy 50 grams of turmeric and add two teaspoons of ghee and fry it. Preserve it in a bottle. Take one half tsp every day with hot water before eating. This will stimulate my pitta and he believes it will really help me with the allergies. He also suggests a ginger based tonic that he is going to prepare for me for Wednesday. Chew it once a day with hot water right when I get up in the morning before I do my practice. He says that raw foods are fine. Just sprinkle a little pepper on fruit or salad and that will act as an anti-vata. Perhaps I won't call him. I'll ask a few questions on Wednesday and then I'll try the tonic and see how it affects me. I feel quite balanced right now.

I come home, clean up and read a little on the porch. Then Carl, Acharya and Jayashree arrive for our discussion. Acharya asks for questions.

Carl explains that he is still suffering from a sore throat and that their friend Sushant has explained that Carl was too hot. He needs to cool his body. His feet are hot and his eyes are red.

Acharya asks questions. "Are you eating a lot of coconut? Your body isn't used to that—it causes pitta in the body. Green chilies, yes, the same. And do you have a fan on your body? When the body sweats this brings pitta down." He tells him that the change in his bed is also probably responsible for it. He must cover the mat he has with cloth. Castor oil also brings heat down. He should use sugar with curd, not salt. Salt with curd brings pitta up. "You can also bring pitta down with pineapple, bananas, pomegranate, etc. Mangos and papaya bring it up."

In the end I think—just switch what you are eating every day.

Then Acharya asks for any other questions.

"Well, I say, I have a question but I don't know if this is the right time since it is about Ramakrishna."

"Go ahead."

So I ask him about "women and gold." I mention that I usually substitute "lust and greed" and that works, but at this point in the book, it has become too much and it is interfering with my reading. "Ramakrishna tells this man that it is perfectly fine if he takes a job in an office to help his mother, but not to help his wife and children. Sannyasis can't even "smell" a woman, he says. Woman is maya. Man is spirit."

"You must realize," Acharya says, "that a teacher's lesson is different for each student. If he is talking to a student where this is a real issue, he may exaggerate and really emphasize the lesson. Sex that is only for enjoyment wastes sperm and is not wise. That person must learn to overcome sex. Take for example someone who likes to drink wine. Even though there are some positives about the wine, it is negative for the person, so the teacher will really concentrate on the negatives. Secondly (and he repeats this over and over in many different ways) one must remember that Ramakrishna was surrounded by the gupta caste of merchants, and because they are materialistic, there may be more craving for sex. So he is stressing these factors for them."

He tells a story about a time when Ramakrishna went to buy some betel leaves from a shopkeeper he knew very well. The shopkeeper wasn't there. Ramakrishna takes the betel leaves and turns around to walk away but his body becomes heavy and frozen until he turns around, goes back, returns the leaves and confesses.

"Now, many other people could walk away and tell their friend later or the next day and not be damaged spiritually at all. But because it was so important to Ramakrishna, he makes it important in his teachings for everyone. For example, I am a hard worker and I automatically transmit my enthusiasm to others."

"So perhaps," I say, "Ramakrishna warned his disciples about the dangers of maya and women and intensely worshiped women as the living embodiments of the divine maternal mystery because this was in part a strength and also a need in his own personality."

Perhaps.

Ok, we only have fifteen minutes left. I apologize for asking the question.

"No," he says, "this question is relevant. It is all in the Gita. It is for the students to ask questions. If you hold a question for a while, that is even better."

Then Jayashree sings with him and he talks about the 17th Shloka.

"Yoga will only work for those who restrict their diet, merry-making, action, sleep and waking. In terms of diet, you must pay most attention to your intention and your constitution."

I'm not sure what intention means now.

He tells a story about a man studying with Krishnamacharya and how he was mad for a little while because he was studying pranayama in a very serious way to quiet his mind. At the same time he was eating garlic and onion, which agitated his mind. It is important to eat suitable food in terms of quantity and quality. And improve the sattvic energy for meditation. "In terms of merrymaking—look at the way you play. How does it relax your mind—if you dance and drink, this will disturb your whole practice. If you go somewhere with a cold wind, it is very vata and more thought will occur . . . Which play relaxes? Which provokes? Which habits are bad? For example leaning as Gina is right now on one side so that her chest does not open. Slowly it will close. Stay balanced."

I ask a question about sleeping on the left or right side or on the back.

"Mostly on the left side but then you can move," he says. "Now it is time to go."

Carl tells me that it is an auspicious day. There is an eclipse at 5:30. It is a very good time to practice. We will meet at 5:30 on Tuesday here at my house. And I will go to Acharya's house at 12:00 noon for my entire practice.

Acharya looks at me. "I had some things I wanted to teach you. I came by yesterday at 9:30 and today at 10:00 am. Sometimes there is a time when things can be taught."

"I wish I had been here," I say, "I wish I had a telephone."

I walk them down the stairs and say goodbye. Back upstairs while practicing, I have a huge coughing fit for five minutes before the eclipse, and then ten minutes of meditation. My pitta is so inflamed today that I feel as if I am burning under the shadow of the eclipse. Soon after that, I ride my bike all over Mysore, stopping at Suhas's fruit stand, and then coming home and typing away on this machine.

Today is Monday. It is already evening. Each day is passing quickly and I am speeding it along by being materialistic. Today I did not see Acharya and I skipped my 12:00 meditation again.

*

At Subrata's, Carl is leaving just as I am arriving. Standing near our scooters, we begin to talk about his experience here with Acharya. Then rain starts falling a little so he decides to come in and eat lunch with me until it stops. Matthew is there and Vanessa comes in shortly thereafter. Matthew asks me if I can pick up the Ramkrishna books for him when I'm at the ashram again. I wasn't planning to, but I will because he wants them and he is reluctant to travel in Indian traffic, even in a rickshaw.

While we are eating Carl notices that there are onions in the potato curry. We are not supposed to eat onions because they increase vata. But more than that, Carl says, the results of eating them takes months to go away. Garlic and onions are to be avoided by yogis from way back. Well maybe that accounts for all my sleepless nights and lots of my overactive thinking. I'll have to experiment with this sometime in the future. We both skip the curry.

I talk a bit about how I think affection and sex can be natural desires if they don't disturb your mind. How I want to talk to Acharya about this. Matthew again asks me if I'll ask Acharya about sex after menopause. I'm not going to ask the question though because it will sound like something I need to consider and I'm avoiding that.

Carl tells us that he would say that our lives are very different in the west. Brahmins have very low sex drives. And Carl tells us that Acharya says a husband should be intimate with his wife if she wants it. It is his duty and if his refusal were to disturb their relationship, that would be worse.

"You're married," I say, "I wonder what he would say to me, an unmarried woman." What I want to say is that I have been somewhat sad about the astrology reading and I would be much happier with some companionship in my life. I don't want to believe the astrology reading, but now that I've listened to it, it may have an affect on the choices I make. I keep wondering if perhaps Acharya thinks I shouldn't remarry and so he is telling me he doesn't see a marriage in my future. Or maybe one of my noble friends will be a man whom I don't marry but have an intimate relationship with.

Vanessa asks Carl what books Harihara would recommend, and he goes through the list: Brunton, Yogananda, Ramakrishna, Ramana Maharshi, Krishna Chaitanya. One in particular by Brunton is good, he says, *Discover Yourself.*

Vanessa finishes eating (she eats her potatoes and onions) and she tells me that Whitney is really ill again. I predict that Whitney will go home with Mary on Thursday and that Vanessa will go home on July 27th. She is surprised but listens to me as if I know what I'm talking about. Maybe I'm developing forecasting skills.

Carl also talks about the effect of beer and marijuana on one's meditation practice. "Alcohol relaxes the mind but brings up images. Marijuana relaxes the mind but brings up ideas. And these mind events are long lasting. When one meditates, one is trying to relax the mind and in that relaxation, there is a kind of discrimination that is screwed up after marijuana and alcohol, even just a little." I think this is Acharya via Carl. He also talks to me about how the Ramakrishnas highly respect Acharya. Carl looks at us over his glasses and says, "There is no doubt in my mind that Acharya is a realized being."

After lunch, I come home and read a little more of Ramakrishna. Then I ride over to typewriter row to pick up my nightgowns from Pradeep. . . they are locked up inside. So I park and walk over to Lakshmi silk. I buy a sari to make the copy of the skirt I brought with me. It is beautiful material, on sale. But I feel a little out of control, shopping like this, and I cannot tolerate store clerks in India. They are very aggressive and they never let you have a minute to decide what you want. "Take this madam, this, this, this." I almost expect them to surround me and attack with their scissors. I am beginning to be a little rude, insisting that they not show me anything. Just let me browse. I know it's like I'm a millionaire who is going to make a good day for them. Then I go to Pradeep again, pull out one of the nightgowns. They look terrible. They are so poorly made. I accept them without saying a word and coast down Sayjayi Road home. When I return to India, I will never ever get caught in this clothes-making activity again.

I prepare my dinner for cooking. Cut up carrots, put them in a pot of water, add spices in a pot for tea, mix up dough for chapattis, and then do my practice. Meditation is about 8 minutes now. It seems like a very long time, but only 8 minutes. I think the evening practice is now about 40 minutes. I feel good, but lack conversation in my daily life. And then reading and preparing for bed. Haven't heard a word from Dimitri for more than two weeks.

Maybe that is the end of that.

*

Twenty four hours later and it's night already. Two weeks from today I will leave Mysore. What was today about? I wake up and decide that even though I have food here, I am going to walk over to Subrata's for breakfast. Just as I walk in, Carl appears in his western dress. He is a messenger (in part, and in part he has his own errands to run) and he is supposed to see if I can meet at 10:15 at his house. Does that mean I will come at 12:00 to do my practice, too? It is possible. Due to Acharya's momentary testing of the environment, his state of mind and when he feels it is best for teaching, things change.

While we're eating breakfast, Mary arrives to settle her account with Jeevesh. I like her. Her body and look are similar to a dear friend Harriette. I walk home, piddle around the house washing things, bringing in clothes from the line. I've decided not to have Bhavini return because I'm pretty sure she is stealing from me, and whether she is or not, I have this feeling, and that means something to me. So if I see her before our appointment, I'll give her the 150 rupees and if not, at 9:00 on Friday I'll tell her and pay her. I don't like having servants or helpers. I feel incredibly awkward around them. That is why I prefer living in this house rather than the hotel. I've even become used to the sounds of traffic so that I imagine returning here next year.

I ride my bike over to Carl's house with my camera around my neck, prepared to take photographs. I hook up the scarf and camera to my neck and just as I begin to take off, I notice the young men across the street with their two elephants. I stop to take their photograph. When they notice me, they start moving toward me, crossing over the border in-between the streets. I am snapping photos when the elephants come stomping right up around my bike and one of the men orders one elephant to put his trunk on my head. I am so frightened that I scream. As soon as I regain my composure, I take a few more shots. Then as I am getting ready to leave, they ask for a tip. I give them ten rupees and they are happy.

*

Today when we meet, Acharya can't stop sneezing. His nose is red and it seems painful for him to concentrate. I wonder what an effect all this sneezing has on his practice. I know I can barely practice when I am overwhelmed with allergies.

*

Carl says, Get ready, I bought new furniture. He has four new little straw mats for sitting. Everyone laughs. We all sit down and then he has to take out the larger mat because we are five, including Ram, a young Indian student of Acharya, who is from the same village where Shivanand's family came from originally.

Carl begins with some questions about eating.

"Ideally, with 8 hours of work and of course depending on one's constitution, there should be two meals of 32 bites each with no breakfast. Upon waking, one should drink eight scoops (with two hands) of water. 99% of the population now eats much more than they need because they are under continual stress. If one is calm and quiet, one eats less—one doesn't need food energy. If one is happy, one needs less food. Because of materialistic tendencies, needing satisfaction and energy, most people go to food. If vata people are overactive and talkative, they need to eat much more—they can't sit still."

He looks at me and I look at him and he says, "She's laughing." I guess I need more food than I would if I were a quieter person. If one has a breakfast (both Carl and I need one, we insist), it should only be about 16-24 bites.

Carl asks whether he should consider computer work as work.

"Yes, it is mental work and therefore it is rajasic—you need to eat a little bit of spicy food to help activate the brain. If one does very heavy physical work, one needs to eat a little tamasic food for muscle development—such as black gram or ragi flour (which perhaps is similar to buckwheat flour). If you are only reading and living a very relaxed householder life, you need to eat only sattvic foods, less spicy. You can remember these things and switch on days you have a lot of physical work. Depending on the climate, this varies, for example in the Himalayas, rice is much harder to digest, so they eat more wheat.

"For the vata practitioner, yoga is difficult because the mind and body are fickle. The vata person should work very hard and then sit down and practice."

In response to my question, he talks a little bit about the description of the three types that evolve into many types and combinations. Vata joints are stiff. Kapha is 100% flexible. Pitta is active mentally, heat in the body—some flexibility. The vata-kapha has vata joints with rigid knees. Pitta-Kapha is not that flexible. Vata-pitta is not as stiff as vata. The questionnaires for ayurveda don't work any more because man is very influenced by other men. He is absolutely convinced that I am vata-pitta almost but not quite even. I mention my stability, commitment and regularity and he says all that is also possible with pitta. I think he knows that I have talked to Dr. Anand. I'm very unsure about whether I should take this mixture made up by Dr. Anand to raise my pitta given the fact that Acharya is trying to reduce it. We finish our meeting without even discussing the Gita.

Carl asks me if I want to stay to learn how to make pallek palya (spinach cooked in a certain way). We end up also cooking a roti. For a roti, first he grates a carrot, chops a little cilantro, scrapes a bunch of coconut (or all three could be other vegetables), adds two pinches of cumin, a lot of salt, a little bit of chili pepper, and 10 big Carl handfuls of rice flour.

"This will make four rotis," he says.

I think we might have made five.

"You add water and keep squishing with your fingers and adding more water until it becomes stiff like a brownie mix." On a cold pan, he puts a little sesame oil and one glop of the mixture, flattens it and adds a little water until the glop is circle like and out to the edge of the pan.

"Try to get it thin. Put five holes and add a little oil in each hole. Use a high flame at first with a lid. Leave it two minutes until it is brown and solid. Another way is to make it on a banana leaf and then throw it in the pan with the leaf on top. It will peel off. In between rotis, turn off the flame and put a little bit of oil on the pan.

"For the pallek, put a tablespoon or so of oil in an iron pot, heat with a tsp of mustard seeds, pop, turn on and off, add chilies a little bit, stir, add a small palmfull of black gram for seasoning, heat until they are brown, dump in spinach, stir fry a few times, add coconut immediately, add salt if you want . . . . . Heat till done."

Ok that is that. A lovely lunch. I leave there with some of the rotis in a container. Then I ride home in the rain. I am wet to the bone. I stop a few times and stand under trees. There are people standing under trees up and down the roads. Upstairs, I peel off my clothes and remember that I must go immediately to Shivanand's.

Work hard, I tell myself, as I head toward Hospital Circle.

Shivanand is walking around the house in his underwear. He takes my hands into his. He is definitely not a Brahmin. "Come in, come in."

We go inside and I ask him to show me which keys are which on the harmonium. I take out my little diagram. Yes, I had one incorrect. I thought PA was a black key, not a white one. He gives me some new tunes.

"Your voice is improving. You practice here. Did you have your lunch?"

"Yes," I say, "in fact I have some rotis here. Do you want them?"

He only wants to take a few.

"No take it all, I say."

"Ok, you practice," he tells me.

And I struggle, finally getting it. When trying to get the key strokes correct, I forget to sing—but it comes with time. "I'll call you tomorrow."

Then I am zooming along home, planning to stop to buy some provisions for dinner when I remember the books for Matthew. So off again, turning my head as the big dirty trucks go by spitting that dust all over my body and face. Work hard, Gina. When I see the little wooden elephant, I go to the right, stop and fill the tank up with gasoline and oil, then turn left into the ashram, down the drive into the gardens, park, and I see the young man in his lungi, hair in a tail, beautiful smile.

"Hello, hello," he says.

"Take off my shoes?"

"Yes, of course." Then I take down the volumes.

"You are buying more gifts for your friends," he says as he reshelves some books in the children's section.

I also decide to buy a little book by Vivekananda and a book about Vivekananda by Romaine Rolland.

"So you will come back, telephone first, and I want to introduce you to the Swami of the ashram. Before ten or after four."

"Yes," I say, "either I will come to you or Shivanand will bring me."

"You are studying tablas?"

"Now I am studying singing."

A big smile. Is it just this young man or am I a bit attached to this ashram?

And then I scoot on home stopping at a metal shop on the way to pick up some tongs for putting covers on pans and a few little saucers, also at a vegetable stand, a milk stand, and a provision store. I am such a spectacle. Everyone stares at me. I don't even order vegetables correctly. I don't recognize the size of a kg so I just buy five beans and two bunches of pallek and so forth.

Home, I practice my meditation and pranayama; and then I cook up a mess and come up with some tolerable, only tolerable rotis—easy but using every dish in the house. Cleaning dishes at the spigot out on the roof and then here I am typing, sitting in half lotus on the floor, continually trying to sit up straight. I've propped the machine up on two pillows and the mattress. Carl and I had a conversation today about how to keep one's back straight so to read and write for hours. Lay down when it starts to hurt.

*

Twenty four hours later, I am sitting on the mat with a big bump on my head, over my right eyebrow and to the left, under the hairline. Earlier in the evening, I decided to take the garbage across the street to the dump and spread it around for the cows. I was wearing a pair of pants I use for yoga—they are much too long—I walked across the first side of the road and climbed up on the platform in the middle. I'm not sure what happened but I am surmising now that my sandal became tangled in my pants. When I stepped off the median, I landed on the cement with my head, the palms of my hands and my knee. I was dazed and terribly frightened that I was going to be run over in the middle of all the traffic. Five or six people came over to help me. I sat up dazed on the median and a boy handed me a paper that had fallen out of the garbage I was holding.

"Where do you live?" I pointed to the house.

"She is all right," I heard someone say in English.

I stood up and continued across the street with the garbage, weaving a little. The crowd dispersed. Then I headed back without falling over, opened the door, swooning and ready to burst into tears.

Why? I think to myself. Misery. It is just one plane of existence. I don't have to let this plane disturb me. But I wanted to—it was objective pain and all the mechanisms of fear asking for the release of a bawl.

No refrigerator, no ice. I ran a towel under cold water and held it to my head. The towel smelled.

I guess I am not so good at washing clothes by hand. These towels need to be beaten on the rock outside. But now I have somewhat recovered, here in my nightgown drinking almond milk and typing about the day.

*

What are you doing? Acharya asks me.

"Shopping."

"Shopping? For what?"

"Things I can't afford in the states—like clothes out of natural fibers."

"What you can use? Yes, that's ok."

I'm relieved. "And I'm going to Shivanand's house for singing."

Good. While he is talking tonight I draw five tunnels coming from a center and then I surround them with a big circle.

"With your senses you only experience knowledge of one tunnel at a time and even if all five are working, there is the whole of knowledge that you are unaware of. . . ." That is pretty astounding.

Why the end before the beginning? I wake up and skip my asana practice because I expect to do it at Acharya's house. I sleep soundly in the last part of the night and that helps me to feel better. I wash clothes and take a bath. I love taking pitchers of hot water and pouring them over my body.

"Do you eat a lot of curd and milk products at home?"

"No. I'm eating a lot here, but I'm not making as much phlegm here as at home."

"Are you under a lot of stress at home?"

"Yes."

"That is why you are making a lot of phlegm."

Again jumping ahead of the day. I do my pranayama practice and then I go to Subrata's and eat flat rice, fruit and curd for breakfast. I talk to Mary for a while about Acharya. She seems like someone who might like studying with him. Then I come home, read and putter around the apartment, cleaning. Finally at 11:30 I leave the house, and just as I go over the hill at the base of this property and on to the road, raindrops start falling. I stop, tuck the plastic bag around my belongings in my bag, a plastic crocheted bag that Jayashree says she can make and her mother used to make. I tell her I bought one for her but I don't think she needs it.

I start off again and rain starts falling harder. I stop, put on my jacket and then head into the rain. It slows down but the clouds are dark, and I think it might be good to arrive at Acharya's as quickly as possible. I don't like being too early and I'm always somewhat early, so I end up riding out into the country behind his house.

When I do arrive, there is a rickshaw in front and an extra scooter. The driver's legs are sticking out of the back of the rickshaw. He is snoring. There are three pairs of sandals sitting outside the door and two of them are very worn. I think I hear Indian voices talking with Acharya. Two women walk out of the front door and put on their sandals. Perhaps they are here for astrological advice about some decision. I am ready to go into the side room when Jayashree steps outside and tells me to wait in the side room. I remove my sandals, straighten out the mat, hang up my jacket and shirt, put a little mosquito repellent on my shoulders and ankles, place the shawl around my shoulders, and then I wait.

I lie down and stare at the cane ladder tied up on the ceiling.

This is where Acharya sees most of his western students.

When he comes in, he sits on the stoop of the door leading into the back of the house. He asks about my practice. "Are there sufficient asanas?"

I tell him I feel fine, but I keep thinking I should have more back bends to strengthen my back. I tell him I am doing extra salabasanas, camels and setubandasanas. That seems to be ok.

He asks me to describe all the back bending.

"That is enough for you," he says. "Someone with a body like yours (vata) and your age should not do a lot of back bending."

In fact, later he tells me that unless someone is extremely flexible, women should not do excessive back bending. Our bodies are not conducive to these asanas. He says I should do more twists. He adds a pose—ardamatsyendrasana—a sitting twist with one leg over the other . . . I remember it but it is very difficult to describe because one is twisted up into a knot. I am to do this after the other twist he gave me.

He asks about my pranayama practice. He tells me that I should identify days of quietness, and on those days it is my duty to sit longer.

I ask him about my friends, Artie and Bill. He tells me I can teach them very light asanas and padmasana, slow breathing for 16 sets, and nada shodana for seven breaths and then rest with no thoughts.

We also talk a lot about when I return home, how I should not criticize the other yoga practices. It is difficult not to, but it will only cause you problems. Only tell someone what you have learned if they are a very good friend and it seems like they want to hear it. I tell him that perhaps I will visit the other yoga centers in the city. He suggests I go to Ananda ashram and the Gurumayi ashram and sing bajans with them, but I should not become attached to them. No problem, I don't want to become attached. He is discouraging me from practicing yoga much in the U.S. in a group setting. After I plead a little, he agrees that I can practice in Manny's studio, but it will be best if I keep doing the same asanas he has given me.

We talk about yoga in the States and the deep need for spiritual life we in the U.S. have. That's why, I say, many will pay large amounts of money to have some attention from an Indian guru. I also ask to talk again about chanting mantras and my mantra. Finally he says that I can say the chant I was given, but not with the sound, "Om." Again we talk about women and yoga and how women's needs are different, how when he traveled he talked to some Indians in the ashrams in the U.S. and asked why they were doing things incorrectly, and they told him that in the U.S. the women will become so angry if they say something should be different for men and for women.

I mention that I was told by Mr. Jayaraj to say Aum, not Om.

Yes, that is all wrong in your country. It has been changed and it is very negative. But it will all resolve. This wave will pass.

Apparently, he believes that the Om energy is not suitable for a female physique, just as certain energies are not appropriate for different constitutions. I remember asking an Indian yoga teacher in a group discussion in New York why Aum instead of Om—and he said very quickly that it had something to do with Indian sexist practices. In this case, I assume that the label "sexist" is a reduction of ancient knowledge for the benefit of modernity. Since I respect Acharya's knowledge about differences between constitutions and genders as they relate to the chakras, I'm happy to chant Aum instead of Om. After all, Om is A-U-M. Maybe feminine energy needs to dwell longer and deeper with the sound.

Acharya leaves and I continue with my pranayama practice. When I finish, Jayashree sits on the stoop and talks to me as I search in my bag for my watch. See you at 5:30 at my house, I say, and then scoot over to Double Road to buy curd and on to Nilgiris for some spices and milk (and I bought cookies which I just finished). I am eating so many sweet things this week.

At 5:00 Carl arrives and we chat. I want to stop talking, especially interrupting a story by someone else to tell my own. This is rude. I am stopping it right now. It's as if my mind is bubbling over with thoughts that I must express. Acharya says it is hereditary, this over-thinking, from one of my parents.

It's a good thing human beings have thick skulls or I'd be in bad shape right now after toppling over in the street.

Carl was the head of a small architectural firm that had to turn over about 30 thousand dollars a month to cover the payroll. He ran this company for ten years, sold it recently and came to India to change his life again, yet he seems pretty busy here, too.

"It is easy to live in the second tier of houses outside big cities, so much cheaper," he says. He's planning to move to a little town outside of Portland, Oregon. When he drove through it with Acharya and Jayashree, he said, they thought it looked like a good town for him.

I wonder where I will be living five years from now.

Then the doorbell rings and I go down to let the rest of the group in.

It is kind of warm in the room with the windows and doors closed, but then with everything closed, you don't hear the traffic and we can hear what Acharya is saying.

He asks if we have any questions. No, not Carl, not me.

"This next shloka is about eating suitable food and having suitable recreation and activities. If one is doing the appropriate work, relaxation will normally follow. Suitable work is work in which you perform your duty automatically. Because it is correct, calm and quiet, it will come without practice. Right action leads to realization. All this is covered in the first six chapters, which address karma yoga. He uses some example about pain. You feel pain, you worry, but then another urgency occurs and the fitness necessary for that urgency is there and the pain is cured automatically."

Stop worrying, then it goes away.

"But the action must be suitable, just as right sleep and the waking state are suitable. A yogi must be disciplined or the yogic techniques get worse. Just as a two-headed snake moves to one side when the other is restricted, so the mind is like this in terms of introversion and extroversion. Cut off the extroverted part. Don't worry about how it will happen, just do it, cut off those thoughts and sense perceptions and it will happen. Introversion will take place. If you cut off movement, automatically there is a dwelling on self. Visualize the self, so visualization."

I'm confused about this one.

"All unnatural desires automatically leave when you cut off the extroverted thought and sense movement. But you must also try to eliminate unnatural desires because they move around. Cut off here, move over there."

5:30 a.m., I happily wake up. Maybe I needed to be knocked on the head by the ground in order to sleep well. Already I have bathed, washed clothes, practiced and meditated—more fulfilling everyday. I found the lost piece of my earring on the bedroom floor. I ride the bike over to the corner, pick up some curd and eat it with the mangos. Enough for breakfast, I think, although I usually need some kind of grain also. Vatas need to eat more.

So now to continue with my memories about the lessons on the Gita. "It is your duty to cut off as much external thought as possible, then to meditate. You will become enlightened about many things. Most unnatural desires will fall away. If you have total contentment, why do you need unnatural desires? They dissolve. In other words if you are looking around and finding a rupee here, fifty there—you keep looking, but if someone gives you a million dollars, you quit looking here and there.

"What is yoga? If there is a lamp in a closed room with no wind, the flame is still. With no unnatural desires, you feel stable and the mind is like that lamp. Yoga is 100% concentration. The mind takes shelter in two ways. One, you may take an object related to the inner truth for meditation. Two, is rather simple—cut off all external activities of the mind. There is the same goal. The first technique is used by many but there is a discipline involved. Deviations can occur. So you must be careful in the selection of the object of meditation. Which object suits who? If it works, your breathing is altered and thoughts will disappear. Changes in breathing determine the length of time in meditation. For some this experience of great joy comes very quickly. They recognize it and instantly hold on to it.

There is a thread to the eternal connected with the breath. If you notice this joy, even a little, catch hold of it. At some point there is a loss of consciousness and no outer awareness—you are in samadhi. Materialistic enjoyment is temporary and noneternal. Samadhi joy is eternal. Total contentment. No more disturbances. Keep it internal and ever existing.

"We cannot understand without the five senses and yet the joy we receive from these is limited just as the senses themselves have their limits. We must stop these senses. The mind wants in fact to be as big as eternal truth with no such limitations. Normally each sense is like a narrow passage and the area is limited—think of the eye—again eliminate these borders and the mind is as big as eternal truth. If you focus on one sense, that narrow passage works and the others shut down.

"Misery for human beings creates an instability—the shivering body is totally out of balance. A yogi however will be unshaken. Just as a child falls down once and cries and then another time falls down without crying, it is psychological. The yogi will not experience that instability. The definition of yoga is 'disconnection with misery.' That in itself is yoga. You must start with joy—don't start with pain. Yoga should give some happiness. It should eliminate misery. Yes—always secure. Never become a yogi to learn to teach. Do it to learn to enjoy. An intention is necessarily perfect so you will grow or there will be no growth. So don't count the number of asanas you do or the number of pranayama."

Ok, I say, ok.

*

I ride the scooter over to Devarajas Road and find the optical place that Carl has been telling me about. I order two pairs of glasses since the lenses cost half what I must pay in the U.S. He is throwing in the frames for nothing. He double checks my eyesight just to make sure the prescription is correct. It is correct. I think the only way to make this trip affordable—in terms of the exorbitant cost of the ticket—is to remember the things you need in the U.S. and buy them in India.

I stop at Upahar's and park the bike on the side road and order

a small cup of almond milk. I'm starting to be tired of everyone staring at me, like the guy in the corner whose eyes are on me while he
is eating. It's amazing his spoon actually arrives at his mouth. And
then in the shops and on the street, the shopkeepers and venders
badger me and other foreigners. It's a good thing peace of mind is
part of the Indian culture because much of the street and shop style
is so intrusive. But perhaps I am calling them to me with the sign
around my neck that says—I am an American. I have a dime.

I ride over to Acharya's. Jayashree sends me into the little room
to wait. I lay down on the mat and rest to try to gain my calm. I
notice that today my coughing is less, but also the weather is dryer
and hotter. Perhaps it is the ginger tonic I am taking.

Acharya comes in, dressed in his white yoga cloth, with a shawla
wrapped around his shoulders. He adjusts it. He has a beautiful
torso.

"Oh you are resting. Rest, I will be back in five minutes."

I rest for five minutes and then review my notes and questions.

He arrives. "Commence," he says.

I have a few questions. I ask him if in the winter, I should
increase the amount of time I stay in an asana.

"There can be some problems with that," he says. "How long is
your winter?"

"Four to five months of cold weather."

"Double your sun salutations or add 50% more. You can do
your asanas twice a day if you want. In the evening, too."

I ask him about some poses that I kind of miss.

"Yes you can include the parvottasana and prasarita padottana-
sona C." But in response to the balancing poses, he says, "Well you
can do them, but you don't want to add too many poses or you will
not gain the benefit of the practice. It takes about six months for the
real benefits to start showing. You will gradually want to raise the
head stand and you will want to slowly develop reverse kurmasana,
yoganidra. But the real message is to accept this practice. The twists
are very good for your body. Others are not so good."

I ask him if I should do the pranayama section in Manny's studio when I am there.

"Better that you go home," he says, "unless it is not practical. Good not to excite anyone else's gaze and questions." Then he gives me the names I need for the asanas and pranayama.

*

I had one of the most beautiful practices I have had so far. Acharya was sitting across from me, my eyes were closed, and I was sending all my thoughts away. There was a large blue and then yellowish circle.

Later he tells me, "That is your soul. These things happen when you first start." He says I am doing much better. Still I must go slower even.

Here in this apartment, the traffic noises stop me from hearing the rhythm. So why am I distracted? I need to concentrate on the meditation. While I was practicing I felt the wind on my body. It was so beautiful and the lights were so large. I felt a bug crawling on my leg and I sent the sensation away. I could feel the wind lift a little bit of my hair and lay it down. I was so happy when I left his house on the scooter. I was moving very slowly and cautiously. That bump I received on my head just going across the street was a little warning.

*

I call Shivanand and he wants me to come right away. So I eat without rushing, and scoot over to his house. He will leave for Bangalore on Sunday and will not return until Saturday next week. That means I will have only a few more lessons from him before he leaves. I sing full and uninhibited and my voice has risen a little bit.

Home I straighten up a bit, take a little warm water bath, pouring pitchers over my body. My face gets so filthy from the dust blowing on it. Then I start working on these notes and preparing for our meeting at 6 p.m.

The doorbell rings and first Justine, a new student, arrives and then Carl. Justine, a tall, willowy pretty young woman from Austin, Texas, wants to know what I have been doing with Acharya and I really don't want to tell her because I love keeping my relationship with him a secret. Nonetheless, she asks, and so I describe my sessions with him.

Carl receives a telephone call on his cell phone—Acharya will be late.

A few minutes later he arrives with Ram and they sit opposite us.

He asks for questions and I begin with one. "Yesterday you were talking about using deities for meditation and you discouraged this—because after all, how do you know which path you are following, Vishnu or Shiva. And so, can you tell me about these two paths?"

He talks a lot about the ways people relax and how different they are. "The whole world can be divided into Brahma, Vishnu and Shiva, and under each deity, or stream of energy, there are many different objects for meditation, different methods of relaxing. Like the branches of a tree. If you are heading down to the roots, you don't begin with someone else's branch. You start right where you are. If you aren't getting calm and quiet, perhaps you are on someone else's branch. If you are chanting a mantra that is not suited to you, it is meaningless. Any object can give some relaxation, but can it give you realization? If you change an activity or change a way of thinking, relaxation can result, but that does not mean it is a path to realization. What is popular now as yoga is really giving people only relaxation. This is not the real goal of yoga. The techniques are limited and unsuitable, so the goal is never reached. Do you understand? Are there any doubts?"

Justine asks how you know if you are on the right branch.

He smiles at her. "Later," he says. It is getting dark. He turns toward me. "You are leaving soon. You do the practice I have taught you, so that you go inside your inner self. It knows where it is. You meditate without thoughts, only on that."

"Anymore questions?" He looks at me.

"Well, I have one more. The other day we were talking and you explained to me that aum is for women and om is for men. And I was wondering if you would elaborate on that. I was wondering about the effects of the particular sounds and how they relate differently according to gender."

"Women have a quality of productiveness—and certain duties connected with pregnancy and feeding—and they are extroverted in their whole constitution. And this part of their constitution can be lost and damaged from the wrong yoga techniques—an imbalance can be created in the constitution. There is always a natural flow of rajas with women. If they chant om, the movement can go up instead of down and menstruation can be affected. This can create adverse affects on their bodies, physically and mentally. Often mental sickness can result. In yoga as practiced by many in the U.S., the rigor causes menstruation to be postponed. This can result in ragasic energy in the body as well as melancholia, uneasiness and other disturbances.

"There is the possibility of realization for each one, but the sexes are different just as the branches are different, and this creates the need for different techniques to reach the goal, bhakti or karma. . . women are not deprived. There are just different paths. Women have more attachment tendencies than men. The father cares much less and therefore the mother has more attachment. For example some people have backaches so they can't sit on a train. They find another vehicle. Device is important because an unsuitable device won't reach a goal. Instead lots of disturbances. Go to the teacher. The teacher should select medium. Om is not the single path. There are hundreds of variations.

"One needs the help of a wise person to help us understand how to find our own relaxation or realization."

Then he begins the next shloka. "Sankalpa are unnatural and natural desires that come from a previous samskara, impressions from an earlier birth. This is when you make a quick decision because of someone else's influences. Eliminate these decisions entirely." He uses an example of a woman who was a musician in a past life and then takes up music thoughtlessly here. "These instructions are directed toward someone who is ready to give up everything for realization, to go into the forest. The direct path. Those who can't do this will instead give up with yoga.

"There are many different paths of yoga—all the eight limbs. But you can work to lessen the amount of decisions you make like this. From ancient times, the sages have told people to realize themselves by sitting somewhere else, lessening or decreasing thought, understanding what is in the mind, withdrawing the mind from the senses, pulling that thought back. Make a firm decision about your meditation. Fix it exactly. Use your intellect. Bring the mind from the senses, gradually with bravery—when you feel confident—fix the mind there. Then you will have internal experiences."

Acharya's cell phone rings as he is leaving the room. He stands at the head of the stairs talking in Kanada, his shadow already on the stairs.

*

This has been a day full of disturbances. I stumble into the bathroom twice in the middle of the night. Then I wake up at 6:30 instead of 5:30. My whole day goes better if I wake up at 5:30. I am groggy. I wash clothes, wash my body and hair, clean dishes, drink eight handfuls of water, chew the ginger tonic from Dr. Anand, and then I prepare for asana practice.

As I begin the pranayama, I realize that Bhavini is going to arrive right in the middle of my practice. I plan to go downstairs, give her the money and come upstairs and finish without disrupting my practice. The doorbell rings and before I can get downstairs, it rings two more times. It is a very loud and noisy doorbell.

I open the door to someone I don't recognize. He is dirty, sparsely dressed and smoking a cigarette, asking for I don't know what. "Sorry, I don't know," I tell him and in an irritated way shut the door. Irritation is not a suitable emotion for yoga practice.

Then I come upstairs, expecting Bhavini any moment. I can't return to my pranayama so I lay down and breathe in and out and relax. I dress. The doorbell rings. I go downstairs. It is Marilyn in a worried state. She needs to reach Acharya and she doesn't know how. His telephone isn't working. I suggest that she try Carl or that she come back here at 12:15 and wait for him outside if she can't reach him in the next hour or so. While Marilyn is here, Bhavini arrives. I pay her for the other three days and today (even though I don't want her to clean) and I tell her I don't need her to clean anymore. I tell her I am going to do it myself.

That is over but I don't feel as great with all those interruptions. If only I could have woken up on my own at 5:30 a.m. all this would not have happened. I go over to Subrata's and then to the bank to cash $500 worth of travelers checks. In the bank I'm behind a very overweight middle aged American woman, decked out with all kinds of Indian gold jewelry, long red nails, and blonde hair in a bun. She is a little frantic—

"I must cash $1600 of traveler's checks," she says explaining that she wants to buy this and go there and there and do all these things today. "Why is there a $200 limit?" She is very nervous. She doesn't wait for the answers.

"After all, I want to enjoy India," she says, lighting a cigarette.

Why, I wonder, did she come to this little out-of-the-way bank? A few weeks ago a western woman went around cashing a bunch of phony traveler's checks and it made the papers. Now it is hard for a stranger to cash them.

I leave her, sitting there arguing, pick up my money and scoot over to Shivanand's. He is very happy today. He starts writing lots of lessons for me in the book since he won't be here very much now: tomorrow and then next weekend and that's it. We make plans to meet tomorrow morning and I scoot on, stopping here and there looking for a wooden book holder for reading on the floor.

I have the computer propped up on it right now as I'm typing this and it is perfect, carved from one piece of wood and opening up into a cradle for a book.

٭

Justine and Carl arrive and talk a little about Colorado, Gortex fabrics for the cold and the Himalayas. Acharya, Jayashree and Ram arrive. It is hot so I try to keep some of the doors open to let air into the room, but the traffic is so loud that I keep wishing I had closed all the windows and doors.

Acharya says something about rajasic energy and the importance of reducing thoughts. "Sattvic energy balances. With less rajasic energy one can focus on any object, anywhere and contemplate. There will be a superior enjoyment then for all. Material enjoyment on the other hand is impure, burdened with other feelings. Most objects that you hold dear also hold the feeling of loss and other problems. For example with sweets, you are happy at first but too much ends in disease. All happiness is followed with some misery. Except for yogi happiness. There is no misery there. Bhoga is enjoyment of the material world and objects. Yoga is an eternal enjoyment. They can work together. You can have both but in balance otherwise the one will destroy the other. Bhoga with discipline and yogic bliss. You can enjoy both.

"A well-developed yogi sees eternal truth everywhere in every object in all materials—I exist everywhere."

A big noisy truck pulls up in front and revs its engine. I imagine it loading and unloading seeds for the business next door. And then there are horns and buses. I am distracted.

"What is the problem?" Acharya asks. He is unaware of the noise.

I mention the distraction.

"A realized person never feels death or destruction. God is eternal—he is good—death is not found—there is no destruction possible—form changes—therefore no fear of death."

This is what I was discovering when Lenny died even though I wept uncontrollably. In the months that followed his death, I learned this—there is no destruction possible.

Acharya explains the behavior of a realized person. "He is so connected with the world, there are heart connections. Others' misery is his also. Others' joy his also. His total knowledge is different from the common man's. Everywhere he experiences eternal truths, in the mind, in the body. Common man has a barrier and no experience about this. The realized man feels a oneness everywhere. He feels, but doesn't experience. He is not tormented by their misery, but in his heart he feels it. His mind is unconditioned and without attachment. Attachment is heavy with selfish tendencies. There is always a benefit, a selfish motive. That's why one feels only the misery of friends and not that of others—it is a selfish motive. This is an illusion. The friends bring no happiness. Happiness comes from within.

"Arjuna says it is difficult to control the mind. Krishna answers: There are two tools for controlling mind, practice and detachment. Practice is a suitable technique constantly repeated. It brings stability of mind and joy and happiness. Detachment brings balance in the mind always. If you have many connections, you have over-attachment to some. Eliminate them. View the importance of materials according to the needs of body and mind. Ask yourself: Without this, can I live? Leave it aside. The burial man has a knowledge about death. We will get this type of knowledge, too, in some areas. Listen to a realized person or a person on a path. This will help you get to an area of knowledge and bring balance."

There is a question about disturbances by Carl. I can't remember his exact question, but I started thinking about my morning practice and all the traffic at the moment.

"When there are disturbances," Acharya says, "you will do something to remedy the problem. Later on, no disturbances. Or you will not hear them. Later on, no real disturbances. You can and should maintain this state all day. The cause of an upset over disturbances is usually some ignorance and lack of practice. Your concern about disturbances will ultimately cause a change in your system that is positive—so it is all a step in the practice. Even sickness is a disturbance, a problem that gives you an opportunity to improve—think, eat, practice. Our reactions to obstacles in our paths come from previous birth experiences. All problems in the system should be corrected. This is the gift. This punishment is a gift because our awareness improves and we make corrections."

Just as we are nearing the end of the discussion, the doorbell rings and someone starts banging on the door. I am disturbed. I expect no one.

Carl looks at me with agony on his face. "Can we just ignore it, please?"

"Ok." Then more rings and knocks.

Jayashree says, "I don't think this one will wait."

So I run down the stairs to see who is there. Two young Indian boys on bikes bringing a message for Justine and they want to talk to her . . . something about Frank. I tell them to stop knocking and wait. They act like they want to burst into the house.

"No," I say, "sit here and wait." Then I shut the door, go upstairs, drop the note in front of Justine and tell her it is for her, some children are waiting downstairs.

She looks perturbed.

Acharya starts talking. I can't hear a word he is saying.

Tears are running down Justine's face.

"Why are you crying?" he asks.

"Joy, this means so much to me," she says when in fact she is terribly tormented by some inability to say—I'm sorry that we were interrupted by someone with a message for me. Tears keep running down her face. I feel compassion for her, but at the same time I don't understand her inability to communicate something this simple.

Acharya departs.

"I don't know any boys so they weren't here for me," she says to me.

"They brought a note for you from Frank," I respond.

"How did he know where I was? He's going to hear about this."

"I'm sorry," I say, "if I was too abrupt when I dropped the note in your lap." I hug her.

And then I am bothered throughout the day by this "disturbance." Yet, I know it is Justine's issue. My disturbance is about feeling guilty for being disturbed about the disturbance and then disturbed by her being disturbed. Freud might call this whole chain reaction neurotic, but here and now I am watching my mind closely as it thinks and interrupts my possibility of experiencing peace. Corrections for the future. Note on the door. Talk softly. Close doors.

After that everyone leaves.

*

Later Saturday evening, all the muscles in my back and neck are tight and sore from driving all over in the dark Indian potholed night without being able to see well while vehicles zoom quickly from every direction. Just for a rava idli and batam milk at Upahar and then a desire to email Josh, which requires that I go all the way to Saraswati Purum.

Frank stops by today. We sit on a mat on the porch and watch the cars go by . . . just relaxed together. . . . I read a few pages today and do not practice at 12:00. Lots of thoughts about going home. Next year I am definitely coming for a much longer time.

Thoughts in my mind this morning. With Brahmins, I wonder if no one is allowed in the kitchen except the cook. Or except other family members? I guess the vibrations from others will cause the cook to lose her steadiness or the food will be tainted. No sex except procreation. I am eating a chocolate bar. I am a woman. I like the pleasures of the world. I like sex, affection and chocolate. Somehow this part of the practice doesn't seem right for me. But then again I am not a monk. I am a single western woman householder with a job in the world. If I argue in favor of sex and desire, I suppose I am also arguing in favor of suffering. Then again, perhaps it is something I don't have to think about anymore. Just follow what feels right for me at the time. Perhaps this practice (which perhaps I will throw off balance today by eating this chocolate) of recognizing my soul will help solve the problem.

*

I look out the window and see Bill approach on his motorcycle. He pulls up in front of my house. I hide in the shadows. He walks down the road and asks some people on the street questions. They point at my house. He is all sweaty. He rings my door bell.

I hide inside the curtains. Why? Something about him frightens me and I don't want him coming into this apartment, so I don't answer. He gets back on his bike and continues along the road. He reminds me of David, his body shape, his smoking. Let him go his way, I think. Then a little while later I see the woman who is now studying with Shivanand. She is riding on the back of his cycle, holding on to him. I have a feeling she was looking for me through him—since I told her nothing about where I live. I think I should drink a big glass of water to try to flush the chocolate out of me. Why sweets? Because they are fake affection . . . they bring disease when overused. I overused it today with three times as much as one bite, which is what feels ok to me.

*

In one week I am leaving. It is a hot afternoon and I am lying here wishing I could leave tomorrow—because of the heat and because today I am lonely.

After Acharya and everyone else leaves, instead of practicing I go over to Subrata's to eat and then I ride over to the center for literature and ethnic studies. The old man is sleeping. His wife shows me the library.

"You must come back after 4:30," she says.

I leave copies of my books, saying, "I will come back later and subscribe so I can use the library." There are lots of old books, worn and well used.

Then as I glide along under the tree-lined road, I remember how irritable he was last year and how much he dislikes American literature and art. "Nothing new," he said.

"Isn't it difficult," his wife asks me, "with no rules, everyone driving everywhere."

"But in fact it isn't like that," I tell her. "There are definite rules of the road that have to do with who yields and who doesn't. And you must be courageous and centered enough to join and yield to the mass of vehicles, pedestrians and animals."

The weather is steadily getting hotter. I go over to the khadi shop and pick up the yoga pants. I turn into typewriter row and encounter the owner of the shop walking down the street. Their gate is down.

"Why?" I ask.

"The roof has fallen and I can't open my shop. Come tomorrow."

Another Indian afternoon. I ride my bike along the palace road moving over for the buses and trucks that have the right of way by sheer size and speed. Home, I come upstairs and lay here reading Romain Rolland on Vivikananda. I don't think very many American fiction writers and poets have written about yoga and India in the 20th Century. When I'm home I will read Ginsberg's India Journals again. It is very hot, and the young man downstairs is practicing his drums.

This morning, Jeevesh asks me what I want—Indian breakfast is idli.

"Yes, idli," I say, noting we had idli yesterday, too. This repetition is uncommon here.

Subrata is in the next room folding clothes on the floor. She doesn't say hello. That is very odd. At first I think it is her servant on the floor. Then she stands up.

"Hello, Subrata. How was your trip?"

It was fine." She comes into the room.

"Matthew told me about your trip to Bangalore. Are you happy about this marriage possibility for Sunanda?"

"Yes, it is my uncle's family. They are so very nice." And then she starts crying. My uncle died a few years ago. Tears and tears. "I have so much problem with attachment," she says.

I ask her how old she is—45 years old.

"Maybe it is pre-menopausal."

"No, I was always like this."

"Maybe you are worried about your daughter. After all she may have to live in California, very far away from you."

"No, I am always like this. Sometimes I do worry about my children." More tears.

I have never seen her like this but I have heard about it. She tells me all about the cousin Sunanda might marry. "He can't come until December. He is thirty years old."

I think if I had to arrange a marriage for my daughter and she had to live with the husband's family, I would surely try to marry her to someone in my own family so I could be sure she'd be ok, or more sure, anyhow. So many girls go to families that use them like slaves and make them feel unwanted. So Subrata's daughter might end up living in the USA—her life will change in so many ways. How lucky Nanda is to marry into Shivanand's family. They are lovely people.

I reach out to touch Subrata and then, remembering she is a Brahmin, I ask, "Is it ok if I touch you?" She says, yes, so I place my hand on her arm. There is an awkwardness, not quite the touch of reassurance we give in the west to someone who is suffering.

Later, I come for lunch and they give me some not-so-delicious food, pullavi (with ground nuts which Acharya has suggested I avoid), beets and two chapattis. I am late so I assume that is why I am being fed scraps.

Sunanda sits down with me to talk about the ways of western women and Indian women. She is surprised that I would even think about going to Chamundi Hill by myself. "There is a cheetah there and so many men who can bother you." She doesn't even know how to get there and it is one of the most celebrated spots in Mysore. She could never ride a scooter either because men will follow you and bother you.

"I see so many women on scooters," I tell her.

"Not me, parents will not allow it. Even on this street here, so many people bother you." She talks about how we have so much freedom compared to Indian women. "Men want to keep us away," she says. "You can do this. You can't do that."

"Yes, I say there are pluses and minuses to it all." Then I ask her if she is worried about the marriage.

"A little," she says. "Parents will take care of it, though."

"Will you meet him? If you don't like him can you say, no?"

"Parents will take care of it."

Suddenly, Subrata comes in and takes her away. I think she must have been listening.

*

Acharya begins by talking about practice and detachment as methods for controlling the mind. "The yoga sutras, later texts, take this up again. Practice—you must do your practice exactly the same way for a long period of time without any change. For an asana to be perfected, it takes about 1000 times or three years. For a simple pranayama like nadi shodana, it takes anywhere from six months to six years. If you are very young or elderly, it takes twelve years. Also, be sure not to break the practice. If it is less than three days, there will be no damage, but more, you will be as if beginning again. Be constant and regular.

"You must also have faith and honor in the teachings and the teacher, otherwise progress will not be found. It is important that you have the right teacher, and it is also essential to have faith and devotion. If you make a lot of changes in your practice, there will be no progress. These changes can be made if you have an injury—a new technique."

I ask about the practice in the west to do open classes, classes that vary from day to day.

"Yes, they are trying to cover the hundred to two hundred poses in ten to fifteen days. This practice changes their system regularly. There is no real stability established. It is only commercial and for physical benefit. They work hard for the purpose of demonstration. It is a circus with physical intention. Asana and pranayama can be practiced objectively and psychologically as a key to open your heart. But you must know how to use the key. Little by little. Sometimes techniques don't work and an immunity develops, then the teacher will suggest a change. But this is usually not necessary. Get the joy out of the technique. If there is a certain strain in the system—asanas can be raised or reduced. But the best is continuity—then joy should arise from the asanas and pranayama. This is most important."

Carl asks some question about washing his face and hands before practicing, something about bringing forward the energy to practice. Acharya talks about the way that even one who feels weak physically can call upon an inner mechanism in the system to create this experience, but that should not happen often. One can also call on that mechanism to shut down.

"Krishna gives Arjuna a warning in the 36th shloka. Along with practice and detachment, one must have control over the senses. One must tame the senses. These two, control of senses and detachment, are mutually dependent. Each helps the other. You can work on one and then work on the other and improvement will occur. There are small differences between them. Just because senses are not active does not mean they are under control. They are like a lion sleeping. One can also have control over the senses, but no real detachment. You can be very contented with your food and health. This creates an illusion of control, but it is only temporary. Keep working on both of these. Eventually it comes."

Carl asks, "What is control of senses?"

"There are instincts for sex, realization, food, material objects. Each must be suitable to each other. One should not hinder the other. If you are going to fulfill one, it should not disturb other aspects of life. Apply the senses to this task. More and more control and you will understand the system."

I ask about the number of times to eat in a day. I thought I remembered him saying once to me that vata people eat more often.

"No," he says emphatically, "eat two times a day, one hour each. Other than that only water. Otherwise your system is working and working and working."

Carl tells him that he is counting the bites and that is working in terms of his hunger (Carl needs to reduce his tamasic energy and lose weight).

Acharya talks about how some people's digestion is taking place due to gravity rather than due to the natural system. "One eats and this pushes the other food out. Change eating habits. It will take ten to fifteen days to put your system in order."

I explain how I am so attracted to sweets if they are around me.

"Some people need a little sweet once in a while. It helps relaxation. For others it is not so good. Generally, not good."

"What happens when someone stops yoga due to an obstacle?"

"Even with a long practice they will lose some benefits, but they never really totally lose it because it is carried over with the samskara to the next birth. People often stop because they don't feel any benefit. A little effort will benefit them now or later in the next birth or now. It will be there as an asset in your life even if you have only practiced for one day."

One question after another. And then it is time to stop for today. After I hear the sound of Acharya's scooter in the distance, I walk into the living room and notice his cell phone on the floor.

I ride out J. Prakash in a light rain. Ram answers the door, adjusting his white shawla over his shoulder. He nods his head and smiles as I give him the phone. Yes, sometimes our dear teacher is absentminded.

On the almost empty streets, I ride very slowly. It is 6 a.m. and I am going slowly so I won't be too early to meet Acharya. A few blocks from their house, I come upon Jayashree walking with her little bag full of vegetables. There are some green leaves flopping over the edge of her worn bag. I slow down.

"Go," she says, "he is waiting for you."

"I want to give you something."

"No, go."

No—I am not going to give her this bag as a gift. It is unwanted and unneeded. Acharya emphasized once in his teaching about the Gita—don't take what you don't need.

In the narrow room, Acharya begins to speak to me. "How is your practice?" He talks about going back and keeping the practice and keeping faith in the teacher. "Even if the results of the practice are not as strong, keep doing it." He says so much more which I can't remember right now.

I ask him about books to read and he talks about the *Life History of Ramakrishna*. Then he talks about reading the *Gospels of Ramakrishna* very slowly and patiently. "Everything is in these books," he says.

"Why does Vivekananda eat meat?" I ask.

"Do not read him now," he suggests.

"I like his emphasis on karma yoga and service."

"Yes, that is his strength."

"Does he eat meat because he comes from the warrior class?"

"Yes, only Brahmins are strict vegetarians."

He emphasizes that I should not talk to others about my practice. "It will create confusions for you. Just say that you have learned some things in India and you are going to stay with that."

I mention that I have been very solitary here.

"That is the way it should be. You should come to India only to learn yoga. Other activities are not necessary. In fact, we don't encourage people to come to India. Carl is here because he has work to do, but he will be returning to his country. You should live in your birth place."

"What about 700 miles away?" I ask because New York is far from Michigan.

"That is close enough as long as the culture is the same." Another person he would like me to read is Krishna Chaitanya, but do not read the Hari Krishna versions. Today he is going to Bangalore and he will look into the stores for me to see which books I should read. But I should not read a lot of other books on yoga— I will receive wrong information and this will confuse my mind and then upset my faith in the teacher and then faith in the practice. If I have questions for him, it is a good idea to send an email and then to telephone one week later, between 9:30 and 10:00 p.m.

When you said to raise headstand, does that mean staying in it for a longer time."

"Yes, but stay where you are for six months and then raise it to 24, after a year to 32. It is very important to go slowly."

"What is reverse kurmasana?".

"It is yoganidrasana. You can find it in the books."

He asks me to make a list of all the pranayama that I am doing with the numbers of breaths. Then I ask him other questions about my astrology chart. He leaves the room to pick up the chart and returns.

"Is it clearly my mother's grace that has brought me to yoga and a quieter life because the week before you began to say it was my father and then you changed to my mother after I reacted."

He studies it and says that very clearly it was mother.

"There is one part of the reading that has bothered me. You say I will not have another husband. I am often lonely and I feel that I would be happier with a companion.

He studies the chart. "There is a possibility of having a companion, but if it is a husband, it will not last for long."

I ask him what the difference is between a companion and a husband.

"A companion could even live with you but you will not have sex and you will not share your property. You should not have sex with the companion. In India, if you are not married and you have sex, that is a sin."

I tell him that I have had lovers and that is the way it is in our country. I tell him about Lenny, how we lived together for so long and stayed friends afterwards.

He studies the chart quizzically. "You are almost fifty and it will be better for you not to have sex, but if you feel a desire to have sex, you should get married rather than having sex out of marriage."

I tell him about Dimitri, not using his name but describing him as someone who lives on the other side of the world, is an advanced yogi, and the sex is more like asanas than wild abandonment.

"It is ok for you to have sex with him," he says.

It's funny these things I already know. Ever since I woke up in the morning and all day yesterday, I have been feeling a little melancholic, perhaps about the coming departure. I feel this sadness as I tell him that I am at times lonely. I forget to ask him about singing. He has told me to include singing in my life, but I didn't ask him what type of singing.

"If you were here for a year of conversations, I would teach you everything and you would even understand why it is ok for a man to remarry when his wife dies, but not for a woman."

"That might take a lot more than a year for me to understand.

Then he studies my chart and tells me, "I am going to tell you something and you are not to feel disappointed. When I did your chart I felt a screen come over me. Also, I came to your house two times and your door was locked. And once I came to you to teach you some more techniques and I did not want to teach them. Perhaps you are not ready." (My heart is falling into the cement.) "Perhaps this will take some time. Often when I have students here, it will be a year before I teach something." (Ok, I tell myself, I am slow like a tortoise, but I continue on my way.) He asks me if I am bothered.

"Yes," I say, "yes." And as soon as I say that I feel less bothered.

"This screen," he says, "might be good and it might be bad. I don't know. Maybe it will be gone next year."

I don't understand this screen and I'm feeling a little unhappy, but I take the unhappiness and set it aside for later. I take out my camera. He sits in half lotus with a serious expression on his face while I take his photograph. "Thank you," I say, "I'll see you in a few hours at my house."

*

This morning (Wednesday, my last Wednesday in Mysore for now), when I start my practice, I am a bit reluctant about starting, but I do and within about two sun salutations, I start feeling this sadness building over the screen between Acharya and me. This thought begins to dominate my practice. I wonder if something is terribly wrong. He did say to me yesterday that when we met, he felt something in his heart, and that he knew we should work together. This is about time. Ok, I say to myself, ok. But when I start practicing, a melancholic mood builds so that tears occasionally stream down my face. When I finish, I hang the clothes on the line and decide to go to Subrata's for breakfast.

I can feel the heavy weight of sadness as I walk into the house. I pick up my email on their computer while I wait for flat rice and fruit. She seems more composed today. On the computer there is a sweet letter from Josh, talking about how his confidence has increased—he is working in a tutoring center at his school and helping a freshman English teacher with his class. Yes, I am happy about Josh. He will be fine. I have so much love for my children. Tears start coming. I am like Subrata. Then there is a little note from my friend Peter in New York with a message for Acharya; a sweet letter from John at school, a young man who several years ago was my student but now is a teacher and friend (I like him more and more every year. It is as if in writing—the heart speaks to the heart); and a sweet letter from my dear friend Artie for whom I have a life love. I do have very good friends.

*

I come to the table. Jeevesh walks by. I think I am earlier than usual because he is not carrying a plate of fire. He is an exceptional looking man, tall, serious and involved in everything in the house, the kitchen, the religious rites. He sits down and asks me questions about my job and my life and the school Josh is attending.

Then Subrata brings him his rice so he goes into the other room. She sits down with me and we talk more about Sunanda's possible matrimonial situation. The parents have decided yes because this young man seems to be very nice (from what she knows—he talks nicely on the telephone to Subrata and the families are agreed), but now it will be up to Sunanda and she did not like the way he spoke to her on the telephone. He was not nice. He was curt. We do not know anything, he says, so why all these questions. They must follow his lead. She cannot call to talk to him unless he invites her telephone call and he has not. She can email but only in response to his email. She is worried.

"Subrata, I would be worried also."

"Why?"

"Because he should especially be nice to her if he wants her to marry him. And she will be going so far away from her home with someone who might have problems."

"He told her he will not interfere with what she does and she is not to interfere with him, ever."

"Oh that sounds frightening."

But it has not been decided fully. He is coming in December, they will meet for one day and then decide and the marriage will be fifteen days later—that sounds frightening. If I were Sunanda, I would feel hesitant to say no, given all that pressure. He works on computers and he has only a few friends. But his family members say he is a very nice boy. What else could they say? When I return to India, this will be resolved, and I will hear news from others beforehand.

*

First Carl arrives, then Justine shortly after. Carl and I are talking about things he wants me to take home for his wife and little details that relate to our already developed friendship while Justine sits on the mat writing in her notebook.

When Acharya arrives, he asks if we have any questions. He looks at me, and continues—"Since this class was started for your benefit."

"Yes, since I am leaving," I say. "None right now. There are some questions forming, but they are not ready."

"Do not try to form questions."

"No, they are there but I can't remember them right now."

"If you leave yoga without reaching the final goal, it will be favorable in your next life. You will be born into a yogi family so you won't need to struggle so hard, you will be ready to experience eternal truths. You will have good parents and a good body—This will be the gift of god for previous yoga practice, a yogi family or a favorable family."

I ask if a favorable family can still be a family which has its own tragic elements.

Perhaps.

I'm not sure he understands me correctly. There is then a lesson about balance. "If you mock people, in the next birth you will be mocked. Everything works out like that although sometimes it happens in this birth and sometimes later. Nature always punishes—sometimes immediately, sometimes in the next birth. Nature punishes sins.

"What are sins?"

"Some damage to nature—even in your own body."

"What do you do about these sins?" I ask.

"Simply realizing they exist is one thing. Or you can correct the damage. Or you can repent, but you should never repent so deeply that you are left with an impression that is unrepairable. Or you can eliminate the error in your system. A yoga student who practices sitting calm and quiet and practicing pranayama solves most sins. If you are calm and quiet with peace of mind, you have lots of capacities of mind. This benefits the soul and the animals that you have hurt. If you have lots of sin, you cannot get calm and quiet. They must all be resolved for realization. Any other questions?"

I mention the image that came vividly to mind while meditating yesterday morning after returning from Acharya's house. "Suddenly there was a bright sun shining through some trees and a mountain and I thought I was really there. Is there any significance to this?"

He begins to talk about the difference between imagination and visualization. For them, the word "visualization" is synonymous with "realization." So at first I am misunderstood. Carl explains and Acharya talks about how imagination comes from a previous birth.

I am a little confused. Perhaps there was a mountain near that desert where I lived in my last life.

"Some yoga practices have no results in this life, but in a higher world there is joy in some other type of body, then birth again in this world with purity and wealth. There are more worlds than just this one, and some offer even more material enjoyment. Purity means he's not attached. Wealth comes and goes easily. When it is needed, it is there. Properly used, wealth brings contentment. He will lose interest very easily in materials. But this is very rare and by the grace of god. If the next birth is pure (not attached), wealthy, and yogic, you will develop interest in yoga the same as in the prior life, with no force. You will experience very deep thinking, sitting calm and quiet, as well as asana experience. Inquiry will be deep with pranayama and meditations."

I ask a question about these types of births for people outside India. I find it hard to believe that there are no "yogic type families" in other parts of the world.

"Yes, there are some but very few. Not like here in India. Even without a teacher the student who practiced yoga in a previous birth will be dragged into the yoga path and will understand easily. Purity in the system is most essential—now or later births—with human effort and intense interest. Those who do penance, who are well versed, those who are karma yogis—A yogi is better than those three. They are good men, but a yogi exceeds these three. He contemplates eternal truth and visualizes eternal truth."

I mention that I have many doubts about rebirth, perhaps because there is no concept of rebirth in the religions of the west or perhaps because my culture is so materialistic. In my rational-logical mind, I am unconvinced, but I can only accept the possibility.

Acharya talks for quite some time about how it is unnecessary that I be convinced by someone else's logic. "To accept the possibility is good and go forward with your practice. Let the experience itself teach you. It doesn't matter whether you believe it or not. It has nothing to do with belief. That is all for today."

*

Suhas arrives in the late afternoon. The clothes he has made are very beautiful and I think I will wear them all the time. But I wish I hadn't put buttons in the front of the pants. The tailors put in strange flaps for buttons and zippers in the front. All I need now is to purchase some saris for Isabella at the store in Saraswati. After traveling in India for an entire year, she sent a trunk home to Mexico but it never arrived. She wants a few red cotton saris.

It's beginning to turn into dusk and I must do my practice and then visit with Dr. Anand. If I could only remember yesterday. Oh yes, I got on the bike and the climate was similar to today—unbearable—and I went into town to pick up some yoga pants from the khadi shop—the same pants I went to pick up the day before when the roof collapsed, and the day before that. No, madam, we are having problems. Only two are completed. The day before in the rain, your partner told me they were all ready. Please just tell me exactly when I can pick them up so I don't have to ride here and ride there and then come back again. Tomorrow at this time, he says. I go to pick up the glasses. Where is your receipt? I can't find it. Where is the owner? He is having lunch. Are the glasses ready? No, only one. I am about ready to yell. A man comes downstairs with a pair of glasses that are roughly shaped but not correct and I'm worried. Madam these are only samples. Your lenses are here. He holds up a bag. Then he wants to measure my eyes again. None of them are ready. Please do not rush this job I tell him, but tell me exactly when they will be ready. Tomorrow this time. (That would be right now, but I am not going to come again until the following day.) I must remember when I return—tomorrow means two or three days at least.

Anything else? Oh yes, I knock on Mr. Utkaresh's door to inquire about his apartments in case I need one next year. He lives in a mansion around the corner from here and is a cousin of Mr. Nutan. He rents to a lot of westerners.

As I sit in his living room, Mr. Utkaresh asks me, "How old are you?"

I feel like saying—Why? What difference does it make? As he sits on his very expensive, dark carved sofa with his bulky body, his gold rings and his wife quietly sitting across the room in her silk sari, I'm sure he is thinking, "Why is a middle-aged woman away from her home and her husband's control?" Yikes. It is almost time to go home. And I think I now look like a fifty year old woman. At least to Indians—they never seem very surprised about my age. Someone told me that my blond hair is the same as gray hair to them.

"Just call me if you want an apartment. I'll take care of you," he says.

*

When I was in the doctor's office tonight, the waiting room was very full and Akasha was kind of quiet. The florescent light wasn't working, so she lit the kerosene lamp and set it on the desk. Her shadow fell on the wall behind her. She was leaning over playing with her long slender fingers in the shadow and they were large in proportion to her body. She's very graceful.

I ask her if I can photograph her.

"Yes, of course." She glides in and out of the doctor's office. Then all the lights go out, so the lamp has to go into the Doctor's office and two candles are put on the table in the waiting room. A thin, very impatient older man with large rimmed glasses returns to the waiting room. He stands before my seat and says, "Excuse me Madam" as he points at the next seat. Perhaps he was sitting there before I arrived, or perhaps women move at the command of a man.

An old woman sits across from me with a red line drawn from the middle of her forehead right into the part of her hair. She is very grim and inward. The young woman she is with is overweight and her sari blouse is so tight and so short that her whole midriff hangs outside the sari. When she has finished reading the *The Star of Mysore*, I pick it up and read a few stories, one covering the anniversary of the victory over Pakistan and a history of the war over Kashmir. The other is the story of an auto rickshaw driver who was murdered by three other men over an argument that started because the driver insisted on serving non-vegetarian food during a celebration. They strangled him and pushed his car and him into the river. An article in the back is about a young couple who commit suicide by poisoning themselves. She is eighteen and he is twenty-one. Apparently they were in love, lived near each other, but came from different castes. I look around the room. The social restrictions are pretty hidden.

A little bell rings and Akasha gracefully ducks into the doctor's office to prepare some medicines for the patients. "Gina," he calls me in. I sit opposite him and take out the sheet of paper with the notes from each visit. The office is crazier than usual today. He is very distracted. I remind him I am here to pick up herbs, and he asks me to come back on Friday at 7:30. (Everything everywhere in India involves coming back and coming back.)

Akasha comes in and out to discuss various appointments, patients and other problems in Kannada. I want to ask questions about my constitution. Suddenly she interrupts again and he says someone is very insistent. He must move his car. I follow him through the waiting room and outside. There is a big truck dumping a pile of gravel into the middle of the lot in front of his office. My scooter has been picked up and moved to a different spot on top of a very high mound of gravel. Oh boy—I have to go down this hill with my feet on the ground and the brakes on continually. I tell him that I left a book of drawings for him and I'll see him on Friday. An Indian experience. This is why you must keep your life uncomplicated here, because people keep postponing, interrupting and rearranging. You'd go crazy if you didn't.

*

Then I scoot over to the eyeglass place. It is 7:30 and he said they'd be open until 9:00. Devaraja Road is a shopping center at night—much more active than in the daytime. Lots more traffic. The glasses are ready and they are exactly what I expected. Back at Iyengar's, I have three chapattis with vegetables and a little curd.

Then I cut down the dusty and busy streets. There is a big celebration going on in the park across from the movie theater. I think it has to do with a victory in Kashmir. Over to the circle and around. The policeman who stands in the middle of the road telling you when you can go—he must recognize me now that he has seen me pass by here so many times. I must stand out because of my blonde hair and my dress and because it is nighttime and I am a woman alone on a scooter. At first I was wobbling, but now I zip around the corner and down to the next intersection.

Here I am home again. Now let me talk about what is perhaps my last meeting with Acharya alone. The room is full of mosquitoes and ants. I am lying on the straw mat in the side room studying a large procession of ants from a corner in the door across the ceiling in a little arc shape, through the light fixture, across the other side and out the door toward the house. Jayashree says they come in for the warmth. Leave them be and they will come and go without hurting anyone. Acharya says there is some food. I say they like the warmth and oil inside the lamp. I can't follow a single one. They move as a group. Before he comes in, I sit up and wave my shawl around as if it is a fan sending the bugs elsewhere. But then they flood back in. I spread the pennyroyal oil over my arms and ankles, sit down and try to forget them. They don't usually bite me very much, but they distract me terribly.

Then Acharya arrives. "How are you? How is your practice?"

"I'm fine," I say, lying, because I feel heavy with melancholia over the things he said about the screen.

"You do not have to feel sad," he says again, "it could be a bad fate, but it could be a good fate. Your chart shows that you will have a strong yoga practice. It is ascending. But I could not give all the details for your astrology chart that I usually can. Something prohibited this. Sometimes there is a screen the first time I meet someone and then the second time when they return there is no screen. I sat with you many times and talked for an hour or an hour and a half about your practice and that is good. There are many secrets I could not teach you now. But there is the future." (All these words are interwoven with my later understanding and so are not entirely accurate).

I tell him that I was perfectly happy with what he had told me until he told me about the screen.

He indicates that he had to tell me so he didn't feel as if he had cheated me.

Ok. I accept his explanation. I ask a few other mundane questions about asanas and then I ask for a beginning chant.

He gives me a chant and I ask him to write it down. He is going to chant it into the tape recorder tomorrow. But he urges me not to say "om" or "aum" with it. I can chant anything as long as I don't say "om" or "aum."

Yogena chittasya padena vacam
malam sarirasya ca vaidyakena
yopakarottam pravaram muninam
patanjlim pranjali ranato'mi

Then he has me do my practice. It is difficult because I am having a little postnasal drip and people keep interrupting him with various problems. He asks me to stop and wait for him, which I do. He makes a few corrections and then at the end he adds two more pranayamas. Also he tells me that I need to breathe quieter so I can be heard from three feet not six feet away. I think I am trying to be louder because of his loud breathing—as a coach—and because of the noise in my apartment. I can't hear myself breathe there, I explain. He nods his head.

Then we talk about some other things—I can't remember exactly—and I ask him if I can talk about something that might have been sinful.

He shuts the door and locks it.

I tell him about Lenny and me and how he was sick for a year and I had to care for him and about some misgivings I'd been mulling over in my mind for several years. Mostly I talk about his death, how in the end he was in a coma, his lungs were full of phlegm, his body was all swollen, his circulation shut down, and he was covered with bed sores. Yet he kept breathing. I'd turn him over and see giant red bruises. Twenty minutes later, I'd turn him again and the same thing would be on the other side. I had given him many injections of morphine to help encourage his death (he had saved it for that purpose) but it wasn't getting into his system anymore. His blood wasn't moving through his body. When he would breathe, yellow pus would fill up his mouth. He had asked me to not let him stay alive in a coma, not to let him linger. That's why he had saved the morphine. A visiting nurse told me he could go on like this for a week or more. She wanted to take him to the hospital. I was distraught. He didn't want to die in the hospital. He wanted to die at home. There was so much misery in the house. Late at night, Josh and Jessie were both in their rooms. I was alone with Lenny. I whispered in his ear, I love you Lenny, and then I took the sheet, folded it, and held it tightly over his face until he stopped breathing and his body became totally silent. I stopped his breath. The rest of his body was already dead. I could feel his spirit as it was released into the room. I was weeping.

Acharya is silent.

Throughout the twenty-five years we had known each other, Lenny was always a bit frozen in terms of movement and I was always helping him with every transition he had to make. I think of myself as a midwife, helping him die. But then I wonder if I couldn't have just been a little more patient. I wonder if doing what he wanted was the right thing to do. And I'm not sure that I was thinking clearly after three days of sleeplessness and misery. I was acting from my emotional center. This couldn't go on any longer.

Acharya looks at me. I am weeping on the straw mat where I usually practice meditation and pranayama. He says, emphatically, "No one can affect the death date of another. You die when you are meant to die. But it is best not to interfere with a natural death. And yet you should not worry about this. You can repent, but if you repent too much, you might disturb his soul."

"He would not want me to be in misery over this," I say.

"On his death date, you should make some food that he would like and give it to poor people. Also you can fast on that day and pray for his soul."

I tell him how Lenny's last words to Josh were "I'm fine. "

"That is a very good sign for a good new birth. It is your duty, Gina, to be happy and to live happily with whatever problems you have. That is what yoga is all about."

"Thank you," I say. "Thank you."

He asks if I have anything else I want to talk about.

"No, nothing else."

Then I coast around the corner with the scooter engine barely running. I am moving very slowly.

After they took his body away, I lit some blue candles in the room. I felt his presence there. At the crematory, I felt his presence in the air around me. In the local Methodist church, they held a mixed service, some Christian rites, some Jewish rituals, and lots of neighbors and customers from his store talked about what Lenny had meant to them. As I planned the funeral service, ordered food, entertained relatives and friends, attended to Josh and Jessie, and cleaned and emptied his apartment of so many collected things, I felt as if I was a robot, waiting. For a while I found it difficult to speak. And then for months I couldn't talk about anything except his death, and yet I couldn't talk about the actual details with anyone except my friend Artie. After a while the death started to fade, as memories do, until some detail calls back the horror and helplessness of watching a loved one's body fail, of helping a loved one die. Fragile like a leaf. Heavy with history. The pages blow down the street.

When I returned to the yoga studio, Manny's wife Sally looked at me and said, "He died. I can tell by looking at you." When I was resting in savasana, I listened to the sound of many people breathing deeply in unison. Sally straightened out my body, rubbed her fingers across my forehead, pressing over the eyebrow center. She covered me with a blanket. Yoga was my solace.

For several years I have longed for someone to talk to about Lenny's death, someone to give me spiritual guidance.

*

On the floor, I'm looking at two photographs of Lenny. One, just a few weeks before he died. Somehow Jessie and I got him down the four flights of stairs and out the door. We had a wheel chair parked in the lobby. He wanted so much to go out in the sun and down the avenue to see people he knew in the neighborhood. He's wearing a big pair of overalls which are hiding his swollen belly. He has his arm around Jessie, his fingers resting on her shoulder. Their heads are tipped together and he has a big smile, so happy to be with her. I notice in the photograph that her right hand is clenched. This was a difficult time for her.

In the other photograph she is about thirteen years old. I think it was taken at summer camp. Her hair is shoulder length and she's a little troubled here, too. Maybe it was just the sun in her eyes. Lenny has his arms in front of her, steadying her as he looks down at her. Her left hand is touching his white shirt on the front, showing her love and dependence with the light touch of her fingers. Hands. Whenever I look at Josh's hands, I see a trace of Lenny. My own hands with my fingers touching this keyboard—If Acharya is correct, I am going to live a long life with these hands. Then I won't need them any longer. I have some of Lenny's ashes in a little container in my room at home. When I look at them I notice little chips of bone. He didn't need his body any longer.

Almost noon. I have three and a half days left in Mysore. Yesterday Acharya told a story about himself and Jayashree. His horoscope predicted no children. But her astrology chart which was done by the palace astrologer in Bangalore indicated, yes, children. So they thought they could twist fate and have children. Then after many different astrologers were consulted, they studied her astrology chart and found that in fact the great astrologist had made an error. For her also, no children. I remember him saying when he met me the first day and I thought the little boy was his—no we have no children, but we have many children. And he does—all these young people who live around and in their house studying yoga.

I stop by the hotel to photograph Mahadeshwara and Rupesh and the others. (I had promised them and also I wanted to use up this role of film so I could see if the photographs I took of Acharya had turned out.) While there, Mahadeshwara asks me to visit his house for only a few minutes for a birthday party and take some photographs. I tell him I am too busy, but he keeps saying, "Come for some sweets, please Madame."

So I think, why not, and I follow him on his scooter to his house. He is wearing a clean white shirt with a puja red mark on his forehead. I ask him if I should pick up some candy for his son.

"No, madam, you just come." So I follow him.

First he goes around the block—he has forgotten something. I wait and he goes back to the hotel. Then he stops at Iyengar's restaurant on double road to buy some sweets for the party. I follow him down the road by the hospital, past the beautiful Hanuman statue, until it became a dirt road and then we turn left and pull up in front of his modest little house.

His wife, mother and sister-in-law are seated on the floor making all kinds of food for the celebration. There is a big happy birthday sign on the wall. I would guess that his son is eight years old, but in fact he is celebrating his fourteenth birthday. I think Indians grow taller later. The boy sits on his father's lap while Mahadeshwara strokes him. The women start bringing sweets for me to eat. . . a cup of some sweet drink .

"Very good for you madam. It will make your body very strong," Mahadeshwara insists.

But it is much too sweet for me. Then they serve me a plate of sugar candies. I simply can't eat this food. I force myself to drink the drink, take a bite of the candy and then I ask if I can take it with me for later.

The cows will eat it, I think to myself.

I take several photos of his family. The one I like best is of his little boy with Chamundi Hill in the background. Then I explain that I must leave because I have another appointment. I would have felt uncomfortable staying there—everyone staring at me without any real conversation (we don't fluently speak each other's language). It's a beautiful place, on the edges of Mysore, quiet, with lots of coconut trees waving in the wind. And that big precious hill in the background no matter where you look.

*

This morning I wake up, practice and my mind is full of worry about a new little pain in my back. (Also during the night I had my first sexual longing in my body since I arrived in Mysore—two months—or did I perhaps suddenly recognize this absence and call on it so I could remember it. It's quite amazing that I could have forgotten sex for this long. Perhaps the diet and practice I have been following is responsible.) How did I do this to my back? I review the entire practice, each pose and can't find a reason. Half way through my pranayama, as I'm on the third round of nadi shodana, it comes to me—I have been picking that scooter up and placing it on the stand rather than leaning it on the kickstand—for two days I have been doing this. The result—a little injury. I must be careful.

*

Sunanda talks to me about the United States, her possible new husband, her worries, her ideas, her views of Indians who leave India and settle in the U.S. I think she is a very strong young woman and she will be fine with whatever they decide. Sometimes I think life might be made easier with these arranged marriages—the astrologers, the parents, an entire combining of the energies of both families. Of course Subrata and Jeevesh let her have some say. Their children have been around too many westerners not to allow that.

Subrata sits down, too. I show them the photographs of my children. Everyone thinks Jessie is beautiful. Subrata talks about some Indians who are visiting their parents for the first time in eight years. They live in Flint, Michigan. He is a corporate executive at General Motors. They know nothing about western yoga students. They don't understand why I want to be here, but they want to meet me. She says they are not as friendly as yoga students.

"Yoga students," I say, "are much different from corporate executives. We are not your average Americans. Most yoga students seek a spiritual side to their lives and are therefore attracted to Indian culture. An Indian going to America for material wealth and embracing western culture is probably quite different."

Today, July 27th, Acharya and Carl arrive at the same time. I leave the door open for Justine, who comes a few minutes later. I yell down asking her to lock the door. We all three sit on the little straw mat across from Acharya. I tell him that I have the tape recorder. He tells me that I should go to his house tomorrow or Saturday so Jayashree can teach me how to sing the chant. Is that ok?

"Yes, of course." Every other scheduled event here takes second place to these yoga lessons.

Then he hands me a paper with the name of a book, *The Science of Yoga* by Taimini and another book that is a commentary on the yoga sutras (he can't remember the title) but the author is Hariharananda and it is published by Anandashram in Calcutta. Also *The Bhagavad Gita* by Dr. RadhaKrishnan. I think I should check Gheeta bookstore tomorrow or some other bookstore over by Dasprakash. He tells me to look in the Vedanta bookstore in Bangalore, which is near the Ramakrishna Ashram, and then another bookstall near the railroad station.

We begin our discussion with a question from Carl: "What is a pure family?"

"A family in which the laws of niyama and yama are naturally found—nonviolence, truthfulness, nonstealing, fewer possessions, celibacy, tapas, contentment, self study, cleanliness, and a natural devotion."

I guess my family wasn't pure—there was some violence as a means of punishing children and animals; contentment was low, and there was much unhappiness due to my mother's illness. The rest of the yamas and niyamas were present in my mother. My father however lacked tapas and a natural devotion. And Lenny and I were certainly not ideal parents.

With a family like the one he is describing, he says, there will not be so many obstructions in the systems—the door for some will open instantly. "All yoga techniques purify. Niyama and yama are like fences. You follow these guidelines and there will be no new obstacles. If you follow these and still there are obstacles and obstructions, then you turn to asana and pranayama to eliminate the obstacles. If you have no impurities, you don't need asana and pranayama. In western countries and much of the world there are so many problems now in thinking. An unnatural lifestyle creates these problems. It is also difficult to follow these guidelines because of the influence one has on the other. If you hurt someone, a block forms in other places in your life. If you steal, your mind is disturbed. But some of these things are inevitable given your situation. Just as strength appears as it is needed, there is so much energy available to help purify."

I ask him about the effect of eating meat for so many years.

He says that I should not worry about that. "It was hereditary. Your family was eating meat for centuries. So you have developed some immunity to the long term effects. Those who consume alcohol and meat can still have some yogic enjoyment, but it is limited." He uses an example of someone who feels joy within but can't express it on her face. Or someone who has knowledge and can't express it. The experience is similar. He also reminds us that garlic and onions are ragasic and should be avoided by those who want to practice yoga.

He talks about different definitions of violence—of body, mind, and words. "Do not hurt others. Do not encourage anyone to hurt others and do not appreciate it if anyone is hurting anyone else. There is so much wickedness in society because there is no moral binding. There is a loss of morality and consciousness and therefore you are sometimes forced to behave rashly. For example, you are on the street and some boys are bothering you. You must speak to them harshly or you must take them to the police. You must do this and yet it is a violence. Or you must kill some mosquitoes or you will die. You could, however, put in a good drainage system so then there will be no mosquitoes. You can avoid the situation. More and more wickedness, more and more violence. First avoid violence. Second, hurt as little as possible, and last, kill for survival. All leave obstructions but some are considered inevitable."

We are at the last stanza in the 6th Chapter. "The mind has extraordinary powers. In philosophy, epics and science, there is some talk about the wish yielding tree. But these stories are not the same in yoga. In yoga the tree is in your mind. You wish and you gain if your system is ready and if not the mind will take you there. But you must have faith. With faith you will obtain liberation and realization very soon. Faith is most important. It helps the wish yielding tree. Faith drives changes in the system. There is a secretion in the mind that happens with intention—faith. You need three things. A clear decision about your goal, the required tools, and faith in the tool. The mind has extraordinary power. With the right goal and the wrong tool, movement is not usually possible. But with extraordinary faith, sometimes you still can achieve your goal.

"With the proper technique and faith: 100%. Pranayama is a tool to help control the mind. The teacher himself can be a tool. Nature is a tool. But you need 100% faith. If no faith, this can still work with a technique like pranayama. But if there is more than the absence of faith, a negative attitude, that will interfere. The whole principle of yoga: According to your desire, prepare your body. All occurs through the body. The body is the medium. When the system is not ready, intentions and decisions will not exhibit until the body is prepared."

And then we stop. He will come tomorrow between twelve and one and Jayashree will come also and then I can make an appointment with her.

Carl says he has a few questions about his practice that he would like to ask outside. They are talking and I turn around and look at Justine. She is laying flat on the mat in the middle of the room.

"Why didn't you take the note off the door, yesterday?" I ask. "I wasn't sure if you had received the message."

"I didn't come yesterday," she says. "I was so sick with food poisoning that I couldn't come. I'm still sick." She is stretched out with her face chalk white.

"Why did you sit here for the whole lesson sick like this without saying a word? What are you taking?"

"Nothing." She tells me she has had diarrhea and she's been vomiting.

"You should ask Acharya what you should take."

"No, I can't".

He is in the hallway, an ayurvedic doctor and she is embarrassed to ask. She says it's ok if I ask, so I step out and say, "Justine is very ill. What should she take?"

"For food poisoning—take lukewarm water as much as you want and then eat hot rice, freshly cooked with curd twice a day. Then take some fenugreek, soaked for two hours in buttermilk and chew it."

"Is someone taking care of you?" I ask

"Yes, two friends."

"Do you want to stay here and let me care for you?"

"Just for a little while."

I take the scooter out to buy some curd and fenugreek while Carl makes the rice. The store keepers don't know what fenugreek is. Someone hands me coriander seeds as if any old herb will help. Not Indian, they say. (I didn't hear Carl say menthi is what they call it.) Back home I look after her while Carl returns to the store. When Justine wakes up, I give her a cup of curd rice.

"If you want to stay here you can. I'll make a place for you in the bedroom, but I will be coming and going."

"No let me try the bathroom and then I'll go home."

I give her some of the Chinese curing pills to try to kill the crap in her stomach and then I walk her home.

*

At night, I join the boys downstairs for dinner at Upahar. Raj, the young American-Indian, promises to give me a list of American novels he has read about India. I am completely comfortable in this restaurant at night with a party of three, especially these two sweet young men. People don't stare at me and I don't look at them. A lone woman eating out, especially at night—this is an occasion for staring in India.

*

I meet for the last time today with Acharya. I write some questions about my practice—the only one I don't really know the answer to is the mudra he was going to teach me for my colon. That will have to wait until next year. He asks for questions and I ask one:

"You have told us that it is better for us to discover our own paths—through our meditation, otherwise someone is forcing the wrong path on us—we don't know what our paths are yet. Don't we follow the path of our teacher? Reading Ramakrishna I note that there are the Saktas who follow Tantra/Shiva/Durga; the Vaishnavas who follow Purana/Krishna/Radha, the Bramajnais, Vedantists, etc. Which path do you follow?"

"Which is your question?" he asks. "Do you want to know my path?"

"Yes, and more, the question is complicated." He laughs and so does Jayashree.

"By birth I followed Shiva, but due to my constitution and fate, I now follow Vishnu. Usually I know which path a student is actually following, but I often don't tell him because it is best if a student discovers his path on his own."

"The intention of reading these books is to end with silence not disturbance. Proper knowledge should end with silence. Don't develop a tendency to question. Try to end with silence. Natural questions are good. But don't provoke the tendency in students to think of questions. They become too much extroverted."

I talk about my students, who watch too much television and who need to learn to question.

"End in a questionless state. When you read a text like Ramakrishna end almost in meditation."

I must admit I feel better with contented introversion.

There is a phone call in the middle of the session on Carl's cell phone, and it is for Acharya. He talks for a very long time. Carl and I exchange email addresses. Acharya apologizes for staying on the phone so long—it is the people he is going to visit when he leaves my house.

He cautions me about reading the Yoga Sutras he's recommended—good but not 100% correct—a lot of imaginative thinking.

"Do your practice and keep doing it even if there are bad days, the good will come. If one day you have particularly good results—you are very calm and quiet—decide to stay in solitude or go to a natural place like the seashore without any contacts. Be sure it is a safe area. Sometimes you can lose consciousness for a half hour or hour. An injury might happen. Do not be near fire or water where you can drown.

"If during your meditation you have feelings, imaginations and experiences, have no curiosity about these. If a suggestion arises that you change your practice in any way, do not listen to it unless you talk to a teacher. Check it out first.

"Go very slowly with your practice in the morning and evening. If you are speedy, you will lose it. If you express the joy and happiness you experience to others, you will lose it. If you explore your experience in words, you will lose it. Sometimes it may not arrive again. Sometimes yogis have become involved in demonstrations, sometimes money and greed become involved, and sometimes their internal progress comes to a halt even though externally, they seem to be practicing."

I mention that I draw and write out of my experience.

"Do not reveal the details of your practice, the secrets or you will lose the experience and sometimes bad things can happen. I might also suffer from it." He asks me how this is with me.

I say I am a bit troubled because I spend my whole life translating and transforming my experience into art and writing. I am an artist."

"How much you learn is not as important as "honor" is. You don't want to damage the wish-fulfilling tree. All will be wasted. It is not important to come and come to India. But honor is important."

I have this all jumbled up because I am a little disturbed. He doesn't know that I have already written 200 or more pages about my experience here. I try to assure him that I will have great honor for him and that I am actually like a tortoise—I continue slowly at whatever I do. I persevere. But I think perhaps we are misunderstanding each other.

*

Carl and I sit on the floor in the kitchen. I'm preparing to leave so I give him things from my kitchen. And we talk about this issue of not discussing your meditative experience and he says one thing that really meant something to me. It is something that Acharya said to him before. You know how you are feeling badly and then you tell someone about it and you feel better. Well when you are very happy and you tell someone about it, you then lose some of the happiness, too. It is probably true. Any use of language—visual or oral— involves loss even though we are often talking to try to regain an earlier loss. Say a word and you lose the experience, the feeling. All seems to be lost with language when we are entangled in it. But then the sound is found. That's why it is so wonderful to sing bajans, Indian devotional songs—in a foreign language without full understanding. This is why I love drawing and poetry. The images point to something while never quite grasping it. I give you this. I give you that. And then this line. And in between maybe the light of the soul.

Carl leaves after indicating that some Indian yogis have problems with Whitman and his attachment to the senses. Why not celebrate the senses too? This doesn't make *sense* to me because I love Whitman. Perhaps I am hopelessly entangled and in love with my material existence.

＊

I finish reading volume one of Ramakrishna.

Whitman's work is about accepting and embracing the whole of existence, the spiritual and the material woven together, senses and all. His "I" includes god and the whole universe, body, mind, spirit—one large awake samadhi. The I has disappeared in the whole.

Regarding Christianity, Ramakrishna says, "The wretch who constantly says, 'I am bound, I am bound' only succeeds in being bound. He who says day after night, I am a sinner, I am a sinner, verily becomes a sinner"(138)

Oh forget it—too many quotes and I found the two I wanted to write inside my book for Carl:

God cannot be seen with these physical eyes. In the course of spiritual discipline one gets a 'love body', endowed with 'love eyes', 'love ears' and so on. One sees God with these 'love eyes. ' One hears the voice of God with those 'love ears'. One even gets a sexual organ made of love . . . With this 'love body' the soul communes with God . . . One sees nothing but God everywhere when one loves Him with great intensity. It is like a person with jaundice, who sees everything yellow. Then one feels, 'I am verily He.'

＊ ＊ ＊

Sometimes I find the universe is saturated with the consciousness of God, as the earth is soaked with water in the rainy season.

I write a note to Carl inside the cover of my book of drawings: "The above quotes remind me so much of Whitman. I search all over for them in Ramakrishna, remembering he is surrounded by merchants who are heavily involved in sakti/maya. I love the world, especially when it is laced with the light of the soul—oh beautiful lust, gold, water, flesh, error, chapatti, old worn cow in the road. Love Gina 7/28"

Yes, I need to be quiet to see the light, and perhaps someday I'll be totally immersed in that light. But then when I stand up, I want to see it in everything. Perhaps some people have to give up sex, but some do not. Do I believe there are calm and quiet people in the U.S. who commune with this light. And embracing couples, too. Yes, hidden, however, much more hidden than here in India and not understood, but they are there. . . . following a yogic way of life.

Before Carl leaves, I photograph him by his scooter. I hug him. He has difficulty hugging today as if he is becoming a Brahmin. Goodbye, dear Carl.

Then I go to Subrata's, driving the scooter into her yard and not closing the door to the gate. While I am eating I look up and a very big black cow walks right through the front door. I yell to her and Sunanda. The cow marches directly into the back room where they store the papayas. Subrata comes running into the back room, swatting the cow on its backside with a tennis racket that must have been hanging by the door for just this kind of thing. As I walk outside with Sunanda to watch some procession for the goddess on Chamundi Hill, she says, "It is a very good sign to have a cow come into your house on Friday because Friday is Lakshmi day and a cow is very sacred."

I eat quickly and scoot around the block to a beauty salon where a woman will give me a manicure and pedicure. What this means in India is a thorough cleaning of your hands and feet, scrubbing them with a pumice stone until there are no calluses. They do very little with your fingernails. Next time I come, I will forget the manicure but come for the pedicure every week. Even without walking the zillions of miles I did last year, my feet have become cracked and full of calluses. The proprietor washes my feet, waiting for hot water to boil on the stove. As she attends to me, she and another woman chat away in Kannada. I tell them I want to know what they are saying. They just laugh.

Later in the evening before going to Dr. Anand's office, I decide to go to the bank and take out some money so Josh has some rupees when he arrives in India. I get there and I can't find my cards. I am a little bit concerned. Did I lose them? Where are they? I go through my bag several times and then go to the doctors. He does not have the medicines ready for me, or at least all of them. I shouldn't call them medicines since they are just herbal/spice concoctions. I sit down and we start deciding how much of each thing. I realize that this is going to be quite expensive.

What I really want to talk to him about is why he might see me as vata-kapha while Acharya sees me as vata-pitta. He considers me kapha because of my precision in making decisions, my lack of involvement in sports as a child, the control over my emotions (I never had any control over my emotions until I started practicing yoga. I told him I used to cry very easily. I just don't feel angry that often or I didn't as a child); my deep sleep as a child, my fine hair (kapha), funny fine hair in the American books means pitta; my oily skin and lack of gray hair; frequent allergies. Whatever—I don't know what to do with all this except to trust Acharya's analysis: vata-pitta, almost 50-50.

At home, I find my credit cards tucked inside a pocket in my wallet. They were with me all the time I was searching in the bank.

*

Today is already tonight—7:30 p.m. and the lights are out and the whole section of town is in darkness. It has been like this for 45 minutes. Where did this day go as morning became noon became afternoon became evening? I wake up and begin cleaning and straightening and rearranging things in my luggage to discover that everything does not fit into the small canvas bag I purchased as an extra bag. I decide to empty it and see if they will take it back in exchange for a bigger one. I'm so preoccupied with tasks that I have gone too late in the morning to do my asana practice so I decide only to do the pranayama and then do asanas in the evening. That way I can do the same tomorrow and the same the next day, working so I end up practicing immediately before I leave. Perhaps this will help me prepare for such a long trip where I can only sit and lean over for over 40 hours.

After running an errand, back home I find Suhas waiting on the stoop for me. We sit on the straw mats on the living room floor and chat. I thank him for all his good work and suggest that he keep a sample bag to show students. (I don't think he can earn enough to buy the fabric for the samples.) He picks up the bag I'm going to return because it is too small and asks how much I paid for it.

"Between 350 and 400 rupees, but I am returning it."

He holds it in his lap and opens every zipper. It is apparent he wants it. "How much do you want?"

"Give me 200 and you can have it."

"One fifty," he says.

I should do that when he makes a price for making clothes, I think to myself. I decide to give it to him for the 150 as a gift and then he is happy and I don't have to go back to the same store. I thank him for all he has done. I wish him the best and away he goes and away I go to pick up my address book off the computer table where I left it at Subrata's.

At Subrata's Matthew and I are talking about Ramakrishna again. He is turned off by his emphasis on "hard work" which I don't remember. Yes, I remember him being awfully hard on some of the people who have done the hardest work for society (karma yoga) because they aren't fully realized, because they haven't gone into solitude enough. Yes, I cringe a little but I think it is important to stand at a distance from these texts and learn something, accept some ideas, reject others, and enjoy a little. Acharya says, be silent after reading. Matthew says he's more interested in a tantra where the everyday world is divine. That was just what I was thinking this morning and last night. I want to know more about tantra. I think in fact Ramakrishna is practicing a type of tantra, but I'm unsure. He definitely sees the everyday world as divine. That's why a word or an image sends him into an ecstatic trance.

At home, as I'm adding some of my things to the closet with all the books and the clothes left from the yoga students who stayed here before me, I notice a book on the shelf by Ramana Maharishi, the guru who Paul Brunton discovered. Acharya mentions Ramana Maharishi often. I open the book and there is a little black and white photo of Ramana slipped inside the book. He is beautiful, his eyes soft and loving. I read an underlined passage in the middle of the book right next to the photograph: "In whatever place in the body one thinks Self to be residing due to the power of that thinking it will appear to the one who thinks thus as if Self is residing in that place. However, the beloved Heart alone is the refuge for the rising and subsiding of that *I*, . . Heart, the source, is the beginning, the middle and the end of all. Heart, the supreme space, is never a form. It is the light of truth." I put the book with the stack of things to take with me on the plane.

*

Carl comes over. He talks about some problems with his marriage. This really is an interlude for him. They may not reunite after his year or years in India. I give him the plastic chair I purchased and he gives me some sweet dessert, which I'm going to eat after I'm finished with these notes. Then he goes and we wish each other adieu. Sweet guy and interesting to talk to, though strangely attracted to Hindu/Brahmin habits that seem wildly incompatible with western life, like washing some dishes outside and others inside, holding one cup with one hand and another with another, sprinkling water in a certain way over the spot where you eat and then spreading the water around with your hand and picking up the particles, and then wiping with a cloth. . . this must be done exactly in Carl's house as it might be done in Acharya's. He says he follows these rituals because Acharya and Jayashree are in his house so often, but I noticed him cringe once in my apartment when I sat down and ate with a spoon and used my left hand. I wonder how he'll make the transition back to living in the States whenever he returns. I have a feeling he will still be here next year when I return.

Off I go on the scooter to the bank to take out 7000 rupees. My balance on the bank machine is 119,000 rupees which comes to about $3,000 U.S. dollars. Hum, I thought I had more than that. I hope everything is ok back at home. I think I really have overspent money here this year. On that note, I decide to buy Isabella a very beautiful red cotton sari at Lakshmi Silk, which I do, and then I come home and put it into the little space left in the suitcase.

I ride over to Roberto's to say goodbye.

"Dear . . ." Roberto steps out of his house in his blue rubber tongs. "You will visit me in the Costa Rica when I return, yes. Or next year you will return and we will spend more time together. Call me before you come and I will try to help you find a house. And perhaps you can bring me some seaweed from New York when you return."

"Yes, Roberto, I will definitely call you."

"And someday we will spend time together on the beach when my wife and I build our little house. You will come to our home." He hugs me and gives me half a loaf of seven-grain bread he has just cooked. "Take this with you for the trip."

"Goodbye dear Roberto."

*

It is very hot in here. I set Ramana's photo on one side of the candle and on the other side the photo of Lenny in the kitchen, looking at the light. Then I do my asana and pranayama practice. It is quite powerful practicing late like this instead of early.

I hold Lenny's photo in my hands.

After the funeral, when I returned home, I pressed the play button on my answering machine and it was Lenny—"Gina," he said, weakly, "I know you'll be back here in a minute and we've gone over everything, over and over again. And I just want to say, I love you, Gina, and I know you know it."

Yes, I'll practice making borscht and knishes this year, Lenny. I've never made them before and then I'll pass them out to the men living in the park across the street from my apartment on your death day.

*

At Upahar, I have a parota and some almond milk. I stop and email Isabella to tell her about the sari and I stop at the hotel and have a club soda. Mahadeshwara wants me to stop by and say goodbye, too. The whole day is a big circle of endings. Tomorrow will be the end of the loop. On the way home, I notice the trees and the wide sky.

I order a little bit of fruit and ginger tea from Subrata. Her neighbors, who now live in Michigan but who grew up in Mysore, come by to talk with me. They are very pleasant people. I recognize the man's gestures and incredible sweetness as an inheritance from Mysore and South India. He gives me his card and I give him my email address in case he ever comes to New York. His wife works in a research section of a medical school and he is involved in some computer consultancy for Chrysler Company. Very nice people. Not really the corporate executive type at all.

Calmness, composure and simplicity. Last year I left India with two inflamed brands on my shoulders. This trip has been an even thread, a calmer narrative.

Matthew tells me he's leaving in a week and having some doubts about the value of his returning to India again. He spends an incredible amount of money and isn't really receiving much. He's thinking it is time to go on his own.

I think he should come back and seek out Acharya.

He might after a year, he says, when he is sure he doesn't want to continue with Ramaji.

We talk a little bit more about Ramakrishna and I mention the criticism of people who concentrate so much on asanas. He talks about how much further he has gotten in his quality of mind from little changes in his asanas. There are probably many different ways to experience contentment (if that isn't exactly realized—and to tell you the truth I don't know what realized means. For me, it has something to do with accepting and experiencing the ordinary and the extraordinary in a blissful, ecstatic way).

Anyhow, we say goodbye and I chat with Jeevesh, planning my trip. I ask him if I can photograph him and Subrata. She is busy in the other room digging through a trunk. She comes out finally for the photograph and gives me a pair of silver earrings, little hoops. I'm shocked. I know I have been eating there and spending money, but I would never expect a gift from her. We have gotten to know each other this year. I take their photograph in front of the doorway to their house. And I snap a photo of Subrata sitting at her table leaning her head on the palm of her hand. That would make an interesting drawing. Later when I'm in the house talking to Jeevesh more about our trip—he is driving me to Bangalore to the airport—I can hear her in the back chanting. She chants for several hours every day. I wonder if there is a penance in it all—for her attachments.

I stop and purchase some jasmine flowers from a woman on the double road and then scoot over to J. Prakash, down the shady road and up the hill. A young man opens the door and tells me to sit on a chair. Finally Jayashree comes out and sits with me. I like her and I think she likes me. It was slow coming though. During my two hours with her, she tells me many things about how to live as a yogi and she sings the chant for me that includes the three lessons of Patanjali—to live correctly with your body, mind and words. And then a tribute to him.

After that, she gives me advice about my practice. "Between nine and five don't do anything that will disturb your calm. Do the minimum possible to complete the tasks you must complete." She tries to explain why a man can marry after his wife dies but she can't—it has something to do with his innate capacity to be more quiet and calm than a woman. I think someday we will continue this conversation because it has become one of the themes running through my experience here this summer.

"Also, dogs," she says, "are very rajasic and they cause you a lot of bad energy."

We talk a bit about Peggy who I say is not so rajasic anymore.

She is old and my pal.

"Don't pet her before you do your practice, she warns. Bathe and wash your hands. Indians have changed in their relationship to dogs to be more like westerners and it is very bad. Let the dog be, but not with you."

I try to tell her about dog as man's best friend.

"No," she says, "not if you are to do yoga. But your dog you have had a long time. Keep her, but when she dies, do not get another one."

I really don't plan to have another dog after Peggy because it makes my life too complicated. But I love Peggy, rajasic or not.

"Yes, make your life simple." She talks about how I talk so fast, and how those who talk fast think too much. "You must go slowly."

I ask her if I can take her photo after she sings the song. She says yes, and I take her photo right in the same spot I took Acharya's.

She mentions that many Americans ask to be Acharya's student, but he only takes a few. "Carl—they have a special relationship."

"Yes, I say, didn't you all travel together?"

"Yes," she says, "Acharya loves Carl."

We also talk about beautiful temples near Mysore. When I come back I'm going to ask her for a list of them and directions on how to get there and I'm going to visit them.

"Some of them won't let westerners in," she says.

"Well, even if I can only see the outside."

I walk down the sidewalk and she walks out on the porch and waves to me.

"Be sure you leave feeling joyful about Mysore and India," she says, "no matter what the little irritations are. When you are buying something, ask yourself—do I need this?"

A very quick ride over to Shivanand's house. Shivanand is in his boxer shorts and a tee-shirt. He's been giving examinations at the ashram all day. I give him 500 rupees for what I still owe him. His mother-in-law is dying and there is some problem with his son. He hardly gets off the couch to say goodbye. There is so much sadness in the house right now. I say goodbye to everyone. I am sad to leave right now with such sorrow and quietness.

Back to Iyengar's to eat some chapattis and then home in the dark, rearranging the suitcases. A little bit of anxiety about the day in Bangalore—I decide I want Jeevesh to stay the whole day there and drop me off at the airport. He will charge me an outrageous amount of rupees, but I am very tired, I don't understand Bangalore, I have so much luggage, and I want to be sure I have a ride to the airport.

The Victoria Hotel. This old hotel was probably established before independence in the forties. Beautiful rooms and gardens. It's 9 p.m., I've been here since noon, and I'll be leaving in an hour and a half. The day has been quite different than I had planned—as are most Indian days.

I wake up at 5 a.m. and take an oil bath and then a regular bath. I straighten out all the little details to close the house and finish packing. I do a pranayama practice, throughout conscious of limited time. The meditation is so different when I'm not limited by time.

I take the suitcase I can carry downstairs and sit on the porch, waiting for Jeevesh. 6:30 a.m., 6:45, 7:00. He comes by in a car that sounds like it won't make it around the corner, smoke pouring out and all kinds of writing on the back window.

"I'll be right back," he yells. "Going for gas."

I wait. 7:15, 7:30. Here he is again, but now in a beautiful deluxe ambassador car with his friend from school, Prabakas, driving.

"Prabakas," he explains, "has three children and he is a very nice man. He can't speak English."

We drive out Sayyaji road and leave behind the buildings and slowly fewer and fewer people selling this and that, carrying this basket, that bunch of vegetables—on head, on back, in cart, truck. I think about taking photographs. Didn't I do this already? I put the camera back into my bag. I am going to return, a year from now. I miss home, but I'm already missing Mysore.

"Will we make it by 10:00?"

"Yes, we'll be at the Vedanta Bookstore by 10:00."

I wonder how, since we are leaving an hour late, but who knows in India. Midway, we stop at his friend's restaurant and have breakfast and then Jeevesh pays for the breakfast and the water I need.

As we approach the city, there are unusually large groups of people milling around. Prabakas pulls over and asks a policeman a question.

"What's going on?" I ask.

"There is a strike. Raj Kumar, a famous Kannada speaking movie star in Karnataka has been kidnapped. Everyone is going home from school. There is a strike organizing. I think we will go straight to the hotel," he says, "because the bookstore will be closed."

Well, that's one of the reasons I came to Bangalore early. And why, I wonder, are they striking and going home over a movie star. Perhaps movie stars are somehow connected to the gods and other mythic figures in India.

The police are stopping and checking all the buses and people are streaming everywhere.

"Wait a minute," I say, "go directly to Elizabeth Road to the American School or I won't be able to drop off this suitcase for Josh." The suitcase I have thought about for two months—stupid me, thinking and thinking.

After lots of maneuvering and questions, we finally find the spot and I climb out of the car and up the stairs to a lovely place with a lot of people highly concerned—"I'm Kirtana," says a very jovial heavy set woman, who is clearly in charge. "We have been waiting for you, Gina. We are all going home because of the strike. It can be dangerous on the streets. We talk for half an hour; I meet the yoga teacher, librarian, secretary, their husbands, and I learn that the fear is that this whole thing can erupt into riots between the Tamil and Kannada speaking peoples. A fast half hour talk. I leave thinking that it seems at first glance like a good school for Josh.

Jeevesh is waiting for me in the car. When I check in at the hotel, the clerk tells me that along the road to his brother's house and to the airport a few buses have been burned and an automobile. Jeevesh was planning to spend the day with his brother. So I invite him and Prabakas to stay in the hotel for lunch. Maybe things will calm down.

While we are eating, a young German man, John, who is working in the one of Tibetan communities on a carpentry project to prepare for the Dali Lama's arrival, comes to talk and to try to figure out what is happening.

Jeevesh tries to convince him to take their car service back to Mysore, of course for a large fee. He isn't interested. Then Jeevesh and Prabakas leave to visit with Jeevesh's brother for the afternoon.

Here I am in this hotel and I will not be going anywhere for the afternoon. We are locked in at the gate and every business in Bangalore is closed. This hasn't happened, a hotel boy tells me, for more than five years. After I finish my pranayama practice and prepack my suitcases, I decide I want to see if the bookstores are open. I start to walk out the gate. John comes running after me, and we walk together a few blocks.

Everything is closed and I don't feel safe because there are no women on the street.

Every so often a hostile young man sneers at us, so we decide to go back inside the gate. We sit at a table and talk with each other, but we really have nothing to say, so we read parts of the newspaper. Then I tell him, I'm going to my room to do my yoga practice.

"Yoga isn't for me," he says with a little bit of a sneer on his face, "the heart's not in the right place."

That's a curious thing to say to me, a yoga practitioner. I wonder if he understands yoga. Maybe he's referring to the hordes of students who only concentrate on improving their bodies and their egotistic relationship to yoga and thinness.

I do my practice, repack and think about the train trip. This takes a few hours. Then I go back to the restaurant to eat. John sits down at my table. His girlfriend has just left on a plane to Germany. We talk about yoga and Buddhism and decide that they are different techniques to get to the same place. We talk about the history of India. He tells me how in Ireland, he stood out and had so much attention because of his different culture and language. Then he went to Berlin and he liked being anonymous.

Yes, I know that feeling.

He told a friend he was going to India and the friend said—Well, there will be no anonymity there.

This was all a result of my telling him that I am returning to Mysore next year. Perhaps he has suffered in India from a lack of privacy.

I stand up and say goodbye and we give each other our best wishes.

In my room there is no hot water for a shower so I call room service. Then they will bring a pail of hot water, but I have to clear my bill because they are closing early due to the strike.

I throw on some clothes, go to the office and John is there, clearing his bill. He has a room for 500 rupees. I guess the travel agents assumed I wanted the deluxe room. As I walk out, he follows me over to my room.

"Do you want to see the room?" I ask. The room is spacious and cool with large high ceilings and a pretty garden outside the window. The porter takes in the hot water.

"If you want to stay here after I leave, you can have the room. I've already paid for it."

No, he explains, he likes his little room, and then we say goodbye and John leaves, kind of reluctantly. If there was more time, perhaps we would have become friends.

Clean and repacked—I'm waiting for Jeevesh. He telephones. He'll be here in fifteen minutes.

I turn off the computer, pack it, unpack my suitcase to find some lotion for my feet to take with me on the plane. Everything ready, I lay down for one half hour to wait and then I remember that I forgot to record something in my notes. Out with the computer.

At dinner, John tells me the reason for the strike is that the outlaw has killed over 200 police. He hates police and he lives in the mountains and does all kinds of violent things. I tell him the person who kidnapped the movie star is a Tamil speaking man. Anyhow he has demanded money this time and the people want the movie star back, want this man stopped, want the government to do something so they are rioting—or some are protesting, others are burning city buses. Off with the computer. Back in my bag.

A day in Bangalore.

*

Jeevesh and Prabakas are honking outside the hotel gate. Finally the guard arrives. The restaurant in the hotel is closing early because of the riots. Jeevesh drives into the hotel grounds. Then he comes into my room to pick up the suitcases. He asks for the money now because there won't be enough time in the airport. I wonder if he doesn't want Prabakas to see what I am paying him for the service. I hand him the 2200 rupees and then he asks for a gratuity.

I look at him and say, "Jeevesh, I can't give you any more than this."

"Ok," he says, picking up a suitcase and smiling.

I indicate that I have some money for Prabakas, also.

When I get into the cab, I give Prabakas 100 rupees and he grabs it like lightening and puts it into his pocket. Perhaps he is hiding his tip from Jeevesh. Sometimes Indians seem perfectly suited—in a hyped up way—for free enterprise and the materialist way.

On the way to the airport, Jeevesh talks a little excitedly, perhaps with some guilt about having asked for more money. After all the going price for a cab from Mysore to Bangalore from an upscale travel agent is 1100 rupees. And a cab on Gandhi Square could probably be negotiated for 800 or less.

He talks about Veerappan, the popular Indian bandit who has kidnapped the movie star. It turns out that some people love both the bandit and the movie star. So everything has become confused. According to Jeevesh, the bandit does things for the poor. It is odd that Jeevesh is so excited by his description of the bandit, because in many ways he is a traditional Brahmin, despite his merchant tendencies, which have probably developed as a result of contact with western yoga students. The longer I stay in India, the less I really understand.

On the way to the airport, there are burnt remains of many vehicles on the roads. A charred skeleton of a bus. Lots of big rocks. In the station I become worried because I have so much luggage. Jeevesh calls over a man, who puts my suitcases on a cart and wheels them into the airport. I say goodbye to Jeevish and wish him and his family the best.

The wait in the airport is long and excruciatingly cold. There are no mosquitoes this year, but it is pouring rain outside now and inside the huge warehouse-size rooms of the airport, air conditioning is pumping extremely cold air out of big vents. This is the only place I have ever experienced public air conditioning since leaving the states and tonight it is unnecessary. There is no one to ask when the plane is leaving and no place to buy a soda or a bottle of water. I step outside because I am cold and ask a policeman if he knows what's going on with the flight. I tell him I am freezing and he invites me to sit at the desk with him.

"Where are you from?" he asks. "How much salary do you earn?" He indicates that he can't travel as I can because he'd have to find a country poorer than India and that's hardly possible. He talks about Kerala, where he is from, and the high literacy rate and all the problems in India. He is also curious about how as a woman I can travel alone. "Where is your husband? Where is your family?"

In India, most women don't have the freedom I have and in exchange they are supposedly taken care of. I like my freedom.

Between Bangalore and London, I fall asleep. There is a breakfast, I think. I am deeply asleep for a while, my head leaning on the window. I am seated beside the people I will spend the rest of my trip with. A woman, eighty years old, wearing a white sari with little flowers, sits in between me and her daughter. She is very small and frail. Her husband died three weeks before and she is a bit lost. Once she falls asleep and lays her head on my shoulder. I am absorbed in reading Ramana Maharishi. The woman's daughter—I think her name is Victoria—has been living in the United States for several years working in an insurance company. Her mother and father visited the U.S. for a year once, but now she is returning without her husband.

I read and sleep for half of the trip so I guess that is my night's sleep. Then in the London airport, a young woman who is traveling to Boston walks with me and all our luggage looking for the lounge and the restaurants. This walk is a complete waste. And I've done it twice before. India Air doesn't allow enough time between the flights to get there and back and to do anything besides go to the bathroom. Yet they encourage you to go.

Back in the airplane, huffing and puffing, I sit down. My nose is running from the air pressure. I take a benadryl and instead of making me sleepy, it makes my body so restless that I can't sit crammed into the seat for eight hours. I will never take benadryl again. Finally, I take some valerian and fall asleep for the rest of the trip.

Then I'm standing in a line at Kennedy Airport, then another line—I am so sleepy. There is Jessie chatting on her cell phone. Mom. Hug, kiss, into the car. She has a new hair cut and blonde color and she seems a little bit older than when I left.

Josh meets us at my apartment later after he's finished with work and we eat carry out Chinese food.

Whoosh, I am pulled right back into life as it was when I left, right through the funnel into another state of consciousness. Peggy is curled up in a ball asleep at my feet. I sit in the rocking chair that I rocked my babies in, the chair my grandmother rocked my mother.

*

The next day, I walk around the East Village in a daze. In the sacred circle of Tompkins Square Park, a fake cow has been left with a shiny leopard skin coat, horns and a face, a caricature of the very human cows I just left behind in India. This funny statue is right inside the area where the Hari Krishnas circle every morning. I notice a fast food hamburger wrapper underneath it.

As I walk around the street with my hair tightly pulled back into a little pony tail, I realize I am out of fashion now in my baggy clothes. The women don't look as beautiful here as they do on the streets of Mysore. They are tightly wrapped and tough looking. So many people on Avenue A seem to have some invisible weight pressing down on them. A lot of serious faces. I go over to Manny's studio to practice my sequence. I can't move very well because my body is stiff after the plane trip.

At home, I clean out my closet, making a big bag to give to the homeless. Something inside warns me though—hold this bag for a few weeks, Gina, until you are really back home. Then look at it again. I clean the house as much as possible, wishing I could throw most of the furniture away, but then I have Peggy here and she brings in dust and leaves her long white hair everywhere. The furniture creates a level where I can escape.

My girlfriends, Vivian and Alisa, come over to hang out in my kitchen at night and we talk about yoga, ayurveda, meditation and all the things I have learned in India. They want to know about my experience. We eat guacamole and chips and Vivian washes her mats in the washing machine. I love this kind of thing, sitting in the kitchen with my women friends.

Monday. I wake up at 4 a.m. in the morning. Last night at 7 p.m. I was so tired that I fell into a deep sleep. I stumbled around the apartment, forgetting to feed and walk Peggy. I think she was stumbling around, too. I remember Vivian phoning me at 9:30 and I told her, "I am ok"—and in the fog I remember talking to her— "It's because you're still recovering from the change of time." She really liked our little kitchen meeting with Alisa, too. We talked about going to a lecture together next Monday. And then back into sleep. 4 a.m. I force myself to stay in bed, dosing until 5:45. It is still dark out.

I throw a few clothes on and walk Peggy down the street. It's very humid with only a little bit of light. No one's on the street except a few men, who look at me with hatred. I am a little bit afraid but I continue to walk. This fear of men on the streets has been with me for a long time as a result of three very frightening incidents in my life. Once in Detroit when I was twenty, I was raped by a man who I let in my house, ten years later a man opened my window and chased me through my apartment, and then a few years ago in Brooklyn, I was chased down the street late at night. These things tend to stay with me.

Safe inside, I make my bed and dust the floor in the bedroom. Perhaps this will be my new morning activity. I drink the hot water, Dr. Anand's ginger tonic and then the large glass of water to start the day. I bathe in the tub with the spray attachment and wash my hair, dry it with a hair dryer, dress in my baggy Indian cotton clothes. Then I sit down on my mat in lotus and practice singing the chant along with Jayashree on the tape. "Yogena chittasya padena vacam/

malam sarirasya ca vaidyakena/ yopakarottam pravaram muninam/
patanjlim pranjali ranato'mi."

It is cooler this morning and of course I can't get as deeply into
kurmasana without Manny's help, but I am better at it than I used
to be. At the end of the asanas, I almost get up and start doing the
list of things in my mind, but then I remember—practice pranayama. As I slowly breathe in one nostril and out the other, I can hear
the people walking by the window, but they are like so many birds.

I check my email. A lovely message from Dimitri—he is sorry
about not writing very frequently, he has been going through some
problems, but he has received a new visa (he was worried about
that) and so he will be returning to New York on October 1st. He
wants to see me. (The other day Alisa told me that I look like I'm
thirty years old.) I suppose that parenthesis indicates a little of my
insecurity. I just pushed the button on the cd player to play a CD
Dimitri gave me in May, *Refuge*, with his countryman, Boris
Grebenshikov, a Russian rock star singing spiritual chants to raise
money for Tibetan Buddhist causes. How could I have stayed in
India for all that time without listening to one CD, especially this
one? Grebenshikov's voice expresses a deep masculine spiritual sexuality.

I dance around my living room.

Maya. Divine maya. I am drawn to the sound and the experience. Is it spiritual-sexuality or a screen, I wonder, like those screens
Acharya talks about, one of many that can prevent one from experiencing the present fully. A fancy delusion I am weaving. A sure
path to suffering. Perhaps I only want a friend from Dimitri now.
But I think not. Instead of giving up your desires, Ramana suggests
giving up the ego-I. All will be solved. Know who you are. A project for the future, I think, as I twirl around the room. For now the
wheel keeps rolling.

I eat some fruit and some toast with tahini. Peggy isn't so interested in sprouted sourdough bread. But it is good. Then I take my
bicycle out and pack the package I have for Carl's wife into my plastic crocheted bag. I start coasting down Avenue A on the bicycle. It
feels so different, riding so high up. It's not a motor scooter. There

are no cows. No red dirt. But instead very fast machines moving in an orderly fashion.

The tires are almost flat, so I coast down Avenue B to the gas station on Houston. A young Latino man with a small bike arrives first.

"What's wrong?" he asks, "It's letting out my air."

"You must tilt it in a different direction so that it will fill up."

I make the wheels on my bike hard, then ride over to the post office on Third Street between C & B. It isn't open yet. I ask three people what time it is. None of us has a watch. In this neighborhood of the young and hip, at 9 a.m., most people are getting ready to go to sleep rather than waking up. So who needs a watch with that kind of upside down schedule. I bike over to the post office on 4th Avenue, pack the package into a priority mail box, pay $4.30 and come back home.

What else? It is now near midnight and I have been out and about all day long. A normal New York day. At school, I open my mail, make out envelopes to mail things to my editor and order desk copies. The months in India now seem like a dream. I leave the building in my squeaky sandals.

Someone says, "Gina, you're looking more and more Eastern every year."

"You should have seen me last week."

Late at night, I sit at an outdoor table and eat a quesadilla. A couple dressed in all black walk down the street arguing and swearing at each other. Then a man passes with a big pit bull. A lot of people with angry facial expressions. Must have something to do with the planets or the kaliyuga. Maybe it's just the rhythm of late summer in the East Village when many people have escaped the city. Those who remain are hot and uncomfortable. So different from India. Must follow Acharya's advice to keep my own joy despite what I see—beggars or angry city folk. In a few years, he sees me living in a little house somewhere in the country, but for now I am here in this city, this microcosm of the world, the place where I have always wanted to live and where in fact I live.

Tuesday. Awake at five a.m., shower, clean the floor in the bedroom with the dust cloth, eat the ayurvedic remedy, drink hot water. Here I am on 7th Street on my mat in padmasana at dawn. The morning light through the venetian blinds leaves a pattern of dark and light on the walls, the floor and on my shoulders. I look at the photographs lined up behind the candle: Ramana Maharshi, Acharya and Jayashree, my childhood family, and Lenny. They shine on me.

Inhale strength, exhale lightness.

Glossary

Dhoti: a formal cloth that men wrap around their hips.

Kaliyuga: the fourth stage in the cycle of human existence, the period when destruction and devastation occur. We are presently living in the era of a kaliyuga.

Kapha: one of the three ayurvedic doshas (humors, constitutions) that regulate the body and keep it healthy. The water element is central to *Kapha*. When natal *Kapha* constitutions are out of balance, they are slow and heavy, producing phlegm. When the dosha is balanced, a strong immunity is created.

Lungi: an informal cloth, often colorful, that men wrap around their hips.

Maya: the material dimension of conventional reality that can sometimes seem like the only dimension, an illusion, in fact.

Pitta: one of the three ayurvedic doshas (humors, constitutions) which regulate the body and keep it healthy. The fire element is central to *Pitta*. When natal *Pitta* constitutions are out of balance, they generate a lot of heat, with anger, argumentation, ulcers, etc. When balanced, the dosha creates a radiance.

Puja: a Hindu devotional ritual that is conducted in temples, homes, streets, businesses, schools, everywhere, in fact. The intent is to honor and appease the deities or the powers they represent. Common offerings include fire, flowers, incense, fruit, money and water.

Rajas (rajasic): one of the three qualities (along with sattva and tamas) that make up everything in nature. *Rajas* is active, passionate, excited and restless.

Sattva (sattvic): one of the three qualities (along with rajas and tamas) that make up everything in nature. *Sattva* is the balance between rajas (activity) and tamas (inertia). It is clarity, lightness and purity.

Tamas (tamasic): one of the three qualities (along with sattva and tamas) that make up everything in nature. *Tamas* is the quality of darkness and inertia, the opposite of rajas. A *tamasic* state would be impure, rotten, lazy or dull.

Vata: one of the three ayurvedic doshas (humors, constitutions) which regulate the body and keep it healthy. The wind element is central to *Vata*. When a natal *Vata* constitution is out of balance, the mind and bodily tissues are aggravated and nervous. When the dosha is balanced, however, there is an increase in energy and creativity.

Barbara Henning was born in Detroit, Michigan. She has lived in New York City since 1984 and is the author of three collections of poetry, *Smoking in the Twilight Bar* (United Artists, 1988) *Love Makes Thinking Dark* (United Artists, 1995), and *Detective Sentences* (Spuyten Duyvil, 2001; a novel *Black Lace* (Spuyten Duyvil, 2001); three artist book collaborations, *Words and Pictures* (with Sally Young), *The Passion of Signs* (with Georgia Marsh, Leave Books), and *How to Read and Write in the Dark* (with Miranda Maher); two pamphlets, *Me and My Dog* (Poetry New York) and *In Between* (Spectacular Diseases, England); and a series of photopoem booklets, *Found in the Park*, *Up North*, *Aerial View*, *Teacher Training*, *Thakita Thaka*, and *My Autobiography*. She teaches at Long Island University in Brooklyn and is the editor of Long News Books.